SPEAR GARDEN

Thomas Tate

Forward

After devoting over eighteen months to meticulously rework each chapter, this enhanced edition of *Spear Garden* represents the culmination of my dedication and growth as a writer. Throughout this process, I've come to appreciate how an author's style can evolve and their writing can elevate to new heights. The compulsion to revisit and refine previously published works can be irresistible at times. I owe immense gratitude to my dear friend and fellow author, Henry Martin, whose unwavering support and encouragement propelled me to strive for excellence and persevere until the very end. I wholeheartedly recommend delving into his captivating literary creations. Some of his published titles include *Element 115 & Sanctuary in Shadows.*

Disclaimer

1

Vasquez Estate
Isle de la Juventud, Cuba
April 9th, 2012
13:00 local (18:00 GMT)

General Hector Vasquez sat in the comfort of his air-conditioned Range Rover and gazed out at his right-hand man, Luca Perez, as he prepared their latest weapon for testing. His eyes narrowed behind his Maui Jim sunglasses, and his teeth bit on his unlit cigar as he fished in his pocket for a lighter while studying the man.

Is it the heat, or is he afraid this thing won't work? He had best get started.

Shielded from the sun by a large canopy, Luca was standing next to a folding table with laptops and monitors scattered about its surface. Palm trees lined the far side of the field past him. He wiped his forehead before heading to the SUV. As he approached, the general rolled open the window and lit his cigar. Adriana, his daughter, would constantly nag him to quit smoking.

What would she say to me now?

"General, we have the armament configured and ready to test."

About fucking time.

Taking a long draw, he savored the tobacco's essence and blew it out. The smoke lingered above his olive-green beret, like a cloud, and swirled as he opened the door and stepped into the heat.

His man beckoned. "Follow me, sir." They walked to the command station, and once there, he lifted a bottle of water and drank most of it.

Vasquez sighed in impatience. "I've never seen a device like this. How does it work?"

Before responding, the man moved to the side to provide his employer with a clear view of the screen. "These weapons don't use a traditional firing pin with a magazine or belt to feed ammunition into the chamber. Instead, these barrels *are* the magazines. The unit, which appears to be a simple black box, contains twenty-four of them stacked in four rows of six."

"Here is one, preloaded." He passed one to his boss, who accepted it and held it with both hands.

"It's heavy."

"Yes, sir. The barrel holds seven forty-millimeter grenades. As do all the others. If you pass it to me, I'll show you how it's loaded into the weapon."

Vasquez handed back the barrel as he blew out a steady stream of smoke. Luca took the cue and moved faster. "Loading the appliance is quick. They're inserted from behind." He dashed into the scorching heat to one of the Metal Storm units a few meters away and unlocked a door at the back of the weapon.

The general spat on the ground. "You are right. It appears to be a plain, black box."

Luca's lips curled.

"Does something amuse you, Mr. Perez?"

He shook his head. "The same idea crossed my mind when I first saw it." He put the barrel into the back end of the casing. When it snapped into place, he closed the door.

Vasquez wiped his forehead with a handkerchief and let out a deep sigh. A sign he was losing his patience. "Get on with it. What's next?"

Luca cleared his throat and hurried back under the welcoming shade of the canopy. "We stack munitions, whether bullets or grenades, in barrels. Projectiles fire using electrical pulses. There is no gunpowder. It's flawless to operate. No jams. You can set it to shoot at your desired pace."

Vasquez chewed on the end of his cigar. His eyes scanned the horizon in thought. "What is the maximum rate?"

"Depending on the projectile caliber, anywhere from two hundred and fifty thousand, to one million rounds per minute."

Luca paused to let the numbers sink in. "The grenades we're launching are at the lower end of the scale. But at such a fast tempo, it will sound like a single shot."

Vasquez rubbed his beard, his mouth agape, and stared over Luca's shoulder.

That's unbelievable. If true, I can raise the price. Or better yet, sell it to the highest bidder.

"Tell me about the kill zones."

Luca pointed to the center monitor. "This section of the display represents the area in the southwest part of the field, out there." He gestured as he spoke to a piece about three hundred meters away.

The general leaned over to read the screen. His gaze moved to the meadow, where indicated. "Continue."

"If I push this button." Vasquez glanced back at the keyboard. "Observe the deadly areas we have established. If anyone enters one of them without wearing a sensor." He handed over a circular token the size of a coin to his employer. He reached out and inspected it. "I programmed the device to shoot all the grenades at the pace specified. Nothing survives."

Colombians will want these to protect their estates. I'll make millions.

"What about animals? Won't they trigger the weapon?"

"No, sir. We can program the unit for a minimum body mass."

Brakes squealed, and an engine stopped as a Jeep halted. The two men turned toward it. Julio Ramirez sat in the passenger seat;

his hands clasped in his lap. The general put the cigar back in his mouth. A cruel smile crossed his face as he walked out into the sun toward the vehicle.

"Mr. Ramirez."

Julio bowed his head. Vasquez enjoyed the man's defeated countenance. One could expect his cowed expression after being locked in a cell, beaten, tortured, and starved for two weeks.

I wonder if it will surprise him when I tell him I'm letting him go.

The man answered in a quiet tone, with a distinct shake in his voice.

"Yes, sir?"

"How long have you worked for me?"

"Six months, general."

"Have I been kind to you—the last two weeks notwithstanding? I provided you with food, shelter, money to send home to your family?"

"You were kind, boss."

He moved closer to the prisoner and reached out, grasping him on the back of his neck. He squeezed. Julio's shoulders tensed, and he closed his eyes. "Then why did you steal from me?"

The man remained silent and became more cowed. He tightened his grip, jammed the cigar into his mouth, and clamped down. He slapped the cowering man in the face. "Answer me!"

The general enjoyed it when the pathetic fool lifted his arms to ward off another blow.

"I—I don't know. I mean—my family. We needed money, and I apologize."

"You're sorry? Is that all you have to say?"

A goddamn traitor, more like it. You'll see how I deal with traitors.

He released his hold.

"I—"

"Shut up!"

Julio inhaled a quick breath and held it. His eyes squinted and his body jerked as his hands raised again.

He laughed. "Relax. I will not hit you."

Yet.

Vasquez took the cigar out of his mouth and spat once more. Julio's chin was dripping with sweat under Vasquez's intense gaze.

God, it's fucking hot. We need to get this over with.

"Trying to work out what to do with you has caused me sleepless nights. People fear me for my sometimes-severe methods, but those strategies are necessary to keep men in line. You understand, Julio?"

"I do, sir."

"Speak up!" The general slapped him again.

"Yes!" He rubbed his cheek. In the reddening face of the condemned man, Vasquez could see the outline of his handprint.

"I'm also thought to be too brutal, according to rumors. Some believe I should be kind and more compassionate. How do you feel?"

The prisoner raised his head with a glimmer of hope in his eyes and attempted a half-toothed grin.

A cruel smile crossed the general's face. "All right, then. It's what I'll do. I forgive you for your crimes against me by letting you go."

Julio's eyes widened, and he lifted his chin toward his captor as his grin grew broader. "You are?"

"Certainly. If you drive this Jeep to the far side of the field and go through those trees," Vasquez pointed. "Someone is waiting for you to take you home. But Julio, there is one thing I demand in return."

He nodded vigorously. "Anything, whatever you want."

"Never come back or ask me for anything again. Understand?"

The man rocked back and forth in excitement. "Yes, thank you."

Vasquez slapped the Jeep's hood. "Go on!"

The driver stepped out and marched over to the canopy as the captive moved into the driver's seat. The engine roared to life. Placing his hand on the gearshift, he paused before raising his head. His eyes were moist.

Vasquez stared into the condemned man's face again. "What?"

"God bless you."

Vasquez waved him forward.

He released the clutch. The tires stirred dust as they turned. Vasquez strolled over to the laptop and examined the screen. One of the kill zones detected a hostile entity within its defined parameters. An alarm sounded.

A fraction of a second later, a single blast startled the general and made him flinch. One hundred and sixty-eight grenades darkened the sky, like a swarm of bats. Vasquez's eyes widened in anticipation.

A thirty-foot fireball was engulfed with dirt, steel, and body parts. Twisted metal, a blood-drenched seat, glass, and something looking like half a leg hit the dirt around a forty-foot crater in the field. Smoke emanated from the blackened pit.

Flickering fires from tiny bits of the Jeep, and Julio's corpse danced on the ground. The general's eyes squinted as a broad smile spread across his face. Laughing out loud, his weathered hand found Luca's shoulder. "You were right. Nothing survived."

2

CIA Headquarters
Langley, VA
April 21st, 2012
08:00 local (13:00 GMT)

Thirty-two-year-old Blake MacKay strolled into the office of his handler, Mike Brennan, the Director of Clandestine Affairs. He was on the phone, pacing around the room. Unsure if he should sit or wait outside, his boss spoke to him.

"Hold on for a sec, Julian." Mike cupped his hand over the mouthpiece. "Have a seat. I'll be with you in a couple of minutes."

He plopped into the overstuffed couch in front of the desk. On the wall facing him, several pictures chronicled his handler's career during the Cold War. It had taken him a few years to get to know Mike well. Not only was he an excellent boss, but he also became a trusted friend.

Among the photos was one of his handler receiving an award from Ronald Reagan. At six feet one, Reagan towered over Mike and his five feet eight-inch frame. Thoughts filled his mind if anyone ever gave him shit for his height?

In another photograph, Mike received his Godan, or fifth-degree black belt, in Ju-Jitsu. He still had the same physique as in the portrait taken so long ago. *Well, if they did, they'd know they made a mistake.*

"Yes, sir. We will discuss it. He walked into my office moments ago. Thanks." Mike disconnected his call. He placed his phone on his desk and ran his hand through his salt and pepper gray flat-top before sighing and slumping into his chair. For a moment, he studied him.

He crossed his legs. "Okay. What's the problem? No beating around the bush."

Mike opened a file and rotated it for his agent to see. "Meet Mr. Prick, otherwise known as General Hector Vasquez, who rose from the Cuban army ranks."

He uncrossed his legs, reached over, lifted the folder, and began reading. After a while, he glanced up. "Gun runner, huh?"

Mike scoffed. "Worse. He used to be a minor nuisance on our radar; we didn't give a shit about him until recently."

"So, what's changed?"

His boss leaned back in his chair and relaxed. "Let me fill you in with a brief background on him. He has always had access to military equipment as a general. That's obvious. His greed, lack of conscience, and appetite for the finer things in life led him to where he is today. He's built an extensive underground enterprise."

He chuckled. "So far, he doesn't sound any different from most of the other assholes I've dealt with." He continued to thumb through the file. His eyebrows raised as he took out an intriguing picture. "Go on."

"He started smuggling weapons to Colombian drug cartels. The income enabled him to buy protection from those in charge of the Cuban government who would turn a blind eye to his operation."

He pulled out an overhead image of a massive house. "Is this his residence?"

"Yes. Gun running earnings permitted Vasquez to purchase real estate and build his property on the southern part of the Isle de la Juventud. It's the biggest and least populated of the three hundred and fifty islands comprising the whole fucking area."

He opened his laptop and accessed the CIA's internal satellite imaging system. He zoomed in on the land. "It appears most inhabitants live on the north side."

Mike nodded. "Right on. This makes it ideal for his operation. The irony is, pirates and other lowlifes used the same segment of the territory back in the day."

"What are these fields?" He turned his computer around.

Mike put on his spectacles, leaned forward, and squinted. "Hmph." He sat back in his chair and tossed his glasses onto the desk. "The funny part is he has a cattle ranch and a pineapple farm. Both are highly lucrative. You and I would be happy with the income generated every year from those."

He frowned as he studied the documents. "I'm guessing he uses those to launder the money he makes from selling arms."

Mike formed a gun with his thumb and index finger and pointed it at his colleague. "Bingo."

Continuing to read the paper in his hand. "This file dates back several years. You still haven't told me why there's a sudden interest?"

"I'm getting to that. General Vasquez soon became the largest supplier of armaments to the Mexican narcotics cartels. Those weapons have been used to attack the U.S. border patrol. They have also smuggled them into the United States and found their way into stateside criminal organizations."

He paused and scratched his nose. "Taking out Vasquez and his enterprise would impact the Mexican drug gang's ability to fight each other, as well as the authorities. It would give Mexican cops a better chance of rounding up and arresting gang members."

He tossed the file folder on Mike's desk and groaned. "Well, I can understand how such an operation would make things easier for the border patrol and the Mexican police. However, I don't have a clue why we need to get involved."

"Do you remember the recent shooting of those two U.S. customs officials?"

He winced. Both officers had families with children. The wife of one had given birth to a baby girl a few weeks before their murder.

"Yes, it was unfortunate. Is this the asshole responsible for this?"

Mike nodded. "The FBI traced those weapons to Vasquez. The president wants this done right, with no connection to us. She insisted on our best man and requested you. It's time he took a dirt nap."

Understanding the need for this guy to go away, he reached for the file again and opened it to read more about his target.

As he sorted through more photographs, he came across one he hadn't seen before. He studied the image for a moment, admiring the woman's features. Her beauty struck him: her olive skin, bright green eyes, and delicate lips.

The tight black top and long brown hair over her shoulder accentuated her body curves.

Holy crap!

He spun the photograph around toward Mike. "Who—is this?"

Mike chuckled. "I wondered when you'd get to that one. She's his daughter, Adriana Vasquez. As far as we know, she's not implicated in her father's operation. She either ignores it out of choice, or out of fear of what happened to her mother."

He glanced again at the picture before setting it on the desk. His eyes narrowed as he searched through more photographs, trying to find Mrs. Vasquez. "Are there any photos of her?"

"His wife? No."

"Where is she now?"

"Well, details are sketchy, but from what we've gathered, Mrs. Vasquez protested when he got involved with the cartels. She contacted Cuban intelligence because she wanted him to stop. Unfortunately for her, the person she reached out to was on the general's payroll. She disappeared soon after. His daughter wasn't happy, but may have taken it as a warning."

I'll enjoy sending this guy to hell. It would be perfect if I could do it in such a way that he can see it coming.

"What does the daughter do?"

"A couple of years ago, she created an organization called Los Niños Primero. It means—"

He interrupted. "Children First. A woman doing this wouldn't be involved in her father's operation. It's possible she's scared to death of him."

"Yeah, she provides food, schooling, and medical supplies to poor villages all over Cuba. A real heartstring puller, if you know what I mean. It's brilliant."

He cocked his head. "How so?"

"Well, this prick gives money to his daughter to do this. He knows the villagers need his charity to survive. He relies on their silence to continue his activities. It's a classic symbiotic relationship. They talk, and they lose support. Also, he promotes what she does, so how do you think he comes across to outsiders?"

He leaned back in his chair with his hands clasped behind his head. "Like a wonderful philanthropist, I imagine."

Mike grinned. "You got it." He laughed out loud. "Hey, like your buddy, Petrovich."

Rolling his eyes as he shook his head. "Ugh! Don't remind me."

"Okay, so what's my cover? The usual?"

"How could it not be? It's perfect. It's like we created him, especially for this assignment."

"What's my timetable?"

"You leave this afternoon."

Shit. So much for finishing my deck. Well, at least I can buy some fine cigars as gifts.

"Do you remember what I told you before leaving Norway?"

His brow furrowed. "You mean Sweden?"

Mike waved it off. "Whatever. Getting near him will be difficult. He's well-guarded. Add to it his paranoia and—this mission won't be quick. If it takes three months, so be it. I need you to complete the job. We figured your cover of being in charge of an organization helping the world's children would impress his daughter. Cozy up to her and she can ensure you get to her father."

"Does she have a boyfriend?"

A grin creased Mike's face. "Hell no! You can bet Vasquez has threatened any man with a slow, painful death, even for staring at her—and they know he'll follow through."

He sighed. "Well, that's fine. At least there won't be any

competition."

Mike pointed a finger at him and grinned while suppressing a laugh. "You're an asshole. I see how women gaze at you when we're out. Hell, half the women here would do you in a heartbeat."

He rolled his eyes. "Well, I'm pleased I'm not the chauvinist pig you are. I actually respect them. I won't make a move until I know that's what they want. It's respectful."

Mike waved a dismissive arm at him. "Aughh! I miss the good ol days. Men were expected to be pigs—and I was."

He expelled a short giggle. "The problem I had was the only gals I dealt with were Russians. And they weren't like the type you've worked with. These galoots were huge and burly."

Mike puffed out his chest and raised his shoulders. "A Russian shot-putter kind of woman. And they were all trying to kill me!"

They both laughed. Blake waved his hand. "Okay, okay. Calm down. I'm not one to kiss and tell either, so you'll just have to use your imagination."

Mike stood, looking incredulous; his lips pursed. "You're still a dick."

He shook his head and smiled. "All right. You feel better?" He cleared his throat and changed to a more official tone. "Anything else we need to discuss?"

"Yeah, there is." Mike scooted his chair closer to the desk and leaned forward. "This guy is well connected and there's been some chatter. He's working with an unidentified weapons dealer from Al-Qaeda. We want you to dig around and gather as much intelligence as you can while you're there. We must find out where—and to whom he has his tentacles stretched."

He grabbed the folder. "If I can get into his estate, I should be able to lay my fingers on any intel he has."

They both stood, and Mike extended his hand. "Best of luck. You still live on your big ass farm?"

Their hands locked, and Blake smiled with a smirk on his face. "Of course. Why would I move from there?"

Mike grinned. "More land than I'd know what to do with. Anyway, go home, get your things ready. I'll have a chopper collect you at thirteen hundred."

3

The Residence of Prime Minister Oleg Shorets
Minsk, Belarus
April 21st
22:40 local (19:40 GMT)

Oleg sat in a plush leather chair and swirled the ice cubes in his crystal tumbler. The clock ticking on the mantle drew his attention.

He's forty minutes late.

A wave of panic washed over him, and sitting only made it intensify. He stood, pacing back and forth as he considered what could delay his colleague. He inverted the glass. A single drop fell to the floor.

Empty! I need another.

Aleksandr Roshenko was deputy prime minister, whom Oleg thought of as a close friend. They were both disgusted at the way President Vladimir Solonovich had hijacked their homeland and turned it into what the rest of the world considered the last dictatorship in Europe.

Belarus gained independence from Russia on July 3rd, 1991. The nation underwent limited structural reform after he put the country on "market socialism" in 1995. He ended presidential term limits, allowing him to run for a third or fourth time, or as often as he wanted. Since then, terrorism threats have risen, and corruption is common. He squashed rampant riots with the dread of arrest, imprisonment, or the coincidental untimely deaths of those organizing them.

Behind closed doors, he and his colleague Aleksandr had discussed what they could do to take back control by getting rid of the dictator president. However, fear has always been an issue. During the latest elections, several competing candidates got arrested or disappeared when they dared to contest the election results. It was because of this that the two friends acted.

He poured himself another drink and gulped it. He wiped sweat from his brow as his anxiety grew.

Where are you, my friend? One last check.

On the bar was a small electronic device capable of detecting surveillance or listening devices. Walking around the room, he held it in the air for the third time in under an hour.

Stealing a glanced at the clock again, headlights raced across the wall. He shuffled toward the window corner and peered out. Half of him expected the KGB to come in with weapons drawn. Then a single car came into view. He ran his hands through his thick, dyed black hair and sighed. A wave of relief washed over him as his anxieties dissipated.

At last!

Proposing a coup, much less getting away with it, requires careful planning and timing. Everything would have to be planned in meticulous detail and executed in the same way. Tonight, was the night he was going to outline his plan for Aleksandr.

The footsteps in the hall grew closer. The door opened, and his friend walked into his office.

He wasted no time scolding him. "You're late."

"I couldn't help it. Minister Litwin would not shut up about the damn power plant."

Oleg's patience was at its limit, and his friend coming in and complaining didn't do much. Before he spoke, his mouth tightened, then relaxed. "The thing you're referring to—"

He paused and raised a finger to his lips. He reached into his pocket and retrieved a small circuit board with a nine-volt battery.

Aleksandr's eyes squinted. "What is that?"

Oleg connected it to the device and flipped a tiny switch. "Laser mic countermeasure. You can never be too safe." He turned around and set it on the bar before continuing.

"As I was saying, the power plant plays a significant role in what I'm about to tell you. That's why I scheduled your meeting with him. Now, how is it progressing?"

"Progress is fine. It's the first nuclear generator in Belarus, so I can understand his attention to detail. I agree it's a high-profile project, but he just kept talking." Aleksandr pointed at him. "I think he wants something from you in return for this. I'm sure of it. He will ask soon."

"If he gets it online in time, I'll give him anything he requires. Is it still on track to go live on July 3rd?"

"Yes."

"Excellent." A wry grin crossed Oleg's face. "One more thing falling into place."

Aleksandr's eyes narrowed. "What do you mean?"

Extending his arm, he grabbed a bottle of Minsk Krystal, which was chilling in a bucket of ice. As he handed one of two full glasses to his friend, he pointed to the chairs in front of the fireplace. "Come, let us be more comfortable."

They both sauntered over and took their seats. Aleksandr placed his drink on the table next to his chair. He retrieved a cigarette from his case, lit it, and took a long drag. The smoke's tendrils lofted toward the ceiling, growing like fingers from some demonic hand before fading into the background. His colleague reached for his glass and sipped it to calm his nerves.

"So, what is this grand plan of yours? I hope you know we're treading on dangerous ground."

Oleg stood and leaned against the mantle. "There is no substantial reward without significant risk, my friend."

The man scoffed. "Save your page-a-day calendar expressions for everyone else. I need to understand what you have in mind so I can evaluate its feasibility."

Oleg's cheeks warmed. He wanted to slap him in the face.

I cannot tolerate your temerity once you find out what I'm planning. Are you really behind me? Perhaps you report to Solonovich? Have they turned you? I'll test you soon.

He frowned at his colleague. "Are you sure you are ready for this? It's possible I read you wrong."

Aleksandr put out his cigarette in the ashtray and stood. "Yes. I am sorry. This is all stressful for me. You, of all people, should know. Plus, the long meeting with Litwin and being late—"

He raised his hands in the air. "Enough."

Okay, it could be stress. I'm paranoid as well.

"Please sit."

As his friend sat, he continued. "We held elections at the end of last year, and the next term began."

Aleksandr shifted in his chair and sipped vodka. "So far, you're not telling me anything most Belarusians don't already know."

"Then you are aware of this as well. If something happened to Solonovich, I would replace him, and you would take my job for the rest of the time. We'd be in those jobs for at least four and a half years. That would give us plenty of time to install our own independent power brokers."

Aleksandr wasn't always a chain smoker. He did this only when he was nervous or anxious. He was relieved to know his friend's anxiety was real. The man lit another cigarette, took a short drag, and exhaled. "And how do you suggest we make this happen? Is your plan nothing more than an assassination of the president?"

He smiled.

There are more positive things coming, my friend.

He walked over behind the leather chair, facing his friend, and gripped the sides until his knuckles turned white.

He leaned in. "This is bigger than the two of us, Comrade." Oleg released his vice-like grip and caressed the soft material as he gloated at the information he was about to share.

"You and I are not alone," he said as he waved his finger back and forth. "There are some of us who feel this is long overdue, so the manpower and infrastructure are already there. For this reason,

I've planned the date."

"When?"

"Independence Day. He speaks at Victory Square every year."

"*Bozhe moy*, that's only a couple of months away. Do you think we could get something organized in such a short amount of time?"

"Yes. I am not worried about time. The problem lies in assigning responsibility. We need to dispel any questions aimed at us. Who do we hire to do it and how do we place the blame on them, so it is irrefutable?"

Aleksandr stubbed his cigarette out in the ashtray. He took a sip of his drink and kept the glass in his hand. "I have no idea, but since you have a group of people, as you claim, already gathered, I assume you have an answer to the question."

A broad grin spread across Oleg's face. "Of course, a terrorist attack."

Aleksandr's eyes widened, and he raised his voice. "A terrorist attack?" He slammed back the remaining vodka and stood. "I'm getting more. Do you want some as well?"

He grinned again, drained his glass, and handed it to his friend.

Aleksandr lounged at the bar and pulled out the chilled Minsk Krystal bottle. "This is almost empty. Got any more?"

Oleg snorted and lifted a finger. "Only one. Another fucking result of the president's incompetence,"

"You mean because of the state taking over private firms? I didn't realize they included the distillery."

"Yes."

Bastard.

"After the government acquired it, Solonovich's assigned minions were guilty of gross mismanagement, like so many other companies. After a while, they could no longer pay the workers, so it was closed and abandoned."

Aleksandr grabbed both glasses and headed to the window behind the massive desk where Oleg had moved. He filled them both and handed one to his friend.

He clasped the glass and raised it. "*yebat' ikh vsekh!* Once this is gone, I'll have to drink that Russian piss."

Aleksandr frowned. "So, what do you have in mind to implement this plan?"

He strode over to a map of the world hanging on the back wall of his home office and pointed to the United States. "I have a contact within the U.S. government who has access to some interesting cutting-edge technology. He has been a trusted friend for years, and with the right inducement, he has agreed to help us."

"What kind of enticement?"

"The license would be granted to him for McDonald's and Starbucks, among other Western businesses. He would lease those rights to those corporations for years. It would make him millions, and, of course, we would get our fair share of the profits."

He eyed his comrade as the idea of so much money seeped through Aleksandr's thoughts. The smile on his friend's face pleased him.

"And what type of revolutionary technological development are you talking about?"

Oleg's lips curled upward as he motioned for Aleksandr to sit again. As his friend followed his instruction, he moved to the front of his desk, leaned back against it, and crossed his arms. "Have you heard of Metal Storm?"

"No, what is it?"

"It is technology out of Australia and the United States. Without entering into detail, it is a weapons system capable of firing one million rounds per minute—and we can do it by remote control."

His friend smirked. "You are joking."

"No. It is real, and we are getting it."

Oleg let the information sink in for a moment. He savored Aleksandr's expression as he contemplated what he had learned.

"My contact in America sold the weapon to an arms dealer in Cuba, who should have received it by now. I have already spoken with the fool who will be both our supplier and our scapegoat."

"And who might this person be?" Aleksandr asked.

"The man who is providing us with this service is Zahmir Al-Hamwi."

Aleksandr pulled out another cigarette and lit it. After a long draw, he exhaled a plume of smoke. "Is this person supposed to mean something to me?"

He couldn't believe he didn't recognize the name. "Do you remember when we supplied munitions to the Kurds in northern Iraq a few years ago?"

"Yes."

"And can you recall how Al-Qaeda was the go-between for us helping the Kurds?"

"I do."

"This man was part of that and will play a vital role in our plan."

"How so?"

"This man is a weapons dealer for Al-Qaeda. He is on the top ten most wanted terrorist lists in the U.S. and Interpol." He studied Alexandr's reaction and, after a moment, asked, "Are you now seeing how things are coming together, comrade?"

Aleksandr glanced up. His eyes were wide. He took another drag on his cigarette, then smiled and nodded approval. "When will we get this weapon? What will we do with it until we are ready to use it?"

"Al-Hamwi will collect the device in early June. He'll have plenty of time to deliver it, and we will only need to store it for a day or two. These are items we can work on as time approaches."

"But we always stand next to him when he speaks. If this is a weapon of mass destruction and you want to make it appear to be a terrorist attack, won't we be in the line of fire?"

He smiled again. "Excellent question. That's why I asked about the nuclear plant timeline. Such a prestigious project needs proper representation. We will attend the opening ceremony. Far away from Minsk."

He raised his glass. "To the future?"

Aleksandr chuckled. *"Vashe zdorov'ye!"*

Both men emptied their glasses in one swig.

4

Villa Clara, Cuba
June 1st
17:30 local (22:30 GMT)

Blake reached for Adriana's backpack. "Here, let me help you."

"Thank you."

The two spent the week giving vaccines to children in outlying villages in Central Cuba. The work was fulfilling, but he was no nearer to completing his mission. He lifted her rucksack, setting it in the back of the pickup they had used for seven and a half weeks. The focus to get closer to his target had become arduous when, a few nights ago, an opportunity emerged.

She was already in the truck waiting when he climbed into the cab and closed the door. Glancing over at her. "Have you thought over what I said the other day about our next location?"

There was an article he'd read, reporting a case of diphtheria on one of the outlying islands, close to Vasquez's estate.

"I have, and it's sad, but to be honest, I was shocked. MEDICC all but wiped out the disease since the turn of the century. I can't believe several cases have popped up."

His brow furrowed. "MEDICC, Isn't that the name of your

country's national immunization program?"

"Yes."

Blake leaned his left arm on the steering wheel and turned to her. A boastful smile appeared on his face. "Well, I've got some connections too, and I've found out it may have come over from Haiti. A whole boatload of people landed, and now they've spread themselves out among the chain of islands down there."

Clipboard in hand, she studied it, twirling the pen in her mouth. As she flipped through the papers, she ticked various checkboxes. She tucked her long, dark hair behind her left ear, letting the rest dangle free.

Didn't you get the hint? I hate to sound pushy, but—.

"So, any more ideas regarding your father's estate as a staging ground?"

Her eyes focused on her documents.

"Adriana."

Nibbling the pen with her teeth, she wasn't paying attention. "Hmm?"

He called her name again, but louder.

"Huh?" She jerked up, eyes turned to him and withdrew the pen from her mouth. "What? I'm sorry, what did you say?"

An errant clump of hair dangled down the middle of her forehead and caught in the corner of her mouth. She crossed her eyes as she gazed at it and blew it out of the way.

She glanced back at him and returned a bubbly schoolgirl smile. It never ceased to amaze him how alluring a woman could be in a dirty green shirt and khaki shorts; despite having worked for nearly twelve hours in the humid Cuban jungles.

"Your father's estate. Can we utilize it?"

She clapped her hand on her head. "Damn, I almost forgot." She placed the clipboard on the dash. "Well—not yet, but I'll talk to him later." She leaned toward him and rested her hands on his. As she did, he experienced a strange tingle in his belly he hadn't had for a long time.

Oh crap. Please don't do this to me now. I cannot fall for this woman.

"He invited us to dinner tonight. He's—" Her eyes danced

back and forth as she searched for what to say. "protective of me and would like to meet you before deciding."

"I'm not sure I follow. Are you saying he tries to protect you?"

This is when he'll threaten to cut my balls off if I touch her.

"Yes." She removed her hands and scrunched her brows. "It may be why I'm still single." Her full lips pouted, and he focused on them.

Well, it isn't your appearance, that's for certain.

"But I told him you were engaged. So, he agreed to think about it." She grinned as he frowned in his mind.

Oh, yeah—my fiancée. I'm glad she reminded me. Dammit!

"We can go back to the hotel and get our things in case he agrees. He's sending an aircraft to the local airport. Home is only forty minutes away by air."

He started the truck and put the vehicle into gear. "Well, all right. Let's try to convince him."

#

The private Citation jet flight was a brief twenty-two minutes. He figured she had taken the journey before, but either on a prop plane or she has a poor sense of time. Perhaps the latter.

An AMG Mercedes CLS collected them at the Vasquez airstrip. When he inspected the car, they had outfitted it with traditional "cartel/mafioso" accoutrements such as bulletproof glass and tires. It was also armor-plated, and packed with other surprises.

"Um, is your father expecting trouble?"

Despite her dark olive features, blood ran to her cheeks. She tilted her head downward and sighed. "Daddy was an army general. Many folks hate him for some things our own government has done to our people. It's only for his protection."

Bullshit. You know what he does.

"It's why he funds my charity. Dad hopes, by giving back to the community, some might forgive him."

Is it something you're trying to convince yourself of?

As he opened the heavy door for her, he nodded. He thought by nodding, she would assume he understood or accepted her explanation. As he gazed out the window, he took note of everything around him on the short two-kilometer drive. When they reached the gate, they were met by a towering structure at least thirteen feet tall, flanked by guardhouses on either side. It was a simple yet astonishing sight, constructed from wood and chain-link fencing.

I guess he's not trying to impress anyone here.

No less than four guards occupied them, and they carried submachine guns. The driveway, long and straight, lined with decorative landscaping, stretched deep through the jungle. Beyond the ornate flowering plants, dense trees and foliage straddled both sides. A massive house filled his view as they entered the clearing.

Wow!

To his left was a dog kennel with some German Shepherds roaming inside.

Fuck. Dogs.

Another one was on a leash, straining and choking, as it pulled an armed guard along for the ride.

A well-trained animal wouldn't do that. It's helpful to know.

Off to the right was a six-door garage and a vast barn, matching the home in color and architecture. At least four horses grazed in the field beyond the fence. The car circled around a massive stone fountain.

The fountain consisted of three huge fish standing on their tails with their 'chests' meeting in the middle. The water spilled out of their mouths and splashed a good couple of feet high before cascading down their backs into the pool below.

What an ugly ass thing.

They entered the residence via an impressive central staircase. Someone he assumed was the head maid met them in the atrium.

"Senorita, your father expects you. I think he started without you."

Adriana turned back to him and grabbed his hand. "Come on, we don't want to keep him waiting."

He took her hand and the strange feeling returned.

Before they stepped into the dining hall, he jerked his hand out of hers. Remembering the façade of being engaged and the certainty Vasquez had already done a background check on him.

Besides, he didn't want to risk not getting his permission to use the estate for staging and giving him his chance to fulfill his objective.

They walked into a spacious room, opening out onto a veranda. Birds chirped in the vegetation next to the immense pool. Further out, the setting sun's orange and violet hues reflected off the water, forming the natural harbor. Nearby was a vast warehouse with its own docks on the seafront.

Hmm. Let me guess what's in there.

Without hesitation, she introduced him. "Daddy, I'd like to present you to David Saye. He is the Director of *Canadians Helping the World's Children*, out of Vancouver. His organization has been assisting me to administer vaccinations for the past seven weeks."

General Vasquez remained seated at the end of a long wooden table. Candlelight illuminated his face, bouncing off the walls and reflecting off the tabletop. His neutral expression remained as he chewed pork and sipped wine. He grunted a greeting, disinterested, and Blake tried to think of something to say to break the ice. Glancing over at the man as he pulled the chair out for Adriana, hoping he would notice his gentle behavior.

Nothing.

He walked to the other side to sit next to his indifferent host. Servants placed plates with jerked pork and plantains, along with a mixed green salad, before the two guests. A plate of bread sat in front of him, and he lifted it and offered it to her.

As they ate, Vasquez remained muted. Blake attempted to break the silence on several occasions, but the man responded with short, neutral responses.

This is going to be tougher than I thought.

After a less-than-successful dinner, coffee was served, and he continued to try to get a response from the general. Something different was necessary, so he came up with another line. "I couldn't help but notice your horses. They remind me of some of my own back home."

Vasquez's brow raised, and he glanced over at him.

Ah ha, got you.

"You have horses, Mister…"

"Saye. David Saye."

Vasquez cleared his throat and sipped his coffee. "What kind do you have?"

"I own two Paints and an Appaloosa. They're boarded on my parents' farm. I'd like more, but work keeps me away. Three is all my folks say they can handle. What I would like to do is take them to shows. They might do well."

Vasquez wiped his mouth with a napkin. He rose. "Come with me. Allow me to show you something."

Holy shit, that was quick.

He stood, turned to Adriana and grinned with widened eyes. She smiled back and waved him on. He guided him to his personal office. Through the substantial wooden double doors, he cast his eyes upon a one-half-scale bronze statue of a horse. Oil paintings of all of his horses covered the walls.

Alongside each painting, he arranged the ribbons the horse won in various competitions. The frames were dark mahogany, decorated with ornate flower carvings along with other equestrian themes like saddles, spurs, and lassos.

Blake walked around the room and took in as much information as he could; computers, file cabinets, the desk; anything able to store intelligence. "These are impressive, sir. Did the same artist do all of your artwork?"

"All but one." The general knocked twice on the statue. There was a dull thud. Not the ringing sound he expected, and he made a mental note. "This is one of my prized possessions. It is a half-scale statue of my most winning horse. She passed away three years ago. It is a fitting way to honor her."

"I'm sorry for your loss. I'm sure she was a wonderful animal. Thank you for showing this to me." He scanned the room.

Vasquez stood with his feet shoulder width apart and crossed his arms in front of his chest. His voice was without kindness. "Mr. Saye."

"Yes?"

"What is your interest in my daughter?"

Here it comes. Off with my balls!

"Strictly professional, sir. I'm getting married this fall. My fiancée and I have been together for around seven years."

He nodded and accepted Blake's answer. "Excellent."

Whew.

"As you can tell, I'm protective of her. She's a grown woman. I may not be able to manage what she does, or with whom she does it when she is out doing charitable work. But when she's here, I have total control."

Blake clasped his hands. "I appreciate that, sir."

"Fine! Now, I understand you are asking to stay here so you and my daughter can check out the surrounding islands with…" He waved his arms back and forth. "…these drugs, or whatever, you have to give to the children."

"Yes. That's correct."

"How long?"

Fuck Dude, until I kill you and steal your shit. I don't know.

"I'm not sure. Perhaps a couple of weeks? We don't know the extent of the situation yet or how many days or weeks it will take. But, to be honest, how long I stay here is up to you. I would greatly appreciate anything."

#

Vasquez stood with a crumpled face. Pacing back and forth before stopping. "I need you to check another thing."

Luca walked around and sat at the desk. He typed on the keyboard as his employer watched from behind. They found an announcement in the Vancouver Sun archives.

He pointed to the monitor. "Here it is."

The general leaned over, squinted and read aloud. "The parents of…Allison Slade…engagement… David Saye…wedding date…October twenty-seventh." He straightened back up. "Is there a photograph?"

He scrolled down to reveal a picture of Blake and a dazzling blonde.

His assistant glanced at his employer. "Is this what you wanted?"

"It is."

#

Blake leaned back in his chair, sipping his cognac, when the host arrived. Vasquez beckoned him.

Turning to Adriana, he stood. "Excuse me."

He strode to Vasquez. A half-smile creased the general's face. "I understand you have an early start tomorrow."

"We do, sir."

The man nodded and ran his hand through his thick beard. "What's your fiancée's name?"

Well, you sneaky fat bastard. You checked up on me.

"Allison. Why?"

"I'm sure you'll be happy together. I have a guest house prepared for you."

Vasquez pivoted and walked away a few paces before he stopped. "One more thing, Mr. Saye."

"Yes?"

"Don't wander around. The guards don't appreciate strangers lurking on the estate grounds after dark."

"I understand."

Thanks for the warning.

5

Isle de la Juventud, Cuba
June 19th
02:00 local (07:00 GMT)

Blake opened his eyes. He had trained his mind to be his internal alarm long before he began serving his country.

An unfortunate mishap with his alarm clock, when he was at the University of Colorado. With no money for a new one, it forced him to wake on his own.

He pulled back the covers and let the ambient moonlight splashing through the open window shine across the naked body of the beautiful Adriana, who slept next to him.

Her room was in the main house near her father's, and he had sneaked his way in from the guest's quarters.

The general's guards weren't as on their toes as Vasquez believed. Too much tequila and a lack of discipline, or perhaps overconfidence, on behalf of the general himself.

It may have been the combination, contributing to their becoming lazy and ineffective. If the rumors held true, he was sure Vasquez would have them beaten or killed for their cavalier behavior. But it wouldn't matter after tonight.

The night had reached a comfortable seventy-three degrees.

The smell of the sea wafted in through the open window as the curtains danced back and forth, casting shadows on the opposing wall from the full moonlight. That he was supposed to be engaged in his cover didn't prevent Adriana's desire for him.

Working together every day for the past two months, he got to understand her, and even though his persona was a ruse, it never prevented her from becoming attracted to him.

She didn't know the real man. He fought against his own appetite to be with her, but it wasn't long before his lust consumed him.

The odd feeling in his gut grew as they kissed. Was he falling for her? They explored each other's bodies with eager anticipation for what was next.

He savored her touch and the gentle way she fulfilled him. This added to his guilt for what he was about to do and the pain of never seeing her again.

It had been a wonderful evening to make love, but not the best night for what was to come.

He would have preferred for it to be as dark as possible, but knowing he would rid the world of a man like Vasquez, he didn't care if the sun shone; he would adjust and get the job completed.

He raised his upper body and gazed at her once more. It sickened him to see how serene and innocent she appeared.

She wasn't yet cynical enough to realize there were bad people on the planet. People who would slip chloral hydrate into an unsuspecting girl's drink.

Unlike his, whose intentions were indeed noble, others might have done things to her while she slept.

He was glad he got the dose right—it would have been a shame to kill her. Not like her scumbag father, she was at least trying to do a little good in the world.

Sliding out of bed, he dressed, and stepped over to the window from where he slipped into her chamber earlier. Outside, on the ground and tethered to a rope, was his gear. He leaned out and pulled it in.

Inside the bag, he had several tactical knives, throwing spikes, primer cord, three small magnetic mines with timers, an experimental set of night-vision glasses, and a package full of raw meat. There were also various electronic items for hacking computers, alarm systems, etcetera.

He strapped on a spring-loaded sheath on both of his forearms and inserted one of the long blades into each of them. He flexed his right forearm, and the blade slid into his hand.

After he snapped the weapon into place, he screwed a silencer onto a Glock 23 and tucked it in the small of his back.

The primary home, from a bird's-eye view, was akin to two Christian crosses connected at the bottom, with the top of the crosses pointing east or west.

On the east wing of the estate, the general, Adriana, and any personal guests slept. Vasquez's room was the on the south tip, closest to the shore, and Adriana's was on the easternmost.

He cracked the door and peered into the hallway. From the time he spent at the property, he observed the general enjoyed his privacy, and it was rare for the guards to come into this wing of the home.

Your love of privacy is going to be your biggest mistake.

He crept along the hall, careful with each placement of his feet. When he reached the general's door, he retrieved his night-vision.

Instead of the bulky kind he was used to, these were like normal, dark-rimmed glasses. Sensors built into the frames, pulled in the light and cast their familiar greenish hue.

From his pants pocket, he extracted a tiny tin of spray lubricant and applied it to all the hinges.

We wouldn't want any squeaks waking you now, would we?

Stuffing the can back, he gripped his Glock, took a deep breath, and opened the door.

The room was cavernous. The only furniture was the bed, a small desk, and a couple of chairs. Tuckedf up in the duvet, the general slept unaware.

This is almost too easy. Be aware of everything.

He crept over to the bed thand inspected his surroundings once more. His heartbeat thumped in his ears. A rush of adrenaline pumped through his veins.

It was rare for him ever to get this close to one of his targets.

Blake raised his weapon to the Vasquez's head, placed his finger on the trigger, and took a deep breath.

#

Light flooded the room. To prevent flash blindness, Blake's glasses went black. He yanked them from his face—a fraction too late to thwart the hold on his arms.

Men on either side grabbed him and held him in a vice-like grip. He curled his fists and shifted his weight. His captor's hold tightened, and a cold, steel gun barrel pressed against the base of his skull. They ripped his Glock from his hands. He glanced to his right. Under the covers were nothing more than pillows positioned in the shape of a sleeping body. Blake closed his eyes.

Fucking stupid!

A hidden door in the wall opened. "Small pockets behind concealed panels in the wall make for an excellent hiding place, wouldn't you say, Agent MacKay."

The blood rushed to his head in anger. His heart sank.

How in the… Someone tipped him off.

His captor approached him. "It would appear your concerns go beyond the poor children of Cuba. Perhaps you'd like to tell me something about it?"

Who the fuck told him? Who?

From his peripheral vision, an arm extended and handed Vasquez Blake's Glock.

He stood, grasped by the two guards. His eyes were staring toward his still-intended target. The wrath of betrayal reached its tipping point. Both men were about the same size, carrying automatic weapons and knives tucked into their tactical vests.

A pair of rent-a-ranger armed thugs and an old fat ass with my Glock stuck in the waistband of his pants.

Given the opportunity, he could take them and still complete his mission. He only needed to wait for the right moment.

Vasquez stepped closer. "I opened my home to you, shared my food, my thoughts, my hospitality—and you do this shit!" The general delivered a blow to Blake's solar plexus. "To me, you son-of-a-bitch?" Another punch made Blake bend over. He coughed. The men holding him intensified their grip.

The pain in his belly subsided. "Who told you I was here?"

The man he'd come to kill squinted his eyes and tightened his jaw. "Let's say someone does not want you to find out where I got my latest weapon from."

The latest weapon?

"I don't know what you're talking about."

The right fist crossed the left side of his cheek as Vasquez followed through. He could feel the swelling start. The next two punches, delivered to the center of his chest, hurt the most.

Blake's knees buckled, and he tried to catch his breath.

Fuck!

The other two men were still grasping his arms tight. The general took a step back. "Stand him up!"

He came in close again and pointed his finger at Blake. "Who gave the order to have me killed?"

He stared at Vasquez and smiled. The slap across the face wiped it away. "Tell me instantly, or I will make this a painful ordeal for you." His captor nodded to one of the pair holding him. Two hefty punches slammed into his kidneys.

The man yelled. "Tell him now!"

The pain from the kidneys pierced through his body. His head spun, making it difficult to stand. He regained his composure. Lifting his head to the general, he smirked. "The Mexican drug gangs—they want a bigger discount on their next shipment."

Loathing eyes stared back at him. The kind condemned men saw right before execution. "How amusing."

Another devastating punch reached deep into Blake's abdomen. "Bullshit! Tell me who called the hit."

Blake was bent over. Bile rolled around in his stomach, threatening to make him spew. He tilted his head upward and snarled, "Fuck you. Ask whoever tipped you off."

The guard behind him slammed the butt of his rifle in the middle of his back, which felled him to his knees. With his eyes closed, he tried to shake away the darkness beginning to envelop his vision. Vasquez stepped forward, kicking him in the upper abdomen, and almost knocking the wind out of him.

"You're trying my patience, Mr. MacKay. Pick his ass up! Hold him!" He punched Blake in the face twice and kneed him in the stomach.

He dropped to his knees again. Blood oozed from the corner of his right brow and nose. It seeped into his mouth. The metallic taste made him salivate.

Okay, I've got to take control. This is enough. I can't stand much more of this. He's not about to tell me who tipped him off.

Blake spat. Both in the field and in training, he'd taken plenty of beatings in the past. He was aware of his limitations. How much he could withstand and retain the capacity to operate. Those limits were closing in fast.

He spat more blood onto the floor.

"For the last time, you're going to tell me what I need to know and you're going to do it…" Vasquez drew his foot back, "Now!" The blow landed square in the middle of his chest, knocking him back. His lungs emptied like a punctured balloon. His eyes opened wide as he gasped for air. Both guards regained their grip on him.

He panicked as he struggled to breathe.

That one did it. I've got to take control.

Vasquez prepped himself for another kick. "You're going to die tonight, but not before you tell me what I want to know!"

As Vasquez cocked his foot back, Blake raised his hand. "Wait!" He coughed. "Please." He held up a single finger while he still fought to breathe. "Hold on, I'll tell you." He swallowed hard. "Please—let me—catch my breath."

The general nodded to both guards to release him.

Oh, you've screwed up now, fat ass.

He'd had the wind knocked out of him but had already composed himself.

I need to stall them a little longer. Keep coughing and gasping for air.

This bought him some time, perhaps ten or fifteen seconds.

"You had better tell me everything I want to know, Mr. MacKay."

Blake continued his charade of choking and wheezing.

"Please." He took two deep breaths. "I promise I will. Just a few more—seconds."

He sat on the floor on his knees and acted as if he were still struggling for breath, stealing a glance at the two armed guys. Each had a Heckler & Koch submachine gun. Excellent weapons, but neither of them had silencers.

Where are the remaining guards? These two are not equipped with radios. Why? I still have a chance to escape if the other men are unaware of this. I mustn't let them use their firearms.

There would be virtually no possibility of his escaping alive if any of the guards fired a shot, since it would draw the attention of all the other guys.

He leaned over and put his hands on the ground. Blood dripped from his cuts and nose.

Vasquez made a fist again. "No more time! Tell me now.".

He acted as if he were still having problems breathing. Motioning for the general to bend down, his voice was a cracked whisper. "Please, come nearer. I can talk better like this."

As his target bent down, he released the tactical knife from his right sleeve. It sprang into his hand. Vasquez moved in closer.

Now you're mine.

He jammed the blade into the center of the soft tissue under the general's jaw and into his brain. He twisted it and ripped it out. His target's eyes were wide with fear as blood pulsed out of the wound and sprayed the room.

Die, you son-of-a-bitch!

He savored the satisfaction of seeing the terror and surprise on his victim's face. Vasquez's hands went to his neck, and all he managed was a gurgled plea.

He retrieved his Glock from Vasquez's waist and shot the guy to his right, with three silenced shots to the chest. The man fell back, letting his weapon fly into the air. He dropped to the floor like a sack of meat.

The other guard was standing close behind him. Still on the ground, he lurched up and backward with all his strength and hoped to throw his adversary off balance. He didn't realize how close he and his assailant were to the wall at their backs. The fellow was smashed into the wall. He spun and banged the H&K into the wall four times before the guard released it. The weapon fired a single shot and fell to the floor.

Oh, shit! I've gotta get outta here fast.

He grabbed the guy's arm and flipped him over his shoulder, slamming him down. As he adjusted to make his next attack, the guy rolled over onto his back and kicked him in the lower abdomen, then delivered a leg sweep, dropping him to the floor again.

He glanced over as the man pulled a combat knife from his hip.

Dammit! You're a better fighter than you appear. It's time to end this.

The assailant lunged at him. He swiftly righted himself, unleashing a sidekick that popped the joint of his attacker's left knee. Ligaments and tendons ripped as the force sent the man crashing to the floor, writhing in agony as he reached desperately for his weapon.

Still on the ground, he spun, booting the blade out of reach. His heel slammed into the man's kidneys twice in rapid succession. Raising his leg high, he dropped his full weight onto the guard's chest, leaving the eyes wide and mouth gasping for air.

He lifted his leg once more, driving his heel with brutal force into the throat to crush the windpipe beneath. crimson gore gurgled from lips as Blake's hands grasped at the ruined neck. Moving in swiftly, he slid behind the now-still head and twisted it hard to the right, ensuring the spine would break. A final glance told him no others were near to engage.

He stood, his breathing heavy. Sweat and blood ran down his face.

What about the shot? Did anyone hear it?

Floodlights illuminated the room and alarms pierced the once silent night.

6

Time was not on Blake's side before more men flooded the room. Having a few more minutes to recover from his beating was not a luxury he could afford. Bolting over to the desk, he rummaged through the drawers.

There must be something here.

He found a thumb drive and put it in his pocket.

Dammit! I've got to get to his office!

He rushed to the door and cracked it open. Six guards were barreling toward the room. He closed it and flipped the lock, then scrambled for a chair and jammed it under the handle to buy a few precious seconds.

Collecting his Glock, night-vision glasses, and the submachine gun, along with extra ammo from the dead bodies, he then hurried out onto the balcony. It was broad, with stone rails and columns. His breathing was still labored as he hid behind the closest column. The sound of barking dogs approaching filled his ears. As he peeked out, they ran in the opposite direction, on the far side of the pool.

Gotta go, now.

To his right was a copper downpipe. He slid on his backpack and winced from the pain in his ribs. With the rifle slung over his shoulder, he grabbed hold of the pipe and shimmied to the ground.

A thick row of bushes provided ample cover.

A brief glance over the shrubs gave him a clearer idea of which way he should go. As he headed toward the west side of the mansion, there was a thunderous crash in the general's quarters as the guards broke through the door he had barred. Voices yelled orders in Spanish. When they discovered the bodies, they would intensify their search.

The meat!

He reached into his pack and, taking out the bag of fresh-cut sirloin, scattered it where he squatted.

As he moved on, he came to the edge of the veranda, looking out over the pool. Two sentries stood in the center, in front of the broad glass doors. They carried automatic weapons.

I've got to get to the other side.

He searched around until he found a medium-sized stone, and he tossed it to the far end of the veranda. One guard put his hand out to stop the other from speaking and lifted his rifle. As the pair raced in the direction of the spot where the rock landed, He drew his Glock and ran across.

His first shot slammed through the side of the guy's head in a sea of red. The closest man turned toward him and raised his weapon. He dropped to his knees and slid while he fired. Two rounds forced his head back, spraying gore and gray matter. His body fell, rolled down the steps, and plunged into the pool. Blood flowing from the dead man's cranium stained the crystal blue water.

Blake jumped off the opposite end of the veranda. He stayed near the ground and did his best to stay concealed. Now on the western side of the mansion, he was closer to Vasquez's office. The shadows from the shrubs were a welcome friend to aid in his concealment.

Voices from two more guards kicked Blake's already-pounding heart into overdrive. In a flash, he sank to his belly, waiting for them to pass. Both men ran by, unaware of his presence. Wishing he could remain there a moment longer and recover, the barking of the dogs convinced him otherwise.

Shit! I hope they find the meat.

Heading toward the general's office in the western direction, he crawled with caution along the rear of the house. Ahead was another doorway into the building near his intended destination. A lone man stood guarding the entrance.

Dammit! Can't I catch a break?

He removed his backpack and slid out one of the throwing spikes. Crouched down, he moved closer to get the perfect angle. When the man turned away, He rose and threw the weapon, embedding it deep into his target's right kidney.

Before the dying man's thrashing and bellowing alerted others of his distress, He leaped to the portico, grabbed his head, and slit his throat. He eased the body into the shadows on the ground. The door was ajar, and he entered the mansion. To his left was the hall leading to Vasquez's office. He sauntered toward the closed double doors so as not to draw attention if the hallway was under electronic surveillance. His all black attire matched those of the guards searching for him.

Vasquez had locked the doors. A quick pry with his knife did the trick. After entering the office, a deep sigh dispersed some of his anxiety.

The night-vision glasses once again filled his view with a green hue. At the general's desk, he found a few folders full of worthless papers. Another flash drive sat in a drawer. He shook his head and scanned the room.

Where's his damn laptop? There's gotta be a safe in here somewhere.

His fingers searched for a button under the edge of the desk. A bead of sweat, mixed with blood, dropped onto the blotter. He wiped his brow with his arm. Behind him, he pulled books off the shelf and probed for a hidden panel. He flipped through the pictures but found nothing. Voices outside the door froze him; his finger ready on the trigger of the H&K. They faded, and he exhaled.

Fuck—me.

His eyes swept the room.

Where would I keep it?

They stopped at the statue of the horse.

Gotcha.

They had bolted the animal to a massive slab of granite. It had real horsehair for the mane and tail. They had made the saddle into a scale model of the one the general used and crafted it of leather. He searched beneath the belly, in the saddle, in the creature's ears, and under the mane. He explored behind its thighs and to the rear.

Dammit. Where is it?

When Blake lifted the tail, he discovered the button and the indentation where the asshole should have been.

Allowing a quiet chuckle, he smiled.

I'll be damned.

He pressed the button. There was a click, and the saddle moved. With a slight pull on the underside, it opened on its hidden hinges and was soon sitting upside down, resting on the horse's side. Inside was the safe door. He didn't have the time or the inclination to attempt cracking it.

He glanced at the door, listening for anyone coming while he removed a roll of high-yield primer cord and a detonator from his pack. With care, he wrapped the cord three times around the edges of the door where it met the body of the safe and inserted the blasting cap. With the detonator in hand, he moved to the other end of the room and ducked behind a couch with his finger on the button. He closed his eyes, taking a deep breath.

Well, they'll know where I'm at now.

The blast, which focused on the safe's door, peeled back the bronze statue's sides like an onion. The smoke and heat sensors in the room activated the alarms. Blake ran to the smoldering statue, unlocked the entrance, and collected everything inside—including a laptop—and stuffed it all into his rucksack as quickly as his arms would allow. As they hurried to the room, voices and footfalls filled the hallway outside the office.

From his bag, he removed an anti-personnel mine and set the timer to fifteen seconds before chucking it to the middle of the floor. He grabbed a bust of Fidel Castro off of a table and threw it through the office's rear window. As he jumped through the shattered glass and out onto the west lawn of the estate, the guards raced into the room.

A quick roll, and then to his feet. He sprinted the short distance to the massive garage and got to the entrance as the mine exploded. Screams from several men filled the air. The heat from the blast warmed his back as it rolled out through the opening. The garage door closed behind him, and he glanced upward as debris from the explosion peppered the roof.

Inside was a menagerie of vehicles; from motorcycles to Ferraris, Lamborghinis and a Bugatti.

He could hear shouting and the footsteps of more guards as they got nearer. "Look in the garage!" Blake's eyes darted back and forth, scanning the interior of the building.

Shit, where is it?

At last, he found the ride he hoped would be there; the bulletproof AMG Mercedes CLS.

As he approached the car, the side garage door burst open, and the sentries started shooting. The men were forced to flee outside once more as he, protected by the car, opened fire with the H&K. He got into the Mercedes, hit the start button.

Nothing happened.

You had to make things more difficult for me, didn't you?

Three men hunched over and re-entered. Bullets ricocheted off the glass and trunk of the vehicle. Blazing steel marched across the hood in a relentless line. The window of the Ferrari next to him shattered. Blake unzipped a pocket in his bag and retrieved a diminutive box. He reached under the dash and connected it to the ODB port. Once in place, he switched it on. As it ran through its sequencing, he shot a glance at the guards as they came closer.

The tiny screen was illuminated: Step 1… Step 2… Step 3…. His adrenaline pumped as his head turned on a swivel, looking out all the windows at the approaching men.

Come on dammit! Get a move on!

The welcoming sound of a chime made him turn his attention away from the hostiles. The screen read, *Start Car*. He pressed the starter. The forceful V-8 roared to life. He withdrew another mine and set the timer for five seconds. Opening the window, he tossed it through the shattered window of the Ferrari. Blake floored the pedal and burst through the garage door as the explosive erupted into a brilliant ball of flame.

7

Off the coast of Isle de la Juventud, Cuba
  02:38 local (07:38 GMT)

Explosions in the distance jolted Zahmir Al-Hamwi from his sleep. Springing from his bed, he darted to the wall, grabbed the intercom, and called the bridge. Mustafa, his right-hand man, answered the com.

He squinted. "What's going on?"

"Something is happening on shore. There was an explosion followed by gunfire."

"We're not being attacked?"

"No. It is all coming from the estate."

"I'm on my way."

He slipped on his sandals, reached for a pair of binoculars, and ran out to the deck.

Someone had better not be stealing the weapons we came for.

Once there, he focused on the general's plantation. The night glowed on the western part of the house, from where, moments ago, a huge fireball engulfed what used to be the massive garage.

Mustafa approached. "Can you tell what is happening?"

His jaw clenched. Anger swelled up from within at the thought of losing his precious cargo. He lowered the binoculars and handed them to Mustafa. "No. Gather the men. Two boats. Everyone armed. We're going ashore now."

"Yes, of course." Mustafa ran off while he went back to his quarters to get his rifle. He was in the lead boat as they made the one-klick ride to shore. Waves lapped against the fiberglass hull as the engine hummed. Despite the silence caused by the breeze, the sight of fires burning reminded him of his youth and how he ended up joining a feared terror network.

#

Zahmir Al-Hamwi was 31 years old and from Khaje Bughra, a suburb of Kabul. He grew up poor, with three brothers and two sisters. He was the third youngest of the four boys and the fifth of six children. They often neglected him because his older brother, Nasir, had severe mental retardation and required constant care.

His youger sister suffered from polio. His mother had no time for him. When he was fourteen, Nasir finally died from a congenital heart defect. It was more of a blessing than anything, but it still upset his parents. His mother lost whatever smile she could sometimes muster when, five months later, someone murdered his older sister.

In order to help the family, she sold herself to anyone who could pay. His father and mother disowned her out of shame, refusing to give her a proper burial. Zahmir took the loss the hardest because she, seven years his elder, raised him and nurtured him more than his mother ever did. He vowed to Allah that he would avenge her death.

Along with his brother, Osama, it took only three weeks for them to find out who murdered her. A new person to the neighborhood, Ayman Mohammed Fadhil, had set up an import/export business in Afshar, an area a few kilometers southeast of Khaje Bughra.

With no planning, the brothers watched the shop for their mark to appear. When he arrived, they crept up on him from outside the premises, pushed him inside, and threw him to the floor. As Osama closed the door behind them, Zahmir approached the confused man.

With wide eyes and a scrunched, weathered brow, Ayman begged with the two youngsters from his position on the ground. "What are you doing? Who are you? Are you aware of who I am?"

The pair took another step closer.

With a raised open hand, the man pleaded, "I demand to know the meaning of this."

He had taken a jambiya from his father's chamber. Without saying a word, showing no emotion or any sorrow, he slammed the nine-inch blade into Ayman's stomach and twisted. He whispered into his victim's ear. "This is for my sister."

The shifting in his victim's eyes showed he was searching his mind for who his attacker was talking about. Ayman gawked at him with the fear of death in his eyes. He struggled to speak, but managed just two words. "The whore?"

He withdrew the blade and screamed. He stabbed the man repeatedly. When Osama pulled him off, their target had over forty stab wounds in his chest and face. What the two brothers didn't realize was that the business was a front for an Al-Qaeda terror operation. They found the boys only hours after the murder, but not by authorities.

He heard the knock and went to the front room of their small home, watching as his father answered the door. Two men stood in the doorway.

His father faced them, his face stern. "What do you want?"

"We wish to talk to your sons."

"What is your interest in them?"

The taller of the two put his hand on the chest of their father, pushing him aside. They entered the house. The other man followed.

"I did not invite you."

The second guy pulled back his robe, revealing an automatic rifle. A wave of terror spread over him when he saw the weapon. *Oh no! They know what we've done.*

"Zahmir! Osama! Come here. There are two men that want to talk to you."

Their father closed the door behind him.

He hung his head. "I am here, father."

Osama came into the room, and Zahmir had an expression of panic on his face. Osama's eyes widened at his brother's countenance and then turned to his father. "Yes?"

Their father gazed upon them. His lips were down turned, and his tone was stern. "These gentlemen want to speak to you."

The taller of the two strode over and circled the boys. The two brothers watched with wide eyes, fear rising in both of them. Finally, from behind them, the tall one spoke.

"My name is Asul. We're here to offer our gratitude."

Confusion replaced Zahmir's panic. His brow furrowed. "For what?"

His father took a step forward. "Zahmir!"

Asul smiled. "It's all right—I appreciate the directness." He strolled around and faced the boys. "You eliminated a problem for us."

Osama's eyes widened. "We did?"

A scowl adorned his face. "Do not play dumb. You killed the murderer of your sister."

Their father's face reddened, and his voice rose. "What have you done? Tell me now!"

"Silence!" Asul raised his hand. "I'll get to the point. He was a thorn in our side. His instructions were to lie low, not draw attention, and he'd been warned too many times. The man whored around. He got sloppy and your sister was on the unfortunate end of that. We planned to eliminate him, but you two did that for us, and for that, we are grateful."

The two stood silent. Zahmir observed with keen interest as Asul gracefully navigated the room, exuding an air of restless energy. *What could they want with us now?*

"We'd like you to come and join our cause. We would train you and treat you well."

Their father stepped closer. "No, they will not be a part of the Jihad! They're still children."

Asul glared at their father. "You have misunderstood. This isn't a request." He focused his attention on his partner. "What's the punishment for murder these days?"

"Public execution by hanging."

He grinned while facing their father. Do you see what I mean? The alternative is far worse. In addition, we will reimburse you. He turned to the young men. "We shall take care of your family, and you have the chance to contribute to the eradication of the infidels from the world."

There was no hesitation. They packed what little belongings they had and left with the two men. Over the course of the following seventeen years, he developed a reputation as an Al-Qaeda soldier who was dependable but deadly, and whom no one should ever cross. He always followed instructions and didn't let anyone get in his way of achieving his goals. Mustafa's hand on his shoulder snapped him back to reality.

#

"Here."

"Zahmir!"

His name resonating over the splash of the sea against the hull brought him back to reality. He faced his friend and peered down as they handed him a rope.

Mustafa pushed it into his hand. "Here. Take it. We're approaching the dock."

"Right." He grabbed it and prepared to exit the boat as they approached the landing.

A loud crash in the distance and automatic weapons fire caused them all to duck.

8

A hail of gunfire met Blake after he burst through the garage door. The sound of bullets ricocheting off the side of the car filled the air.

It was a natural reaction to duck, even though the car's armor was more than efficient.

Shit!

Another explosion ripped through the building as fuel tanks ruptured from the searing heat and flames.

He glanced in the mirror. As the fire enveloped the structure, another explosion further decimated the already engulfed structure. The concussion flung bodies in all directions, slamming them into the walls and trees like worthless bags of sand.

From the side of the burning garage, two SUVs emerged in pursuit. He pointed the Mercedes toward the ugly fish fountain in the middle of the driveway. Past the statue, along the path, and then on to the main gate.

Floodlights lit everything in the yard. About three meters beyond was nothing but jungle. He had the opportunity to flee through a natural avenue made of bushes and trees.

Perhaps this was a bad idea.

Had he not been in a bulletproof vehicle, a motorcycle to escape through the dense woodland would have been a better choice.

He steered the Mercedes around the fish sculpture. The tires smoked and created a thick white fog he used as cover. He could smell the rubber as the smoke permeated the cabin of the car. The act taunted the men in the SUV to catch up.

Come and get me assholes.

As he came back to face the garage, two SUVs barreled in his direction at breakneck speed. Sentries poured out of the house to his left like ants on a disturbed hill. Four guards ran toward him.

As he made another circuit of the fountain, a man raced into the driveway and opened fire.

"You're an idiot!" He swerved over and nailed the fool head-on with the front of his car. The simpleton leaped to his feet; his legs twisted at an odd angle. He tumbled off the rear of the automobile after rolling across the roof.

Blake ejected a half-spent clip from his H&K and replaced it with a fresh one. He went around the circle again. The SUVs were getting closer.

Okay, enough of the smoke. Time to get the hell outta here.

The Mercedes sped toward the gate, along the long driveway. Another glance in the mirror. The grill of a Range Rover was close behind him. He swerved from left to right. Bullets plinked off the back of the motorcar. Another brief peek revealed a man climbing from the side window of the other SUV.

Oh shit! RPG!

The SUV approached him from the right. He weaved the car into the SUV.

"Get over you son-of-a-bitch!" With a rapid turn to the left, the Mercedes veered off the path to the edge of the jungle. Another glance in the mirror showed the man at his rear aiming the rocket-propelled grenade.

The RPG launched from its cradle. He swung hard right as the explosive hit a tree and detonated. The overwhelming impact of the concussion proved to be too formidable for the bulletproof rear window, causing it to fracture into countless fragments throughout the car's interior. "Shit!"

As Blake swerved back onto the road, he crashed into the

Range Rover, forcing it to brake and return to a trailing position. The automatic guns firing smashed his rear-view mirror. Blood dripped from his forehead.

"Son-of-a-bitch! Now you've pissed me off!"

He wiped his face, then grabbed the H&K. Adrenaline pumped at full capacity as he turned and fired out through the back window while trying to control the vehicle. Lead peppered the front grill of the Chevy. The headlights shattered and steam pushed outward as it escaped from the punctured radiator.

He returned to steering his car. The main gate was in sight. Sentry's scattered about. He twisted round and opened fire on the Chevy again. With the front tires blown out, somehow it kept coming.

"You like that? Come on!"

He refocused on the roadway and headed for the exit. Bullets ricocheted off the hood. As the firing intensified, he veered hard right. The crossfire from the guards at the gate went straight through the windshield of the trailing vehicle. Riddled with holes, it veered to the left and lurched off the road.

The truck hit a palm tree, snapping it in half and the impact sent it back onto the track where it rolled. Bodies flew from the windows like rag dolls and the wagon continued rolling.

The Range Rover swerved to avoid the wrecked truck. In doing so, a surviving guard smashed through the windscreen. The vehicle took a sharp turn and slammed into a palm tree.

In the melee, the guards at the front gate stopped shooting, watching the turmoil unfold before them. He seized the moment. Opening the sunroof, he stuck the H&K out, and mashed the gas pedal to the floor while firing at the men standing by his only exit. The Mercedes burst through the gate and tore off along the road.

He killed the lights and drove only by the moonlight. The car covered the two kilometers to the airfield in record time. A glance in the side mirrors revealed nobody was following him. The tightness in his shoulders loosened. He breathed a sigh of relief when the outline of the control tower was stark against the moonlit sky.

To his left was a heavy cluster of trees, so he steered the car toward them, pulled in as far as it would go, and abandoned it. He grabbed his bag and dug for his night-vision binoculars.

Ok, you dead fat bastard, I know you've got people there. The small hangar appeared with the familiar greenish hue. *No movement.*

He scanned to the right. The silhouette of an MD 530F and an older Huey came into view. *Bingo.* With his rifle in hand, he dashed across the road toward the airport.

Keeping low was key as he approached the fence. Prone on the ground, he withdrew a pair of wire cutters and cut his way through the chain-link. Blake crept to the first helicopter, the MD. Staying in the shadows, he glanced through the binoculars. *There you are.*

There was movement inside the hangar. Several men and a Jeep with a fifty-caliber machine gun mounted on the rear. He reached into his bag and removed the last mine. Keeping on his belly, he crawled the ten meters to the Huey, set the explosive to manual detonation and placed it on the bottom of the chopper.

Back in the MD, Blake rummaged through his things once more.

Two and a half clips for the HK. Three for the Glock.

His finger was on the first switch, engaging the start-up sequence for the helicopter, when he stopped. More movement from the hangar caught his eye. A quick glance through the binoculars showed more men. "Shit!"

With his pistol in his hand, he jumped out of the chopper, scampered over to the Huey and removed the mine. He opened the chopper's passenger door and pulled out his knife. From under the dash, he grabbed a handful of wires and cut them.

Still leaning over, he ran back through the fence and out to the car. The distance between the Mercedes and the hangar was too far for anyone to hear it start. He backed the auto out of its concealment and drove it to the opposite side of the hangar.

Parked out of view of the men inside the hangar, Blake stepped out and placed the mine on the fuel tank.

This should distract you idiots as I fly away.

He navigated his way back to the MD as quickly as he could, staying low and out of sight.

The start-up would take about one minute. He would have to get the engine to temperature and wait for the oil pressure to build. His decision to use the car as a deviation while the bird started was a bright one.

Air filled his lungs as he took a deep breath. Holding his phone in one hand, he flipped the first switch to start. Seconds later, he hit the detonator button. The explosion created an orange-and-white glow on the opposite side of the building, where it got brighter as it mushroomed over the tin roof.

Vasquez's followers darted out and headed for the commotion. The Jeep followed. Blake counted down the time until the rotor speed was high enough for him to take off. Approaching headlights appeared in his peripheral. A truck veered off the road and blew through the fence onto the tarmac.

The MD roared to life and lifted off. He spun the chopper to his left and aimed the bird at the truck. Guards jumped and dodged for cover. With both hands on the stick, he gained as much altitude as he could.

As he cleared the area, the men, previously distracted by the explosion, opened fire. Blake took evasive action. Bullets plinked off the bottom. *Dammit!* A quick glance at the gauges revealed no immediate damage. He pointed north and set a course for NAS Key West.

The base was 350 clicks away. The MD could cruise at almost 250 kilometers per hour. He glanced at his watch. Based on his fuel level, he calculated an ETA.

It's going to be too close for comfort.

As he headed for Key West, his mind returned to the time he had spent there a few years ago. It's the home of the U.S. Army Special Forces Underwater Operations School, or (SFUWO). He filled in for a pal who was recovering from a torn Achilles tendon he got while water skiing.

During the weeks Blake was there, he facilitated the *Combat Diving Supervisor* course; one of three courses taught there. The other two were the *Special Forces Combat Diver Qualification* and the *Special Forces Diving Medical Technician.*

All three were required for graduation, and he was one of only a handful of people qualified. He was also available to teach and fill in, as his friend recovered from his injury.

Jack Thieme served as the base Command Master Chief and was still there. He would help him out of this sticky situation.

Projectiles plinked off the side of the chopper and jolted him from his thoughts. "Shit!" He flew in a defensive move and turned around to see where the shots came from.

Beneath him and to his left were the nav lights on another aircraft. "Son-of-a-bitch! Where did he come from?" He pulled back and banked hard right. Bullets whizzed by and ricocheted off the rotors. He made a steep dive and kept evading his pursuer behind him. He switched on the radio.

"NAS Key West, this is CU-H133. I have an emergency." There was no reply. "NAS Key West, this is CU-H133. I am taking fire and need help!" As he continued to maneuver the bird back and forth, he used the cover of darkness and quick evasive moves to lose his pursuers.

"NAS Key West. Hello! Answer the fucking call!"
Silence.

He scanned his gauges. There wasn't enough fuel, and he still had a hundred and eighty kilometers to go.

9

Isle de la Juventud, Cuba
June 19th
03:00 local (08:00 GMT)

Everyone chambered rounds into their firearms before they pulled the boats close to the docks. The sound of gunfire had ceased, and the focus had now changed to putting out the fires on the west end of the estate. A warehouse where General Vasquez stored a respectable number of his weapons sat next to the dock. Boasting the same Venetian-style architecture, it was equally impressive as the home. Built from light-colored bricks, it was three hundred feet long and fifty feet high.

Zamir addressed one of his men in Pashto. "Go!" He motioned with his chin. "Check if anyone is there."

The man ran off. Moments later, he came back shaking his head. "Locked! I glanced in the window. It was too dark to see anything."

Zahmir peered toward the burning house. The fires from the garage and the far side of the mansion were raging. Embers soared into the dull morning sky before fluttering down and out in the surrounding jungle. Men were scampering around, yelling orders in Spanish, while others tended to hoses and extinguishers.

The weapons dealer shook his head. "We will get no help from them. Come, let's go search for our shipment."

Once at the storage building, they pried open the door. It was dark and the brackish air was overpowering. Flashlights illuminated and beams of light went in all directions. Above their heads was a crane on tracks. Shelving, full of wooded crates lined the walls. Labels on the boxes showed them all to be holding rifles, grenades, RPGs or various types of ammunition.

"Everyone explore! Find it!"

Tension grew as time passed and they had not found his precious cargo. Zahmir tightened his fists and clenched his jaw. "I do not see it. It must be somewhere else." The fire outside continued to burn and cast a faint orange glow inside the building. Movement from beyond the window caught his attention.

He removed the AK-101 from around his shoulder. "We will get our what we came for. Come! Now!"

As they approached the door, five armed guys came through the door, shouting in Spanish.

Zahmir's men, prepared to shoot, shouted back. Every man had their finger on their trigger. They could decipher nothing among the yelling. A sixth person entered and turned on a light. His voice boomed above all the others.

"Silence!"

There was quiet. The only sound was the subtle rattle a rifle made as whoever held it flinched or readjusted their grip. Luca's eyes squinted and his head tilted as he gazed at the weapons dealer and his men. He carried a pistol in his right hand and pointed it at the man he recognized.

"You must be Al-Hamwi."

Zahmir and his followers all stood still. Their firearms were aimed at the six men entering the building. Questions rolled through his mind.

"Who wants to know? You are not General Vasquez, are you?"

He shook his head. "No. My name is Luca Perez, and I… was the his second in command."

He cocked his head. "Was?"

"He's dead. Professional hit. Perhaps you know something

about it?"

Zahmir's temples thumped as the blood rushed to it from his rising anger. "Why would I do that? He has my money *and* my package!" He raised his rifle toward Luca. "Do not attempt to cheat me or I will kill you this instant!"

All the al Quaeda leader's people reaffirmed their grip on their rifles. Luca's men did likewise. Heads darted in every direction as each man eyed the other, waiting for someone to fire first.

Luca yelled and lowered his arms. "Hang on, wait a moment." As the commotion died down, he raised his hands, but his right hand continued to grip the.45.

"Observe." He holstered his pistol. He turned his head to his people surrounding him, motioning for them to do the same.

Zahmir eased his stance, yet his rifle remained firmly pointed at Luca.

"We know who did it. It was an American."

Zahmir shouted in fury. "An American infidel? Why did you blame me then? Once more enraged, he prepared to shoot. Everyone followed suit and began aiming them at one another as the clamor started over.

"Please! Calm down! I was testing you. I'm sure you can understand that. Besides, we didn't store your package here. You'll need me to get them."

You'd better not be playing me infidel, or you will die in agony.

He finally relaxed and gestured to his men to do the same. "Where is this American? Is he dead? What does he know about me and this transaction?"

Luca shook his head. "I have no idea where he is or if he is dead. I've been tackling this fire. As far as your involvement and the weapon, he knows nothing about it."

"How can you be so sure?"

"Because I am! Now, do you want it or not?"

Infidel pig!

The terrorist leader let his assault rifle drape at his side. As he attempted to ease the tension within himself, air filled his lungs. He slung his rifle over his shoulder and stepped over to face the general's assistant. While smiling, he placed his left hand on

Luca's upper arm. Luca smiled in return.

The grin vanished when Zahmir drew his pistol and pressed the barrel into Luca's eye socket. He leaned in and grasped the back of Luca's head. "Do not—speak to me—with such disrespect."

Again, weapons rose and pointed toward Zahmir. Luca's brow perspired. He was shaking and his one open eye was wide with fright.

"Do you understand?"

Luca nodded in short, quick jerks. "Yes! Yes, I'm sorry."

The terrorist withdrew the pistol from the frightened man's eye. "Perfect, now take me to my package and I'll be gone."

Luca took a deep breath and wiped his forehead. Motioned once again for his people to back down. "Everything is okay. Let them get what they paid for so they can be on their way." He turned to the weapons dealer. "Follow me."

Luca had ordered his other men to go back to battle the inferno. He hoped it would also show the man who threatened his life some trust. They entered the home at the midway point and descended a flight of stairs. He keyed a code into a security system. The door unlocked with a loud click and opened outward to reveal a long hallway with an arched stone ceiling.

He motioned with his arm. "This way."

Zahmir removed his pistol from his holster and pressed it against Luca's kidneys. "Hold on."

"What are you doing?"

"I don't trust you. How do I know you're not leading us into a trap?"

"There are only two ways in here. The way we just came and there's a larger door along the hall. It's on the right and leads to a spacious elevator. There's a steel gate you can only open from within."

Zahmir nodded to his closest man to check out the room.

Emphasizing who was in charge, he pressed the barrel harder into Luca's kidney. "We will find out soon enough if you are speaking with honesty. In the meantime, move inside."

He prodded his hostage with the pistol, and they stepped into the room.

Smaller rooms with vaulted ceilings running parallel to the central arched hallway framed the walls on either side. Iron bars separated each chamber. It gave off the vibe of a combination of a medieval prison and an antique French vineyard.

Footsteps echoed as the guy Zahmir had sent returned.

"He speaks the truth. No one is down here and there is a locked gate at the end. We must unlock it to remove what we came for."

Once again, showing no fear, he leaned in. "So far, so good. Now where to?"

He pointed. "It's the third one on the left. I'll have to unlock it for you. Everything you paid for is inside. You can load it on the lift. It will take you to the main level, and there is a door facing the warehouse. There is a Cushman Truckster parked adjacent to the door. You can use it to take your shipment to the docks. The keys are in it."

Zahmir encouraged him forward with a bit of pressure from the gun. "Okay. Let's go."

They walked along to the proper stall. Luca unlocked the traditional padlock with his keys and grabbed the bar door. The squeak echoed throughout the dungeon, as rusty metal scraped against the hinges. The leader snapped his fingers and pointed to the cell. His men started loading the crates on carts.

He inspected the other locked cells. "What are in these other chambers?"

"His personal cache. Now please, you got what you've come for. Get it and leave so I can attend to the estate."

His temper was at its tipping point. *Such Insolence!* As Zahmir wildly gripped his pistol, he took a steady aim at Luca's head. With a deafening blast, his bullet pierced through the target's skull, causing an explosion of blood and tissue. His lifeless corpse crumpled onto the floor.

Satisfaction flowed through Zahmir as blood oozed out of the hole in the infidel's skull. The expression of shock remained in his eyes.

Bastard Pig! He reached down and grabbed the keys from Luca's still twitching body. He threw them to one of his men.

"Take everything."

10

NAS Key West
June 19
03:40 local (08:40 GMT)

Petty Officer Second Class Raymond Shulster was on his first night of working the graveyard shift. So far, the night was muted with nothing on the radio. He leaned back in his chair and daydreamed about his afternoon. His heavy eyes reminded him he should have gone to sleep instead. But the invitation from the two women he and a friend had met earlier in the week was too tempting to turn down. "Oh Ray, you're such a doll. Would you please put some sunblock on my back and legs?"

Would I? Hell, yeah.

"Sure thing."

He grabbed the almost empty bottle of *Hawaiian Tropic* and shook it well before he popped the lid. When he squeezed the tube, it made a farting noise and splattered lotion...

His head jerked as he woke from his dream. Taking a deep breath, he forced his eyes open wide while he ran his fingers through his sandy brown hair.

"Shit!"

I should have gone to sleep instead. Perhaps some coffee will help.

In the break room, Raymond plopped himself into a chair next to a small round table with a fresh booster of caffeine and a *Road & Track*. He turned to the article on the Geneva Auto Show to check out all the new cars debuting. Halfway through the piece, he stopped. "Oh God." He rubbed his eyes. "Just five minutes. That's all I require."

I'll let my head down and snooze for a short while.

Half an hour later, the radio woke him. "Somebody answer, goddammit! This is an emergency!"

Ray's eyes sprang open as he leaped from his position. "Shit!"

The voice continued to plead for help as he put on his headphones. "This is NAS Key West. State your name and the purpose of your emergency."

"This is CU-H133. I'm on special assignment and I'm taking hostile fire. I want assistance. Now!"

Shulster tried to shake the cobwebs from his head. "Uh. Are you serious? Are you joking with me? If this is a joke, we can have you arrested for—"

The radio squawked. "Listen to me! I'm a federal officer and I am about to get shot down. I know Commander Thieme. Wake him!"

"And who is this again?"

"I'm not going to tell you my— Shit!"

He could hear the bullets hitting the side of the chopper over the radio. "Hello? You there?"

"Rouse the fucking commander. Tell him—Blake MacKay is on the line. Wait! Call in the support first, *then* get him. Do it now, soldier!"

"Coordinates?"

"Check the goddamn radar! I'm around twenty-three degrees north by eighty-two west. I'm heading right for you! Send me F18s. I can't hold these guys off much longer!"

"Yes, sir! Hang on, please!"

The petty officer lifted the phone and dialed Commander Thieme. "Sir, sorry to disturb you. I've got a guy on the radio who says he needs F18s for assistance. He reckons someone is trying to shoot him down."

"What? Who is it?"

"Blake MacKay? He said you'd know him."

"Affirmative. Scramble the Gladiators! Give him whatever help he requires. I'm on my way."

#

The Navy Air Station (NAS) was also the home of the Strike Fighter Squadron 106 (VFA-106), the *Gladiators*. Captain Donald "Donny" Donaldson was a twenty-five-year veteran. His new "wingman" was thirty-three-year-old Lieutenant Stacy "Luke" Luking. She was a real hotshot known not only for her outstanding flying prowess, but more so, her capacity to keep a calm demeanor in combat situations.

They both scrambled out onto the tarmacs and climbed into their aircraft. Ten minutes later, two F/A18 Super Hornets took off in formation and made radio contact with Blake. Commander Thieme ran into the operations room.

#

Blake checked his six. The nav lights of the chopper showed them still in pursuit. "CU-H133, this is RedCloud from NAS Key West. We are en route. What are your coordinates?"

Thank God!

"RedCloud, this is CU-H133. I'm heading straight for you at twenty-four degrees, three minutes north by eighty-one degrees, fifty-five minutes west. There's a hostile on my tail and I am taking fire! Repeat. I am taking fire."

"Copy that. We have you confirmed on the radar. Visual in three minutes."

#

Commander Thieme grabbed the radio mic. "Blake, this is Jack. What's going on?"

"Long story. Thanks for the support. I'll be happier once these guys on my ass are gone. But I've got another snafu. I'm almost black on fuel. I'll need to ditch this bird in the drink. Can you send someone to pick me up?"

"Not a problem. I'll get a SAR in the air asap."

#

Even though he kept his distance, the spray from the automatic weapons still found him. He made a hard right and one slammed through the front canopy. Alarms sounded, and the chopper shook.

"Jack! they've scored a hit on me. I'm losing oil pressure!"

"We've got a cutter heading back. It's close to your position. It's launching its SAR as we speak. ETA is fifteen minutes."

He fought the stick to increase his altitude. "Roger that."

Lieutenant Luking came on the radio. "CU-H133, we have visual, three seconds to target."

His heart pounded. Sweat ran down his neck.

"Hurry!"

The other helicopter closed its distance. He lost the fight for altitude. The sound of bullets, as they hit the fuselage, ceased. He turned hard left and glanced back at his pursuer. It had stopped firing and leveled out a hundred meters away.

What are they doing? Shit. I've got a bad feeling…

An AIM-9 sidewinder missile, fired from one of the F/A–18s, headed toward the copter. Blake angled his head in time to see an RPG launch from the other chopper.

Oh, holy hell!

#

Zahmir and Mustafa followed the other boats containing the last of the weapons they took from the warehouse. As they approached, in the early morning's dark sky, their ship's silhouette was only a black outline.

They classified their ship as a 'handy-size'. Constructed 180 meters long and 20 meters wide, it had four cargo holds with three cranes of twenty-eight metric ton lifting capacity. They had already filled one hold with tobacco and other products, purchased in the off chance Customs boarded and searched their vessel.

She was called the "Angel van de zee", which translated from Dutch meant "Angel of the sea".

Both men steadied themselves as they stepped off the small boat and onto the ship's landing platform. The chains attached to the crates on the other tinders rattled before the crane pulled them taught. Zahmir smiled as his prized possession rose and disappeared over the railing.

With a broad grin, Mustafa clapped his hands together. "It was a brilliant move when you took the other weapons."

"Yes. They will go a long way to help our cause. Ever since the infidel Americans murdered bin Laden, it has been difficult to raise funding and buy weapons. This will aid us immensely."

And they will well reward me.

"Is our Automatic Identification System disabled?"

"Of course, they can't track us. Nobody will know where we are."

Zahmir placed his hand on his friend's shoulder. "Come, let us go for some tea and re-estimate our time of arrival in Croatia. Loading our extra cargo has delayed our departure."

#

The missile fired from the pursuing aircraft detonated less than thirty meters away. Blake's helicopter convulsed violently from the concussion. It intensified as one of the F/A—18s blew past him, overhead.

The sidewinder, fired by Lieutenant Luking, engulfed the enemy into a blazing ball of fire. Burning aluminum and body parts flew everywhere, but as they dropped into the water fifteen hundred feet below, the fires went out.

Captain Donaldson shot down the shoulder-fired missile.

"Whoo hooo! Red Cloud a flaming! Nice shooting Luke," called out Capt. Donaldson over the radio.

Luking's voice cracked through his headset. "CU-H133, you're on your own now. NAS Key West, this is Gladiators six and eighteen. Target destroyed; I repeat, target destroyed. We'll circle until help arrives."

Jack's voice filled the airwaves. "Roger that, Gladiators, six and eighteen. Target Destroyed. Great job! Over and out—Blake, are you ok?"

"Yes, I am. Tell both of them I owe them a beer when I'm back on dry land."

"Will do. What's your status now?"

More alarms sounded, and his eyes darted across the array of gauges in front of him, looking for the culprit. "The damage I took did me in. I'm high enough to get the rotors to auto rotate. I'm shutting the engine off and going in here."

"Affirmative, give me your coordinates and I'll relay it to SAR."

Blake relayed his latest position and shut off the motor.

The sound of the engine faded to nothing, and Blake's stomach rose as the chopper dropped.

It had been quite a few years since he learned to pilot a chopper, and he hadn't had to fly one without power since then. He was relieved after the wind rushed through the rotors and caused them to auto rotate faster as the bird descended. The additional weights in the tips helped to increase the autorotation as it plunged to the sea. When the blades reached the correct speed, he gained enough control to help guide his damaged aircraft into the water.

It crashed into the ocean and bobbled for a while. The restraints pulled hard on his shoulders. Water rushed in at his feet.

Which way was this going to roll?

He grabbed the backpack containing the intelligence he'd collected and waited for the craft to sink. As it listed to his left, he climbed over the other seat, ripped the cushion off, threw it out, and jumped into the sea.

He swam as fast as he could, careful to keep the pack from getting drenched. The heavy rhythmic thump of the blades hitting the water told him he was far enough away and safe from their potential deadly blow. As he turned back, they sliced through the water on the opposite side of the sinking craft. They came to an abrupt halt when the water's drag became too much.

His pack was water resistant, but not waterproof. He did his best to tread water and keep his cargo over his head. The seat cushion he tossed floated nearby. He swam over and rest the pack on it until the search and rescue team arrived.

The whine of the Jayhawks' rotors grew louder as the helicopter approached and brought him some comfort. A minute later, it was hovering above. A frogman jumped in, followed by a buoy attached to a cable from the helicopter's winch.

"Are you okay? Are you wounded?"

"I think I'm fine."

He nodded his understanding and helped him into the harness.

Once on board, Blake breathed a heavy sigh. "Thanks guys. You were right on time."

The co-pilot turned back to him. "Where to, sir?"

"NAS Key West."

11

NAS Key West
June 19th
07:00 local (12:00 GMT)

The Jayhawk landed, and Blake stepped out onto the tarmac. The heat from the morning summer sun had warmed the pavement, but it was a tremendous feeling against his soaking clothes. He was thanking his rescuers in the Jayhawk when he recognized a familiar voice behind him.

"Blake."

He turned around, and a smile creased his face. Extending both arms as he approached his old friend, he hugged him, then shook his hand.

"Boy, are you a sight for sore eyes. Fantastic to see you, Mate."

He winced from the pain in his ribs but reflected on dinner at Jack's house with his beautiful wife and two kids several years ago when he filled in for him.

"You too." Jack smiled with genuine glee in his expression. "Wow! It's been forever since I've seen you."

He took a step back and cocked his head. "Still a tan, chiseled motherfucker, I see."

They both laughed, and he reached for his ribs. "Stop. Don't make me laugh."

Jack scrunched his lips. "Even super models can have their shit days and today, my friend—is your day."

Blake flipped him his middle finger while he smirked. "Fuck you."

He's right. I look like shit.

He shrugged. "Well, I'll ignore your man crush on me, but I will say, yeah, it's been a long time and second, I do feel like crap. So, you happy?"

"Anyone would think you've been in a bar fight against six guys—and lost."

He grinned. "Sure, I know, but you should see the other fellows."

Jack put his hands on his hips and studied his friend. His eyebrows shot up. "So, what in the hell was that all about?"

He laughed. "Company business. You know I can't say."

Jack's smile vanished, and he pursed his lips for a moment. "Yeah… I figured. Well, at any rate, I'm glad you're here. Can you hang around—at least for the day? Hey, you haven't seen my youngest yet. We had another boy. His name is Connor and he can throw a football like you wouldn't believe—well, for a three-year-old."

"That's fantastic. Congratulations. I would love to stay here, but—" He patted his bag "Duty calls."

"Well, if you can stay, we'll grill out and I'll invite the two pilots who saved your ass over, and you might want to thank them. Whadaya say?"

Damn, it sounds wonderful, but this intel can't wait.

"Let's see how things go."

"Ok, I understand. However, I'd be willing to bet you're a little hungry?"

Blake was unfocused, his brain miles away. He'd lost track of how long it had been since his last meal amid all the commotion he had been involved in.

"I am, but I have to study what's in this bag." He displayed the damp rucksack to him. "I must make a call on a secure line, and I need a quiet spot to analyze this. Do you think you could fix some place for me?"

"Not in *my* office, but over in the Command Center. I can patch you through to MTAC and they'll establish the connection from there."

"Yeah, it would be fine. Thanks."

MTAC was the Department of Navy's Multiple Threat Alert Center. It provides indications and warnings for an extensive range of threats to Navy and Marine Corps personnel and assets worldwide. During the walkover, Jack called the Command Center on his cell and had them prep the room and get MTAC on the line. They entered the building through a set of double doors.

Jack followed him. "We go all the way to the end." He opened the end door for them with his keycard. A huge oval conference table occupied much of the space in the middle of the room. Three doors were located against the far wall. Jack pointed. "Any of those offices are available to you."

Blake nodded. "Perfect. I'll take the one on the left."

He dashed over to the office. Inside, he put the pack on the desk and unzipped it. "Could you give me thirty, perhaps forty-five minutes to dissect some of this and patch a call through to Langley?"

Jack let out a small chuckle and grinned, shaking his head.

It caught Blake's attention. "What?"

"Nothing. I'll relay the message to MTAC. I don't know how the hell you do what you do." He raised his hands in the air. "Whatever it is."

He gave a bitter laugh. "It is what it is."

"Yeah. We'll, you're still soaking wet. I'll have some fresh clothes and chow sent over, okay?"

He breathed a deep sigh and smiled. He'd silently hoped his friend would do just that. "Wow, it would be fantastic. Thanks."

"No problem, catch you later."

"Yep." He waved as Jack walked out of the room and closed the door.

The backpack had done a better than expected job of its contents from getting wet. Only a small bit of moisture formed around the file folders, and the machine remained dry. For the next thirty-five minutes, he searched through the files and laptop for anything he considered a threat to national security. When he got to one of the thumb drives, he found something suspicious. The telephone on the table rang. It was MTAC patching through his call from Langley.

What perfect timing!

He grabbed the phone. "Blake MacKay."

"Mr. Mackay, sir, I have Langley for you. Director Brennan, go ahead."

They both waited for the familiar click in the line, informing them they had made the connection and they could now freely speak in private on an encrypted line. Mike snorted. "So, what the hell happened? You were supposed to go to GITMO?"

He debated telling his handler he believed someone had given the general a tipoff, but opted against it. He trusted Mike one hundred percent, but there could be somebody he worked with who may be feeding information to the wrong people. He didn't want to risk tipping the guy off. "Well, things didn't go as planned. I must have been careless and missed something. A guard caught me coming out of the his room and all hell broke loose. I was lucky to get out of there alive."

"Did you meet the objective?"

"Affirmative."

"Any intel?"

"I've spent the last thirty minutes going through what I got and—we've got a problem."

Mike's voice took on a somber tone. "What is it?"

"Does the name Zahmir Al-Hamwi ring any bells?"

"Fuck yeah! He's one of the largest arms dealers for Al-Qaeda. What's he got to do with this?"

Blake ran his fingers through his thick, black hair. "I haven't decided yet. There's more digging to do, but from what I can tell, he's purchased something significant from the general. I don't know if they've already delivered it, or if it's still at the estate or what. It's gonna take some time to investigate further."

"Okay, this new intel takes precedence. I need you back here for a formal debrief and I want the data for complete analysis. I'm dispatching a plane to Key West and it should be there in a couple of hours."

Dammit. So much for the cookout. Now I have time for one more thing.

"See you this afternoon." He replaced the receiver and walked out of the room. Sitting on the floor was a full set of BDUs, including clean underwear, socks, and boots. Next to them was a tray with a plate of covered food. Blake smelled the bacon, and his stomach growled.

He bent and removed the lid. His eyes shone at the sight of the pancakes, two eggs, toast with jelly, and four strips of bacon. He took the tray, along with the dry garments, back inside. A knock on the door came as he finished tying the laces on his right boot. "Come in."

Jack stepped in. "All done?"

"Yep. Thanks for the food and clothes. I feel a lot better. I know it's a shame, but I'll have to take a rain check on the barbecue."

"Yeah, I figured so. Is there anything further I can do for you during your stay here? Like, get you patched up? They should examine you to make sure you haven't broken something."

"Yes, I will, but first there's something else you can do."

"What would that be?"

"Where might I find Petty Officer, Shulster?"

#

Shulster was in the locker room about to go home. As exhausted as he was, he guessed it would be a while before he could sleep. The conversation with Blake MacKay kept running through his head.

The youngster stood in front of his locker as he walked in.

"Hey, I'm looking for Petty Officer Shulster. Are you him?"

He closed the locker door and paused. "Yes."

He extended his hand. "Hi."

Shulster accepted his hand and shook it. "Hello."

He grinned. "I'm the guy on the radio."

The smile faded from the young man's face as Blake delivered a left cross to his jaw. He gripped him with his right, yanked him in close, and hissed into his ear. "Never leave your fucking post again."

He shoved him back and walked away. Halfway to the door, he turned back as Raymond sat and put his face in his hands. Blake's lips curled with satisfaction.

#

After his attitude adjustment meeting with Shulster, he went to the infirmary to have his ribs checked out and repair some of his cuts and bruises. He had to hurry to finish so he could fly back to Langley.

Thirty minutes later, he and Jack were in the central hangar. The Gulfstream G650 stood on the tarmac outside the door. A smile tugged at Jack's lips. "Wow, when you travel, you go in style."

"Yeah. One of the perks of the job, I suppose."

"How did your little conversation with Shulster go?"

"Not the way I wanted. I would have liked to beat the crap out of him."

"You mean you didn't?"

"No. I didn't want to cause you any problems." He chuckled. "I think I scared the piss out of him, though."

Jack laughed back. "Yeah, you have a knack for doing such things. We will discipline him. Not sure what it will be yet, but it won't be fun for him, regardless."

He held out his hand. "Jack."

Jack shook his hand. "Take care, buddy."

He turned and boarded the plane.

12

CIA Headquarters
Langley, VA
June 19th
14:00 local (19:00 GMT)

Mike Brennan, along with CIA Director Julian Thomas, sat in Mike's office. There was an oscillating fan atop the beige filing cabinet, squeaking as it slowly made its cycle.

Julian took a sip of coffee and wiped his mouth. "Well, we got him. Not quite the way we wanted, but at least he's no longer around."

Mike grinned. "Damn straight. The bastard's out of the picture."

Julian frowned. "What do you imagine the fallout's going to be now?"

He shrugged. "I don't know. Every bit of intel we have points to the fact the Cuban government were aware of General Vasquez and his minor operation the whole time. Besides, what can the Cubans say? There's nobody down there who could point a finger at us."

Mike's eyebrows raised. "Well, no one we are cognizant of, anyhow."

"Right."

Mike drummed his fingers on his desk, then loosened his tie. The fan continued to make noises.

Julian shook his head. "You need to oil that fucking thing."

"Yeah."

"You okay? You seem—anxious." Setting the mug down, he pressed. "Don't tell me it's Veronica that's got you acting this way."

Mike glanced up and scowled. "What? That bitch? No!" He stood and walked to the other side of his desk.

He peered out through the window in his office door. The Director of National Intelligence, or DNI, Veronica Slocum approached. He tensed as he prepared himself for any ensuing verbal battle. From the day they met, they didn't click.

Almost everything he proposed for different clandestine missions, she opposed and his '*the end justifies the means*' attitude didn't cut it with her. Anytime one of his assets used violence to get the task completed, she would threaten to bring criminal charges against them. He didn't understand her at all. Nor did he care to.

At National Intelligence, the supervisor's position or the Principal Deputy Director's job can be an active-duty commissioned officer, and she supervised Julian in the government hierarchy. They only permitted a military officer to hold one of the two roles simultaneously. Veronica graduated with degrees from Harvard and UPenn. She had never, in her life, served a day of service in the armed forces.

Her profound lack of understanding of military protocol infuriated him. He was a former member of the tenth Special Forces Group headquartered out of Fort Carson, Colorado. He'd served in Europe during the Cold War. Violence, death, torture; it was all part of how they played the game in the covert world of espionage and intel gathering.

Veronica believed in handling matters through civilized diplomacy. She thought if you treated enemy combatants humanely and asked them nicely, they would give you whatever information you wanted. Mike was thankful because Julien and

Blake both agreed with him. He referred to her as *The Liberal Bitch* or *The Red Headed Whack Job,* among other uncomplimentary names.

He frowned and mumbled, "My favorite person is here."

Julian chuckled, shook his head, and collected his mug from the desk. She opened the door and stepped in. Mike drew out the name while he extended his hand. "Veronica, great to see you. How are activities on The Hill today?"

She turned to Julian as she spoke. "Busy as hell. Hello Director."

He took another swig of coffee, raised his mug and tilted his head with a grin.

She removed a file folder from her satchel. "Let's get this over with, as I'm sure I'll be busy trying to fix this shit storm you two created."

Mike shook his head and sighed. "Shit storm? What are you talking about?"

"The one you started when this little mission of yours didn't go quite as planned. It was supposed to be a silent job. In and out undetected, you said." She snapped her fingers. "A piece of cake." She scratched her nose. "I've got word the AP is reporting a story about some fishing charters seeing a dogfight between two helicopters off the Keys. After which, one of our jets blew a chopper out of the sky with air-to-air missiles."

Several of the people on the charter boats have already tweeted it. One person posted a damn video of the missile blowing the thing out of the sky to his Facebook page and TikTok. The bloody things went viral, and by the end of the day, tens of thousands of people will have seen it. What the fuck, Mike? What—the—fuck?"

Julian raised his hands. "Relax Veronica, I'll contact NAS Key West and have them post a statement to their website. Then, we'll disseminate a press release stating it was an advanced tactical training program. They'll proclaim it was a live round exercise and the second bird was flown via remote control. The other copter was an inadvertent casualty when it got engine failure due to the concussion of the other one exploding so close to it."

She frowned and glared at him. "Are you serious? Do you think something so corny will work? The American people aren't as stupid as you think. This thing will have gone viral over the whole world by the time you get such a release out."

He smirked. "Hell yeah, we do it all the time." He paused for a moment. "I'll have my people write it for them." Julian turned to Mike. "When is Blake supposed to get here?"

"He landed on the heliport a short while ago. Probably five minutes, ten at most."

"I'll be back in a sec." Julian took out his phone and left the office.

She glowered. "Mike, I hope for your sake, this works."

He forced a smile. "It'll work, don't worry."

She shook her head. "I dunno. I think this could have been handled in a different manner. Diplomatically, perhaps."

"Director, with all due respect, we slapped sanctions on them for—how many years now?

"They don't give a rat's ass about what we do diplomatically. Besides, they would have denied any and all of it anyhow. This was a private, illegal venture of the general's: even if he *was* giving kickbacks to the Cuban government to keep quiet."

She sighed. "I'll be interested to hear what MacKay has to say about it and if he dredged anything more, we could find useful. For instance, where he's getting these weapons and who else is he selling them to?"

Mike tapped his fingers on the desk and straightened his tie. "We'll uncover it soon enough."

#

On the ride over to Langley. Mentally, Blake reviewed the intelligence he had glanced through on the aircraft. He only kept a few items in the back of his mind. The sale of the lethal Metal Storm weapon was significant. The company's website listed its technology and deadly capabilities.

The worst part about it was the fact it was sold to a known Al-Qaeda weapons dealer, who is on the top ten of the FBI's most wanted terrorist list. He wasn't sure if Al-Hamwi had picked up the package or if it was still on the estate.

When did he get it if he did? Where was he getting it from and why? Where was he taking it and for what use? Also, how did Vasquez get his hands on this weapon?

These were all important questions needing answers post haste. The last question was the one eating at him the most and the one he would keep to himself for the moment. How did the general find out he was there to take him out? Who was the traitor who gave him away?

13

Home of Prime Minister Oleg Shorets
  Minsk, Belarus
  June 19th
  22:15 local (19:15 GMT)

Oleg sat in his home office with Aleksandr. The Prime Minister's mansion was aglow with the soft radiance of landscape lights. They cast a subtle luminescence on the voluminous curtains concealing the expansive windows. Both men had finished discussing President Solonovich's proposal of additional sanctions their government had planned to place on privately run companies. Frustration had reached a new high level and the toll on their minds was precise.

More than two months had elapsed since he introduced his plan to Aleksandr to overthrow the regime and eliminate Solonovich. They hadn't spoken of it up to this point. A lull in their current conversation allowed him the opportunity to bring it back up.

Now I will find out where your allegiance lies.

He rose from his chair in front of the fireplace. Walking to the nearest window, he peeled back the curtain.

"It's been scorching this year. Would you agree?"

His companion nodded and offered a faint grunt in agreement.

He let the drapes fall back into place and strolled across the room to his bar on the opposite side of the room. The shelves contained limited edition bourbons, exclusive single malts, and unique rums.

There was also a collection of countless bottles of Belarusian vodkas on most of them. Before the wall sat a tacky bar covered in padded gold vinyl in a quilted pattern with a black quartz counter. With a wry smile, he picked out a bottle of Platinka vodka, pursed his lips, and chuckled.

Alexandr raised his bushy eyebrows. "What is it?"

Oleg spun around, showing the label to his friend. "I now must drink this—swill"

"Yes. So? It's a fine vodka. They make it in Brest, do they not?"

"Correct, but it is owned by a company out of Atlanta, Georgia." He sniffed at the contents. "The time cannot get here quick enough. Would you like one as well?"

Alexandr shook his head as he pulled another cigarette from his case and lit it. As he did so, he took a deep, satisfying drag and exhaled a plume of smoke. His eyes met Oleg's. "Have you heard from your contact?"

After pouring some into a glass filled with ice, he turned back to Aleksandr and leaned against the bar. He took a sip of his spirit, rolling it around in his mouth to savor it before swallowing.

Well, that's a surprise. It's not bad.

Downing the rest of the vodka, he placed the empty glass on the counter and went to retrieve the bottle. "Not yet, but I am waiting for him to check in soon. He should already be on the way."

A frown creased Aleksandr's forehead. "Can't you call him?"

"I can, but I won't. You will."

His friend's eyes widened as he took another drag and spoke prior to exhaling. "Me?"

"Yes. I told him you would be his intermediary the last time I conversed with him. He is expecting to talk to you the next time there is communication between us."

The smoke trickled out of his lungs with his words. "But how do I get in touch with him?"

Leaving the bar and walking to his desk, Oleg retrieved an encrypted satellite phone and tossed it to Aleksandr. "Use this and call him now."

"Now? How do I identify myself?"

"Tell him, *Spear Garden*."

#

Zahmir finished his afternoon praise to Allah and returned his prayer rug and Koran back to his stateroom. Prior to departing, he demanded they stock the ship's galley with plenty of the foods he and his men enjoyed. He ordered them to prepare chicken shawarma for him.

It comprised grilled lamb or chicken, mixed with salad and spices, rolled inside a pocket of traditional Arabic bread. His stomach let out a gentle reminder. Under normal circumstances, he ate earlier in the day, so he was starving and anticipated his meal and coffee.

As he turned to leave his room, the satellite phone, sent to him by Oleg, rang. He retrieved it from the desk and answered it. "Yes."

The speaker on the other end sounded demanding. "You were supposed to call us when you were on your way. Where are you? Have you left? We have a tight schedule."

Who is this infidel daring to speak to me in such a manner?

"Who is this? I do not recognize your voice."

"I am with Operation Spear Garden."

He frowned. "So, you are my contact?"

"Yes."

There was some static on the line. He tapped the cell phone. "Everything is running according to plan. Wait—there is some interference in this vessel from the steel and wires. Let me go to the deck so I can get a clearer signal."

"Fine, but hurry."

Zahmir went down two flights of stairs to a small hallway and out to the main deck. It irritated him to be spoken to in such a manner, but he accepted it. After all, these were the people hiring him and they would provide the funding their organization desperately needed. He put the phone back to his ear. "I am here."

Aleksandr sighed with relief. He stood and walked to Oleg's desk. Placing the instrument on speaker, he held it out so his friend could listen to the conversation. "Yes, can you hear me better? Now tell me where you are."

"Much clearer. We are about one hundred and seventy nautical miles south of the Turks and Caicos traveling at twenty-three knots. We will be at our destination in ten days. Everything is on schedule."

"What is your timeline?"

"We will dock in Rijeka. From there, we have secured air transport into Lithuania. We will bring the shipment across the border near Hieraniony. Have you safeguarded the area?"

Aleksandr focused on Oleg, who returned his gaze with a confident nod. "You let me worry about such details. It will be ready. Call in and give me an update in five days. Do not make me contact you."

Zahmir bit his tongue. He imagined choking the attitude out of the voice on the other end of the line. "I understand."

#

Aleksandr hung up and tamped out his smoke in the ashtray on the desk.

Oleg raised his eyebrows. "Well?"

"You heard him. They are passing the Turks and Caicos. They are on schedule to dock in Rijeka in ten days."

"Right. But how do you feel? Are you ready for this?"

He cleared his throat while nodding. "I am ready. We need to do this."

"Excellent." He swirled the cubes in his glass.

Everything is aligning according to plan.

Aleksandr reached into his pocket and retrieved another cigarette. He tapped it on the back of his case and glanced at Oleg.

"He mentioned Hieraniony and asked if we had secured the area. Is it something you were going to do?"

A smile creased his lips. "Yes. It's part of the Parks and Preservation Board. I have someone who owes me a favor, and he has assured me he will secure it before the time comes. I've arranged every little thing so we can gain access."

He smiled as he stood. "Excellent." He placed the cigarette behind his ear as he walked over to the bar to fix himself a drink. Oleg studied his companion. Aleksandr handled the call with Al-Hamwi to Oleg's satisfaction.

Now you are truly with me, Comrade. Together, we will take back this country.

He turned and raised his glass. His friend reciprocated.

"Now we wait."

14

CIA Headquarters
  Langley, Virginia
  June 19th
  14:25 local (19:25 GMT)

Blake arrived at Langley, took the elevator, and made the short walk to his boss's office for his debriefing. As he entered, Director Slocum was sitting on the sofa to his left. His boss walked around his desk with a broad smile, his hand extended.

"Blake. Wonderful to see you!" He moved his head from side to side as he inspected the cuts and bruises on his agent's face. "You look like hell, though."

"Thanks for that. Yeah, I feel better than it appears, but it's healing. Just give it time."

They shook hands and his boss directed him to the couch.

He nodded. "Hello, Director Slocum."

"Mr. MacKay. Glad you're here to join us."

She recoiled a little at his battered appearance. He sat, trying hard not to disturb his bruised ribs too much. He could sense some tension in the room. The mission hadn't gone according to plan, and he was about to find out about any blowback.

Veronica swapped her crossed legs and cleared her throat.

"Director Thomas stepped out for a moment to quell some media clamor on the petty incident you had over the water."

Minor, my ass. You should have been there.

"Yeah, well, it's a pity, but I couldn't prevent it. I'm grateful the boys—and gal at NAS could help me out."

He bent forward, putting the file of intel he carried on the table. He stood, grunting to hold back the pain, and walked over to the bureau and poured a cup of coffee.

Mike rose and propped himself against the front of his desk. Leaning back, he folded his arms. "It's a shame you ran into so much trouble down there. I'm happy you're back safe."

Veronica chipped in. "Me too."

There was a certain *tone* in her voice, which didn't escape him.

Are you sure? Hard to believe.

He nodded an acknowledgment. "Thank you both."

Julian stepped back into the office. Blake waved from the opposite side of the room. The man snorted. "You look like shit."

"So I've been told, but you should see the other guys."

"Well, damn fine to have you back." He extended his arm to the couch. "Please. Take a seat and let's get down to business."

Mike walked around to his chair and seated himself. He leaned forward on rested elbows. "What did you find in the intelligence you gained from our dead general friend?"

"Most of it listed his interactions and connections with the Mexican gangs and Colombian drug cartels, much of which we already knew."

Veronica stroked back a stray wisp of hair. "We can turn the intel over to the correct departments handling such data after we've inspected it."

The experienced field agent waved a folder. "Right, but the one thing I think *we* need to handle involves this." He reached in and pulled out a piece of paper. "Vasquez had got his hands on a weapon called Metal Storm. Have any of you ever heard of it before?"

Mike nodded. "Yes. It's quite new, but short-lived at the same time. They've used it as countermeasures to missile attacks on ships, armored personal carriers and tanks. The Navy can use it against torpedoes as well. I understand they developed it in Australia, but the company has since filed for bankruptcy."

Blake fidgeted with his watch and glanced around at the others in the room. "True, but there is an American manufacturer and they're currently in business."

Mike rapped his fingers on the desk. "Give us all a review of what this is, or if there are any new capabilities."

Julian waved a dismissive hand. "We know about such a weapon."

Veronica frowned. "Not me. What's so special about it? Are they using it out in the field now?"

Mike broke in. "Not really. It was in its experimental phase when the Australian company folded, but when you hear about its potential, you'll realize it could still be a game-changer. Sorry, Blake. Go ahead."

"No worries. In a nutshell, the device is brutal. It can fire any caliber from nine millimeter to forty millimeter armor piercing grenades at a rate of up to a million rounds per minute."

She stared at him and shook her head. "What, wait. A million?" drawing out the word. "That can't be right."

He leaned forward. "It is, I'm afraid. Now, obviously, it can't discharge a million rounds. It only discharges the projectiles at that pace. I printed the data I obtained from the company's official website."

He handed them the material. "This intelligence is based on the small caliber model. The amount of ammunition and number of barrels changes depending on the caliber used." He allowed them all a second to let the information sink in.

"When you load it to its maximum, each of its thirty-six barrels will hold fifteen rounds, for a total of five hundred and forty rounds."

He paused for effect. "They can set the thing to fire at various rates from as little as six-hundred and forty per minute to a ridiculous one million. At the top rate, every projectile literally fires at once and it sounds like a single shotgun blast."

Her face paled as he continued. "The result is a relentless hailstorm of flying lead and explosive grenades raining down on unsuspecting targets. It obliterates everything in its path." He glanced around at the three directors to get a gauge of what they were thinking. All were in deep contemplation.

"Here's the most concerning part. They can fire them either on manual or automatic by turning their sensors on and then defining an unbreakable perimeter. So, if something breaches the invisible wall, the sensors see it and then unleash hell."

Mike bobbed his head. "Correct. They can use the device on armored vehicles, choppers and ships as a self-defense weapon. They designate the border around the vehicle or ship and then it can detect any incoming projectile. Then the objective gets obliterated before hitting its intended target."

He nodded. "Right, and with the proper combination of differing calibers and armor piercing grenades, there isn't anything out there capable of surviving an attack from a set of these things. A convoy of tanks, even with their current counter-strike protection systems, couldn't stop everything coming in."

Mike stood, his eyes wide. "Holy crap!" He walked around the back of his desk, running his hand through his hair. "What the hell else?"

He rose to his feet. "Well, it gets worse. There are no moving parts in these guns. As a result, they would just seem to be a steel box when subjected to x-rays or a visual check by someone seeking weapons. Their dimensions are anything but typical."

Veronica's eyes narrowed as she stared at him. "How so? How can a mechanical device function with no moving parts?"

"You've got to remember the technology is in the way they fire. There's no firing pin, no springs, etcetera. It's only a box with a bunch of gun barrels in it. They stack the projectiles—or bullets—on top of each other."

His brows pinched together in a frown. "There is no casing, or shell, because it doesn't need one. They're fired by an electrical pulse. So, an unarmed metal storm weapon under X-ray would appear to be a metal box with some tubes in it and some wires. Nothing else."

She nodded. "Yes, I've got it now. And their dimensions? How are they not typical?"

"For one, the smaller caliber models are about as big as a toaster in height, and the length varies depending on how long the barrels are. Again, it's just a rectangular box with a bunch of holes in the end. The ones firing the forty-millimeter grenades are about the size of a medium to sizable moving box, so we wouldn't be looking for the distinctive long package containing rifles or rockets. They can use the small models with their limited range to position and conceal in unusual locations."

Julian closed his eyes and rubbed his temples. "Jesus. Tell me we know who bought them?"

He studied the faces of the directors in the room before giving his answer.

They won't like this at all.

"Yes. Zahmir Al-Hamwi."

Veronica gasped, and her eyes widened in shock. "Al-Hamwi? Zahmir Al-Hamwi? Top ten most wanted list, Al-Hamwi?"

A trace of a smile crossed Blake's face. "The one and only."

She shot a glance at Mike. "Shit. Please tell me he hasn't collected them yet. Do we have a last known location for him?"

"The moment they informed us we were dealing with Al-Hamwi, I put a call into my contact in the Middle East. I haven't heard from him. Let me see if I can light a few fires."

As soon as Mike lifted the telephone, she turned to Blake. He could see the concern on her face.

"Sorry, ma'am. I don't know if he had or not. The intel I gained didn't mention a pickup date. It may still be there, or it could be long gone."

Her eyes moved to Blake's boss as he spoke on the phone, then shifted to Julian and back to him. "Gentleman, we *will* find out where he is. Julian, do you have any contacts you could reach out to?"

He gestured to Mike with his coffee cup. "Let's see what he finds out first. Those are the first people I'd contact."

She then focused on the field agent. "Hopefully, you heal fast. I have a feeling you're about to get busy." She placed a gentle hand on his shoulder. "If you're ready for it."

He sensed for a moment she had some concern for him.

Perhaps she's not all that bad.

The clunk of Mike's phone turned everyone's attention to him. "His last location was in Sabzawar, Afghanistan. It's about a hundred and ninety klicks east of the Iranian border in the northern part of the country. There is a well-known group there that we have seen him with several times."

Veronica was visibly relieved and less tense when she learned Al-Hamwi hadn't yet collected the weapon. "That's a relief. It must still be still in Cuba."

Mike put his elbow on the desk, bent, and rubbed his face. "Well—not so fast."

It was obvious he was aware of something, and they would not like the answer.

Blake scanned the faces of all around the room. "Isn't there an asset on the ground nearby able to verify if he's still there, or if he left?"

Brennan's eyes traveled to each of the guests in his office. They continued to dart between the three of them. He was like a doctor delivering an unwelcome outcome to a family after surgery. "That's the bad news. NCS says their operative didn't contact them at the last required check in."

Julian rubbed his eyes. "And when was that supposed to be?"

"Two days ago."

He frowned. "When was the previous communication?"

Mike hesitated for a moment. "More than two weeks."

He cocked his head in disbelief. "That long?"

Either someone killed him or took him prisoner.

MacKay leaned forward and winced from the pain in his ribs. "So, we don't know if this guy has been missing for two days or over two weeks? It makes me nervous."

Mike shrugged. "I agree, but perhaps the circumstances only permitted him once every fourteen days. Unless you're there, you can't determine if the time frame is unrealistic."

"So you want me to go to Afghanistan and see what I can dig up?"

"Yes. I'll call NCS back and get as much info on Al-Hamwi's last known whereabouts."

Blake's hand went to one of the bruises on his face. He took a deep breath and winced again. "It might be possible I can get some intel on what he's got planned with these weapons."

Mike poured some water from the bottle in front of him and took a swig. "By the way. Right after we got word of your departure from Cuba, we sent a team over from Guantanamo to clean things up. The Cubans have been helping us."

Julian's eyes lit up. "You know—since the relationship has improved between the U.S. and Cuba, it's *not* surprising they're being so cooperative. I have a feeling they're hoping this new attitude will go some distance with us, lifting some of these sanctions we've had on them for so long."

Veronica's eyes met his, and she frowned. "So, what are you saying, Julian?"

"We should take advantage of this and check out what we can find. Blake's mission was obvious. Finding this intel was an afterthought. Now we know what to search for. There could be more there. It might lead us to what Al-Hamwi is up to. Mike, I suggest you get on a flight there and see what you can dig up. Blake, prep for Afghanistan."

She held up her hand. "Whoa, hold on a second. No disrespect, but I think we need to press the pause button on Afghanistan."

Mike lost his patience with her. "Yes, and I suppose you've got a better idea? You're the one panicking when you discovered it was Al-Hamwi who has this weapon. If you have a sounder plan, then fine—what is it?"

Blake's eyes traveled between the two.

Oh, boy. Here we go.

She stood with her arms crossed, trading glances with her in-office adversary for several seconds. "Okay, let's see what kind of plan you come up with. If it appears to be feasible, then I'll agree to it."

He sat back, the rigidness of his spine softened. "All right. Give us a couple of hours to figure out our best course of action. When we do, we'll go over it with you, agreed?"

Julian plucked at the cuff of his shirt. "Sounds fine to me. I'll leave it to you two. In the meantime, I'll check in with the guys in

Key West and make sure they get the press release out within the next thirty minutes."

She raised her eyebrows and offered a questioning gaze. "Anything I can do?"

Blake expected his boss to respond with a *Fuck no*. Instead, he stayed professional. "Nothing I can think of at the moment, but if something comes up, we'll call you."

#

A few hours later, all four met and sat in Julian's office. Mike stood at a map of the Middle East, projected on the wall.

"We've contacted NCS in Afghanistan and it's confirmed we have a missing operative. He still hasn't checked in and they've not been able to get any kind of signal from his cell."

He then pointed a laser at the map. "Here is what we've got."

"He will fly to Al-Ueid Air Base, west of Doha, Qatar. We've established a relationship with one of the locals in Sabzawar. He's proven to be an excellent asset. I'll tell you how he's going to help in a moment. Blake, go over what your plan is first."

Clearing his throat. "Sure thing." He rose and took the pointer from the table. "Because of rising tensions in Iran and proximity to the Iranian border, I think the best way for insertion is for me to HAHO into—"

Veronica frowned and tilted her head in confusion. "I'm sorry to interrupt. What the hell is HAHO?"

Oh Jesus.

He glanced over at Mike as he rolled his eyes.

Suppressing the urge to smile at his boss's reaction, he focused on her. "That's a perfectly valid question. It's a high altitude, high open jump."

"How high?"

The veteran agent shifted on his feet. "Under normal conditions, around twenty-seven thousand feet. I'll open my chute about fifteen seconds after I jump. It will be a little under fifty klicks, or thirty miles from my target. I'll have GPS on my arm and will steer to my…"

Should I say LZ or will that confuse her more?

"…landing zone."

She squinted as she stared at the map. "Why is this the best way in?"

Mike fidgeted in his chair before speaking. "Because at twenty-seven thousand feet, the plane won't be seen as a threat on radar, and being fifty klicks away, no one within miles of his LZ will even know there is an aircraft in the air. It's clandestine, it's what we do."

Mike waved his hands. "Will you just please continue?"

He continued to mumble under his breath. "For fuck's sake, Jesus."

With a sharp glance directed toward him, she could have sliced through solid stone. "Right. Our local asset will meet me at my LZ and then get me in touch with an all Afghan Special Forces team. I'll be hand-picking them once I land at Al-Ueid. They have dossiers on all the locals. I want to interview them in person."

She rubbed her chin while scribbling notes on a pad. "Um, what then?"

"From there, it's only a matter of reconnaissance and trying to find Al-Hamwi or some clue to his whereabouts."

Mike rose to his feet, turning to the others in the room. "Questions?"

They both shook their heads.

"Excellent." He turned to his agent. "I need you at Langley Air Force Base at oh-six-hundred."

"Right."

"Now go home and rest."

<h1 style="text-align:center">15</h1>

Home of Blake MacKay
   Centreville, VA
   June 19th
   16:30 local (21:30 GMT)

Blake owned a farm about thirty kilometers southwest of Centreville, Virginia. Broad, open meadows stretched across the driveway in front of the house. Beyond, a substantial hardwood forest encircled the plot.

Although it appeared remote, all the airports were never more than a ten-minute helicopter flight away. The property made it simple for choppers to land, and they visited regularly.

Despite having only fifty acres, there was a barn, a modest-sized two-story residence with a partial basement, and a wraparound porch. Scattered around the site were smaller outbuildings used for storage. About sixty meters west of the main house was a charming groundskeeper's cottage.

He found an older, but active, retired couple to live there for no charge. All they had to do was care for the grounds during his absence.

They kept the location in excellent condition, got the mail, and he'd even set up a separate bank account they could use to keep the utility bills paid while he was gone.

Stanley and Irene Fischer solved the problem of looking after his place during his travels. The Fischer's believed he was a consultant for the DOD on security protocols for foreign military bases, hence the helicopters landing, and the long trips away from the house.

A Company car drove along the half-kilometer gravel driveway to the house. Sitting outside on the small porch of their cottage, relaxing, the old couple were reading the paper. They waved to him as he entered his residence.

He went up his front steps, disarmed his alarm system, and entered the house. Dropping his bag in the foyer, he glanced around to ensure that everything was in order.

It's wonderful to be home. Even if only for a few hours.

After sifting through the mail, he shuffled into his bedroom and undressed for a quick shower. As he stepped into the bathroom, his private cell phone rang. His best childhood friend, Joe Silver, was calling. He smiled as he replied, "Hi, Buddy, what's up?"

"Hey man, whatchadoin?"

"I'm getting ready to hop in the shower and get something to eat. How about you?"

"I'm in town for a convention and I've got some free time tonight. Feel like some dinner and a couple of cocktails? I've got a new bourbon we're releasing. You need to taste it."

"I didn't know you were going to be here."

"Well, perhaps if you checked your voicemails or answered your damn telephone, you'd know."

He needed the rest, but it had been two years since he'd seen Joe.

"Uh—yeah, sure. It sounds perfect. Listen, can I meet you about halfway? I know an excellent little pub we can get a drink and some food in Fairfax."

"No problem. Text me the address and I'll see you there in about forty-five minutes. Cool?"

"You got it, buddy."

Mashing the 'End' button, he put his phone on the nightstand.

It would be amazing to check out how Joe was doing, along with the distillery he opened a couple of years ago.

Joe was the one- and the only individual alive he trusted absolutely. On Blake's imaginary confidence scale of zero to one hundred, the only other person even coming close was his boss, Mike, and Blake reckoned he only measured about ninety-four. The other people he worked with came somewhere between eighty and ninety. Director Slocum was about forty.

It wasn't the fact he didn't entrust her with his secrets; he didn't depend on her to do what he considered was the right thing for national security and dealing with enemy combatants. They had opposite political views, and they didn't always see eye-to-eye on how he handled some of his assignments.

His other colleagues in the field, he trusted one hundred percent with his life, especially on top secret clandestine missions. Trusting someone to tell him when his life was in danger didn't mean he would spill everything to them with his private, intimate feelings and thoughts.

After his shower, he got dressed and meandered into the kitchen. He pulled out a 5-Hour Energy drink from the refrigerator and tossed it back. If this night turned out to be like most evenings when he met with his buddy, he would need it. He rushed out the door after grabbing his Glock and keys off the counter.

#

Blake set his mental alarm for four in the morning so he could jog five miles in the dark. He cursed his friend for forcing him to remain longer for *one more round*. He knew better.

Last night's 'one' evolved into two, and he lost count after that. Shuffling over to the medicine cabinet, he took three aspirin and splashed his face with cold water.

For most of his life, he was unsuccessful in his attempts to convince himself he loved to run, but in fact, he loathed it. His survival, however, depended on keeping himself in top physical condition. This had proven to be true on multiple occasions.

Reminiscing about his night with Joe seemed to make it

somewhat bearable.

His parents raised him in the higher altitudes of Colorado, which enabled his body to adapt to running at peak performance with less oxygen.

He had often pondered whether this was the reason for his exceptional athletic ability. Or, perhaps, was he one of the fortunate few with a circulatory system that carried more oxygen in his hemoglobin?

Blake finished his run in his driveway and walked the rest of the way in. The sun crested the horizon. It was a comfortable seventy-three degrees, and he took in the beauty surrounding him.

The dense woods hugged the drive and formed a natural tunnel. At the end, it opened to reveal the open pasture where the helicopters landed. Once at the house, he leaped onto the porch and went inside.

Hanging from the oven door, he grasped a towel and wiped the sweat away. From the fridge, he grabbed a bottle of water and chugged it as he strolled into his bedroom. There he turned on the television and the shower.

He showered but didn't shave; he needed to be as gruff-looking as possible to blend in the best he could in Afghanistan. His Scottish heritage acquired from his father allowed him to grow a thick beard. His Native American ancestry he had inherited from his mother imbued his skin with a dark olive tone.

It would take a day to get to Qatar, a day of prep at the base and after that, in the middle of the night, HAHO into Afghanistan. By that time, he'd have the making of a decent growth. He'd packed his bag the night before, so after getting dressed, he brewed himself a cup of coffee.

While sitting in the kitchen and sipping his drink, the television in his bedroom made an announcement he wasn't expecting. The newscast broke the story of helicopter dogfights near Key West.

'All right, now check out this exciting clip of what appears to be a dogfight between two helicopters. Then, we see one of them being shot down by a fighter jet. It's dark and a little hard to make out, but watch. A tourist that was out in the keys on a fishing

charter captured it.'

He set his coffee on the table and ran into the bedroom. On the television was a shaky video with a grainy texture of a missile fired by Lieutenant Luking. It hit the chopper and exploded.

'The military is saying it was a training exercise and the downed helicopter had no pilot. They flew it remotely.'

He couldn't contain his laughter. "Good one, Julian." He turned off the TV and tossed the remote onto the bed. With his bag in hand, he locked the house. When he pulled back the garage door, the early morning light illuminated the black Jeep Wrangler Unlimited, four by four.

Customization included a lift kit, oversized tires, chrome wheels, lights and the other things, customary for vehicles of this type. During the summer, the top and the doors came off and didn't go back on until the fall. It got horrible gas mileage, but he didn't care. It was awesome.

On the way in, he attempted to clear his mind and inserted a compilation mix of his most loved tunes. He had a broad range of musical tastes and enjoyed all different styles, but people could describe his favorite as *sui generis*.

His ex-girlfriend in college hated it and called it "Teutonic Hate Rock" because a lot of the music he listened to was German. In reality, the bands were from all over the world, including the U.S. Besides, He was fluent in the language, so he didn't see what the problem was.

When he got to the airport, the same G650 that had picked him up from NAS Key West waited for him on the tarmac. The two, who have been Blake's pilots for the past two years, offered their usual greetings and questions.

"Good morning. Here, give me your luggage."

The pilot grabbed his bag and took it onto the plane. "So, what crazy mission are you off to now, Mr. MacKay?"

Chuckling, he gave his normal answer. "Now you know, if I told you, I'd have to kill you."

They both laughed back. "Right. Okay, we're almost finished with the pre-flight list. Get comfortable and we'll be outta here in about five to ten minutes."

"Thanks Randy, Chuck."

He used the time to warm a croissant in the microwave and pour a glass of juice. Sitting on the plush leather couch, he dug into his backpack and retrieved the mission folder, but then placed it back. He'd scrutinize it later.

The intercom squawked. "Buckle up, here we go."

The jet taxied out onto the runway, powered up, and accelerated. He peered out the window and focused on CIA Headquarters when it came into view as the plane gained altitude. Thoughts of General Vasquez came to mind, and that same feeling in his gut appeared.

How in the hell did he find out? Somebody fed him information. But who?

#

After a restless sleep, Blake forced himself to stand and walk around the plane's cabin. He went forward to the galley and started some coffee.

The flight to Qatar was under fifteen hours, giving him plenty of time to study his mission briefing. Someone would also discuss the operation with him when he got to Al-Ueid AFB to review everything again and to notify him of anything new of possible significance.

He was the only one on the plane, save for the two pilots. While the coffee brewed, he opened the cockpit door. At the controls were two familiar faces, Randy Emerson and Charles "Chuck" Donovan. Both had formerly flown aircraft for the Navy. but now worked privately for the CIA. They had flown him to countless locations over the past several years and had become trusted colleagues.

He grinned. "Hey guys, good morning."

The two men spoke in unison. "Morning."

"I'm brewing some fresh java. Would either of you like some?"

Randy, sitting in the captain's seat, shook his head. "No, I'm fine."

Chuck nodded. "Sure thing, I'd take some. Black, please."

"Okay. How are we doing?"

The captain checked the instruments. "A little over twelve more hour's flight time. The weather ahead is clear, and we shouldn't encounter any rough air. We should have you there right on time."

Blake stepped back a few steps into the galley. He poured Chuck a cup, brought it to the front, and handed it to him. "I'll be in back reviewing some notes if you need me for anything."

Laughing, Chuck took a sip. "Well, no shit, Shirlock. Where else would you be?" "Well, I have been known to jump out of these from time-to-time." He shut the cockpit door, moved to get his drink, and strolled to the back to read about the asset he was meeting in Afghanistan.

The CIA had informants all over the world, they were referred to as 'Human intelligence', or, 'HUMINT assets'. These are people either working at present or have worked for a foreign government, or other targets of interest.

They may observe and report on the sightings or behavior of a specific individual or group. This might be the number of ships in a port or where a particular bunch of people stay or work. They convey the findings back to the Company. Rafaela Delatam was one such asset.

He was forty-eight years old, married and had three children, all in their teens. He and his wife owned a restaurant in Sabzawar, Afghanistan, where they all worked hard and earned about five hundred and twenty dollars a year, which is above the average annual income for most workers in the country.

Rafaela once provided intel on an IED—improvised explosive device—and its location to a U.S. soldier who patrolled outside his business. He had overheard some men talking about it in his diner he'd suspected of working with the Taliban.

After they had proved the report he'd given the military was true, they recruited him into the CIA as a human asset. After several years of productive service, he would get payment and have the chance to move to the United States with his family. Rafaela had been doing this for close to six years and had become a top aid.

After reading about Rafaela, he studied maps of the region where he would be landing, as well as Sabzawar. A few more hours had passed. Blake picked up the satellite phone and called his boss. As usual, Mike answered on the first ring.

"Hi man, how's the flight?"

"It's fine. You said our operative was going to provide me with a team, but I don't have any data about them in my packet. Was there supposed to be something in there?"

"No. Once you land, they should get all of that for you. There are several ANA Commando and Special Forces units we use and we don't know which one it will be yet."

There were loud familiar whirling and exhaust notes of a Black Hawk helicopter through the receiver and Mike raised his voice. "My connection in Qatar is working on it as we speak! I'll forward you his contact info and you can call him in a few hours! Right now, I'm in Guantanamo getting on a bird and headed to the general's estate to assess the situation! Gotta run!" The phone went dead as his boss disconnected.

Blake put the sat phone back in his bag. He leaned back in his chair and rubbed the stubble on his face as he stared out the window and thought about the validity of this group of Afghans he would entrust his life to. After reading the history, worry crept into his mind.

ANA, or Afghan National Army Commandos and Special Forces, did not have the same training or know how as those from the USA. The Commando units have only been around since 2007 and the Special Forces graduated its first-class in 2010.

The SF teams trained and based in America. have a higher level of expertise and experience compared to the ones in question. Special Forces only require fifteen weeks of instruction.

With such knowledge, along with the fact they had limited involvement and had about a fifty percent literacy rate, Blake had plenty of reasons to be concerned. Until he received his contact information from Mike and could talk to him, there wasn't anything else he could do.

He fixed himself a ham and cheese sandwich while he

pondered on his mission.

I imagined I was going to review some dossiers before I landed. This doesn't bode well.

He took a bite of his food, walked back, and sat down.

Well, I can't do shit until I get there. Might as well watch a movie.

He made a selection from the plane's extensive library and leaned back to enjoy the rest of the flight.

16

The White House
June 20th
14:11 local (19:11 GMT)

Directors Slocum and Thomas both arrived at the White House. Their cars stopped under the portico on the North side of the West Wing. They were meeting with President Rebecca Pennington and the Chairman of the Joint Chiefs, General Andrews.

They were to discuss the findings at Vasquez's estate and updates on the Metal Storm weapon investigation and how it ties in with Al-Qaeda.

The Secret Service escorted the two directors to the Roosevelt Room, adjacent to the Oval Office. There they waited and reviewed their notes until POTUS was prepared to receive them.

Veronica wished to ensure she had all the information necessary to offer the president. She despised surprises and strived to project an image of complete control, even when it was not always true.

Deep in thought, she stood while she stirred the sugar in her tea. "Julian, you have the latest intel we received from the intelligence call this morning, correct?"

Sitting with his back to her, he turned to talk over his shoulder. "Naturally."

Not convinced, she walked over to speak to him face-to-face. "And you haven't heard of any further developments in the last hour?"

"No. If I did, I'd tell you." His brow furrowed. "Why? Should I? Is there something you're not telling me?"

She sighed, placing her blue mug with the POTUS emblem on it on the end table. "No. Of course not. I want to make sure we keep her briefed. You know, she can be a real vixen sometimes. You don't want to get on her bad side. Let me answer the questions about what we know. You can reply to any queries she has about our asset. It's your show."

Julian shrugged. "It's fine by me."

She stared into Julian's eyes, seeking signs of deception, but she found none. The tension in her shoulders subsided.

Ten minutes later, the president's secretary came in and told them she and the Chairman were ready to receive them. Collecting their briefcases, they followed her to the Oval Office.

The president and General Andrews were sitting on the couches facing one another. They both stood, and Pennington approached them with her hand extended. "Veronica—Julian. Good morning."

She shook her hand and returned the greeting, then shifted her eyes toward the general and nodded.

He sniffed, his face devoid of expression, and mumbled a greeting.

Director Thomas also exchanged pleasantries. For the next few minutes, she went through the essential points of her summary one more time in her mind and prepared herself for the meeting. POTUS extended her arm to direct them to sit on the couch and she took one of the two armchairs facing the pair of sofas.

Pennington's eyes swept around the room. "I read the security brief first thing this morning. What do we have on Al-Hamwi? Do we know what he's doing?"

Veronica fidgeted with her bracelet. "Madam President, we've discovered he has purchased a weapons system called Metal

Storm. It is a—"

"I am well aware of what it is, Veronica. As I said, I've studied the communique. So please, don't give me a synopsis of what I'm already cognizant of. Tell me something I don't know. Like, does he have it, or what he's going to do with it?"

Veronica felt the blood rush to her cheeks. Thirty seconds into her address and it wasn't going well. She cleared her throat. "We cannot answer either of those questions, Madam President."

General Andrews' face flushed.

"For Christ's sake, Director, what *do* you know?"

From across the room, everyone present could see the blush on her face. She sat with her mouth agape when Julian swooped in for the rescue.

"Mike Brennan has flown to Guantanamo to meet a team and then on to Vasquez's estate to verify if the weapon is still there. He will attempt to gather any additional data our operative may have missed in his hurried exit." He paused and glanced around the room.

"The Cubans are cooperative and granting us access. We have information on the whereabouts of Al-Hamwi and his known accomplices. We're sending our man in there to find him to collect further intelligence."

Veronica's embarrassment converted to anger. The benefit was the blood went from her cheeks to the back of her head.

The general's eyes moved to Julian. "When is the agent being dropped in?"

He tried to suppress a smile. "He is on his way to Qatar as we speak, sir. We'll inform him of any additional data we procure while he is en route."

The president nodded. "Okay. Go on. What's the plan once he arrives in at his destination?"

"At Oh-two hundred, local Afghan time, our operative will HAHO into Afghanistan to meet with another asset, who will then take our man to the last known location of Al-Hamwi. From there, he'll make an assessment and get back to us. Until then, I'm afraid it's a waiting game."

POTUS tapped her fingers on the chair as if giving thought to her next reply. "Ok. I demand an update every twelve hours, no matter how insignificant. Anything more significant you discover. I want to learn about forthwith. Understood?"

Julian nodded his head. "Yes, Madam President," Pennington held his eyes. "Have we found out how Vasquez got his greedy paws on this weapon to begin with?"

Veronica broke in. "No, but we've started looking into it."

"Fine, I need to be updated about what you find out concerning that as well. The sooner the better." POTUS stood and glanced back and forth at both directors. "Thank you for your time this morning." They shook each other's hands and left the Oval Office. The entire meeting lasted six minutes.

On their way out, she grasped Julian's arm. "Follow me."

They walked along the hallway and back into the Roosevelt room. She couldn't wait to chew him out. As soon as the door was closed, she pointed an accusatory finger at his chest. "Never butt into my conversation again unless I give you a nod. You made me appear to be a stupid ass in front of both of them."

His eyes narrowed. He took a deep breath. "Seriously? Perhaps you should—"

"Don't fucking do it again. Understand? Now, do we have any kind of lead to find out how he got these weapons in the first place?"

She sensed the contempt in his voice. "No. I'll get someone to contact the manufacturer and check if there is anything there that we might be able to study to get a clue."

She brushed her palms together. "Fine. Call me as soon as you get any additional information." Pleased with how she had handled him, she stormed out of the room. Once outside, she stepped into her car and departed.

#

Julian stayed in the Roosevelt room alone to let his agitation subside. He pulled out his phone, his face red with rage. "What a bitch!"

He dialed Mike. As usual, he answered on the first ring.

Julian's voice rasped. "We may have a problem."

#

The president walked around to her desk and sat in the plush black leather chair. General Andrews approached and spoke before sitting in the chair facing her.

"Something's on your mind. What are you thinking?"

She twisted her pearls while her eyes danced around the room in heavy thought. "I don't know. I can't put my finger on it."

"Well, if it's your confidence level waning on Veronica, you're not alone."

She immediately abandoned her necklace and focused on him. "It's not her. I have all the confidence in the world in Director Slocum. She's under a tremendous amount of stress. No. This is something else. Something about this mission just seems—off."

He licked his finger and rubbed at a spot on his tie. "Well, if you figure it out, let me know."

17

Al-Ueid Air Base, Qatar
    June 21st
    05:10 local (02:10 GMT)

The Gulfstream landed at Al-Ueid Air Base and taxied to the end of the runway. Off to the right were multiple rows of C130s and C5 Galaxy's waiting for duty in perfect formation. The jet came to rest outside one of two hangars at the northernmost part of the tarmac. Blake gathered his things, thanked the pilots, and exited the plane.

The U.S., UK, Australia, and Qatari have all used the base since it was finished in the middle of the 1990s. Now, it served primarily as a supply and operations center for American missions in Afghanistan and Iraq. An officer of the RAF stood by to welcome him. "Mr. MacKay, I'm Colonel John Smyth. It's a pleasure to make your acquaintance."

He shook Blake's hand. "Commander Jameson sends his apologies for not being here to greet you, but he had pressing matters demanding his attention. He's asked me to liaise with you in his stead and prepare you for your mission."

Smyth marched out of the hangar's side door, followed closely by Blake, who threw his gear in the back of the Humvee. After a brief ride to the administration buildings, He was shown into his quarters.

"I hope you find this to your satisfaction."

The room was small and as vanilla, as they came. Bunk, locker, desk, lamp.

"It's fine. Thank you."

"I know it's short notice, but we need to talk. My office, five minutes?"

It was difficult to suppress a chuckle, but he smiled. "I'll be there."

A few moments later, he met with the colonel. It was a bland room with a workstation, a beige couch with two other seats, and a coffee table. To his right was a circular conference table with four green vinyl padded metal chairs. A gigantic cartographic display of Afghanistan hung on the wall.

As the working spaces changed hands frequently among different commands, it remained devoid of personal effects, except for a solitary photograph of the colonel's family resting on his desk. The Brit was standing reviewing the map when Blake entered.

"Mr. MacKay, come in. Please." He made a gesture with his hand for him to have a seat.

"Call me Blake, sir."

"I will do so. You may address me as colonel or commander."

He raised his eyebrows, taken aback by the man's less-than-friendly response, but he dismissed it and listened to his briefing.

As they sat, Smyth handed him a pile of manilla folders. "These are all dossiers on the men comprising your team once you land in Afghanistan." The sizable stack comprised somewhere in the region of twenty records.

A frown formed on his face as he regarded the heap. "Why so many? I gathered from the intel I read on the plane there would be only ten of Al-Hamwi's people; eleven, in the off chance their leader is there in person."

"At present, there are four A-teams of ANA Special Forces. Each unit comprises fifteen soldiers with at least one woman."

A wry smile crossed the commander's face. He cleared his

throat as if for dramatic effect. "Do you know—why there is a woman in every group, Mr. MacKay?"

What's with this guy's arrogance?

Not missing a beat, he looked him in the eye and responded. "Their culture allows another woman to conduct the search or handling of women without violating their religious beliefs."

Smyth's smug grin disappeared. Blake hoped the arrogant jerk felt somewhat defeated.

"Correct. Things such as this need to be handled with decorum."

"Right. If I may, I'd like to study these and break the team into about five or six."

The man leaned back in his chair. "It's your call. It's your mission. But *do* know they are all well taught by your own Special Forces teams and much of it came *on the job*. They have proven themselves to be trustworthy and will battle to the death if necessary. No cowering wimps among them."

I'll believe it when I see it.

The commander was referring to problems the U.S. and Royal Army had with many of the soldiers they had trained. Often, they found Afghan fighters cringing in ditches, hiding instead of joining in the fighting.

It was also reported that during a fight in 2009, when the Taliban attacked a fort, the local troops ran away and hid under their beds. To add insult to injury, they stole the personal property of American warriors fighting hand-to-hand to defend the outpost while they were out of the barracks.

The incident caused the death of eight U.S. servicemen and wounded many more. Stories like this made Blake speculate about what kind of trust factor he could put on these men; and women. There were twenty at the moment, which wasn't ideal. He would have to review their backgrounds before deciding.

The base leader leaned in. "Let me point out a few things for you." He stood and grabbed a laser pointer. "Presently, we are here." The light flickered on the map, pointing to their location.

"I studied the area on the flight over. Show me in more detail where you think Al-Hamwi might be and where I'm to rendezvous with our asset."

The Colonel smiled an unfriendly smile. The kind where the lips made the movement, but the eyes said something different. Blake didn't care. If the guy was going to be rude or a jerk to him, then he could dish it right back.

He directed the laser light to another coordinate. "This is where we suspect they might be holed up." He moved the pointer again. "And this is where you will liaise with your operative. It's in the middle of nowhere and there shouldn't be anyone for miles. While you make your descent, he'll be arriving in an old lorry and will take you into Sabzawar, where you will meet with the team you assemble."

"Okay. How soon do you need my recommendations?"

"It was three days ago." The Colonel's eyes squinted as if to apologize.

Blake let out a heavy sigh.

Wonderful.

"Fantastic! I'll get them to you as quick as possible."

#

It was a little under fourteen hundred kilometers to his jump point and the flight would take about two and a half hours, plus another thirty minutes to get on the ground. His departure would be at 23:00, and his planned touchdown time would be at 02:00.

He would use the next day or two for reconnaissance and planning and also to report his findings and wait for his orders before making any kind of assault.

Blake read the dossiers, looking for anything to help him get to know the fourteen men and one woman better and increase their trust factor with him. He was interested in those affected by personal tragedies involving the Taliban, Al-Qaeda, or any other terrorist organization.

Whenever there was a family tragedy that took place, like a relative or spouse getting killed or tortured by one of these groups, sympathy was in short supply, and almost always a burning desire for some kind of vengeance.

A high rate of illiteracy dominated the country, so it meant having the basics of being able to read and communicate was essential. In an ideal world, all of them would be fluent in English.

Colonel Smyth was right. They all had proven themselves worthy on the battlefield, so now Blake had to decide on whom to choose to accompany him on this mission. He must make sure his team was well-rounded, so he picked five to make six, including himself.

Among them, he had chosen two medics, one sniper, one demolitions expert and one woman, who, much to his delight, was the team's master in hand-to-hand combat.

Hmm, such a skill might come in useful.

He got up, walked along the hall, and presented his choices to the colonel.

Back in his quarters, he changed clothes, then did his usual run outside to get his body acclimatized to the searing temperatures. The time was only ten in the morning, but the temperature was already in the thirties, Celsius.

The heat further solidified his hatred of running. After his exercise, he went into the gym, worked out with some weights and used the heavy bag. Following his workout and shower, his stomach growled, so he sought the mess hall.

The colonel entered and sat across from him as he focused on his breakfast. "I've been in contact with your asset, and he is assembling the team and getting the additional equipment you requested."

Blake glanced at the officer. "Thank you."

The man leaned forward. "So, what are your feelings about all of this? Do you think Al-Hamwi is there? What do you imagine they are planning?"

Resting his fork on his plate, he took a sip of water. "I don't know, Colonel. It's what I'm here to find out. I'm concerned no one has seen him for a while and I'm also troubled we have a man in our organization who hasn't been in contact in over two weeks."

The colonel's brow furrowed. "Do you suppose Al-Hamwi was involved?"

"I don't know, but my gut feeling says yes. Whether this man is there or not, I plan on discovering what he is planning, and I hope to discover what happened to our operative."

"But Mr. MacKay, finding this—this missing agent of yours isn't an element of your mission."

Blake fixed his gaze on the officer sitting across from him. The suggestion he should somehow forget about one of his colleagues made him furious.

"Colonel, no disrespect sir, but I don't give a rat's ass if it's part of my operation or not. Somewhere out there, dead or alive, is an American, and I will do whatever is required to find out what happened to him. I would pray to God, if I were in his shoes, someone would do the same for me."

The colonel's voice was stern, and he glowered at Blake. "None taken, but your military *is* looking for him. *Your* orders are to observe and destroy Al-Hamwi's men and we hope, also the man himself. Then you are to gather any intel. This isn't a search and rescue mission. Do we understand one another, Mr. Mackay?"

Blake's head tingled. Something about the colonel raised his ire. He wanted to tell the arrogant prick to shove it, but what good would it do? It would only warrant a call by the commander, eventually making its way back to Mike. Or worse, to Veronica, which would give her fodder to make life a living hell for his boss. Instead. he took the high road and allowed it to run off his back.

He shoved the remaining food in his mouth and chewed while Smyth gazed on. "Perfectly."

He stood and grabbed his tray.

"Excuse me, Colonel. I need to get my things and prepare for my trip."

He turned and walked away. Finding the missing agent wasn't part of his mission, but he didn't care. He would adhere to the directives for his assignment and perform it effectively.

But if he learned any further information on the latter and the chance arose, he would seize it. He left the mess hall and went back to his quarters. He called Mike to report about his team and the current situation.

18

Al-Ueid Air Base, Qatar
June 21st
21:00 local (18:00 GMT)

Blake awoke at twenty-one hundred after eight solid hours of sleep. He felt rejuvenated and ready for the mission. After he showered, he packed only the things he needed; Glock 23 with a silencer, night-vision equipment, tactical radio and throat microphone, GPS and a few other items. His left-over personal effects went into a locker and he locked it before heading to the hangar for his final briefing.

As he approached the tarmac, the mighty C-17 Globemaster III stood in all its glory, awaiting its mission to transport him to his designated drop site. An ideal aircraft, as it only required three crew to run it - two pilots, all that was necessary for this trip and a loadmaster when needed.

Blake was connected to the cockpit via wireless. At the rear of the airplane stood Smyth, with the two airmen. At their feet was the other gear he'd requested.

"Colonel."

"Mr. MacKay." The response was as dry and lifeless as the terrain beyond the runway. He gestured to the two men beside him.

"This is Major Henry Talbot and Captain Donovan Stewart. They'll be taking you to your destination tonight."

He shook their hands and exchanged pleasantries.

"Gentleman." The commander nodded as if to say 'dismissed' and the two aviators exited and went into the jet via the loading ramp in the rear.

Blake could sense the enmity in the colonel's voice. The man realized he was going to search for the missing agent anyway and already made the call.

Who cares? Let him kiss my ass.

Instead, he focused on the gear he'd asked for to make certain everything was there.

"I've got all the things you asked for, your assault weapon, grenades, sat phone and the M82. The sniper rifle is going to add a lot of weight. Are you positive you want to take it with you? I can get you a firearm from the team meeting you."

"No, thank you, Commander. I'm familiar with this piece of equipment and I've requested the proper chute to adjust for the additional mass. It's one less thing I'll need to learn or get used to while I'm there. Having a new unit of 'Ghanni' soldiers will already be a challenge."

Blake appreciated the colonel's offer but wanted to stick with what he was accustomed to. The more control he had over his gear, the better off he'd be. In addition, he possessed some cutting-edge technology the colonel was unaware of and that might prove useful.

"Fair enough. Your flight suit, helmet and oxygen are all on board. The extraction squad will be there to collect you at Shinidad Airbase on the north side of the city at oh-two hundred local time in four days. Best of luck."

The Brit shook Blake's hand and then saluted him. Blake wasn't officially in the military, so it was rare for him to salute. Taking it as a sign of respect from the man, he returned the gesture.

"Thank you, sir." After gathering all his equipment, he headed into the belly of the plane.

#

Two hours later, the aircraft was thirty-five thousand feet over Afghanistan. The cargo area was bathed in an eerie crimson glow, as the red light cast its luminous veil. Abruptly, a squawk erupted from his radio. "Three minutes, Mr. MacKay"

"Thanks, Captain."

After donning his helmet and oxygen mask, he rechecked all his gear in preparation for his jump. The high-pitched shrill of the hydraulics filled the void as he lowered the ramp. Even with his suit, the rush of cold air chilled him, but he shook it off and focused on the task at hand.

His adrenaline started to pump as the time to leave the aircraft grew nearer and helped to warm him. This was the part he hated. A chute not opening, or becoming tangled, entered his mind. Now—now he was safe. It wouldn't matter after he jumped. There was some comfort in knowing everyone else he ever accompanied had the same thoughts.

Captain Stewart's voice came over his headset. "Fifteen seconds." *Too late to back out now.* "Ten... five, four, three, two..." The red light flickered to green. With no time to waste, he charged toward the ramp and flung himself into the frigid abyss below, hurtling through the atmosphere to the uncertain fate that awaited him.

As the plane's engines went silent, an eerie hush descended upon the sky, broken only by the sound of his own labored breathing inside the oxygen mask and the rustling of his suit flapping in the wind.

At this altitude, the temperature was minus thirty-two degrees Celsius. The whoosh of the air and the change in pressure as his body fell and increased its speed was a unique feeling. The rush was exhilarating, and something he never got tired of.

Looking into the darkness, he could make out some of the topography. A few small fires burned in the desert night. Some belonged to the shepherds or nomads in the area for sure, but some—some were possible terrorist training camps. Although it was a task for another day, he wished he had a crew with him so they could go in and eradicate them.

The glow of his altimeter showed he was at thirty thousand

feet. He waited until he passed twenty-eight, and pulled the cord. His body jerked upward as his fall was slowed from the open chute.

Blake had his GPS strapped to his left arm. Based on his current position, he would have to control his decent speed and direction. He estimated he should be on the ground in approximately eighteen minutes; twelve ahead of schedule, which was how he liked it. He hated being late for anything. It would also give him a brief period to scout the terrain and make sure it wasn't an ambush.

As he predicted, he landed at the exact time and spot they had pinpointed. It took him a few minutes to remove his chute and jumpsuit. The desert air was pleasant and helped warm him as he dragged his gear behind a small outcrop of rocks for cover. With his night-vision binoculars, he scanned the area.

Nothing yet. You'd better be here, Rafala.

The rumble of a four-cylinder engine approaching from the east had him straining to see through his binoculars. It approached with its lights off. He yanked out his pistol and chambered a round. The truck stopped eight meters away, and he continued to study it from his rocky hiding place.

A gentleman dressed in a kondura stepped out and scrutinized the terrain. Although he recognized him from the photo in his dossier, Blake steadily drew closer to him until he was just half a meter to his rear. With his firearm pointed at his asset, he told the man to 'stop' in perfect Pashto.

"Wadrega."

The man spun around and raised his arms. "Are you the American?"

"I'll ask the questions. Hands on your head. Face the truck." He frisked the man, searching for weapons and any type of monitoring device while he kept his weapon trained on him. Satisfied, he turned the man to face him. "What's your name?"

"I am Rafaela Delatam, your liaison. I came to escort you to your place of safety."

"Where is the safe house?"

"I do not understand. I thought you were apprised of this."

Blake rolled his eyes and shook his head. "I *do* know. I'm checking to make sure you are who you say you are. Now tell me the address of the house."

His captive told him and several other tidbits of information only his contact would have known. It was enough to make him lower his pistol.

"Tell me about the team. When do we meet them?"

"They are to come to the location before first light. It is the four soldiers and the woman you selected."

Blake cracked a smile and made a dismissive shake of his head. "You know she's a soldier, too. What about Al-Hamwi and his crew? Any changes? Have you spotted him?"

The man blinked. "Of course. As for Al-Hamwi, no. Everything is the same. There are still ten Al-Qaeda there and no sign of their leader."

Blake started to ask Rafaela another question when a familiar whishing sound came in, and then the crack of a high-powered rifle.

Rafaela's head exploded and splatted blood and gray matter on Blake's face. He dove to the ground on his left, where he had placed his gear and unclipped his Barrett sniper rifle from his pack. Switching on the night-vision scope, he scanned the area where the noise originated. His heart thumped in his chest.

There were outcroppings of rocks and hills everywhere. At this point, the shooter could be behind any of them.

Where are you, you son-of-a-bitch?

He had to force the hidden assassin to take another shot in order to get his bearings. Because of the crack/thump, and the timing between when Rafaela was hit and the blast of the rifle, he had a fair idea of the distance and it was close.

Grabbing a rock, he lobbed it into the back of the pickup, hoping the noise would startle the shooter into taking another attempt. It worked. Not only did he get a better bearing on where the shot was coming from based on the sound, but he was looking in the right direction at the perfect time to see the muzzle flash.

Through the scope was movement behind an enormous boulder, one-tenth of a klick away. *There you are.* He lined the crosshairs on his target, used tactical breathing to slow his heart rate, and waited. When a head popped up, he squeezed the trigger.

The bullet hit the top of the rocks. The person who was there concealed themselves even further out of his line of sight.

Dammit.

He had sighted the gun in for targets at a greater distance away. His manual adjustment was too much, and he cursed at himself.

He had no idea what type of rifle they were using or if it had night-vision. One thing was certain—there could only be one of them. Any more, and they would have flanked him by now.

Blake peered through his scope again. From his shirt pocket, he retrieved a notebook he utilized to take a record of his settings from past engagements. It's used to track the configurations based on terrain, humidity, temperature and other environmental measures. He learned from his training with the SEAL snipers, you use this data to "DOPE your scope," in all shooting scenarios to make the proper adjustments, and it can be a lifesaver.

Okay, asshole. It's you and me. Let's see who the better man is. I've got a little surprise for you.

He pulled a new piece of technology out of his bag. It was the latest bit of techno-wizardry developed by the brilliant young scientist, Alice, whom the CIA snatched from DARPA, the Defense Advanced Research Projects Agency.

Glancing to his left and down, about three meters, was a perfect place for cover. A natural indention in the desert floor surrounded by rocks standing under two meters high. Blake jumped down. Another shot hit the top of the landscape as he landed.

Dammit!

He unfolded and fastened the brace he would use to hold his gun stable. The legs resembled tiny shock absorbers and were designed to absorb the recoil from the fifty-caliber.

Looking everywhere, he checked he wasn't being flanked. He placed a tiny box around the trigger guard and connected the box to the scope with a short cord. The semi-automatic Barret had nine rounds left.

Ok Alice, let's hope this thing works.

He pulled out his phone and opened the impressive program Alice had installed. The monitor glowed in the same greenish hue as the night scope. He adjusted the rifle. His mobile reacted. The rock where the sniper was came into view. Blake smiled.

Now to keep you there for a while.

He pressed the button on his phone, and it took control of his weapon. It let off a shot in the direction where the assassin was dug in.

Brilliant!

He fingered a sub-menu in the application and a circle appeared on the screen. With his finger, he touched the middle of it and slid it to the left. The legs on the brace adjusted, and the barrel moved.

Perfect. Fantastic job, Alice.

Blake drew his Glock and fired two shots toward the boulder. Then, he raced to the rear of the truck and hunched over. He glanced at his monitor. There was motion behind the rock. He pushed the button on his device and his rifle ripped out another shot. Seizing the moment, he ran for another outcropping to flank the man.

He scrambled and allowed another pile of rocks to provide him cover. Focusing on the phone again, whenever there was the slightest bit of movement, he would fire the Barret. After about fifty meters, he turned toward the shooter.

He crept along while he kept an eye on the image on his phone, watching for shifts behind the boulders. He fired again sixty meters later, but this time the bullet impacted a massive rock lower down an embankment. It was fifteen meters ahead of him.

When stones shuffled below his target's feet, he stopped.

You're still there, aren't you, you little bastard?

He concentrated on his breathing and calmed himself. He put on his night-vision goggles and peered in the shooter's direction. Huge rocks surrounded him and his view was obstructed on all sides. In front of him, the ground angled down to where his adversary was.

There was an alleyway with tall rock formations on either side, heading down toward the shooter.

Crap! Last place I want to be is in there. Let's see if I can get you to come to me.

The image on his screen was grainy. He hit the fire button and nothing happened. He glanced down and tried again. Nothing.

Shit! These boulders are blocking the signal. All right, asshole. You want me, here I come.

He tucked his device away and raised his pistol. He took a deep breath and prepared to head down between the rocks. When he peered down, his target was coming at him.

Oh Shit!

He fired two quick rounds into the guy's knees. A dead man can't be questioned, and he had questions.

The man screamed and dropped to the ground. He holstered his firearm and drew his knife. In less than a second, he was on top of his assailant. He elbowed him in the face twice. There was a crack as the man's nose went crooked and he yelled in Pashto, "Who are you? Who sent you?"

The man struggled under Blake's vice-like grip but got free. He rolled over and away. He produced a grenade and yanked the pin. "Allahu Akbar!" Blake dove toward the man and tried to grab it before the man released the handle, starting the timer, but it was too late.

The man attempted a shaky throw toward him. Unable to stop due to his momentum, he grabbed the shooter as he flew over him and used him as a human shield. The grenade exploded as he started to pinch his nose and open his mouth to minimize the pressure of the concussion.

A high pitch filled his ears. He experienced an unusual numbness, as though there were hundreds of tiny needles piercing the skin beneath the surface. Similar to, but more painful than, the "needle effect" one experiences as blood is pumped back into a sleeping limb.

He rolled his assailant over, who fared far worse. Shrapnel covered the man's head and back. He was dead.

"Dammit!" By now, it was obvious the man was there alone.

He searched him for any intel, but found nothing. His weapon was an old Tokarev SVT-40, used by the Soviets as early as

WWII. It was eventually replaced because of complaints of too much muzzle flash. Blake now understood first-hand why.

He took the rifle and headed back to the truck, but not before taking pictures of the face of the man dispatched to slay him and his contact. He gathered his gear and put it in the cab, along with the old Soviet gun.

Questions, worry and concern all filled his head as he wrapped Rafala's body in his parachute and placed him in the bed of the vehicle.

He found the address of the safe house on his phone and began to drive into Sabzawar, all the while wondering who sent the man to his rendezvous to kill him and if his mission was compromised before it even started?

19

Sabzawar, Afghanistan
June 22nd
04:14 local (01:14 GMT)

The old truck rattled and squeaked as he drove into Sabzawar and located the safe house. The absence of headlights behind him didn't mean he wasn't being followed. Only constant observation in his mirrors ensured he didn't have a tail.

Underestimating your enemy was one of the biggest factors leading to defeat. Someone who knew the location of his rendezvous with Rafaela sharpened his senses. The incident made him visualize danger and death around every corner and in the faces of each man he saw. The implication was clear - the site of the house could be compromised. He'd have to put in safeguards to be sure.

The entire region was run down, much like the majority of Afghanistan, but this area was closer to the bottom. He was certain that its residents envied the people in the other areas.

A rundown structure could be seen across the street. Half of its roof had caved in from neglect. Next to it stood an empty lot, dotted with various merchant tents made with torn and tattered canvas many used as their homes.

He backed the vehicle into a building whose front façade was missing. A collapsed wall leaned against the adjacent one and provided him with dark cover but still a clear line of sight to the house on the other side of the road. His watch ticked away the minutes until first light.

Twenty more to wait.

He scrunched down in his seat, pistol in hand, and waited for the team of Afghan Soldiers to arrive.

It hadn't been a quarter of an hour when two sets of headlights caught his eye. They drove in two separate vehicles, each approaching from a different direction to avoid any suspicion. One vehicle came to a halt in the alley next to the house and the other in the lot, out of his view.

The first group entered the home. Moments later, the rest came into sight while they crossed the street. Ten more minutes passed before he exited the truck with a vague idea of what he was going to do.

With his pack on his back and rifle in his hand, Blake ran across the road and peeked into the motorcar parked in the passageway to make sure it was empty. The door to the house was next to the car.

The approaching men were talking. He ducked into the shadows past the opening. He set his weapon down and drew his knife. A soldier came out of the house and retrieved a bag from the auto.

He crept to the guy's rear and pressed the blade to his throat. He grabbed the soldier's arm and pinned it behind his back. "I'm assuming you understand me?"

"Yes… I do. You are the American we are supposed to connect with?"

"I am, but we've already run into a problem. The man you sent to meet me—"

"Rafaela?"

"He's dead. Someone was there to confront us and tried to kill us both. Now you know nothing about it, do you?"

The man didn't move his head. Blake assumed he was correct, and the razor-sharp blade pressed against his throat had something to do with it.

"I do not. I was unaware of your meeting place with him. We were to rendezvous with you here before the sun rises. They call me Akbar Khan and I am here with the team you selected."

The name rang a bell. He had read his dossier. The Taliban tortured and murdered his father after they suspected him of giving information to U.S. soldiers.

When the United States came in to help rid the country of the enemy, they located some of the men who committed the crimes against his family. Prior to executing them, he discovered they also raped his fourteen-year-old sister and practically beat her to death and then sold her as a sex slave. Nobody ever heard from her again.

He released the man. "I'm sorry. You'll have to forgive me if I'm not too confident because they murdered Rafaela less than two minutes after I arrived."

Akbar turned around to face him. He swallowed hard and sighed. "I understand. Come. We are fixing breakfast and tea. Are you hungry?"

Almost serendipitously, his stomach growled, so he put his knife away. "Yes, thank you."

"Okay. Follow me and I'll introduce you to the rest of the team."

He kept his hand near the butt of his Glock strapped to his thigh. He didn't want to enter in a threatening manner. It wouldn't impress his new squad, but he maintained all his senses on full alert. He motioned for Akbar to proceed, and he followed behind.

The house had the typical sand-colored brick walls, but was bigger on the inside compared to other dwellings in the area. It had a shabby linoleum floor looking like something from the 70s.

Bits and pieces of it were missing in most of the high-traffic areas, and the plywood was visible below it. There was a central living room with two couches and three battered armchairs. A small television with aluminum foil covered rabbit ears rested on a rickety bench in the corner.

The kitchen had a sink, running water, which was also a luxury; a stove with only two cooking eyes, a refrigerator, and even a microwave oven. In the middle of the room were a well-worn wooden table and six chairs. They used the rest of the house for bedrooms and one squat toilet.

When he entered the side door behind Akbar, there were three other members of his new "crew" in the kitchen unpacking the supplies they had brought in. They all turned toward him. Akbar wasted no time in introducing him to the group.

Abdul Sabur Amin and Barbrak Zahir Shah were the two doctors and Sardar Kamal was the demolition expert. Akbar was the sniper. Blake selected the four individuals because they were all professionals in their respective fields and proficient in tactical operations. He picked two medics since someone would certainly get hurt in this area of the globe, and he wanted to ensure that everyone on his team survived.

Abdul was the first to speak. He was of average height for males in this part of the world, but his stature was nothing less than impressive. He weighed every bit of two hundred and thirty pounds, and it was all muscle. His voice was gruff. "Where is Rafaela?"

Blake's lips curled, and he took a deep breath. "Dead, I'm afraid. Someone shot him only two minutes after I met him. Which reminds me; his body is in the back of his truck. It's parked across the street. We'll need to get him out of there as soon as possible."

Footsteps came in from the living room and turned to see Farishta Taraki, the female member of the team. It enlightened Blake to see how attractive she was. Most of the women, when out in public, wore burqas covering them from head to toe. They had to abide by strict Sharia law, and they had nothing but a tiny slit for their eyes.

He often wondered how awkward it must be when meeting a woman for an arranged marriage for the first time. They could be beauty queens or coyote ugly; you had no way of knowing. Being a member of the ASA elite forces, she was exempt from having to wear traditional clothing, something not passed without vehement opposition.

Farishta had thick black hair, reaching her mid-back and fell loose. Her green eyes bore into him with an intensity making it difficult to be the first to break eye contact. The BDUs and tight-fitting tee shirt did little to hide her alluring physique.

Once he broke from her enticing glare, he found it hard to keep his eyes off her. She reminded him of Adriana and his mind drifted even further away. It wasn't until she spoke and introduced herself; he snapped out of his daze.

He placed the last of the new team's gear in a corner of the kitchen. He lifted an eyebrow. "Have we got everything?"

Akbar nodded. "Yes,"

"Excellent. I need you, Abdul and Sardar, to help me with Rafala's corpse."

After backing his truck up to the door, he and the other three men carried and stored his things in his room. Next, they grabbed the remains of Rafaela, which were still wrapped in the parachute.

They made it snug and duct-taped the ends and middle to keep his body protected. The best place for it was in the back of the vehicle until they could get it back to his family.

They ate breakfast comprising hard-boiled eggs, bread, jam and tea.

Blake finished swallowing and took a sip of tea. "So, you are all aware of why we are here. I want to hear what you all know of Al-Hamwi's men, where they stay and if you have any information regarding his location."

Akbar licked his lips. "The property is on the Northwest side of the city, roughly eight kilometers from here. It is a two-story office building in a district which is a mix of residences and businesses. We are uncertain, but we think there is a basement."

Blake rubbed his chin. "What makes you say that?"

Akbar stroked his beard. "Because we've been in the buildings flanking it and they both possess basements. We are also in possession of the schematics of the structure to its north, if that will help you."

Blake pulled out a map of the city. As he unrolled it, the others removed the crockery and glasses. He spread it across the table. "Farishta, can you show me where the building is?"

As she pointed to the coordinates, he took out his laptop and booted it up.

He connected to the internet through the satellite phone and opened the CIA's version of Google Maps. The picture was more detailed and could zoom in and read license plates with ease. It updated the photos with each overhead passing instead of years. With special clearance, he could even call for a live shot, complete with infrared and night-vision. This was not one of those times.

He zoomed into the location to get a bird's eye view of the building. "There's a narrow alley behind it as well as one to the south. Inside, to the north, you can see from the shadows that the structure is taller. We'd have an excellent vantage point from there."

Farishta nodded. "Correct. The space has three stories,"

He raised his eyebrows. "What kind of facility is it? Is this a residence or a business?"

"It is a merchant selling silks, baskets and other general merchandise,"

"What's upstairs? Is this place the dwelling or is it offices, or used for storage?"

She shook her head. "Mmm, I do not know."

Blake inclined his head. "Okay, well, it's one thing we'll need to find out. If we can get on top of it, we can get above Al-Hamwi's and use that as another entry point in our attack. Tell me about the occupants."

Akbar tapped his feet. "From our observations, we have confirmed ten men entering or leaving the premises."

It pleased Blake the intel he was getting from this team fell in line with the other information he'd received. So far, there was nothing to give him any doubt or suspicion. "How long have you been observing the place?"

Akbar thought for a moment. "Two weeks. Ever since the disappearance of the other American who was keeping an eye on them."

Blake paused for a second. "And you've seen no sign showing they have him?"

Akbar shook his head. "No. Nothing."

Blake rubbed his hand down his chin through his emerging beard.

There's got to be something in the building that can tell me what happened to Jim.

"Okay. What else can you tell me?"

"There is no continuity to their behavior. They come and go at different times all throughout the day."

Abdul broke in. "That is not true. They send someone to either of the two shops on the corner for lunch. They go around a quarter after twelve, every day. One of those café's was Rafaela's."

He stared at the man. "Would you recognize any of his guys from a photograph?"

Akbar nodded. "Of course, we took photos of all of them over the past two weeks."

Blake took out his phone and revealed to them the picture of the man he'd killed a few hours earlier. "How about him? Is he one of them?" He showed the photo to the team. They all shook their heads.

Blake's eyes swept around the members of his squad. "How about at night? Do they have anyone stand guard?"

Akbar cocked his head. "Sometimes they do and other times no."

"Okay then. We need to head over there anyway to deliver Rafaela's body to his family."

"You want to do this now?"

"Yes, now. Akbar, you drive your car and I'll follow. Farishta—please come with me. I have an idea I want to run by you."

20

Office of Prime Minister Oleg Shorets
  Minsk, Belarus
  June 22nd
  14:00 local (11:00 GMT)

One of Shorets' assistants showed Vasily Litwin, Minister of Energy, into his boss' office. He had never been in there before. They had always met with other officials in conference rooms or other venues.

They covered its walls, twelve feet tall, with walnut paneling, and they put thick red velvet curtains held back by gilt braided cords in the windows. The floors had light maple coloring, with designs in a darker color inlaid into the wood.

The Prime Minister's desk was mahogany with gilded accents. In the center were a gold pen set and a clock. Although the surface was far messier, it made him think of one he had himself.

#

The languid little man came into his office, glancing around in apparent adolescent amazement. His expression was that of a child going to an amusement park or huge toy store for the first time.

"Minister Litwin."

"Yes?"

Oleg directed Vasily to one of the leather chairs in front of his desk. "Thank you for coming. Please sit and make yourself comfortable. Can I get you a drink?"

"No. I never imbibe during the day."

"Then perhaps some tea?"

"Water would be fine."

His eyes rolled as he turned and went to the bar. Bending, he retrieved a bottle of water from the refrigerator and handed it to him. After that, he returned and poured himself a shot of vodka. "First, I want to congratulate you on your progress with bringing Belarus into the nuclear age."

The minister smiled; the wrinkles on his face almost objecting to it. "You are most kind."

"Tell me. How did you become the lucky man to head such a visible and important undertaking?" There were suspicions Vasily got into his position only because his father had served in the Soviet Army with President Solonovich and had called in a favor.

"The circumstances were distressing, I'm sorry to say. I was to be the second in charge. I was supposed to work under Gregory Davydov when the project was first announced, and the team created it. Unfortunately, he was involved in the horrific hit-and-run accident."

Oleg took a sip of his vodka and nodded his head. "Yes. I remember."

"They never discovered who ran into him."

A tiny hint of a smile crossed Oleg's face. "So, it was unfortunate for him. Not you."

"I suppose you could say that."

You are such a fool. No wonder people take advantage of you.

Olegs raised his eyebrows. "Do you not find it interesting they never found out who drove the car?"

"No—why would I?"

For a few seconds, he stared at Vasily.

Or—perhaps you were part of it and are slyer than I thought. Hmmm.

"Never mind. I understand you are close to bringing the reactors online. Is this true?"

"Yes, it was in my last report. We should be ready by July 3rd. It's what we have planned."

He was going to tell the minister he hadn't read his pointless reports. There were more important things to take care of, but the thought vanished from his head as he listened. "Planning? Is it not certain?"

"Well, there are a series of trials necessary. Prior to the tests, there are a number of items needing to be checked and rechecked. All of those tasks will take days. These are matters we can't shortcut. The evaluations are extensive. Any miscalculations or shortcuts of any kind could end in being catastrophic. But so far, the entire project *is* on the timeline."

Dziarbo! I cannot have any delays.

He pointed at Vasily and raised his voice. "You make sure it stays on schedule, Minister. I am planning a grand celebration to coincide with our Independence Day. You would be like a hero to the people of Belarus if the reactors were to be put online the same day. You'd be famous. Fame is something you would like, is it not?"

The man seemed to be in deep thought as he sat and pondered the moment. Oleg knew he was single, so he stoked the fire.

"The honor alone would be grandiose. Women would flock to you. *And* it would secure your place in Belarusian history."

He could almost read his mind.

Vasily refocused on him. "Mr. Prime Minister, I give you my personal guarantee the plant will be ready to be brought online by the third."

"Excellent!" Oleg drew out the word. Stepping to the side, he motioned with his arm to show the end of the meeting. "Now, I will have my people contact you regarding the plans for the grand celebration. It will be a massive day for you, Litwin." He walked the fellow to the door, thanked him, and strode out of the office.

After the minister had departed, He strolled over, withdrew the encrypted phone from his desk drawer and called Aleksandr. "Come to my office." After ending the call, he poured himself another vodka. Only after sweeping his room for bugs again, did he wait for his partner in crime.

Aleksandr entered and meandered to the chair in front of Oleg's desk. The flame cast an orange glow on his face as lit a cigarette. The smoke's tendrils danced like ethereal specters, weaving a mysterious tapestry before fading into the stale air. "So, what did you need?"

"I have set in motion the beginning of our plan."

"How so?"

"I had a meeting with Minister Litwin a few minutes ago. He has assured me the power plant will be operational on August twenty-fifth. *We* will be there commemorating the opening on Independence Day."

"Right, but you still haven't explained to me how we can get out of being on the podium with Solonovich when he gives his speech. He always likes us standing behind him."

He waved him off. "The arrogant fuck is telling you lies. Do you know how often he has complained to me about having to share the stage on that day? He wants all the attention to himself. This will be perfect."

He walked over to the window and gazed out. "My plan is to have a video simulcast. There will be giant screens set up in Victory Square showing us with Minister Litwin as we turn on the reactors."

He smiled. "Solonovich can carry on about how wonderful he was to initiate nuclear energy for Belarus and then we can bring the plant online. We'll be safe; far away from the mayhem we will deliver to him."

He turned to his friend, who had a scrunched brow and a blank stare. "What is the matter?"

"This weapon you told me about—the one we are bringing into the country. Is it what you are plotting on using to do the job?"

"Yes, of course. What else would it be for?"

"Are you planning on zeroing in only on him, or are you going to make it widespread? If you do, it will slaughter thousands of people."

He scoffed and dismissed the comment with a wave of his

hand. "Collateral damage. You yourself said it needed to appear to be a terrorist attack. If we do it any other way, it will seem to be a political assassination. There can be no questions. There is no other way."

"But excluding the strikes on America, the majority of such attacks kill fifty, perhaps a hundred people, two at the most. Not thousands."

He walked over to Aleksandr. "My friend. This is the best *and* only way to do this, where we can get away with it. Yes—it will be bloody. It will—lots of people will perish. The more people die, the more compassion we'll get. We will have the sympathy of the world!"

He scowled and slammed his flat hand on the table. "The first step is to capture and hold Al-Hamwi when he delivers the weapon. After we take power, people will be demanding justice."

He pointed to himself and Aleksandr. "They'll be looking at us. In a week's time after the attack, we will have miraculously captured and killed the terrorists that brought this inhumanity to the people of Belarus. We will be heroes."

Aleksandr continued to sit in his chair. He pulled out another cigarette and lit it, but said nothing.

"What are you thinking?"

"I'm reflecting on the deaths of thousands of our countrymen we have sworn to protect."

"It's not all you're contemplating."

Don't turn on me now, Comrade.

Aleksandr tapped his fingers on the slick leather. His eyes darted back and forth in thought. They met Aleksandr's. "You're right." He nodded his approval. "This is the only way."

He stood and extinguished his smoke in the ashtray on the conference table.

"Yes!" He clenched his fist and smiled. "I will notify Solonovich of this at our next meeting. He will be most pleased not to have to share the stage with us. His arrogance will be his undoing."

21

The White House
June 23rd
07:30 local (12:30 GMT, 07:30 AFT)

Director Slocum, along with Directors Brennan and Thomas, sat in a conference room in the White House with the Joint Chiefs and waited on the president. The FBI Director joined them as well. They were grateful to have a couple of moments to cool off before their meeting. The last few days, the thermometer had peaked at 103 degrees and there was no rain in sight for the foreseeable future.

Strolling to the buffet to pour himself some water, He used a napkin with the presidential seal to wipe the sweat off his neck and face.

"I can not wait until this damn heatwave ends. Do we know when it might break?"

Deciding to join him, Veronica headed over. "They said sometime next week. Perhaps Tuesday or Wednesday."

Mike stepped aside while she poured a glass of water. Placing the cool surface on her forehead, she mentally prepared for the session.

The plan was to review the daily threat assessment for all

things related to terrorism and the security of the United States. She opened her folder and perused the topics to calm her nerves. Something about meeting with her ultimate boss disagreed with her psyche.

The one thing she was desperate for was to do her job well and impress the commander-in-chief. A strong woman like President Pennington would recognize the strength in her, and it would help her to advance her career. For whatever reason, her desperation always manifested against her. She felt as if she continued to screw up at each turn and it ate away at her constantly. Perhaps she was trying too hard? Today, she hoped, would be a better day.

First on the agenda was a report on any home-grown security threats. There are over six-hundred militia, terror and hate groups they kept their eye on.

The Ku Klux Klan, Neo Nazis, Skinheads, The Nation of Islam, and The New Black Panthers, to name a few. Every state had them, and they were all being surveilled.

Unfortunately, with the Internet and the dark web, small factions would pop up much faster than before. Some would be a mere four to five members and most of the time, each member would reside states away.

Regardless of their size, they couldn't ignore them. The FBI recently stopped a plot from a couple of men planning to bring down the power grid of half the country by blowing up three substations simultaneously. Had they ignored them simply because of their size, the results would have been catastrophic.

After the internal terror parties, they talked about international bodies such as Hamas, Al- Qaeda, Isis, and the Taliban.

However, if there were any imminent dangers, domestic or foreign, those went to the top of the list and today; Al-Hamwi had won the honor.

She remembered what had unfolded in the previous meeting. An annoying tingle crept into her nerves.

She wanted to give her what she needed. Her worry grew with each ticking minute. The feeling intensified when, at last, the door opened.

The commander-in-chief hurried into the room. "Sorry, I'm

late. Jezebel vomited, and I accidentally stepped into it, so I had to change my shoes and call to have it cleaned up."

Veronica tried her best to stifle her amusement when she realized the story eased her anxiety. Jezebel was the president's beloved cocker spaniel. It either slept or barked and if you touched it, it would squat and pee all over the floor, a trait common among the breed.

Pennington turned to her. "So, Director, tell me what you have on Al-Hamwi, and it'd better be interesting."

Oh-oh. What did she mean?

"Well, Madam President, we have inserted our asset into Afghanistan. However," she cleared her throat and swallowed, "he ran into trouble right away, and he witnessed his contact's murder."

"Murdered? When?"

"Soon after he landed. Within a few minutes, at least. A sniper shot him from less than a kilometer away." Veronica's anxiety rose again.

Pennington frowned. "And *our* operative?"

"As you know, Blake is an exceptional field agent, and he's fine."

Thank God.

"He eliminated the threat and made his way into Sabzawar. He has been surveying the last known location of Al-Hamwi for the past two days. However, ever since, there has been no sign of him."

When Pennington turned to her with narrowed eyes, Veronica braced herself. She scowled. "How the hell did our guy in Afghanistan get killed and how did they uncover *where* he'd be and when? Something doesn't smell right."

There was a pause in the room, and everyone glanced at each other for some kind of reply. Soon after, all eyes were on her.

I've got to say something. She will not like this answer.

"We don't know Ma—"

POTUS slammed her palm on the table and glared around the room.

Dammit, I was correct. Why do I keep doing this?

A vein made its appearance on the side of the president's neck. "Well, pardon my French, but that's not fucking acceptable! Someone is feeding these sons of bitches' information! Find out who the hell it is and deal with them! What's the next action on Al-Hamwi's men?"

Mike Brennan stepped in for the rescue. He cleared his throat. "Madam President. Our asset has met with his team of Ghanni Special Forces. As Director Slocum said, they've been monitoring them and have gathered enough intel to make their move."

He steepled his fingers and rained his eyebrows. "They plan on striking this evening at around 19:00, our time, or 03:00 tomorrow, Afghanistan time. I should receive information from the mission by 21:00. If you like, I can order a satellite and we can view it live."

Veronica's jaw tightened as she gritted her teeth. Although she didn't like the interruption, she welcomed it. The information was relevant, and Mike did a fine job of delivering it without a shake in his voice. The last thing she wanted to do was show any fear or insecurity to POTUS. She was still going to crap on Mike at the end of the session.

"No, it isn't necessary. I will not squander money and resources on a basic terrorist raid. Had it been Al-Hamwi, I'd do it. This mission now is to gather intel in the *hope* we find out where Al-Hamwi is and what he's planning. Call me when it's over and tell me if they get anything worthwhile."

Mike nodded. "Yes, Ma'am."

The conference continued with the discussion of other potential threats at the top of the list. As the meeting adjourned and the Joint Chiefs and Pennington had gone, Veronica leaned in toward Mike. "For fuck's sake. Will you let me finish my own goddamn report?"

Her face flushed and veins throbbed in her neck. "Between you and Julian, I'm not sure which one of you is trying the hardest to make a fool of me. In the future, shut the hell up. If I need your fucking help, I'll ask you for it!"

Before he could respond, she gathered her Samsung tablet and briefcase and left the room.

On the ride back to Langley, she pontificated the mission in Afghanistan and what would be a key indicator of success. Every scenario she ran through her mind ended with one of two possibilities; Al-Hamwi was either dead or captured, nothing less.

And how in the name of God did someone know when and where Blake would be meeting his asset? There might be an entirely new situation developing and it needed to be brought under control immediately. She had to get this right.

22

After lunch, Blake assisted Farishta in cleaning up in the kitchen. She wasn't able to escape the stigma associated with being a woman, despite the fact she was as formidable as her male colleagues. The four other members of her team reminded her she lived in a nation where respect was scarce. They expected her to cook and clean after every meal, as well as perform other traditional womanly tasks.

He lifted an eyebrow. "Does it bother you they treat you this way?"

She handed him a washed plate. "What's the problem?"

"Making you do all the cleaning and cooking."

"No. My parents raised me to expect this. Besides, I've grown close to all of them. They're like my family, so I don't care."

"If you don't mind me saying, you appear Westernized compared to other women I've met serving in the military."

Farishta smiled, and he knew he'd hit on something from her past.

"When I was eight, we moved to America. My father taught

economics at the University of Arkansas. We were there until I reached seventeen."

Well, that explains it.

He put the last of the clean dishes away.

"Now we're finished, we can relax for a while before they get back."

His idea was to remain unseen in public as much as possible, so he ordered Abdul and Sardar to go out for supplies. Akbar had gone to relieve Barbrak as he studied the suspected Al-Hamwi hideout. Someone should be there at all times to check on Al-Hamwi's men to see if there have been any changes in behavior or headcount. He told Barbrak to be back by 15:00 so they could review their plan of attack intended for early the following morning.

Over the past few days, they had been viewing the building the terrorist leader's known associates had been occupying. He made detailed notes of the building's dimensions, the position of its exits and windows; the height of the structure next-door and anything else to help them design their plans.

The previous day, he'd gained entrance to the adjacent business and found they used the second and third floors for storage. It was easy to pick the old lock and enter at the rear. The back staircase leading to the upper floor was on his left. No one saw him go in. A tattered silk curtain obstructed the view of the back door, hanging in the doorway of the short hallway before it.

The owners of the premises closed at 21:00 and went to their apartment several blocks down. When he climbed the stairs to the roof, he dropped on his belly and shimmied to the edge to observe the top of Al-Hamwi's stronghold. It was an eight-foot drop and they could make it with ease and with minimal noise.

There was roof access to the adjacent building, another stroke of luck, but it appeared as if they wired the door with some kind of alarm. From his vantage point, it was archaic and easy to bypass, but he would have to investigate closer prior to beginning the attack. This would be where he would enter, as he didn't trust the others to disarm it.

After his reconnaissance, he met up with Farishta, where she'd been his lookout. Blake had dressed in traditional Afghan clothing and accompanied her as her cousin. They made a purchase from the silk and basket merchant next-door to their target and then left the area to go back to the safe house.

Before proceeding with their planned raid, they walked in front of the selected building to gain an understanding of its layout. However, their attempt to peek inside through the windows was thwarted as the view was cleverly concealed with old newspapers.

I can't see a damn thing in there.

He gestured toward the window. "I don't like it at all."

"The papers covering the windows?"

"Correct. I'd like to have seen the interior to get some idea of the arrangement. I'm not sure if there's a hallway or an open room. We haven't a clue if it's empty or cluttered with furniture. It all sets me on edge."

Her forehead creased. "But if we take them by surprise, what's the problem?"

The statement alone was unsettling for him. She never would have said such a thing if she had received the right training.

"It makes an enormous difference. Perhaps they set up sandbags in front of different rooms for all we know. There could be furnishings or boxes blocking our path or any number of things. Their ideals might be crazy, but they're far from stupid. Never underestimate them."

After they cleared up from lunch, Blake went back to his bedroom to prepare for the mission. He had laid out most of his weapons on the bed. Everything underwent cleaning and oiling, checking and rechecking. The slide of his Glock clicked back together when Farishta walked into the room and leaned against the doorway. Her curves made his mind wander to other base pleasures.

Her forehead puckered. "Do you ever get accustomed to this?"

He moved the slide back on his firearm, held it up to the light, and stared down the barrel with one eye closed. "Used to what?"

"Coming into foreign lands and killing people."

He lowered his pistol and turned to her with narrowed eyes. A tinge of anger replaced the visions of intimate actions. "Are you serious? Are you looking at this as some kind of invasion or something?"

"No. But it always appears it's America breaking the borders. Not the other way around."

He rose and stepped over to her. "Farishta. Are you with us? Are you on our side—meaning our team? The one we have right now. Because if you're not, I want an answer and I need one now."

She popped up and was no longer leaning against the doorway, and her brow furrowed. "What? Of course, I am with you!" She turned away for a moment before turning back. "You misunderstood the question."

He grabbed the bottom of her jaw and forced her attention. "I didn't misunderstand anything. Listen, we had *our* borders broken. On September 11th, 2001. Perhaps you heard about it?"

She waved his hand from her jaw, and he put it right back up, this time lightly pinching her chin with his thumb and forefinger. "I had friends die that day. When it happened, we, America, vowed never to have it happen on our soil again, and so far, it hasn't."

He spoke with passion. "I and thousands of my countrymen promised we would bring the fight to them wherever it may be. Not the other way around, and I make no apologies for it."

Blake waited for her answer, but none came. He found himself in one of those awkward moments of silence as he stared into her lustful green eyes-only inches from her. Her essence invited him in; full lips begging to be kissed. He knew he shouldn't do this, but the attraction was too much. She made the decision for him. Grasping the back of his head, she pulled him to her. Her mouth was warm and soft.

He tugged her close. She willingly pressed up to him. Wrapping his arm around her to her lower back, he ran his hand down to her butt and squeezed. She yelped with glee and kissed him harder, silently asking for more.

She shoved him back and pushed him onto the bed. With a sly grin on her face, she straddled his upper right thigh as she kissed him more intensely. He put his left hand on her rear as he slid his hand up under her top and grasped her firm breast.

Her breathing intensified while she clenched her thighs around his. Nibbling his lower lip, she made her way down to his pants. After tearing open his shirt, she ran her tongue down the center of his chest and licked his belly button. She grabbed his crotch, and she could feel his excitement. She undid his trousers….

The door to the safe house opened and Barbrak announced he had returned from a final reconnaissance of the Al-Hamwi house. "Hello?"

She jumped off him.

"Shit!" He sat up and buttoned his pants. He felt like a schoolboy getting busted by his girlfriend's parents.

Tucking in her shirt and heading out of the room. "Back here!" she yelled as she glanced back to make sure he had put himself back together.

He fidgeted with his gear as if he was organizing it when Barbrak came back and announced, "Everything is the same at the house. They sent someone to get food at the normal hour and it's all we saw."

He nodded. "Okay. Let's wait for the other two to return and we'll go over the plan again to make certain we all have our roles and times down." He glanced past Barbrak to Farishta, and she smiled.

Dammit, Barbrak! Your timing sucks.

Ten minutes later, the rest of his team, minus Akbar, arrived back at the house. Blake had made a mockup of the buildings earlier from various things he'd found around the house. He placed them on the coffee table in the living room. For the next two and a half hours, they went over the plan again and again, so they all had it memorized and timed.

"Remember, we're looking for any kind of intelligence we can get on Al-Hamwi; where he is at or anything on the weapons he purchased in the past weeks. Leave at least three men alive so we can interrogate and cross-reference our findings for additional intel: Non-lethal wounds if possible. Akbar is well-informed as I went over this with him before he left for his shift."

Everyone agreed. "Now, get something to eat and go and get

some rest. It's going to be a busy night."

23

Sabzawar, Afghanistan
    June 25th
    01:45 local (22:45 June 24th, GMT)

Blake opened his eyes and let them adjust to the dark while he shook the cobwebs from his mind. He pulled the cover back, twisted his body, and pressed his feet to the grainy wood surface. The sand and grit from the unforgiving terrain outside always found their way everywhere and collected in between his toes.

God, I hate this place.

Slipping on his clothes, he stretched out on the floor. The short yoga exercises got his blood flowing and allowed him to clear his brain and prepare for the mission.

He was eager to uncover any intel on the disappearance of Jim Dunn, but was also nervous about working with an unknown team. Once he felt awake, he went to make sure everyone else was preparing to go.

Sardar was standing in the living room. He'd returned from his sentry shift.

Blake raised his eyebrows. "Everything is still the same?"

"They do have one person on the outside. When I left, he was sitting on a bucket, not moving. Could be asleep."

He was silent for a moment. "Don't assume he's sleeping, but it's acceptable intel. Thanks Sardar. Akbar, you said we don't have to worry about local authorities. I'm hoping we get in and out undetected, but you never know how things go."

"Correct. The area is under Sharia law, and the police will not go into it."

"Okay. Fine."

They gathered in the kitchen. Dressed in black BDUs, and carrying silenced assault rifles with Glock 23 pistols, Blake handed out throat microphones and radios to everyone, in the hope he wouldn't have to give crash courses. "I assume all of you have used these before?"

Akbar inspected them, turning them over in his hand. "I think we've all operated something similar, but not this model. Is there something unusual about them?"

"Yes. You can whisper and we'll hear you, so be aware of how loud you talk. The operation will be on channel eleven. 467.6375 megahertz. Make sure you lock it at that frequency. In case coms get compromised, switch over to twenty-three. We will do a radio check on the way over."

Blake's eyes scanned the group. "Farishta, Abdul and Barbrak, for confirmation, you're Charlie squad."

A chorus of "okay" filled his ears.

Blake glanced at Sardar, who grinned before responding. "I am Bravo."

"Right. I know it's strange to be alone, but it's only in the beginning until you get the charge on the back door planted. Then you'll slip around the front and meet with the others."

Sardar nodded.

"Akbar and I comprise Alpha. Does anybody have questions prior to leaving?"

Everyone shook their heads.

As the mission commander of an untested team, he took a deep breath with a modicum of apprehension. Regardless of how he felt about his untested squad, the time had arrived to execute their plan. No turning back. "Ok, let's load up."

They drove across Sabzawar and headed south toward their

target. Blake and Akbar rode in one vehicle and the rest of the crew crammed into the following car. Thoughts raced through his mind about his unknown unit.

Did they possess the capabilities and the will to get the job done? Could he trust them if all hell broke loose and things turned to shit? They were close to their goal when a pothole jarred him back.

Radio check. I almost forgot.

"Alpha to Bravo, do you read?"

" Loud and clear,"

"Check. Alpha to Charlie?"

All three members of Charlie checked without any problem.

"At the next intersection, we break off to the east and you all head west. Go to your destinations and we'll continue on foot."

Barbrak's voice came over the speaker. "Understood, Alpha."

After a few more minutes, they came to their destination. They all ensured their weapons were ready and stepped out into the cool desert air. Clouds shaded the half-moon, blessing the ground with darkness. There was a subtle breeze, and the noise of barking dogs came from the distance. A slight stench of urine burned his nostrils.

He waited with Akbar until the other teams notified them they were in position. The two men sneaked to the rear of the next-door building after they had confirmation. He turned and raised his hand. "Keep watch."

Akbar nodded while Blake picked the lock. He lubricated the hinges to eliminate any squeaking it might make as it opened. He took a deep breath as he pushed the door. His lips curled at the stillness. They slipped inside and took a quick left prior to ascending the stairs to the roof.

Barbrak broke radio silence. "Alpha, this is Charlie. There is a sentry outside."

"Affirmative. Hold your position and standby." He lay on the top and belly-crawled over to the front edge of the structure before peering down. A single guard with an AK-47 sat on an overturned bucket, and from his lack of movement, He couldn't tell if the man was asleep or not.

Gesturing to Akbar to proceed to the roof, they both dropped to the adjacent building. He crept over to the door he'd seen alarmed the previous day. Once he was on the roof and no one popped out of the door, and there was no detonation, he let out a breath he didn't realize he'd held.

Blake's voice lowered to a whisper. He displayed a piece of wire to the alarm system that had signs of being cut months prior. "How about this? One less thing we have to be concerned about."

Akbar nodded.

Turning the knob, he found it locked. Then another worry crept into the back of his mind.

What if they rigged this door to explode?

Alice had given him an experimental handheld ion mobility spectrometer, which compared reflected, infrared, and visible light measurements on multiple areas of the suspected area. After what might have been an eternity, the device showed him the answer he hoped to see.

"It's clear."

He pulled out his pick kit and picked the lock. More lubricant on all the hinges and a gentle pull to open it. The door broke its seal, and he stopped it when it opened a crack.

Sweat ran down his back as he removed a snake camera from his pack and slid it into the gap of the door. He displayed a greenish-hued image of an empty stairwell on the tiny screen. He showed it to Akbar, who responded with a 'thumbs up.'

"Alpha to Charlie, baby-baby. Prepare and get ready."

"Baby-baby," Farishta confirmed.

He hit send on his radio. "Bravo, sitrep?"

Sardar's voice. "Almost finished. Ten seconds—wait."

Sardar rigged the back door to explode if one of the terrorists attempted to escape. He was to stay in the rear until he got word to come around the front and join the team before going inside.

"Alpha. This is Bravo. The package is prepared."

He took a deep breath. "Understood. Charlie, okay?"

"We're good to go."

Even though Akbar was the designated sniper of the group, because of the close quarters and general makeup of the area,

Blake deemed it unnecessary to bring a bulky sniper rifle on the mission. From the reconnaissance they'd done, there wasn't any viable tactical spot for him to set up and provide cover. Since Akbar was on the roof with him, he chose the next best shot.

Farishta was an excellent marksman and was tasked to take down the sleeping guard. He watched through his night-vision as he saw her take her position from across the street. She raised to take aim with her M4A1 assault rifle. He moved his focus to the unsuspecting man who would be dead in mere seconds.

Nothing more than a silent *whap* of her slide opening and ejecting the spent cartridge. The man fell over into a hump on the ground. Abdul and Barbrak raced in, seized the body, and moved it to the alley, out of sight.

He had to smile.

Great shot.

So far, his team worked well together. He crawled the three meters back over to the door.

"Charlie, sitrep."

Barbrak's soft voice came over the radio. "We are green. Getting into place now."

He paused and glanced around. "Bravo. Time to move."

Sardar responded. "This is Bravo. Moving into position now. Over."

Abdul and Farishta were outside the front door. Abdul had picked the lock. Barbrak and Sardar followed them.

"Alpha, this is Bravo and Charlie. We are in position. Over"

"Copy Bravo and Chalie. Standby. Do not go until I give the word, understand? Over."

Farishta's voice filled his ears. "Alpha, this is Bravo and Charlie. Understood. Over."

"This is Alpha. Copy that, Bravo and Charlie. Stand by." Blake positioned himself by the door on the roof. He whispered as he peered at Akbar. "We could have used the help of the satellite to view the inside."

"Why was it not?"

"A mission to rescue some kidnapped girls in Africa got priority. We'll be ok, though."

Akbar nodded.

He got on the radio. "Okay, everyone. On three."

Soon he received a flurry of confirmations.

"One…two…"

#

Bullets whizzed through the front door and struck Abdul in the side of his head, under his ear. He dropped dead in an instant. Splinters of wood filled the air. Farishta and Barbrak ducked back left around the side of the building as Sardar went right.

More rounds sprayed out of the front glass toward Sardar. Half ran up his Kevlar vest and the rest through his neck and head. They blew off the left side of his face. Farishta grabbed a grenade and threw it into the room. The concussion blew out the rest of the glass. After it exploded, she dove in the door as Barbrak followed her, laying down suppressing cover fire.

#

Up top, Blake couldn't believe what he had heard.

What the fuck? They knew we were here! How the hell did they know that?

He barreled his way through the door and down the small flight of steps. Akbar followed. Blake stopped at the bottom of the stairs and peeked around the corner, but a hail of bullets met him.

Son-of-a-bitch!

He grabbed a grenade and threw it to his right where the shooting came from. It detonated. Two voices cried out in pain. There was movement on his left. He ducked back into the doorway as weapons fire erupted and ripped through the wall. Blake stepped out and shot several three-round bursts and took out two more terrorists.

He rushed back to the location where the grenade had detonated and there lay the corpses of two men. He checked both. No pulse! He turned back to where Akbar was. "Akbar? Akbar! Where you at?"

No answer!

After returning to the stairwell, he glanced up. Akbar's lifeless body was on the staircase.

God dammit!

Gunfire and yelling filled the air. He grabbed Akbar's ammo and grenades and headed for the ground level. There was gunfire. "Bravo, Charlie. What's going on down there? Anyone!"

"Alpha! This is Barbrak. Farishta is in the hall and I am in the living room. There are two men in the kitchen. We're pinned down! We are having difficulty getting to them."

"Understood. I'm on my way down. Where do the stairs come out in relation to the kitchen?"

"Hold on!" He blindly fired several busts in the direction of the kitchen and stole a quick glance. "Uh, from what I can tell, in the passageway to the right of the kitchen." Three puffs came over the frequency of his MP5 firing. "You can come down and they won't see you."

"Copy. I'm coming down. Cover me."

There was the iconic note of the silenced shots as he descended the stairs. When he reached the landing, Barbrak was in the living room crouching behind a couch; his weapon popping up to deliver Blake more cover. There was no sign of Farishta or the individuals in the kitchen. He informed Barbrak of his plans in a hushed voice through his microphone.

There was a pause and a sigh before he received an answer. "I understand."

Taking the two grenades he'd retrieved from Akbar's body, he pulled the pins. His adrenaline was at full throttle.

Sons of bitches. See how you like this!

He dove down the hallway to the other side of the door where the men fired from.

As he flew by the doorway, he threw in both grenades. As soon as they yelled *'grenade'*, Barbrak opened fire toward the kitchen. The grenades exploded, and Blake grabbed his weapon and unloaded the rest of his magazine into the kitchen.

The sound of brass from the last few shots plinking on the floor and debris from the explosion landing were the only sounds. Blake stood in front of the kitchen. When there was no sound or movement, he focused on Barbrak. His eyes were wide.

"I got two more. I got four upstairs, plus the one Farishta got outside makes seven. How many did you get?"

Blake caught his breath as Barbrak spun around. "There is one in here, plus I think she got one in the hall."

Blake scanned the area. "That's only nine! Where's the tenth?"

A closet door in the front hallway burst open and the tenth man burst out. He was unarmed. When he moved to go out the front, Barbrak stepped in his path. Panicked, the man turned and ran toward the back door.

Blake yelled. "Get down!"

The explosion ripped through the front hallway. It obliterated the fleeing man and took out the back door and part of the outside kitchen wall. As the debris still settled, Blake went into the hallway. In front of him was Farishta.

"Farishta!"

She was on her back and her head rested on the back of a man she had killed moments earlier. She clutched her stomach under her Kevlar vest. He knelt, and she removed her hand, covered in dark crimson.

"Barbrak! Get your ass in here now!"

He rushed to his commander's side and knelt beside him. He grabbed Barbrak's arm. "Fix her!"

The medic nodded, retrieved his medical kit and gave her a shot of morphine. Blake helped her to her feet and took off the Kevlar vest. She screamed in pain. There were no markings on it.

The medic stared and wiped his forehead. "Whatever got her came up at a sharp angle and got in under her protection."

He grabbed Barbrak's shoulders. "What can you do for her?"

He shook his head. "Dark blood. It hit her liver. There is nothing I can do."

Blake gently laid her back on the ground and held her hand.

Oh shit. What did I miss? There's got to be something he can do.

"What the hell do you mean? There is nothing you can do? You're a damn medic, for Christ's sake!"

"A shot to the stomach, a sucking chest wound, yes I could help, but this injury is too bad. There is no way I can stop the bleeding. It's possible only to ease the pain."

Barbrak gazed down at her. "I regret this, sister. You fought valiantly. You are a true warrior, and I'm proud to have served with you."

Tear-filled eyes focused on him while she smiled. Some life came into her eyes that had already begun to dim.

For the next few minutes, he sat with her and did his best to keep her comfortable.

His eyes were desolate and conveyed infinite sadness. "I'm so sorry."

Someone compromised this mission.

She moved in and out of consciousness for the following moments. Then she took her last breath.

In anger, Blake stood and kicked the body of the dead Al-Qaeda operative. Picking up a chair, he hurled it into the living room.

"Shit! How the hell did they know we were here?" He ripped off his helmet and slammed it to the ground. "Dammit!"

He checked all the bodies to find out if any of them were still alive. Barbrak searched the building for anything that might give them information on the whereabouts of Al-Hamwi or what he was doing with the weapons.

When he stepped back into the main room, He was bent over the body of one of the men when his medic called out.

He didn't move or turn his head. "What?"

"I've found something. They have a cellar here and there is something you should see."

The old wooden steps moaned as they went lower. He stopped when he reached the bottom step. It fit what one would expect a basement would be in a building occupied by terrorists; dark and dirty, with a single chair in the middle of the room, chains hanging from the ceiling and strung along the base. It smelled of urine and human excrement.

The blood-stained instruments on the rusted table brought back terrible memories. Underneath was an accumulation of various chemicals, rags and a steel wire brush. To the right, on the floor, was a car battery and cables. They had tortured someone here and turned this place into a dungeon.

24

The dungeon-like area Blake inspected had a couple of doors on his left. The solid wood door of the first one went ajar when he turned the knob. He drew his pistol and cracked it open further.

Stacks of newspapers, empty boxes and trash filled the closet size space. The second one had a window and didn't budge when he tried. Cupping his hands, he peered through the filthy, soot stained glass.

"Son-of-a-bitch!"

He stood back, fired three shots into the lock and kicked in the door.

On the far side was Jim Dunn, the agent who had vanished over two weeks ago. He was suspended by chains that tightly bound his wrists, leaving him no room for movement.

"Barbrak! Search for a set of keys that might unlock some iron cuffs and get in here. Hurry!"

He was unresponsive to his touch or voice. Containers hit the floor from his teammate's rummaging while he checked the man for a pulse. There was one, but it was weak. He called the medic again.

"I got some. I'm coming." The medic entered the room, holding a bunch of keys. "Who is this? Is he your missing man?"

"Yes. Get a move on. Toss those things to me."

Blake laughed, delighted to have found the agent. If one good thing came out of this night, it was this. He hoped Jim could give him some valuable information if he survived.

With the chains unlocked, he lowered the man down. "Okay, get an IV in him. Do whatever you have to. I'll be right back."

He darted up the stairs, skipping every other one. When he reached the living room, he checked the two terrorists. Both were dead. He ran across the hall to the kitchen. One terrorist had his head blown off. The next man had a pulse.

Alive!

Checking the man's injuries, he found they were incidental shrapnel wounds to his back and hamstrings. The other guy took the brunt of the two grenades.

Swearing at him in Pashtu, Blake kicked him. "You playing possum? You faking it, asshole?"

The man put his arms up in a defensive block. He grabbed him by the collar and dragged him out of the room. When they got to the hallway, he stood him up and elbowed him in the face twice. The man stumbled backward and back to the floor. Rushing to him, he lifted him and punched him in the gut.

The anger he felt from the loss of his team and the condition of Jim Dunn came through, and he relished taking it out on this sick bastard.

"I've got some questions for you that you're going to answer!" He reared back and knocked him along the hall in the direction of the basement door.

Marching toward his prisoner with adrenaline pumping through him, he yanked him up by his shirt. The young jihadi coughed and tried to catch his breath. He had a bleeding cut under his eye.

"Come with me, dickhead." Dragging him through the doorway to the cellar entrance, he kicked him down the stairs.

Leaping down the staircase after him, he pulled the man to his feet and pushed him back into the lone seat. The man's body was limp as he bound his hands with the cord he found on the dusty floor. He slapped the jihadi's cheeks. "You're not out. Come on. Wake up, you bastard."

The man spat in Blake's face. Without wiping it off, he delivered a punch to the helpless guy's nose so hard the chair lifted before toppling him over backward.

Enhanced Interrogation, as they called it, in the world of political correctness. Blake always thought that it was a kind of an oxymoron to call it "politically correct". He guessed it was more to make it sound friendlier, or not as harsh. Regardless of the words, torture still sucked, and he hated doing it. However, this time, his fists connected without thought or repulsion.

He knew people who were specialists in extracting information from unwilling participants. Taking several months' time or even years, depriving people of sleep and food. Breaking them down, little by little, until they cracked.

Others could do unspeakable things that would make the Nazis cringe. When reading or even seeing these techniques, he was glad it hadn't been the career path chosen for him; he had neither the patience nor the desire. However, if he needed to get down and nasty, he would. This was one of those times.

"Tell me where Al-Hamwi is."

The man stared straight ahead.

"Come on! I know you understand me."

The man was silent, then gave him a toothy grin. Blake's eyes narrowed. "Oh, well, perhaps this will make it clearer."

He pulled out his suppressed Glock, shot the man in the kneecap, and prepared for his screams. He grabbed a rag from the table and stuffed it in the terrorist's mouth. "Where is Al-Hamwi? You know what I'm saying, I'm sure, and I'm too pissed off to speak your language. Now tell me!"

The man glared up at him. Eyes wide. Blake yanked out the rag.

"I do not k—." He put a round in the guy's other kneecap and rammed the cloth back in to quiet the screams of pain.

When his prisoner finally stopped screaming through the gag, he stared into the man's eyes. "I can do this for a while. There are ten more places where I can shoot you that will cause significant pain but won't kill you. Next one goes in your ankle." He pulled out the gag again.

The man only communicated in bad, broken English. "Please. I tell you true when I say I do not kno—"

He stuffed the rag back into his captive's mouth. He raised his pistol, paused, and then put it on the table.

"Perhaps you'll like what your asshole jihadis did to my friend."

He didn't want to go where he was going, but perhaps if his captive thought he was crazy or lost it, he'd come around quicker. He drew his knife and rested it by the prisoner's ear. The jihadi's eyes widened as he wiggled in the seat, so Blake delivered a hard punch to his prisoner's groin.

"Hey! Get in here and hold this prick for me!" Barbrak exited the other room and gave pause when he saw the man tied to the chair.

"Come on, goddammit, I don't have time for you to search your morales."

He hurried over and held the terrorist. His eyes were almost as wide with fear as the man in the chair.

Blake scowled. "I know what you're thinking, but it needs to be done."

He placed the blade on the top of the man's ear and carved it off like a chunk of holiday ham. Blood flowed down his shoulder and collected on the floor into a small crimson pool.

The scream echoed, despite the gag. After removing the cloth, he shoved the severed piece of flesh into the young jihadi's mouth.

"Chew on that!" He grabbed his prisoner by the back of the head and leaned down next to him. "I do not have any patience today. You're going to tell me everything you know, or I am going to cut you up little by little and make you swallow the bits."

The man spit out his ear. "Fuck you, American infidel!"

"No. Fuck *you*! Where is Al-Hamwi? Tell me now!"

"Go to hell!"

Reaching over to the table, he seized a machete and hacked off the guy's thumb. Raising his pistol, he shot him in the thigh. He reached down, picked up the severed item and shoved it, followed by the rag, back into the squirming guy's mouth.

Fists clenched; he went around to the man's back. His evil side was coming out in full force. It grew in him the way he'd only experienced a couple of other times in his life. Nothing suppressed it from consuming him. He gestured toward a bottle on the table. "Hand me that kerosene."

Barbrak stood still.

Blake turned to him. He could see the stunned expression on his face, but didn't care. "Hey! Get me the damn kerosene. What's the matter? Never seen an interrogation before?"

His teammate remained still. "Not like this."

Well, I guess I shouldn't have expected them to understand everything.

He let out a frustrated sigh and took the few steps needed to retrieve the fuel. Doubt of Barbrak's allegiance crept in. "You're still with me, right? They *did* just kill all your teammates up there." He raised his arm and pointed toward the ground floor with the bottle.

Barbrak snapped back from his shock. His eyes narrowed as he stared at Blake. "Yes. One hundred percent. What do you need me to do?"

"Grab his feet up when I tip him back."

He pulled the chair over backward and the man hit the ground. He lifted him from his shoulder. "Grab his ankles and hold him at this angle."

His partner snatched onto the jihadi's pant legs and held him. Blake grabbed another rag and put it over the man's nose while he poured the kerosene over his face. The man flailed. "You know this is a flammable liquid, don't you?"

The man tried to mumble, begging them to stop. He noticed him struggling to get something down his throat and winced at the thought of him swallowing his own thumb. The fluid ran out, and he propped the chair back up and walked back to the front.

"Five seconds from now, I'm going to shoot you again, unless you talk."

He removed the rag.

"Please! Wait! I know what he is busy with. I don't know where he is, but I know what he is doing."

He waved his pistol at him. "Go on. Keep talking."

"He went to Cuba to get something."

"I already know about the weapon, asshole! That's why I'm here. Who is he planning on attacking? When is the attack taking place?"

The man shook his head. "No, you don't understand. He is selling it."

Blake's brow furrowed. It made little sense. "Who is going to purchase it?"

"I do not know."

He pointed his firearm down and shot him in the ankle. His prisoner screamed.

The rag went back into his mouth and he waited for the cries to subside.

"One more time."

He jerked the cloth out. "Please! Russians, I think. I heard them mention Russians."

Blake's eyes narrowed. Now this is getting even crazier. "The Russkis sell weapons to you assholes, not the other way around."

The agonizing injury caused the man to lose focus. "All I know is what Zahmir called them. He said he did it to anger them."

Blake stepped back.

Crazy! Why would a Russian get pissed off at being called a Russian?

He turned and walked toward the room where Jim was. He peeked in. Clear liquid dripped from the IV bag hanging from one of the chains.

Why wouldn't I want to be called a Russian?

He spun back around and headed to his captive. The thought slammed into the front of his mind.

Because I'm from Belarus or Ukraine.

That made more sense. Ever since the Eastern bloc countries seceded from Russia, they hated the name 'Russians'.

He didn't let his prisoner realize he'd figured it out. He took three quick steps back toward him.

"How is he getting the weapons over here?"

"By boat. That is all I know. I swear." He shot him in the other ankle, then stuffed the rag in his mouth. He screamed and cried.

"God, will you shut the fuck up!" He backhanded him.

Perhaps a bribe will work.

"Would you like some painkiller? Some morphine?"

The man's eyes widened. "Yes."

"Barbrak, hand me some, please."

The medic returned to the back room and retrieved his bag. He handed him a filled syringe and hurried back to treat his patient.

Dangling it in front of his prisoner's face. "Is this what you want?" The man nodded. He removed the rag from the jihadi's mouth.

"Where and when are they docking?"

"I swear to Allah! That is all. Stop the pain."

"Are you sure that is everything?"

"I am."

"You're lying."

Blake put a bullet through his left foot.

As his prisoner screamed, He pressed on.

I don't believe it. This guy is tough. There has to be more he can give me.

"That is all you know?"

"Yes. There is nothing more."

He stepped back and shot him through his other foot.

"Aughhh! Stop! Pleeaaasssee!" Tears ran down the man's disfigured face as he pleaded in agony. The realization that he had probably gotten all he was going to get finally set in.

"There's nothing else you can tell me?"

"I swear! The morphine!"

Images of the pain that they had caused Jim flashed through his mind; the relentless torture. The inhumanity they gave to others. His anger boiled. The hatred. It numbed his humanity.

"No." He lit a match and flicked it onto his prisoner. The kerosene ignited. His clothes and face soon became engulfed in the blaze, and the man screamed in agony.

He raised his pistol, let the man suffer a few seconds more, and then put a slug between the terrorist's eyes.

The impact knocked the chair over. He stared down at the blazing man's body, emotionless. Barbrak darted out from the other room and dropped a blanket over the man to extinguish the flames. The stench of roasting flesh filled the air. Both men were silent.

They went back into the room where Jim Dunn was. He bent beside him. "How's he doing?"

The medic wouldn't return his gaze. Perhaps he decided Blake was some kind of animal. He didn't care, he had got what he needed.

"This IV will help the severely dehydrated man. He has seven cracked ribs, ten broken fingers, no finger or toenails, and they cut off his right ear. I've set all his joints and placed splints on them. Everything but the ear will heal, but I assume they will have a prosthetic for him back in America."

Blake chuckled and put his hands on his hips. "Yeah, maybe, but here come sirens. Akbar said they wouldn't come to this area. We need to get him and us the hell outta here. Once we get him in the car, I can reach out for a medevac."

Barbrak stood and met eyes with him. "My friend. Do not worry. We're not on some clandestine mission in hostile territory. You forget I am a Major for the ASA Special Forces and I have jurisdiction here. After radioing my commanding officer, he has already dispatched them. If you like, I can contact an ambulance to take us back to the base."

In all the commotion, he had indeed forgotten. "Right. When they arrive, we'll get out of here and get Jim to the base as soon as possible."

Police came minutes afterwards and entered the house. He dispatched Barbrak upstairs to speak with the officers while he remained with Jim.

There were voices on the ground floor, but he couldn't make out what they said. Jim was still lying unconscious on the floor, but his pulse had strengthened. He examined Jim's toes and fingertips, stained with dried blood where his nails used to be.

He had himself been the subject of interrogations in the past. Although they beat him, they never tore out his fingernails. He was lucky enough to escape or someone saved him before any of that happened. It struck him that he couldn't remember which. It was probably his mind burying it deep to protect him,

After a few minutes, the clump of footsteps from several people coming down the stairs filled the space. It was his medic and three other people. Two EMTs lifted Jim onto a stretcher and took him upstairs to the waiting ambulance.

Barbrak caught his attention. "I'd like to introduce to you Mohammad Al-Aziz. He is the captain of the police force here."

He extended his bruised hand. "It's a pleasure to meet you." Al-Aziz turned to Blake and shook his hand, scrunching his nose as he peered at the burned body on the floor.

He met the man's eyes. "We need to go to the Shinidad Airbase. Are you familiar with it?"

"Of course. We will be happy to take you. But your man should have immediate attention. The hospital is—"

"I'm sorry to interrupt you, sir, but there is a complete medical staff at the base and I'm sure that they will handle anything that he requires. No disrespect to your facilities."

Al-Aziz raised his hand. "None taken."

Shinidad was one of the first airbases built during the U.S. insertion in the War on Terrorism. It is one of the best and most modern air bases in Afghanistan, with full concrete runways. They operated it to bring in troops and multiple aircraft like the C-17 Globemaster III, the same type of plane that he had used.

The captain smiled. "I believe they have your man loaded by now. We should go up and make certain. We can give you an escort from here."

Blake tugged at his earlobe. "Right. Thank you."

He put his hand on Barbrak's arm. "Stay here a minute."

After the police had left the basement, he turned to his medic. "Are you positive about these guys? I know a lot of them get bankrolled and paid off by some of the local radical groups."

Barbrak cocked his head and squinted. "I have no suspicions."

He hesitated. There was something in his gut that said no, but he had no reason *not* to trust his teammate. "All right."

Barbrak was about to leave when he stopped him again.

"I want you to keep your guard up, okay? Just in case."

He nodded, and they both hurried to the stairs.

#

The EMTs loaded the injured agent into the back of an old Citroën ambulance. It was narrow and long to navigate the narrower roads and alleys that Sabzawar offered. Barbrak stayed in the back to monitor him while Blake rode with the driver. They headed north through the city and they had a police escort of two cars ahead of them and another behind.

When they turned west at the top of a hill, he began to worry. There was no reason for turning. The number of people along the road had also thinned out. It was late enough in the early morning and he should have seen more people as they started their day.

That uneasy feeling coursed through his veins. It would not be unusual for the Taliban or Al-Qaeda to infiltrate the cops or even local military units of Afghan troops, and they would warn the civilians to stay off the streets. Recently, there were increasing reports of them as well as local police turning their weapons on their U.S. trainers or leaders.

He shot a quick glance in the side mirror and saw a panel truck had driven into the road and stopped to block a rear exit. His heartbeat sped up and his senses became more aware. Situational awareness and just plain instinct had been what had saved him many times in the past. Ahead and to the left, another vehicle drove across their path.

There is no such thing as coincidences.

Blake eyed the driver, then reached over and jerked the wheel toward him. The driver swung at him and connected with his cheek. He shook it off and punched the man twice, just above the temple.

"What is going on?" Barbrak screamed.

He tried to open the driver's door. "It's an ambush!"

The man wedged his arms under his passenger and pushed him back. Blake drew his firearm and received an elbow in the nose and a strike to his arm. The pistol clattered to the floor, and the ambulance lurched from one side of the road to the other.

After hitting him once more, the guy driving reached for his own weapon. Blake grabbed him from behind the neck and slammed his head into the steering wheel, twice. The truck sideswiped a parked car, jarring the occupants inside.

He fumbled for the latch and got the driver's door opened. The emergency brake handle clicked when he yanked on it. The vehicle jerked to a stop, and the door flew open. He karate chopped the guy, crushing his windpipe. The man's hands went to his throat, gasping for air. A swift kick and the man tumbled out. Blake hopped over the center and into the driving seat.

"Hold on! It's about to get bumpy!"

He released the brake, slammed the truck in reverse, and floored the accelerator. His adrenaline was pumping at full steam again. He collided with the car that followed them and kept his foot on the gas, pushing it into the window of a café.

Barbrak peered out the windshield. "We're blocked both front and rear! Where can we go?"

Blake grinned. "There's almost always a way out."

He snorted, put the ambulance into first gear, and floored it. He drove up onto the sidewalk and slammed through several café tables and chairs, scattering them into the buildings and road. "See, that was easy."

Barbrak grabbed his arm. "Watch out."

A police van sped around a corner toward them. The doors opened and three men began firing.

He yelled as he jerked hard on the parking brake and slid the vehicle sideways. "Get down!"

Hot lead shattered his side window and plinked its way down the panel of the vehicle.

While he sought for a way out. Barbrak pointed forward. "Over there. Head for that alley."

Flooring the accelerator, he steered for it. "It's narrow! Hang on!"

As he drove into the opening, it ripped both mirrors from the vehicle. Bullets pinged into their rear. He was thankful they had retrofitted this wagon with armor on the inside, but they hadn't upgraded the engine to compensate for the added weight.

Ahead was a set of steps going down. He slowed enough so the ambulance wouldn't launch and catch too much air as it connected with the stairs.

"Shit!"

They hit the stone walkway and recovered. When they came to a road, they flew out onto the pavement without slowing down. Turning a hard left, they sideswiped a compact car and pushed it into one that was parked. He made a right and entered another alley.

"Fuck! More steps. Hold on!"

The vehicle launched into space and slammed into the ground. Agent Dunn's body lifted and fell back against the floor of the ambulance.

Barbrak grabbed Blake's arm. His voice rose. "Careful!"

They turned north on the next street. He gave it full throttle and drove two more blocks when two cars came around the corner and closed in behind them.

Are you kidding me?

He maneuvered through the slower motorcars, scooters, and bicycles that dotted the road.

"Hey, you're going to need to assist me to get them off our backs. I'm going to call the base, get some help, and let them know we are on the way!"

As he crossed another intersection, a motorist turned, inadvertently blocking them. He swerved, but it wasn't enough. The ambulance slammed into the right front quarter panel of the other vehicle and made it spin out of control. The two cars chasing them dodged and continued their pursuit.

He got on his radio and dialed in the frequency of the air base. When he got through, he talked to Lt. Cmdr. John Thielen.

"Commander, this is Blake MacKay. I'm supposed to be arriving there to get my ride back to Al-Ueid."

"Yes, we're expecting—"

"Sorry to interrupt you, but I'm coming in hot. I've got some dirty cops on my ass and they're plugging our vehicle full of holes. I'm driving an old ambulance and I have passengers. One is a missing asset of ours. Situation is Fubar. Send me some backup."

"Jim Dunn?"

"Affirmative."

"I'll have a bird in the air in three minutes."

He tossed the radio mic into the passenger seat and yelled to the back, "Five or six minutes until we get some assistance. Do what you can to buy us some time."

#

Barbrak re-strapped his patient to the gurney and then secured it to the floor. Making sure he had a full magazine in his submachine gun, he kicked open the double back doors of the ambulance, opened fire into the windshield of the pursuing motorcar and killed the driver.

A well-aimed shot blew out the front passenger tire. Both incidents caused the car to slow and lurch to its right. The one behind it slammed into the swerving vehicle so hard, it flipped it and rolled. He fired and a round hit the gas tank, rupturing it.

Waiting for it to roll again, he unloaded his weapon on its rear chassis. Hoping to generate a spark and ignite the fuel. After about eight more shots, the wagon erupted into a ball of flame. The second one bashed into it as it exploded.

Barbrak grinned. "Two down."

"That's awesome. Any more?"

From around a corner came a pickup, followed by two more cars. They closed in behind them. Two fighters in the pickup's bed fired AK-47s over the roof.

Yelling once more. "Sharp right coming up!"

His medic held on tight.

"That's the last turn. We're on the main road to the base. We should see help any minute now!"

"Affirmative!" He raised his weapon and fired, hitting the man on his left. Watching as one assailant fell out of the truck, the remaining gunman shot and scored a hit passing through Barbrak's shoulder. He winced but recovered and unloaded the remainder of his magazine at the other man in the truck's bed. Another shooter leaned out of the passenger window and opened fire at them.

Barbrak unclipped his last grenade, pulled the pin, and released the handle. Counting down and just before exploding in his hand, he threw it onto the ground. It detonated under the back of the trailing truck, sending it flying into the air, tumbling until it finally came to rest on its roof.

The second car increased its speed toward the ambulance. Bullets flew out of both rear door windows. Barbrak picked up his rifle and fired in controlled bursts.

Blake yelled back to him, "We're getting near! There's the base entrance, and a helo is headed our way!"

"That is good, my friend, because I am almost out of ammunition!" He emptied his weapon and threw it down. Reaching for his pistol, he shot at the vehicle behind him.

"We're close. A hundred meters!"

Just as Barbrak's slide locked open, he heard what sounded like a chainsaw.

It was the minigun, a GAU-17. A Gatling-style machine gun firing 7.62 mm bullets at a rate of up to six thousand rounds per minute. They mounted it on an Apache helicopter that was now unleashing hell. The car disintegrated as they pummeled it with flying lead.

Blake had the gas pedal to the floor. He maxed the little Citroën at seventy miles an hour as he drove through the front gate. The chopper couldn't get turned around fast enough to fire on the remaining pursuers.

Military personnel filed in to protect the base. The terrorists were still in pursuit of what was now a suicide mission for them. Little did they know how fast their death would arrive.

A Hearld Roadblocker system protected the entrance. It was a spring-loaded barricade lying flat but can deploy instantly when triggered. It can stop a thirty-ton truck traveling at fifty miles per hour in less than a quarter of a second.

The moment Blake's ambulance passed over the barricades, the guards in the guard house activated it. In an instant, they sprung up. The remaining car hit the barricade at almost eighty miles per hour and crushed in on itself, killing the occupants instantly.

25

Blake raced through the base to the hospital and skid to a stop by the emergency entrance. The medical staff met them with a stretcher. They removed Jim from the ambulance and took him inside to be cared for. On their way in, he grabbed the last EMT by the arm and asked for regular updates. The man nodded as he turned to follow the others.

With a limp, Barbrak made his way over to him. His hand grasped his bloody shoulder. "I think he will be fine. Even after all the bumps you put him through, he should recover."

Blake pulled his gaze from the emergency room doors. "Hey man, I want to thank you. The way you handled yourself—especially after everyone else on our team got killed. You're a valiant soldier and I'd be proud to serve with you anytime." The two reached out and exchanged handshakes.

The battle-tested medic's eyes and nose crinkled. "Thanks."

Blake gestured to his shoulder. "You'd better get your wound treated."

"I will. Do you have an idea of what you are planning to do now?"

In the back of his mind, he had decided what his next move would be, but shook his head. "No. I'm going to call my boss and ask what he wants me to do. The first thing is to get a ride to Qatar and then I'll head back to Washington."

Barbrak winced when he put his hands on Blake's shoulders. "All right, my friend. If I don't see you before you take off, safe travels and all the best of luck."

"I appreciate it. And all the best to you as well."

Blake got back into the beat-up ambulance and drove over to the administration building. Lt. Cmdr. Thielen stood in his office, finishing a phone call. When he hung up, he directed his attention to his visitor. "I was speaking to Langley. They are now aware you found and rescued Jim Dunn. You should get a commendation for it, you know?"

Smiling, he shrugged. "I would hope he, or anyone else, would do the same for me."

"Regardless of what you think, it was heroic, and I commend you for it. So, what can I do for you, Mr. MacKay?"

The coffee pot to his left called to him, so he strolled over to grab a cup. "I was hoping for a lift to Al-Ueid." He took a sip, grimaced, and poured it into the sink.

Thielen frowned. "Yeah, nasty stuff. It takes some getting used to. I can arrange transportation for you. When did you want to go?"

"Now."

"Now? Hold on a second." He stepped over to a file cabinet, opened a drawer, and removed a folder. "Tomorrow. I've got a group of guys ending their tour. They're scheduled to fly out of here to Al-Ueid at first light."

"My apologies, Commander, but it's not quick enough. I extracted vital intelligence from one of Al-Hamwi's men, and time isn't on our side. I need to leave as soon as possible."

"What kind of information did you get?"

Blake shook his head.

Everybody wants to know something.

"Sorry, sir. Classified. National security is on the line."

Thielen stood and tapped the folder on his desk, gazing at him for a few moments. "This is most unusual, but…" He picked up the phone and ordered the plane to be fueled and prepped for the transport to Al-Ueid. He made arrangements for the two dozen soldiers to depart a day ahead of schedule.

"Okay, Mr. MacKay, you've got your early flight. It leaves in an hour."

"Thanks, and if you catch heat, have whoever it is, call Director Thomas. He'll have your back."

"Oh, trust me—I will."

#

Blake was exhausted and sore. Since the trip had only twenty-four men on it, there were plenty of empty seats. Lying across a full row, he closed his eyes and pondered about events from the past two days.

How did this mission get compromised in the beginning? There were only a few people who knew the details. Who would have had the intel *and* the connection to leak to Al-Hamwi's team?

Farishta straddled him. Her soft lips caressed his as her thick black hair brushed his skin. Her eyes were in a panic; the life fading away.

He reared up and rubbed his hand through his disheveled hair as his eyes darted around the plane. The hum of the engines echoed throughout the cabin. Her death had disturbed him and he had to find some way to distract himself from the last painful day.

A group of young guys and one woman were playing cards. He decided a chat would help. The rest of the flight was uneventful, and he had a chance to enjoy the ride, talking to the soldiers going home to their families. They showed him a collection of photos of girlfriends, boyfriends, wives, husbands, and children.

Three hours later, the plane touched down and Blake said his farewells to the youthful men and women he'd made friends with. He wondered if he'd ever meet any of them again on some mission in the future.

He walked to the building where he stored his other gear and retrieved it. Colonel Smyth didn't appear to be around, which was fine with him. The last thing he wanted was another distraction and someone trying to extract classified information.

Outside the hangar, Randy and Chuck were waiting for him.

They trudged up the stairs and Randy turned to face him.

"Ready to head back, sir?"

"What's with the *sir*, shit?"

They both chuckled. He stowed his luggage while the pilots prepped the aircraft for takeoff. After a few minutes, they taxied down the runway and were off toward Andrews AFB.

A jolt of turbulence startled him out of a sound sleep. A glance at his watch told him he'd been asleep for a couple of hours. He walked gingerly to the front of the plane and started a fresh batch of coffee. Opening the cabin door, he poked his head inside. "Hello, boys."

The two pilots reciprocated the greeting.

He pointed at the instrument panel. "How are we doing?" A smile creased Randy's face. "We're fine. We might hit a little bit more of this turbulence in about half an hour, but it shouldn't be too terrible and should only last ten minutes or so."

"Okay." He paused a moment before continuing. "Hey, I need to take a detour and not head right back to Langley."

Both pilots shot a quick glance at each other. Randy raised his eyebrows. "So, where to?"

Blake stared straight out the cockpit window for a few seconds.

I'm going to catch hell for this.

"Cuba."

26

Minsk, Belarus
June 25th
13:00 local (10:00 GMT)

Aleksandr Roshenko sat in the back of his car on his way to a daily briefing with Prime Minister Shorets and President Solonovich when his satellite phone rang. A wave of excitement flowed through him. It could only be one person. He erected the divider between himself and his driver and picked up his telephone. "Vitayu."

"Hello Minister Roshenko. I am calling you as you requested."

He was relieved he was speaking to their contact. "Fine, and you can skip the formalities of the title. Tell me where you are."

"We are off the South-West coast of Morocco, near the Isla de la Palma. We should pass through the strait of Gibraltar in one day's time."

"So you are making good time?"

"Yes. We are on schedule. I will call you as we head into port."

He disconnected and put the phone away as they pulled into their destination at The Palace of the Republic, on Oktabratska Square. A trace of a smile developed across his face.

Oleg will be pleased with this information.

The building was a commanding piece of architecture, compared to the smaller ones surrounding it. Instead of a palatial home, the structure resembled a museum or library, rising three stories high with a rectangular shape. Columns adorned all four sides, while behind them stretched a massive row of glass windows.

Upon entering the president's office, the rich hue of scarlet would greet one. It painted the walls, which were decorated with immense oil paintings depicting former Russian rulers and notable Belarusian heroes.

The drapes were luxurious crimson velvet, and the hardwood floors, with inlaid patterns, were covered with huge red and black Persian rugs. The grand meeting room featured two enormous stone fireplaces standing across from each other on opposite sides of the room.

A table, at least six meters long, had twenty seats around it, spaced perfectly, like an orchestra of precision. Adjacent to the table were two plush couches and a couple of wingback chairs, which circled a central coffee table. It was at this spot the president and prime minister sat when Aleksandr entered the room.

The three men exchanged pleasantries and began their agenda. The first to speak was Solonovich, who turned to catch Aleksandr's eye.

"These protests from the people, still complaining about the election results, I am tired of them. Despite the arrests and police presence, they continue. What do you suggest we do to put them behind us and move on? I've heard from Oleg, so I would be interested in hearing your ideas."

He knew the 'riots' his boss talked about were peaceful demonstrations. They only erupted into chaos after the KGB and police were dispatched and started to beat and arrest protesters.

He cleared his throat. There was a strong desire to tell the dictator it was because his actions had caused this, but justice would be served soon enough.

"Mr. President, perhaps a showing of goodwill to the people would help settle them down."

Solonovich peered back at him with narrowed eyes and a

furrowed brow. "Like what?"

"Sir, we could—*you* could announce the release of some of the protesters. Tell them you have hired an outside team to do a full investigation of the election results, which, of course, would drag on and find nothing."

"You're not suggesting I let some of my adversaries from the opposition go, are you?"

Pausing to think through how he should respond, he glanced at Oleg for some sign of support but got none.

"Perhaps the least threatening of them. They would know not to say or do anything. We know who their families are and where they live. They would be reminded of the fact."

The president sat for a moment. Aleksandr decided to take a chance. "It would give the impression to the people you are taking them seriously and would get them to back off. Many of these people are protesting because their friends and family have been arrested. Free them, and they go away."

Solonovich pounded his fist on the table. "No! It shows weakness. I will not show them any sign of breaking down."

He frowned. "Sir, with all due respect, I think you are looking at it from the wrong point of view. The people will see it as a token of openness and honesty, something you pledged during the last election."

"Enough! I will not tolerate rioters. I promised them leadership. But… I will take your suggestion under advisement."

He knew they were words used as a dismissal of the thought.

Arrogant bastard. You know I'm right.

The two schemers eyed one another. Aleksandr was almost certain his partner was thinking the same thing.

Solonovich rose. "Now, on to other things. I want to talk about Independence Day. *This*, I believe, will be an excellent day to get the people on our side."

The two met eyes once more and Oleg stood. "Mr. President. I have glorious information. The nuclear plant will be operational, and the two reactors will be ready to come online on such an important day. The announcement will come over as positive to the people, knowing they will no longer be relying on Russia and

Ukraine for their power. This will be a compelling statement *you* can make during your celebration speech in Victory Square."

The president smiled. "Yes, it is excellent news. This could be the thing to turn people's opinion about me."

Oleg nodded. "It's a shame—all three of us have to be at the Square and we couldn't give it the proper attention it deserves." Oleg planted the seed. Both men silently hoped the arrogant bastard would take it and bite hard.

Solonovich was turning his gears in thought. "I have an idea. You and Aleksandr should be at the power plant to represent the people during its opening. We can arrange a two-way broadcast from there so you two can—throw the switch—or whatever the hell it is to turn it on."

Oleg lifted his head and gazed at their leader. "Like a simulcast. We could erect giant screens in the square so all the people could see this. You could make the order for us to activate it, and everyone with their eyes on a television could see it. It would be a glorious day: one for Belarus as well as for you, Mr. President."

Solonovich turned his attention to the ceiling. A broad smile spread across his weathered face. He clapped his hands. "Yes. It is perfect. Organize it."

Oleg strode over to him, smiled, and placed his hand on his shoulder. "Excellent suggestion, sir! We will get started right away."

After the meeting, Oleg and Aleksandr walked along the hall and went into a private room. It was soundproofed and often swept for bugs. There was a log on the wall indicating the most recent sweep had been an hour earlier, so they were certain it was safe to talk.

Aleksandr lowered his voice to a whisper. "It was brilliant! You made him think it was his idea."

A broad grin spread across Oleg's face. "What is it the Americans say? Hook, line, and sinker? In fact, it *was* his suggestion. I only planted the seed."

Aleksandr leaned in and spoke softly. "By the way, I heard from our contact. He is on schedule and will call when he is in port. Everything is coming together."

Oleg beamed with excitement. "Excellent news, my friend! Get in touch with Minister Litwin. Let him know about our broadcast from the power plant. Have him coordinate things and tell him we will be there soon to aid in the logistics."

27

CIA Headquarters
   Langley, Virginia
   June 25th
   16:00 local (21:00 GMT)

Mike Brennan sat glossing over some reports on his computer when Veronica Slocum walked into his office with her usual frustrated expression.

Oh shit, what now?

With an air of frustration, she flung her bag onto the couch and fixed him with an intense glare. "Well, I had an unpleasant meeting with the president. She expected an update on what the situation was with Al-Hamwi, and I didn't have a damn thing to tell her. What the hell is happening, Mike? Is there some reason you couldn't fill me in?"

Wanting to suppress his frustration the best he could, he avoided her death stare. Swiveling his chair around to retrieve the printed statement from the printer tray, he rolled his eyes. *This stupid bitch doesn't understand how things work.*

He turned back and extended the latest report to her. "Here. I just received this a little while ago. Somebody killed his asset as soon as he landed. There was an ambush, it was a sniper, and there was nothing he could have done to prevent it. We're fortunate he didn't get Blake, either."

She perused the paperwork and glanced up. "I know about this, Mike. We've already told POTUS. Are you telling me *you* got this information minutes ago? You're his goddamn handler. You should be the first to learn about it."

Letting some of his frustration slip, he jabbed back. "I only just received the *full* debrief. If you read further, it gives the complete account of what happened." He stood and went to a mini-fridge next to his file cabinet. Retrieving a bottled water, he used it to refill the reservoir on his coffee maker.

She tossed the folder on his desk. "Okay, you know so much, then give me the entire picture. Was it a failure or a success? Did he abort after they murdered our asset?"

Mike started the coffeemaker. "Hell no. A minor mishap wouldn't turn Blake back. It turns out there was only one sniper, and he eliminated him. There's a photo of him in the file. Unfortunately, we don't know who he is or how he found out about their rendezvous. After the ambush, he went into Sabzawar and met with the squad of ASA Special Forces he hand-picked."

"So, the mission was successful? He discovered something about Al-Hamwi?"

He strolled over and poured a fresh cup of coffee. "No. They infiltrated the target location, but Blake lost four of the five members of his team. It appears they were aware he was coming, and when."

Her jaw dropped, muscles tensing in a momentary freeze of shock. "What? How? How in the name of God did this happen?"

Mike walked back behind his desk and plopped into his chair. "There's only one answer." Placing his left hand over his temples, he began to rub. "We have a mole."

Veronica scowled. "What? How the f—dammit! Well, we need to discover who it is and deal with them. Right now!"

He released an audible sigh, louder than usual, and tilted his head to the side. "Gee, ya think?" She shot him a scornful glare.

Holding up his palms in a manner of surrender, he avoided a verbal onslaught. "I'm working on it, and I promise you'll be the first person I call when we locate him or her." He paused for a moment. "Now—I have some better info."

"Okay! I could use some good news. What is it?"

"When Blake went into the basement of Al-Hamwi's, he found Jim Dunn. He's in lousy shape. They tortured him and he lost all of his finger and toenails, broke all his fingers, cracked some ribs and—they cut off his ear."

Veronica cupped her hand to her mouth; horror filled her eyes. "Those animals! Oh my God! Where is Blake now? Is he on his way back here for debriefing? I want to talk to him as soon as he gets back."

"Well, he was supposed to be, but he diverted the aircraft." He glanced at the report he'd received from Blake in order to avoid Veronica's stare.

Wait for it… It's coming.

Veronica scowled. "Diverted the plane? Where did he go?"

And… there it is. I shouldn't need to cover for him like this. She needs to let him do his job.

He met her gaze from behind his desk. "Nowhere yet. He's still en route. But he's scheduled to land in Cuba in about an hour."

"Why is he going to Cuba? I thought you got all the intel from there when you had to clean up his mess?"

"I did, but he must have a reason."

Veronica shook her head. "No. There is no sense for him to go to Cuba. Have him re-diverted back to Langley. I want to debrief him right now." She grabbed her bag and opened the door. Halfway out, she stopped and turned back. "Call me when he gets here. And that's an order." She slammed the door shut as she left.

Bitch!

"Yes, ma'am." Mike lifted the phone. Faking as if he was dialing a number, he glared at her through the door's window. When she turned the corner, he banged the receiver down.

This is ridiculous. She is more of a problem than an asset.

He stood and left for Julian's office.

#

Over the Atlantic
   16:34 EST (21:34 GMT)
   June 25th

Blake settled comfortably in the rear of the plane with his seat reclined. His eyes remained peacefully shut as he rhythmically tapped his fingers on the armrest to the beat of the music resonating through his headphones. His mind drifted to attempt to connect all the dots and make some sense out of everything he'd learned.

If Al-Hamwi came to Cuba to meet with Adriana's father, there must be something he'd missed; something not in the intel he'd taken. There had to be some kind of clue, and Adriana was the only person who might assist him. However, approaching her and asking for help would not only be challenging, but problematic. After all, he killed her father about a week ago.

The first thing she'll want to do is knock my head off.

He would have to breach the subject with a lot of diplomacy.

His thoughts drifted back to when he was undercover as David Saye, from Canada. Reminiscing about how he helped her distribute food and medical supplies in one of the many villages she visited every month.

He recalled an incident when she cut her palm with a box cutter. Acting on instinct, he grabbed her hand and led her over to the only supply of fresh water, a hand pump in the middle of the village. It washed away the blood and grime as he cleaned her wound. While he bandaged her injury, he sensed her gaze on him.

When he glanced up, he caught how striking she was, her dark hair, green eyes, and tanned olive complexion. As thoughts often dance from one to another for no reason, his mind returned to Farishta and how he'd hoped they had given her a proper funeral. He then realized how similar the two women were, with their dark hair and exotic features.

When the aircraft made a correction and changed directions, it threw him from his reverie. Curious, he rose with a grunt, still sore from his battle scars, and went to the cockpit. "Why did we change direction?"

Chuck, who was piloting the plane, glanced over his shoulder. "Sorry buddy. I got a direct order from Langley. We're supposed to bring you back."

"By who's orders?"

"Director Slocum. She said she wants you there ASAP."

Blake considered what to do for a few seconds. "Hang on a minute, I'll be right back."

In the cabin, he paced around several times. *I can't go back to Langley. I've got to get back to Cuba. What's going on at Langley, making them force me back?* He needed to find out more information about Al-Hamwi and the shipment. So far, his only viable lead was turning him back to Cuba. Another day or two at home could have drastic consequences.

He went back to the cockpit. "Turn back toward Cuba. Do it now."

Randy turned to him and licked his lips. "And disobey a direct order? Not a hope in hell. Sorry, pal, we've got to do what we're told."

Blake gripped his pilot's shoulder. "Do you guys trust me?"

Randy kept his gaze on the instrument panel. "Well, yeah, but this has nothing to do with trust. It's us keeping our jobs."

"Ok, tell them I threatened you. Tell them I pulled a gun and forced you to go to Cuba. If I discover what I believe is there, this won't be a problem. And they will hold neither of you responsible."

The two pilots chuckled. Randy turned to him and stared into his face. "HA! Come off it, man. We've known you too long. You wouldn't do anything so stupid."

Blake drew his Glock, pressing the weapon to the back of Chuck's head. "You mean like this?" Randy gazed wide-eyed at him and then at the gun pointed at the back of his partner's head.

"Dude, what the fuck?"

"Let me make this as clear as possible. I will incapacitate you both and fly this plane myself. You know I can do it, so let's make this simple, ok?"

Randy nodded and Chuck grinned, "Okay." The pilot then focused on the instrument panel and pointed to the EICAS. "Oh dear, it appears we've got a sudden drop in oil pressure. We're going to need to land at the nearest base. Where might that be, Chuck?"

"I believe it's Guantanamo."

He removed the gun from the back of Chuck's head. "Thanks, guys. I'll take all the heat for this. If you don't mind, I'll stay right here until we touch down at GITMO."

After taking a deep sigh, Chuck turned to him. "You're fucking crazy, you know that?"

A smile danced on his lips. "Yeah, well, ya gotta be a little insane to do what I do. Don't ya think?"

28

Guantanamo Bay Naval Base, Cuba
June 25th
17:20 local (22:20 GMT)

The aircraft landed on the single airstrip, running east/west on the forty-five square mile base. As the plane taxied, the buildings surrounded by razor wire appeared into view. They have held enemy combatants, suspected of terrorist activity against the United States, since the attack on the World Trade Towers in 2001.

The Gulfstream came to rest in front of a small hangar. Blake elected not to check in with his boss. Mike was probably getting heat from Veronica for his failure to return to D.C. But, if he could find out something substantial, it would dissipate some of the intensity.

He called in a favor from an old colleague stationed on the base and had organized a more civilian car. Looking cocky as ever, Doug was leaning against a lemon-colored Ford Mustang Convertible.

Blake strolled over and fist-pumped him, followed by a quick hug.

His friend had a lopsided grin. "Hey buddy, glad to see you. What the fuck kind of mess are you starting now? You look like shit."

He smiled and diverted the question. "If you only knew. It appears you want me to start more disruption with this bad boy. Yellow? Is this for real?"

"Well, you said you wanted something touristy." The guy spread open his arms. "Viola! Nothing says *crazy, dumb tourist* like a lemon-colored convertible."

The corners of Blake's mouth turned up. "Hmm, it's not the most inconspicuous car on the road, but it beats an ugly gray Crown Vic with government tags."

"There you are. I did you a solid."

"Whose is it? Because I know you wouldn't own something this flashy."

"It belongs to a buddy of mine. They've deployed him to Kuwait. Posh, straightforward assignment. Anyway, he's gone for six months, and he asked me to run it for him sometimes. So, what are you here for?"

"I can't discuss official business. Let's say I'm here to talk to someone and leave it there."

"All right, I get it." He shooed away a bug. "So, you gonna be here long? Am I allowed to ask you? Any time to have a drink or something?"

"Nothing I'd rather do, but things might change. I'm not sure—we can only wait and see."

"Okay. No problem." He eyed the same pestering fly landing on the car. Lowering his hand, not to scare it. In a flash, he slapped the fender and inspected his palm. His brows knitted while he frowned.

"Still slow as shit, I see."

Doug chuckled and waved him off. "Fuck it. All right, so keep it as an open invitation. I know you've got to head out, so with luck, we'll catch up later—or in a few days, or whatever."

"Yep. I'll be in touch."

Blake took a seat, feeling the scorching heat radiate from the seats, as if the fiery sun itself had touched them. In a desperate bid to escape the oppressive heat, he cranked the air conditioner, hoping for a refreshing gust of coolness to wash over him. He drove until he was well away from the base and arrived at an abandoned melon and pineapple roadside market.

It made for a decent spot to pull over and examine his map. It was over eight hundred kilometers from Havana, and he didn't have an idea if it was the right place to go or not. Another colleague at Langley came to mind who could help him.

Greg Steffins worked there for the Directorate of Intelligence, known as the DI. Their function is to anticipate and assess any rapidly developing international situations. They decided whether they would have a positive or negative impact, following which, they wrote the president's daily briefs and World Intelligence Reviews.

His friend had access to top secret materials when they applied to whatever POTUS needed to know. They included such information in her brief. The two became friends about seven years prior, when they were on a mission together in Syria. He was an avid climber and got injured when he fell seventy feet in a freak accident.

It was a miracle he survived at all, let alone walk. Had it not been for Blake, who carried him out and got him to the hospital, he would have died. After the tragedy, Greg's field days were over, and he took a desk job at the agency instead of being out with *"the normal folk."*

A familiar voice answered the phone. "Greg Steffins."

"Hi, pal. Guess who?"

"Hey man, old buddy, what's up?"

"Ah, you know—a little of this, a little of everything."

"Uh, yeah. I'm acquainted with the vague, dismissive answer. So how ya been?"

"I've been good. But, sorry dude, this isn't a social call. I need some information."

"Oh, one of *those* kinds of calls. Ok, what do you want?"

"This has to do with the Al-Hamwi situation. General Vasquez had a daughter, Adriana. I have to discover what happened to her and where I can find her."

He could hear typing on the computer. "Yes, I included her in the last brief—my God, she's beautiful. Please tell me she's single and get me her number. You think you could hook me up?."

Blake enjoyed the playful attitude of his friend and if he had time, he'd play along, but now was neither the time nor the place, and his patience was growing thin. "Dude, give me the damn information."

"Okay, don't get your panties in a wad, I'm looking."

While he waited, he reached into the vehicle, grabbed the map, and unfolded it on the hood of the car. He hoped Greg would provide him with her last known whereabouts, and, with some luck, be a *lot* closer than Havana.

"Right, let's see—it appears she moved to stay with an associate of hers working for her charity. She's legit buddy. She had nothing to do with her father's illegal trade."

Blake snorted and rolled his eyes. "You're not telling me where she went."

His friend continued typing. "She's in Sancti Spiritus. Staying with some guy named Javier Ramirez. I'll send his address to your phone."

"No. Give it to me." In his shirt pocket, he kept a tiny notebook. He whipped it out, along with a pen.

His friend read out the details, and he wrote it in his book. "Thanks, pal. I owe you. Gotta run."

It was still over five hundred kilometers to where he needed to go, but at least he didn't have to drive all the way to Havana. Sancti Spiritus, which in Latin means "holy spirit", is the capital of the province with the same name.

Founded in 1514, it is one of the best-preserved cities in the Caribbean from the time of the sugar trade. The Mustang's exhaust spit out a deep growl as he tore off.

Halfway there, he stopped and bought a map of the city. He had removed the battery from his phone earlier, so its navigation was worthless. It was well past nightfall when he arrived. A streetlight with a vacant spot underneath was ideal. He unfolded the map and got his bearings.

Driving for another fifteen minutes, he found the address. The home's entrance was in a narrow alleyway, lined with multi-colored homes and businesses in green, white, light, and dark blue. Across the alley from where she stayed was a two-story motel called "Casa Azul."

Blake walked around the perimeter of the place and glanced toward the roof. Two rooms were providing a perfect vantage point to her residence. One of the two suites facing the alley also had a rooftop deck.

Perfect.

The faint smell of spices and soft music warmed him as he stepped inside. An older woman behind the desk greeted him.

He returned her greeting in Spanish. "There is a room with a balcony."

"Señor. Do you mind if I talk to you in English? I am trying to learn the language."

He smiled. "Of course. It's my pleasure."

"Ah, *un balcón,* Yes. we have such a room."

"Is it available?"

The woman cocked her head.

"Is it empty—*vacio?*"

"S*i, señor.* It is ready for you."

Blake paid for the room in advance and inquired if there was anywhere still open to eat. The woman shook her head. She handed him a piece of paper, supposed to be a menu. It had a list of food she would cook for him.

She motioned she would bring it to his room. He perused the sheet and placed his order, avoiding any alcohol in the event he needed to leave in a hurry.

The room was plain with hardwood floors. The walls were dingy white, and the plaster had cracks spreading out like a major river and its tributaries. On the side facing the alley were two windows and an easy chair sat with its back to the wall between them. The entrance to the bathroom was to the left of the bed and the exit out to the patio was to the right.

He went to the bathroom and washed his hands and face. As he shut off the flowing water, the distinct sound of a truck coming to a halt outside caught his attention. Moments later, he discerned the faint creak of two doors being opened and then firmly closed.

Dousing the lights, he rushed to the window and peeked into the alley. It was Adriana and a man who he took to be Javier. Blake had a funny feeling, deep inside again. His eyes sparkled and his feet wiggled at the sight of her, even from afar.

They removed their gear from the back of the truck and stacked it by the door. He listened to their conversation as best as he could, but all he made out was they planned to go somewhere tomorrow morning. He studied them as they carried in the boxes and equipment and shut the door.

A knock startled him. He drew his pistol and moved over to the door. He positioned himself against the wall.

"Yes?"

"Señor Saye, dinner."

Tucking his firearm into the back of his pants, he opened the door and accepted the tray. He handed her a generous tip.

"Oh, *thank you. Muchas gracias.* You are a rare guest. Anything you want, I get for you."

He thanked her and closed the door. The jerked chicken was moist and flavorful. It carried more spice than he cared for and wished for a moment he'd ordered a beer. The plantains were sweet and cooked to perfection. After he finished his meal, he took the easy chair and turned it to face out the window, into the alley. He sat and settled in for a long night. His thoughts drifted to Adriana.

29

Sancti Spiritus, Cuba
June 26th
06:30 local (11:30 GMT)

Voices coming from the alley below stirred Blake from his trance. Rubbing the sleep from his eyes, he leaned forward to get a glance out the window. The sun had crested the horizon a few minutes prior and the smell of beans, frittatas and other spices filled the warming air. His sleeping accommodations hadn't been kind, and he cocked his head from side to side to crack his neck.

He hated sleeping in a damn chair when there was a comfortable bed available, but he wanted to make sure he could get away fast. As he gazed at the street below, Adriana and Javier were loading supplies and food into the back of the truck. He sprang to his feet, grabbed his things, and left the room.

The woman behind the desk wiped the already clean counter. Blake suspected it was her way of appearing busy.

"What time will you be returning for dinner, Señor?"

He shook his head as he rushed by her. "Sorry, but I'm checking out." She ducked her chin and continued her *work*.

The morning light hit his eyes, and he lowered his sunglasses. He tossed his bag into the car and got in before Adriana returned to the alley and recognized him. He couldn't approach her until she was alone. The last thing he needed was to be interrupted by new friend. His mind wandered to thoughts of this new helper taking his place in hear heart. Could she be forming a relationship with him? Her father was no longer in the way to intimidate and run interference. We waved it away when another blank cloud filled his mind. The canvas of what he must tell her was clean, so he followed them as he pondered.

They headed south on Highway twelve toward the city of Bango. The traffic was light, so he did his best to keep his distance. About twenty kilometers before Sancti Spiritis they turned off. After another eight klicks, they made a left onto an unpaved road.

Blake kept well back, so he drove past the dusty roadway and waited for about a minute prior to turning around in pursuit. The dust hadn't settled from when they passed through, so it was easy to follow. It also provided him with some cover in case they glanced in their mirrors.

After a few kilometers, some facilities came into view and beyond, there was an open field of tobacco. The wealthy farmers would erect shanty towns of shacks and other poorly constructed buildings for their workers to live in.

The idea was if the workmen lived on location, they would never be late to work. They could start early and finish later; making enough to survive while the plantation owners got rich exporting their famous Cuban cigars. He imagined how hard such a life must be.

He stopped his car in a grove of trees on the south side of the road and walked the rest of the way. As he approached the village, he recognized the truck he followed parked next to an open-air building, like a pavilion you'd find in any city park, near the edge of the street. Inside it, Adriana set out her supplies.

He observed as she inoculated the children. She spent extra time nurturing the ones crying. He admired her dedication and thoughtfulness about her mission. She was a blessing to the people she cared about. Blake's stomach churned and his entire body tensed.

How in the world am I going to do this? Never have I been so damn nervous.

After she gave a shot to the last child, she turned and mumbled something to Javier, who nodded and went off in the other direction while she walked back to the truck.

Well, it's now or never.

She finished putting something in the front seat of the vehicle, backed out, and closed the door. When she pivoted to walk back to the pavilion, he stepped out from his hiding place. Facing her back, he spoke.

"Hello, Adriana."

She stopped. Her head didn't twist to glance back. After a long moment, her hands at her sides balled into fists.

Why doesn't she say something? I know she knows it's me.

As he began to speak, she spun around, took three quick steps, and slapped him in the face.

"You bastard!"

He could have blocked her from hitting him, but from her point of view, he deserved it. There was also hope it would let off some of her steam. He was incorrect. She started to pound him in the chest. "You lying swine! You think I don't know what you did! Who the hell do you think you are?"

She reared back to punch him again. "I *hate* you!" Those words hit harder than her fists. Blake refused to take anymore. He grasped her arm. "Okay, I understand why you feel that way, but after I tell you what you have to hear, I think—no hope—you'll change your mind. You must give me a minute to explain."

She stepped back and glared at him; her eyes narrowed, and her teeth clenched. The uninvited pest on her arm felt her full wrath as she squashed it with her other hand. "What do you mean? Who are you?" She pointed at him. "And do *not* lie to me, because I'm sick of these lies!"

Javier ran over. "Are you ok? Who is this?"

"He's the bastard who killed my father."

The man confronted him. "You had better go."

He shook his head. "Listen, I have to talk to her. It's vital."

Javier came at him and pushed him. "You must leave, now!"

He raised his hands. "I don't want any trouble, but I have to speak to her. It's urgent. There are things she doesn't know."

"All you need to know is she doesn't want you here! Now, get out of here!"

The guy lunged at him.

He dodged and grabbed the man's arm and twisted his wrists back behind him. With a swift and calculated move, he skillfully swept the legs of his assailant, swiftly bringing him down to the ground in a matter of seconds. Javiar winced. "You're hurting me!"

Blake glanced at Adriana. "There are terrible crimes you think I've committed, but you don't know the truth. There are facts you need to know. It's why I came back here."

Her stare was cold and hateful. He could sense she needed more.

Time to tell her everything.

"My real name is Blake MacKay, and I work for the CIA. Will you please listen?"

His assailant groaned in pain and gazed up at him. "Ok, spy man. You're hurting me."

"If I let you go, will you behave?"

Javier stared at the ground. "Yes." He released his arms and helped him to his feet.

Adriana scoffed at him. "How do I know you're not lying to me again? How do I know you aren't called Jeff or Steve or something else? You need to prove to me you're telling the truth."

He leaned in toward her. "Okay, fair enough. Did you notice your charity's bank account got a lot bigger after all this went down?"

She paused for a moment. Her eyes showed she was in deep thought. "Yes."

He resumed, "And by what amount?"

"You know so much. Why don't you tell me?"

"Fine. How's ten million bucks grab ya?"

She scrunched her lips and squinted. "Given to me by my father in case something like this happened."

He shook his head. "No—no, it wasn't. It was me. I asked for seized money to be transferred into your account."

She stood frozen as she contemplated what he had said.

"If you want, I can tell you the bank, its address, and your account number. But I did it. Not your father."

She glared at him. "You killed my father! Do you deny it? Why did you do it, you… you bastard. And to think I trusted you."

This isn't going well. He placed his hands on his face in frustration. "He had a gun to *my* head and was planning on shooting me dead. Allow me to at least tell you what occurred. Besides, for the tenth time, there are important things you don't know."

He pinched the bridge of his nose as he glanced back at her to get a read on what she was thinking.

"You want more? I can tell you what happened to your mother."

She crossed her arms in front of her. The right side of her mouth curled with arrogant confidence. "My mother abandoned me. She left me a hateful note telling me so."

He shook his head. "No! It's what your father wanted you to believe. If you want the truth, you'll have to pay attention to me."

For what gave the impression of forever, she stood statuesque. In the end, she unfolded her arms. "Ok, I will listen to what you have to say, but only for a moment."

"Thank you." He motioned along the road. "Do you have a few moments to walk with me so we can talk privately?"

Javier reached out to Adriana. She shook it away. He gazed at her with concern. She stared at her colleague and addressed him in a matter-of-fact tone. "It's okay. Can you please take the additional carton of medicine to the pavilion? I *won't* be long."

He gave a reluctant nod, bent, grabbed the box, and walked off, looking over his shoulder at them. Blake gestured at the street. "Come on. Let's walk."

They strolled along the road, past the village, before he started to speak. He'd run through what he was going to say on the ride over and had so much to tell her. But would it be enough? Would she help him, and most of all, forgive him?

He told Adriana about the things her father was involved in; the Colombian and Mexican drug cartels, Al-Hamwi, Al-Qaeda.

As painful as it was for her to hear, she needed to know.

Her gaze stared off onto the horizon with no particular focus. A shimmering pool of tears formed in the corners of her eyes, revealing her complete unawareness of the situation. After a significant pause, she eventually directed her attention toward him. "Can you prove all of this is true?"

Blake sighed. "On my laptop, I have detailed files going back at *least* twenty years. I will show them to you. They're not only reports, but pictures of your father with cartel leaders, and statements from witnesses who disappeared before they could have brought any charges against him. It would probably take you days, if not weeks, to sift through all we have."

Her eyes darted back and forth at the ground. She was trying to take it all in. Blake's strategy was simple; the more he could get her to hate her father, the faster she would forgive him and the more willing she'd be to help.

He could sense her internal struggle to untwist the memories of who she thought her father was, with the additional details of what she had only today learned. And now, the bombshell.

He explained to her how her father was responsible for her mother's disappearance after she went to the authorities and turned him in. The broad bough of a banyan tree provided a welcoming place to stop and escape the heat.

Placing the palm of her hand on her forehead, she shook her head. "I can't believe it all—I mean—I suppose I had my suspicions, but I had no idea of how deep it all went."

"This is a lot to take in, but please accept what I'm telling you. As I said, I have detailed files. Everything I've mentioned, as difficult as it is to believe, I have documented proof."

With evident hesitation, her gaze gradually shifted toward Blake, locking onto his eyes. Tears cascaded down her cheeks, mirroring the depth of her emotions. "My mother. He killed my mother." She cupped her hands and covered her face as she started to cry.

The pain must have been unbearable. To learn these things about your father had to be weighing heavy on her, but this was what he wanted. Soon, her sorrow would turn to anger, and, as if on cue, her ire shocked him as it raised to a level he had never imagined.

She bent and grasped onto a fallen branch and swung it at the base of the tree, yelling expletives in Spanish so fast; he could only make out a few words. She screamed and after the fourth swing; the bough snapped in half. Gasping for air, she leaned over to catch her breath. Her face nestled in her palms, and she began to weep again.

His hand rested on her shoulder. "Adriana, I apologize for the deception. And I am sorry to be the one telling you all of this. I can assure you the feelings I projected toward you were genuine. I cared. It's what makes this so difficult for me."

She raised her head from her hands and gazed deep into his eyes. "Cared?"

He paused before answering. The admiration he had for her rose from giving him this chance. If he could only tell her what he was truly feeling. "You know what I mean. I still care or I wouldn't have had the money deposited and I wouldn't be here now."

She lifted her hair and fanned her neck with it. "Do you? Do you really, or is it only another line?"

Without giving him time to reply, she asked the question he knew he would have to answer. "I have to know. Did you kill my father?"

Shit!

The urge to break eye contact was strong, but he knew how it would be interpreted. He drew in a deep breath. "I did. And I won't apologize for killing him. It was my duty. But I *am* sorry for the man he turned into. I can only imagine how difficult this is for you."

Adriana stared at him for what appeared to last for an eternity. Her green eyes were full of pain and sadness. The joy once filling them was gone. Another tear formed in the corner, and her lips tightened.

"I...I forgive you." Her body shook. With a deep breath, she extended her arms to embrace him. "It was more painless than I thought. It's so much easier to absolve than to hate. Forgiving is the Christian thing to do. Can we walk some more? I need to know everything."

It shocked him at how willingly she accepted his apology. All the worry and anxiety faded away. She was a remarkable woman.

They continued to stroll along the road and came to a barn they used during the tobacco harvest. They strolled under a shaded area utilized to park tractors they operated on the plantation. She sat on the bench of a picnic table and Blake perched on the table. She straightened herself and cleared her throat while she wiped away her tears. "What do you want from me? Why are you here?"

Finally.

He took a deep breath. "I need your assistance."

She cocked her head and brushed the hair from her face. "What can I do? I had nothing to do with anything my father did."

"I know you didn't, but I'm hoping you can give me some information. Something which would help me to stop a potential disaster."

She shook her head. "I still don't understand how I can be of any use to you."

"Your father acquired a lethal weapon. I won't go into details, but picture an enormous gathering of innocent people, perhaps even thousands." He took a moment to reflect on the idea. "Now imagine firing thousands of grenades and bullets into the crowd in a matter of seconds."

She didn't say anything and allowed him to continue.

"Your father sold the armament to a known Al-Qaeda weapons dealer named Zahmir Al-Hamwi."

She put her hand on his knee. She straightened as if a distant memory slammed into the forefront of her mind. "I've heard his name before."

"You have? Fantastic! What can you remember? The slightest bit of information could be helpful."

"The morning—after—after you killed my father, I had no idea what had happened. I searched for Luca but didn't find him. Another one of my father's men told me he, too, was slaughtered."

"Luca was slain? How?"

Perhaps I did it when I was trying to get away.

"A Middle Eastern man and his crew were on the estate for something. His name was Al-Hamwi."

This was a breakthrough. It was confirmation his quarry was there and collected the weapon. He could now start a timeline and begin to track him.

"Is it everything you know? How did he get there? Trucks? By boat, by—"

"Yes. By sea. They loaded the crates on a ship."

"This is valuable information. I need you to tell me anything you can about the vessel."

"Like I said, when I awoke, I was drowsy, like I'd been drugged." Her nose crinkled, and she tilted her head away from him.

He lied. "It must have been the champagne. I was the same."

"I went outside, and the sun had started to rise and a vessel was anchored in the harbor."

"Adriana, this is important. What did it look like? Was it a yacht, a trawler?"

"Oh, it was a cargo ship. Not a giant one. I think I remember seeing perhaps—three cranes on it?"

"Three. Are you sure?"

She shifted her gaze out over the fields for a few seconds. "Yes. There were three. I'm positive."

He stood and dusted off his hands. "Okay, this is a brilliant start. Now, try to think. Did your father keep any personal journals or laptops or tablets anywhere other than the safe in his office, his desk in his bedroom, or the warehouse?"

Adriana shook her head, "No, but—"

"But what?"

"I got a letter from my bank stating a safe deposit box in my name was being held pending an investigation."

"Did you know you had one?"

She thought for a second. "Yes, but I'd forgotten about it. My father got it for me soon after we built the estate. I kept one of two keys in my jewelry box in my room."

"And where is it now?"

"It's at Javier's."

Blake grabbed her hand and pulled her off the table. "Come on, we gotta go."

"Where are we going?"

"To the bank."

30

Banco Nacional de Cuba
  Sancti Spiritus, Cuba
  June 26th
  14:22 local (19:22 GMT)

Their ruse at the bank had to be played to perfection. Beforehand, they stopped at a clothier to get appropriate attire for themselves, and then on to Javier's to change and for Blake to outline his strategy to Adriana.

As the day grew hotter, the air filled with the tantalizing scents of barbecues, wood smoke, and fresh-cut grass. They'd opened all the windows. Several fans hummed as they created a pleasant breeze in the room, as well as muffling the sound of children playing in the alley.

While sitting at the kitchen table and discussing their plan, her eyes drifted off, along with her thoughts. Had she forgiven him? Her face contorted as a tear formed and trickled down her cheek.

With a gentle gesture, he reached out to grasp her hand, only to have it swiftly pulled away by her. "I don't know if I can do this. I'm having second thoughts."

"You are? Why? About what?"

The chair screeched as she scooted away and rose to her feet.

"This—this whole thing. You! My father! You killed him! He—he had my mother murdered." She turned and walked into the living room.

Shit! I thought we were through all of this.

He removed himself from the table and followed her to where she stood. Her back was to him, and she wept. Wanting to console her, he considered touching her shoulders, but withdrew. Taking a deep breath, he slid around to face her.

He rested his hand on her shoulder. "Listen. I said I was sorry for the deception. Your father was going to put a bullet in my head, and I've explained the other—"

"I know!" She brushed him away. "I've been through hell this past week and now you add to it by dumping all this horrible new information on me. I—I can't process it all."

He hung his head. "I understand this has been a tremendous amount of crap that's fallen into your lap, but let's examine the items we can't reverse. Your father is dead. It is what it is."

He maintained eye contact with her. "Your mother is gone, and that's not going to alter either, and the fact he was responsible for it is something you'll have to live with. But use it. It can be fuel to get you through this and do the things needing to be done to fix what we *can* change."

"Like what?"

"The truth is, an Al-Qaeda terrorist has a weapon of mass destruction and is planning on using it. You enjoy saving people. Well, here's your chance to protect thousands of them."

She glanced at him and wiped away a tear. He was getting to her; he hoped. "Do you want to be a part of the operation? Preserving the lives of so many people?"

He grabbed a tissue and handed it to her.

She sniffled and nodded. "Yes."

"I know you do. I don't think you've forgiven me yet."

She bowed her head and glanced away. "It's hard. I'm trying, I genuinely am."

He reached out to her again. She let his hand stay this time.

"It's going to take time, okay?"

Her tear-reddened eyes stared into his. "Fine. I can do this."

#

The bank was on Independencia Norte Street across from an old cathedral. Adjacent to it was an arched entrance gracing the front of the two-story white stone building. The second level had a covered balcony overlooking a park where children were playing *Futbol* and they could hear their laughter over the chirping birds perched in the various trees lining the road.

They sat outside the bank and went through what he wanted her to do a few more times until she was comfortable.

Blake's eyes shifted to two people parking their scooters near a café on the opposite side of the street. He turned back to her. "I've been thinking. With all the banking regulations, I think telling them you're going to move ten million dollars is suspicious."

He scratched his chin and paused for a moment. "I think we should lower the amount to fifty thousand. It's still a lot of money for here, and it will allow us to get the same result without all the fanfare."

To lighten the solemn mood hanging between them, he joked. "You never know. If this goes well, there could be a future for you in Hollywood. I have connections, ya know?"

She grinned and used her best southern drawl. "Well, Mr. MacKay, I do declare."

He laughed. "Yeah—don't use the accent."

She playfully slapped him on the arm while she grinned. It was wonderful seeing her smile. All the information she has had to absorb about her father and why he was killed must be overwhelming. He wondered how she felt deep inside. If there was any animosity toward him, she was doing an excellent job of hiding it.

He gazed at her face and into her eyes. "Ready for this?"

Nodding, she tightened her lips. "Let's do it."

Upon entering the Banco Nacional de Cuba, an employee greeted them. "Buenas tardes, ¿Cómo estás?"

Adriana smiled and held out her hand. "Good afternoon to you, too. I am fine, thank you."

The banker changed to English. "How may I be of service to you two on this lovely day?" The man was short but stringy. He had a mustache and thick dark hair on the sides but was going for the 'comb over of the year' award on top. Blake thought to himself to try and get a picture so he could post it on his alias's Facebook page.

His friends back at the agency would have a riot with this one. He wore a tan linen suit with light brown loafers, a white shirt, and a blue tie. All he was missing was the hat and monocle and he could pass for the Panama Jack guy.

Adriana studied the man. "I have a sizable amount of money I would like to withdraw from another bank. Their service has been lacking and I've heard excellent things about your establishment. What could you offer me to earn my business?"

"And how much are we talking about?"

"Fifty thousand dollars."

Blake regarded the facial expression on the banker and was pleased when the man's eyes widened.

The clap of his hands echoed in the marble-clad lobby. "Please. Follow me to my office and we can get started."

Blake was the last to enter. As he did, the little man turned and extended his hand. "Be seated. Allow me to introduce myself. I am called Caesar Romero, and I'm the chief executive."

He suppressed a chuckle as he pictured the actor with the same name in costume playing *The Joker* in the 1960s *Batman* TV series.

The man raised his eyebrows. "Can I get you something to drink?"

Blake tapped her on the thigh. She glanced at him. "Please. I would like a coffee black. No—on second thought, make it two sugars and one cream, and my assistant would like the same, with two creams and one sugar."

The banker walked out the door.

"Oh, Mr. Romero?" She waited for him to come back.

"Yes?"

"I hate to ask, but can I trouble you to bring me some information on various accounts you offer and some history of the bank?"

A broad smile crossed his face. "Of course,"

He left the room to get their drinks. Blake's eyes squinted shut. "What the hell did you order? I'm not going to drink swill."

"I know it, but I figured it would buy us an extra twenty seconds or so."

His lips curled up.

Smart girl—but what's this assistant shit?

He vacated the chair, shuffled over to the banker's terminal, and started to type.

Adriana's brow furrowed. "Do you know what you're doing?"

"Sort of. My degree is in computer science. Let's say for extracurricular fun, some friends and I learned a few tricks along the way."

He kept typing. "Ever hear of the Cult of the Dead Cow?"

"No. What is it?"

"It's a group of what they say are the most elite hackers in the world. In any case—a teammate of mine back in school—his father was one of the founding members. The kid could hack almost anything and his father was a hundred times more talented than he was."

"That's a weird name."

"Well, whadaya expect from a bizarre bunch of guys? Ok, I'm in. Keep a lookout, will ya?"

He hacked into the part of the system showing details on the safe deposit boxes, while she stood and kept a watchful eye along the hallway.

"Tell me more about this letter you got. Why did they say it was being held?"

"It didn't go into details. Only it was on hold pending an investigation. I suppose it is related to all the illegal activities my father was doing."

After clicking through a few layers, he found her information, and sure enough, in a red rectangle with black letters, it was clearly marked to "HOLD" the box and not release it.

She leaned over and placed her lips close to his ear. "He's coming."

"Think of something. Stall him. I need one more minute." He took a deep breath and popped his knuckles before placing them back on the keyboard. He could feel his shirt starting to stick to his back. *Come on...*

She went out the door, and he could hear her talking. "Mr. Romero, I'm so sorry. I forgot to tell you. My assistant needs decaffeinated coffee. Caffeine makes him—twitchy."

She stepped back into the office. He stared at her in disapproval. "So, not only am I your assistant, but now I'm twitchy?"

She smiled and took a sip of her drink. Her nose wrinkled and her lips curled down.

He smirked at her expression of disgust.

It's what you get for putting all the crap in there.

He refocused on the screen and changed the status on the box from a red "HOLD" to a plain "OK." He backed out of the system and darted back to his seat before "The Joker" came back in.

The bank executive stepped into his office and handed him his coffee. She continued to sip hers while he used his as a prop. The banker went over the multitude of accounts she could put her money in. When he was done, he asked her if she had any questions.

"Well, you've been thorough, Mr. Romero. I have a lot of information to examine. Give me a day or two to process this data and I will get back to you."

As they rose, Blake gave her another tap on her thigh. "Oh, there is one more thing, Mr. Romero. I have a safe deposit box here, and I wanted to get something from it. Could you get it for me, please?"

"Yes, of course. May I have the number and your key?"

She wrote it on a piece of paper and handed him the key. He went around to his computer, checked the status and saw everything was clear. The banker stood and beckoned. "Follow me."

They both exchanged a smile and followed him to the secure room.

The safe was typical of one you'd find at any bank. They

walked in and the banker used the banks and Adriana's keys to unlock the container. He slid it out and passed it to her.

They escorted them to a private room to use. Inside the box was an envelope containing no less than three dozen loose diamonds, a rose gold Patek Philippe wristwatch, twenty-five thousand U.S. dollars in cash, and an inconspicuous black journal.

She held it up. "This is it."

After glancing at the timepiece, she handed it to him. "Here. You can have this for me calling you twitchy."

He loved watches and considered himself an aficionado. He scrutinized the watch. It was a triple-date split-second chronograph. "This is worth at least a hundred and fifty grand. I can't accept this."

She turned to him. "You deposited ten million into my organization's account. I think you've bought it many times over. Besides, it was purchased with the money my father made from selling weapons. I don't want it."

He accepted it and reminded her they needed to hurry. "Since this box was on hold, we don't know when someone could arrive to get access to it. We need to leave now." They grabbed everything and put it in her purse. They handed the empty container back to the clerk, thanked them, and left the bank.

On the way back to Javier's, she read through the journal while Blake drove. Her eyes opened wide, and she shook his arm. "I think I have something."

"Ok, what did you find?"

"It appears my father would pay off the Coast Guard so they wouldn't stop certain ships from coming or going. He has the names of the people he paid off and the amounts."

"It sounds about right. Perhaps he kept those records to use as blackmail in the future."

"Are you positive?"

"Hell yeah. It's what I'd do. Always helps to have an ace up your sleeve."

"There is a ship in here named the *Angel van de Zee* and it was here at the exact time Al-Hamwi was here."

"It's got to be it. Anything else?"

She rifled through the pages. "There doesn't appear to be. However, there are some codes on the next page."

"Read them to me, please?"

"BZI zero, zero, nine, nine, nine—"

"That's fine. You don't have to continue. I know what it is."

"I don't. What kind of numbers are they?

"They're for a Swiss bank account out of Zurich. The 'BZ' is for the Bank of Zurich. The 'I' is for an international. I'll require those for later, though. They could lead to something. You know what they say—follow the money."

They arrived at Javier's and went inside.

"Hey, if you don't mind, I need some privacy to call my director."

She pointed. "In the back room."

He hurried into the room and prepared himself to contact his boss. He knew he was in deep trouble, but hoped this new intel would bring him and Mike out of the doghouse.

31

The White House
June 26th
15:45 local (20:45 GMT)

Mike finished an afternoon meeting with the head of the NSA and was walking to his next one. Together with Veronica and Julien, they were to update the president on the status of the Al-Hamwi situation. As he walked along the hallway, he glanced up to see his favorite person motion him into another room.

Oh crap!

"What the hell is MacKay doing? I gave him a direct order to return to Langley, and he disobeyed it."

He was going to have to deal with this eventually. Now was as well as any, since it wasn't in front of the commander-in-chief. "Veronica, the last I heard was they had a drop in oil pressure and had to make an emergency landing. It doesn't sound like insubordination to me; it sounds like they had a legitimate problem that needed to be dealt with."

Shaking a liver-spotted finger at him. "Emergency landing my ass! It's a brand-new sixty-million-dollar jet. His story is bullshit and you know it. I have half a mind to have him arrested when he returns."

His top agent was being his regular, thorough self. It aggravated the crap out of him realizing she didn't understand it.

"The plane's age has nothing to do with it. Haven't you ever had a new car? The first few months, you always have to take it in for minor problems here and there. You know—work the bugs out. It will be repaired, and he'll be back here by tomorrow, I'm sure."

She shook her head in disgust. "You need to keep your dog on a better leash, or you are going to lose him." She turned and stormed out the door.

Letting out a deep sigh, he waited a second for her to get further along the hall.

God, she's incorrigible.

He pondered for a few more seconds about how he could brush the heat off Blake before he left to go meet with the president.

As he meandered across the corridor, Veronica went into the meeting. The Chairman of the Joint Chiefs and Director Thomas spoke to each other in quiet voices outside the room. He was about to say hello when his secure phone rang. He stepped to the side to answer.

"Mike Brennan."

"Hey, it's me."

"About damn time I heard from you. How's the *oil pressure problem?*"

"Yeah, it's all fixed."

"Fine. When are you coming back? I covered your ass. The bitch is calling for your head, so I hope you have something solid."

"I do. You know I wouldn't do this if I didn't think I had a proper lead."

"Go on."

"Al-Hamwi, in fact, loaded the weapons and put them on a cargo ship called the *Angel van de Zee* on the morning I was there. I got on the marine traffic website and tried to track it, but I think they disabled their transponder. Where it went from there, I don't know."

"Not a problem. I'll call satellite images from the day and will get a visual on their bearing. I'm about to head into a meeting with POTUS now on this topic; as a matter-of-fact, I'm late. I'll get on it and let you know what I find out. Anything else?"

"I'm afraid so. It appears he purchased around twenty-five of these weapons, all in different caliber sizes with the biggest being the forty-millimeter grenades. And, they are what he bought the most of; fifteen units of the grenade launchers."

#

The attendees were already engaged when Mike opened the door. Veronica had no compunction in telling POTUS what she thought of the current situation or throwing him and his agent under the bus.

"Madam President, so far this mission has been a disaster. Blake MacKay has managed to get his entire team in Afghanistan killed. It included a valuable asset we've had for a couple of years. He's all but hijacked a company jet and he has yet to report with any new information."

The commander-in-chief sat back in her chair and intertwined her fingers. "Veronica, I understand your frustration. These things can get hairy. I can recall plenty of times when we lost outstanding soldiers defending the Afghans when their men were either hiding under beds or running away. Let's wait and see where this goes."

She shook her head. "With all due respect, he disobeyed a direct order. It is a punishable offense."

Mike butted in after the comment. "Madam President, everyone, I apologize but I need to speak to Director Slocum. It's about this situation. It will be only a minute."

"It's okay Mike. I understand the chain of command. No sense in telling any intel you have twice. We're wasting valuable time. Come on in and inform us what you have. We realize this would be coming from her under normal conditions."

Veronica sat back in her chair with her lips pursed and a stare that could melt ice.

Mike took a seat and addressed them all. "Madam President, general, everyone. I got off the phone with our asset. It turns out his instincts were right. He followed a potential lead in Cuba and he was able to glean some frightening stuff. Al-Hamwi did buy those weapons and take possession at the Vasquez estate. He purchased twenty-five of them in assorted calibers, with the majority of them being grenade launchers."

They spoke a few choice expletives around the room, including some from the president.

"He loaded them on a cargo ship called the *'Angel van de zee'*. They disabled the onboard transponder, so it couldn't be tracked. His destination at this point is unknown."

General Andrews leaned forward and put his palms on the table. "If this is the beginning stages of a long-term plan, he may be acquiring them. He'll store them away somewhere until they're ready to use them."

Pennington frowned. "Perhaps we're being too vain gentlemen—and lady. What if the arrangement is for something else? Not meant for an attack on us?"

Mike nodded. "It's an excellent question, ma'am. They're all questions we don't have answers for, but only speculative at this point. I'm calling NRO the moment we're done here to study satellite imagery so we can track this ship's path. Until we know where it's headed, it's only a guess as to what he's up to. Madam President, with your permission?"

#

She glanced around the room. "That will be fine, Mike. I want to stay close to this. As soon as you find that ship and where it's heading, let me know."

He bobbed his head, grabbed his folders, and left.

POTUS waited for him to turn and vacate the room. "Perhaps you jumped the gun on Mr. MacKay, director."

Veronica could feel her face start to flush with anger and embarrassment, but she held it in.

Oil pressure problems. I knew it was bullshit.

"Yes, ma'am, it would appear I did."

32

Nuclear Power Plant
   Astravets, Hrodna Voblast, Belarus
   June 27th
   11:00 local (08:00 GMT)

The first Belarusian nuclear power plant was nearing completion. At a cost of six billion dollars U.S. It will house two reactors with a combined capacity of twenty-four hundred MegaWatts. The contractor for the project was a Russian company owned by an ex-KGB officer who served with Solonovich in the Red Army and Spetsnaz.

There were proposals to add two more reactors by 2024 if the system proved to be successful. Located in Hrodna Voblast, in the Astravets district in the northwest part of the country, the plant was only forty-five kilometers from Vilnius, Lithuania, a mere six klicks from the Lithuanian border.

Oleg and Aleksandr were getting ready to meet with Minister Litwin during their car ride on the poor Belarusian highways. Discussing and perfecting the arrangements for the opening celebration on Independence Day was a top priority. The occasional bumps from potholes and the decaying infrastructure made relaxing problematic.

Oleg scowled. "God damn roads!" He sat with a smug expression in the back seat. His lips pouted and his thoughts wandered back to when he was a boy and was happier. "I hate this drive. Flat, boring. Nothing but farms and trees."

Aleksandr raised an eyebrow. "I thought you liked forests?" He fixed his attention on his phone.

Oleg swatted his comrade on the arm. "Did you see the condition of the village we went through a short while back? Did you see how sad and dilapidated it was?"

He let out a heavy sigh. "Yes, and your point?"

He pointed a crooked finger in the air. "Solonovich is responsible for everything. His policies and implementation of market socialism have all but collapsed our economy. If we went and drove through parts of Russia similar to these ten years ago, you'd see a significant difference. Villages like the one we went through are now growing."

"People are opening businesses. They've built new buildings, and old ones repaired. Their factories are churning out products, many of which are sold to the West. They are thriving, Comrade." He stopped to gaze out the window as if begging for a reminder to keep him on his rant. "They are flourishing while we are wallowing in a quagmire of self-destruction at the hands of a fascist pig!"

Even though the divider was up, giving them privacy, Aleksandr pointed with his thumb toward the driver. "Careful what you say."

Oleg laughed. "You think I haven't vetted him? His thoughts are probably even more hard-core than mine. Do not worry, you are among friends."

They spent the remaining part of the drive in relative silence. He would give Aleksandr an occasional stare. He wanted verification his friend was still with him, but ignored it. When they arrived at their destination, their caravan of vehicles carrying security and advisers all went around to the front entrance.

They were met by Minister Litwin and Dr. Ivan Sakevich, plus many other employees of the soon-to-be operational power plant. A band played the national anthem as they stepped out of their car and onto a red carpet.

Oleg suppressed rolling his eyes at the fanfare as the annoying Litwin approached and greeted them. "Prime Minister Shorets and First Deputy Prime Minister Roshenko, it is a pleasure to have you here. Please, let me introduce you to Dr. Ivan Sakevich. He will be the man in charge and will be managing everything once we are up and running. He reports directly to me."

The two men went through the motions of the formal introductions and shook hands with many of the staff until Oleg's impatience got to him. "Minister, can you show me where the switch is to turn this thing on?"

Litwin's face creased into an enigmatic smile. "Yes, sir, but it is not that simple. There are several processes and procedures that must be done. One person can't do it; it takes an entire team to—."

He hoped the scowl on his face was telling. It wasn't. "I know, you idiot. I was speaking metaphorically. Take me to the control room."

The blushing on Vasily's face was obvious. "But of course. I'm sorry. Please follow me."

Both men and a slew of KGB agents followed Minister Litwin and Dr. Sakevich inside to the operations center. It was deep within the bowels, under tons of concrete and steel. It was designed to withstand earthquakes with a magnitude of 9.2, higher than the 9.0 quake that hit Japan in March 2011.

Oleg frowned and shook his head. "No, this will not be sufficient."

Vasily raised his eyebrows. "Excuse me?"

"For the simulcast with the president when he is giving his speech; this will not work. This space is too tiny and too boring to be shown all over our country for people to see. Besides, this far underground, the signal won't make it out of here to the truck to be broadcast. Am I right?"

Oleg narrowed his eyes at one of the newscast advisers. His tone was clear as he demanded a firm confirmation of whether it was true or not. "Uh…yes, sir. You are correct."

The little man stared at him. "Then what shall we do?"

A broad grin spread across Oleg's face. "It's simple. We'll erect a stage—a grand one outside, and you'll make a switch with a green light on it. It will symbolize then for your team to start the reactor down here. We can even have your band playing. It will be much nicer, don't you think?"

He smiled. "It's an excellent idea, Prime Minister!"

Of course, it is, you ass-sucking little man. "Come, let us celebrate. Have a vodka with us. I have a very fine bottle in my vehicle." Oleg put his arm around Vasily as they exited the control room. Snapping his fingers at the broadcast members. "Begin putting things together for this."

As the three men strolled toward the car, Aleksandr's SAT phone rang. "Excuse me. I must answer this call." As Aleksandr distanced himself from the others, Oleg turned to Minister Litwin. "I want you to know, a day or two before the third, I am going to have a truck make a delivery here."

A broad grin spread across his face. "It is a surprise for the president on our day of celebration. It will only be to hold it. I don't want him to find out. You understand, right?" He opened the door and motioned for Vasily to step in.

Once they were both inside, the annoying little man answered. "But of course. No one will go near it. Our facility is for the people of Belarus. We are most proud to help out in this matter."

A smile creased Oleg's face as he nodded his approval.

Aleksandr stepped in from the other door and acknowledged the other two with a wave.

Oleg poured everyone a vodka and raised his glass in the air. "Excellent! Budzma!" They all shot back their drinks.

Ok. Time for you to go.

Oleg reached for Vasily's empty and took it. "I am sorry to leave so soon, minister, but we have a meeting with Solonovich we need to attend. Part of it will be to let him know of your progress here. I know he will be pleased."

He could see the pride in the little man's eyes when he mentioned it. "Yes, thank you, Mr. Prime Minister. Have a safe journey back to Minsk."

The entourage of vehicles left the plant and headed back to the capital.

Oleg raised a questioning eyebrow. "Your call. It was our contact, was it not?"

"It was."

"And everything is on schedule, I presume?"

"It is. He will be at port at the designated time, and he should have no problem making the meeting for delivery."

"Excellent. I have arranged to have the weapons stored here before we proceed."

Aleksandr scrunched his brow. Oleg could sense his comrade's concern. He held up a hand. "I can see your unease. Trust me. This is the best location for it. It's fenced-in and guarded. Besides, Minister Litwin wouldn't dare go against my wishes. He's too busy kissing my ass. Everything is indeed falling into place. We now need to discuss another item on the agenda."

He cocked his head. "What is that?"

"When to kill and dispose of Al-Hamwi?"

33

At Javier's, all three had finished breakfast. The lingering aroma of sizzling bacon, crispy fried green plantains, and rich café con leche filled the kitchen as Blake's secure phone chimed to life. Removing it from his pocket, intuition told him who was calling, and a brief glance at the screen confirmed it.

He stood. "Excuse me."

Outside, he hurried along the alley. "What's up?" The white ginger lilies lining the edge of the neighbor's small yard filled his senses with their fragrance.

The caller was Mike. "We got a message from NRO, and they tracked your ship to its current location."

"Where is it?"

"In the Ionian Sea, headed north into the Adriatic. We don't have a final destination yet. Get in the air and head toward Croatia. I'll contact you as soon as I find out."

"Okay, I'm on my way."

NRO or The National Reconnaissance Office is in Chantilly, Virginia. They design, build, and operate the spy satellites of the

U.S. Government. Several intelligence and military agencies rely on them to coordinate and analyze their surveillance and satellite imagery. Mike had the authority to call in extraordinary requests to reposition them when there were matters of national security.

Back inside, Javier and Adriana had cleared away the dishes from breakfast. She was washing them when she set her inquisitive eyes on him, making his stomach tighten. It was impossible to hold her stare, and he busied himself with gathering his personal effects. "Sorry, but I've got to go. Thanks for your help."

She flipped her hair back over her shoulder while she removed the rubber gloves from her delicate hands. "That's all? '*I've got to go*' and you leave? Wait a minute."

She was lurking behind him.

Oh, shit. Here we go.

He turned back to her. "You know I can't talk about it. It's part of the job."

"But you've told me a lot of stuff already; the weapon, Al-Hamwi, my father."

There was a hint of desperation in her voice. He liked it, and it kept him in control. Stuffing the last of his things in his backpack, he grabbed it and glanced back over his shoulder. "Sorry." He brushed past her and out the door.

The deep, throaty note of the Mustang's exhaust masked the sound of the passenger door opening. She plopped into the seat next to him. "You can't get rid of me so easy. I'm going with you."

He cracked a brief smile, which quickly faded. "No, you're not. You don't know where I'm going."

She smiled and shrugged her shoulders. "So?"

"But I'm not coming back."

"I don't care." She fastened her seatbelt. "You never know. Perhaps I could be helpful to you."

So much for control.

He curled up his eyebrows and shook his head. "What in the *hell* could you do to help me?"

"Uh—the bank, for starters. You wouldn't have known about my safe deposit box. Nor would you have discovered the name of the ship—or those Swiss account numbers."

Shit. She's got a fair point.

"Okay, I admit it. You helped me back there. But that's because we're here, in Cuba." He pointed down with both hands. "I'm going halfway around the world. There isn't anything you can do for me where I'm headed. Now, stop being stubborn and get out. I'm not joking."

Her voice was defiant. "No."

He threw his arms up. "I don't have time for this."

The car lurched forward as it went into gear.

"Where are we going?"

"The airport. I had my plane moved over there yesterday from GITMO and I am going to get on it. In the meantime, you stay here."

She smirked. "We'll see."

The thought of having her eyes sparkle when her gaze rested on him, or her long dark hair cascading over him while they... he shook his head to clear his thoughts.

How would he explain her presence to Mike? It would be impossible to babysit her at his destination. What if something happened to her because he was too weak to say no? He didn't know if he was falling in love or not, but one thing was for sure; he didn't want to separate himself from her. The image of Farishta lying dead on the floor flashed into his mind. He flushed the idea away.

She won this battle.

"Screw it." He glanced over as her long hair danced in the wind.

"What did you say?" She leaned in toward him and stopped her hair from blowing back with her hand.

"I said, screw it. If you want to come along, you can come. But you're not going like it."

The transformation from a defiant woman to a giddy little girl who talked her father into buying her an ice cream excited him. He called ahead so the pilots could prep the aircraft and told them they would need to take off immediately. When they arrived at the plane and approached it, both flyers quirked their eyebrows at Adriana's pajamas and bare feet. Blake scowled at the pair of them. "Don't ask."

Once everyone was on board, he went to the cockpit. "Okay, before you say a word, she is General Vasquez's daughter and helped me gather some valuable intel. She has contacts in Croatia, Montenegro, and Slovenia. If when we get over there, it doesn't appear as if she can help, we'll fly her back home. Questions?"

Randy and Chuck regarded each other and grinned. "Nope!"

In the cabin, he dug out a duffel bag and tossed it to her. "Here you go. See if there is anything in there you can wear?"

"What is this?"

"We call it a go bag. All the agents using the plane have one on board. You'll find a change of clothes inside and the female agent who owns it is about the same size as you." He sat and fastened his seat belt.

"Oh, if one of those two pilots asks you about contacts in Europe, say you know an extensive network of people. I had to invent a reason for bringing you along."

The giddy schoolgirl was back. "Okay, it shouldn't be too difficult."

"All right. Now buckle up, we're about to take off."

Seven hours into the flight, the in-cabin phone rang. He glanced over at a sleeping Adriana before he answered. "MacKay."

"Mike here. We've got a bead on your ship. It appears it is going to be docking in Rijeka, Slovenia."

He pulled out a pen and scribbled the information in his notebook. "Sounds fine. We're about three hours out." On his laptop, he opened the CIA's version of Google Earth. "There is an airport a few klicks from the chief port. Send me their exact coordinates to my phone once they dock, and I'll head there and see what I can find out. In the meantime, I'll get Chuck to change the flight plan."

34

Port of Rijeka, Slovenia
June 29th
01:20 local (22:20 GMT)

The captain eyed the Port Authority supervisor as he came into the wheelhouse of the ship. His eyes met those of the captains. "I have completed the inspection of your cargo and they have approved you to dock and unload your containers. We can release the majority of it right away."

He raised his eyebrows. "What do you mean, *the majority*? Why can't we take possession of everything?"

"Since the tobacco is organic, it is required to be quarantined in a bonded warehouse for three days. After it passes random sampling and is free of pests and illegal content, it will be authorized for release."

"What if we have a deadline for our final delivery? It will cost us money."

"I am sorry. It's the law. You should have checked the laws at your port of arrival before leaving. I'll have the harbor pilot dock you and then you can begin your work. Welcome to Slovenia."

The captain's lips tightened and his nostrils flared as the supervisor left and boarded his boat back to the docks. He turned to his first mate and held up his hand. "Wait here for the harbor pilot. I'll be right back."

#

In his cabin, Zahmir went over their route to Hieraniony. He sighed when a knock on the door startled him. "What is it?"

The door opened, and the captain stood in the doorway with his hand on the knob. "We are here, but we have difficulties."

"What sort of problems do we have now?

"The tobacco we have on board is an organic farm product. It has to be quarantined for three days and inspected. They won't release the containers to us until then."

He pondered for a moment.

How foolish of me not to oversee which container they put the weapons in.

"It is indeed an unfortunate situation. What are we waiting for now?"

"The harbor pilot to dock the ship."

"Have you seen Mustafa?"

"I passed him on my way here. He should be on the bridge."

An uneasy feeling came over him.

What if they find all the armaments we packed in with the tobacco?

He grabbed the com, called the bridge, and ordered Mustafa to his cabin.

The knock on the door stopped his frantic pacing. He met eyes with his friend when he entered. "What container did you tell the men to pack the weapons in?"

He raised his shoulders and held out his hands. "You mean the number? Where it is on the—"

His impatience grew. "No! What other cargo did you put with them?"

"The cigars. We had to, in order to throw off any dogs, sniffing for explosives."

Zahmir closed his eyes. The deep breath failed to slow the anxiety as it swelled within him. His emotions turned to anger and then panic. His eyes snapped open and found the nearest thing not bolted down. Reaching for the chair, he hurled it across his cabin. *Lewanaya!*

His friend rolled his eyes. "Brother, what is it?"

His blood was boiling. "Did you not come from the bridge? Did you not hear?"

He shook his head back and forth. "I was only—"

"Shut up! It's our cargo. Some of it is organic and needs to be held for inspection. It is tobacco. They want to hold it for three days! We do not have such a luxury!"

Mustafa stood silent. Zahmir whirled as he sought a solution. "Show the crane operator which container to pull out first. The one with the weapons. Afterward, gather all the men in the mess hall. I know what we'll do."

After all his team had gathered, he explained the situation and then went into detail about what he needed them to do next. The captain entered the gathering of his team members. "We have docked. We're ready to remove the payload."

He stared out at his squad with pride. "You know what we have to do. Let's get started."

Zahmir went back on top as the crane operator unloaded the container holding the weapons, buried deep within pallets of cigars. They loaded it onto the back of a flatbed truck, which proceeded to the quarantine area. He lifted the two-way radio to his lips and barked an order to Mohammad.

#

As he was told, he followed the vehicle on foot, careful to stay in the shadows. It drove past a stack of cargo, then to the left, out of sight of the ship. A hiss of its air brakes made him peer from a distance. The driver stepped out and strolled toward a reach stacker; the machines used to lift and move the massive shipping crates.

He sprinted to the opposite side of the truck, out of the man's view. Another quick peek showed the worker walking to the back of the stacking machine. The sharpened blade, sheathed in the small of his back, came out as he crept ever slowly to his target.

Shadows, cast from the columns of stacked containers, suppressed his movement.

When the man turned his back to him, he thrust the knife deep into the driver's kidneys. He clamped his left hand over his victim's mouth from behind. He withdrew the weapon from poor sap's back and slit his throat. After disposing of the body in between two stacks of crates, he ran to the vehicle and radioed Zahmir. "I have the truck."

#

Al-Hamwi chambered a round in his rifle and the two others followed his lead. "This is another reason I selected this port. There is an ongoing strike for the dock workers. These people are a skeleton crew of replacements. Under normal conditions, there would be close to thirty longshoremen. But tonight—there are only five."

He held out his hand. "Allahu Akbar."

The men replied. "Allahu Akbar."

He and the other two walked off the ship and into the office of the Port Authority. They wore traditional thawbs, or tunics, and concealed their AK-47s underneath them.

Inside, the supervisor and harbor pilot lifted their gazes from their desks. "Gentlemen, I'm in the process of entering your cargo into the system for inspection. We'll send the pickup notice to the bill of lading party as soon as it's ready."

Al-Hamwi scowled. "I am sorry. Such a method will not work for us." All three terrorists withdrew their weapons and opened fire. Footsteps running away caught Zahmir's attention. He turned as someone ran out of the back door. "Both of you. Quick!"

The two chased after the fleeing man. Zahmir bent and grabbed a set of keys from the dead supervisor. He checked through his pockets and took all of his cash.

He did the same for the other man. After he stole what he could use, he went to the supervisor's desk. The freighter's entry was still on the screen. He ripped out the hard drive and kept it to dispose of later.

\#

The stevedore on the gantry crane spotted his colleague barreling out of the warehouse door. Two men from the freighter chased after him. One of them stopped and brought his arms up.

Gunfire echoed around the docks. His jaw dropped as his co-worker stumbled, then fell, his shirt soaked dark from blood. "Holy shit!" He cupped his hand over his mouth, pulled out his cell phone, and dialed the cops.

"State your emergency."

"I am employed at the dockyard. Send police now—terrorists, or something. They've killed someone. They've got machine guns and—Oh my God! I've got to get—get here. Now!"

He panicked and leaped out of his chair and out of the operating booth. Once on the steel platform, gunfire came from below. A hot, searing pain erupted from his leg up through his chest. "Shit. No!" He stumbled, flipped over the safety rail, and tumbled fifty feet to the pavement.

\#

Five minutes later, sirens sounded. "Come! Now! The pair of you! Quick!"

The two men ran to their leader. Al-Hamwi handed Mohammad the sets of keys he took from the dead supervisor in the office. "Go to the car park and find the vehicles these belong to. Bring them out here, by the door. Now!"

They rushed off to complete their task. Zahmir called another man over and told him to drive the flatbed with the container on it. He put his radio to his mouth. "Captain."

"Yes, brother."

"We're leaving within the minute. The law is on its way."

"Understood."

Mohammad and Rafala had brought two cars around and parked adjacent to the ship.

"Everyone in." He opened the driver's door to the first car. "Rafala, out. I'll drive. Go back, ride in the flatbed, and follow me. Mohammad, when you leave here, go in the opposite direction from me. We'll meet at the airport we talked about earlier. Everybody switch your radios off."

Two minutes after they left, the local authorities arrived.

35

Rijeka, Slovenia
June 30th
04:00 local (01:00 GMT)

Dressed in all black, Blake retrieved a suppressed Glock, checking if he'd loaded it before slipping it into his holster.

He had called ahead to the U.S. Embassy and arranged for a car to be left for him at the airport. Adriana raised her eyebrows. "Where are we going?"

He chuckled. "*We* are not going anywhere. *You* are staying on the aircraft. I'll be back as soon as I can. The pilots can order a restock of the plane and you can fix yourself something to eat. Relax, be patient, and wait."

"Based on how you're dressed, I think I'll be fine staying put. Are you expecting trouble?"

He dipped his chin. "In my line of work, I always expect it. However, I'm going to avoid it if I can. I only want to find out if Al-Hamwi is here. If he is, I can come back, regroup, and plan out a course of action. This is a simple reconnaissance operation."

The airplane rolled to a stop beside a black Chevy Suburban. He turned to her. "I'll be back soon."

"Okay, be careful."

It amused him they sounded like a married couple. The sound of her warning him to use caution made his soul dance with joy.

#

Blake steered toward the harbor. When within a few hundred meters away, he studied the police lights reflecting off the nearby buildings.

"Oh… no, what is this shit?"

With his headlights off, he continued to the cul-de-sac at the end of the block and parked.

#

Retrieving his binoculars from the glove box, he exited the car and walked to the chain-link fence that marked the ports property line. Heavy police activity dotted the docks near the ship and an ambulance sat with its lights flashing under the gantry crane.

Another EMT vehicle appeared from behind the vessel and backed into its slip. He turned on the night-vision and searched for the stern of the boat. Below the rear deck, the name stood out. *Angel van de zee.*

Gotcha. So—what in the hell happened? Could they have been careless? Is this mission already over or is it about to get stranger? Shit. Time to get into the water.

He returned to the Chevy, spun the truck around and drove two blocks away, parking facing the direction he was going to leave.

The area was a warehouse district. There were no streetlights, but there were a few lights dotted on the tops of some buildings.

He found the darkest spot and changed into his wet suit. Staying in the shadows, he crept back to the fence separating the street from the docks and scanned along the dockyard for movement. The last thing he needed was a wandering police officer stumbling onto him. It wouldn't be the first time.

The multi-tool made quick work of the fencing. Moments later, he was on the wharf, crouching to avoid detection toward a ladder leading into the sea. A thin coating of Liquipel protected all of Blake's gear. Mindful not to create any waves, he climbed down while monitoring all the activity on the dock to his left.

A tingling sensation hit his body as he slipped into the water. It was warm, and he felt the pressure as it rose against his suit. The smell of diesel filled his nostrils close to the surface. He had to swim two hundred meters to the vessel.

The distance took more time than usual; an unfortunate result of the pace to prevent ripples and noise.

They moored the ship with the starboard side next to the quay, so he swam around to the bow, the furthest point away from the police.

A ladder on the end made it easy for him to climb to the dock. Staying crouched, he crept over to the bow mooring line and shimmied his way up to the deck.

Distractions to his right forced him to stop multiple times while he dangled from the rope. He was glad to have had all the upper body workouts. Most people couldn't hang on for this length of time. Several people shuffled along the gangplank as they carried out their investigation.

At last, on deck, a life raft was there to use as shelter. A glance at his watch told him he had between thirty and forty minutes prior to sunrise.

He was more upset with himself because the swim took so much time. Now he was under pressure to find something of value and get out before he lost the cover of darkness.

The lights of the dock illuminated the ship's starboard. Blake lurked around and found an open doorway on its port side. The most likely spot someone would make a mistake and leave behind some kind of clue was the crew's quarters, so he made it his destination.

He trod with caution through the echoing halls, his every step accompanied by a subtle squishing sound beneath his shoes. The distant symphony of voices and approaching footsteps elevated his senses and catapulted him into a state of heightened awareness.

He ducked into a room, closed the door, and waited for the police to pass. A map of the ship mounted to the wall captured his attention. Yanking it from its mount, he studied it.

I'm guessing you took the captain's cabin.

The two men passed the room. He held back for a short time and listened. When he was sure they were gone, a slight crack of the door gave him ample view along the corridor.

He made his way to the crew's quarters. They were around the next junction, but voices stopped him again.

Blake peeked around the corner. Two police officers stood in the hallway outside several of the cabins. Not knowing Slovenian, but by judging their body language, he could tell they were going to be there for a while.

Panic set in as he glanced at his watch. Another officer came to the cabin door and gestured for the other two policemen to come in.

Shit.

Time was running out quick, so he focused on the map of the ship again and changed his plan. The trek to the captain's quarters was lengthy. He had to duck in and out of rooms to avoid detection. When he reached the location, the sound of voices emanating from the cabin stopped him once more.

Slipping silently into a room, he cracked the door. Shadows moving in the area he wished to go caught his attention.

Two men stood speaking to one another when the radio one of them carried squawked. They exchanged a few words, and both exited the room. He took a deep breath.

Now or never.

He hurried along the hall. The inside of the stateroom was sparse, but he could tell someone had stayed there recently. The bunk appeared disheveled, with an unmade bed. A plate of half-eaten food and a partially filled coffee mug rested on the desk. Trash littered the floor.

Searching the various closets and storage compartments in the cabin resulted in nothing new. There were papers taped to the wall, comprising schedules for maintenance and crew shifts.

He sifted through the rubbish, looking for anything of value. Most of it was junk, but one piece he unwrapped had something handwritten on it.

Hieraniony. Old castle site. 30th 23:00.

He folded it and put it in his waterproof pouch.

A voice in Slovenian. "Stop! Who are you?" caused Blake's head to jerk, and he stared into the face of a policeman in the doorway.

Busted.

"Well, I…" Lowering his head, he charged him and delivered a blow to the man's sternum. The officer gasped for air. No holding back. He slammed him in the jaw with an uppercut from his right elbow.

Blake grabbed the officer's arm and flipped him over his shoulder, onto the floor. The noise was going to get attention. He rushed out of the room and turned left along the hall. Seconds later, the blaring of a whistle and shouts for help filled the ship's narrow halls. Two policemen advancing on him stopped him as he ran down the hallway.

He reached for some pipes on the ceiling, pulled up, and kicked both men as they entered the doorway. He sprinted back toward the captain's quarters, completing a one-eighty. The officer he'd earlier floored staggered out of Al-Hamwi's former cabin. Blake elbowed him in the forehead as he passed by and knocked him back to the ground.

The rhythmic thumping of feet across the metal deck increased. He turned to his left and went down a steep set of stairs to another level. One more flight to go and he would be on the main deck.

He took a right and ran along the corridor. As he went by a hallway, an arm extended out, catching him in the neck. His head jerked backward as his body continued forward until he fell onto the steel plating. Anger and adrenaline pumped through him. He hopped up and charged his attacker.

Like a defensive end rushing for the ball, he tackled the officer, slammed him into the adjacent wall, and buried his head in the guy's stomach. He rushed in hard and banged the top of his head into the bottom of the guy's jaw.

The man drew his pistol and pointed it at him. With instinct, he grabbed the man's wrist with his left hand and elbowed his assailant in the belly. Still holding on, he brought his attacker's arm up over his shoulder and pulled down with force, snapping it at the elbow.

An agonizing scream soon followed. The broken bone poked out through the skin. The officer yelled in agony. MacKay turned back to face him, ripped a fire extinguisher off the wall, and slammed it into his opponent's face.

Blake's breathing got heavier. He dropped the makeshift weapon and ran. The throbbing in his neck and pain in his back encouraged him to go faster—the next set of stairs led to the main deck.

At the bottom of the staircase was a welcoming door to lead him to freedom. Somehow, he'd lost his sense of direction while inside, when he exited; he was on the starboard edge of the vessel, facing the docks.

Oh shit. Wrong side.

Three men below pointed and blew their whistles. Small arms fire peppered Blake's position. Automatic weapons followed. Thoughts of Adriana waiting for him on the plane and him not returning entered his mind.

A new feeling of urgency renewed his aching muscles. He ran the width of the boat. Hot lead plinked off the steel walls behind him. The railing was only a few meters in front of him.

He dove over and into the bay. As soon as he splashed down, he submerged and turned back toward the hull. Bullets ripped through the water.

Their trails were like a shower of meteoroids in the night sky. Blake groped for the ship. Rough barnacles attached to the hull never felt so pleasant. He surfaced and kept close and out of sight.

Revving engines cut through the air. Tires squealed and headlights appeared near the stern of the boat. He slid beneath the surface, swimming aft as fast as possible.

Surfacing to take a peek, a spotlight shone on the back of the vessel and dipped toward the waterline. Taking a deep breath, he ducked back underwater. He swam over to the dock, where a crowd of people and parked cars had assembled.

When he surfaced, he was below the pier, hanging out over the bay. He glanced out to where he was moments ago, and the area was flooded with lights. Voices continued to speak, in a language he didn't understand, although he was sure they spoke about him.

He submerged again and kept his hand against the wall as a guide. Sore, stiff, and out of breath. At last, he reached the ladder. While keeping an eye on the police, he slipped up to the pavement and ran crouched across the dock and back through the hole in the fence.

The silhouette of the Suburban was a welcome sight. He pulled out his phone and called his pilots. "Start dinner. I'm coming, and I'm in a hurry."

Randy chuckled. "Hot or cold?"

"Cold, but it might change."

"Got it."

Ten minutes passed, and he stopped next to the jet. Holding his ribs, he gingerly stepped up the stairs into the plane. She grasped his arm. "You're all wet! What happened?"

"I'll tell you in a minute." He ducked into the cockpit. "Okay, let's get outta here."

Chuck tilted his head. "Destination?"

"Hieraniony. Have you ever heard of the place?"

"No clue."

Randy frowned. "Can you check its location?"

Blake pulled out his device and did a quick search.

"Here you go. Hieraniony is the site of an old castle in the Northwest corner of Belarus." Blake cocked his head. "Belarus? It matches what someone in Afghanistan told me. Who would Al-Hamwi be meeting there?"

Chuck shrugged. "No idea. That's your job."

Blake pointed at the screen. "It's a few clicks inside the border from Lithuania."

Chuck nodded and started toggling some switches. "Okay, we can be over it in about two and a half hours."

"Over it?"

"Yeah. No airports in the vicinity, and because of diplomatic relations, or the lack thereof, the U.S. has with Belarus, we couldn't land even if there was one. So—you know what you have to do?"

He smiled, "Yep."

"I don't. I don't understand what you must do," Adriana proclaimed.

He hadn't noticed she had slipped in behind him and was eavesdropping on the conversation. He twisted around and placed his hands on the side of her shoulders. "You need to take a seat and not butt into my conversations."

Refocusing back on his pilots. "You've got your destination. Time to take off."

The engines whined as the plane moved. He pointed at the seat. "Sit and buckle up."

"Are you going to tell me what you meant?"

He sighed. "All it means is I have to jump."

"Jump? Are you crazy? What about me?"

"It's easy; I do it all the time. Besides, you're not coming. I'm having the guys fly you to Rammstein Air Base in Germany."

"I don't want to go there. I came along to help you."

"Listen, you *are* helping me. You'd be out of my way and safe." He lied to her. "As soon as I need you, I'll have them bring you to me, okay?"

"Isn't there another airpo—"

"Wait a minute, I think we've got another chute in here you could use. I want to tell you this will be as scary as hell for your first time."

Her eyes went wide. "What? Me? Forget..." her eyes narrowed, and her lips scrunched. "I know what you're doing. Fine. We'll do it your way."

Blake smiled. "It's the only way."

36

12,000ft above Hieraniony, Belarus
   June 30th
   08:00 local (03:00 GMT)

Blake stood balanced, with legs wide apart in the cockpit's doorway. He'd changed into his jumpsuit and briefed his pilots on what needed to be done to make it a successful jump.

"When we're within range, there are some things I'm going to need you to do to minimize me killing myself as soon as I exit out of this jet."

Chuck frowned. "All right, what's your first issue?"

"The door is forward of the wing, and I don't want to leap out and slam into it."

Randy grinned. "Yeah, no shit? I know what your next problem is too, and I know how we handle both of them."

Blake's eyebrows shot up. "What?"

"The engine. It's attached to the back of the fuselage. You stand a fair chance of getting sucked into it."

"Correct. So, you have an idea how I can avoid it?"

"I do. Understand this jet isn't conducive for jumping out of, but it's built to withstand a lot. When we get close, I'll drop her down to under eight thousand feet. I'll make sure the cabin is depressurized and then slow us to MCA and then cut the port side motor."

"How much time will it give me before you stall?"

Randy frowned. "All the time we want. Although we'd prefer you to get the hell out of here as fast as you can."

Chuck broke in. "No—I don't like it,"

Blake turned to him. "What's your concern?"

"I don't think minimum controllable airspeed for this aircraft is going to be enough for you to jump out safely. I think you'll still slam into the wing, but I have an idea. Come with me."

After his co-pilot got out of his seat, he followed him to the left side door, where Chuck tapped a handle on the wall.

"This thing here, it's bolted to the frame. It's not going anywhere."

"I already know where you're going with this. You're going to suggest I tether myself to it and slip out slo—"

Chucked nodded. "Slowly, yes. Until you pass the port engine and then you glide away."

Blake slapped him on the back. "I like it."

"And there's an added benefit too."

"How so?"

"Since you'll have a controlled exit, we can fly above MCA and we won't have the risk of a stall."

He let out a sigh. "Excellent. Even better. Tell me when we're ready."

#

He sat next to Adriana on the couch at the back of the plane. Chuck called out. "One minute, Mr. MacKay."

She gazed into his eyes and put her hand on his. "Please be careful."

Unable to resist the magnetic pull between them, he leaned in and gently pressed his lips against hers. In that intimate moment, he savored the alluring fragrance that enveloped her and reveled in the soft silkiness of her hair beneath his fingertips.

"I will. Buckle up."

She fastened her belt as he stood and went to the front of the cabin. He inserted his earpiece.

"Radio check."

Randy replied. "Loud and clear. Depressurizing now. Give it a minute."

The carabiner snapped closed as he clipped it to the handle. "I'm opening the door."

The roar of the wind rushing by at one hundred and twenty knots became pronounced as the door opened. It sucked several loose pieces of paper out.

Randy's voice came over the radio. "Cutting the engine now." A few seconds passed. "On my mark; three, two, one, go."

Blake eased himself out of the door. His body extended out along the side of the jet. Adriana watched him wide-eyed through the cabin windows. The rope slid through his gloved hands until he was next to the left engine.

The plane started to shake. Internal organs jiggled as the craft lost altitude. He slammed against the back of the engine. A hard tug on his vest caused him to glance up. Part of his gear had wedged in between the rear flaps of the wing.

Randy's speech was harsh. "You've got to go."

He could hear the alarms through his earpiece warning of a potential stall.

"One more second. I'm snagged!"

He yanked on the vest. He struggled, defying the force of the gusts as it willed him back.

The tone of Chuck's voice had an edge of desperation. "Now! You've got to go now!"

He unsheathed his knife and reached up against the forces working against him.

"We can't hold it for much longer. We'll have to put it in a steep dive if you don't hurry!"

He stretched out and cut out the diminutive pack of gear holding him to the plane. As soon as he was free, he released the tether. His body flipped through the air as it caught in the jet stream.

"I'm off!"

Chuck's voice came over the radio. "Pulling up, now. Best of luck."

As he dropped, he yelled as the jet's left side engine wound up. "Sitrep!"

"Hold on!"

There was nothing on the radio.

Then Randy's voice. "Engine's back up. We've got control and gaining speed and altitude. Damn, it was close. Remind me not to let you do it again."

He didn't bother with a reply.

#

He fell for thirty seconds and released his parachute. As he glided down, he identified the area where the castle ruins were supposed to be. He planned to make land about two kilometers to the east of the site and then proceed from there. The town was three kilometers to the west.

He touched down in the middle of a field, near a clump of trees. The buckles on his harness clicked, then dropped to the ground. After hiding the chute in some bushes, Blake peered off in the distance. There was a farm to the west and headed in its direction.

After hurrying along for half a klick inside the tree line adjacent to the dirt road, a woman's scream south of his position reached him. He stopped and listened. The rambling of a man's voice and then another cry came through the forest. It appeared to be a few hundred meters away. He maneuvered through the thick brush, careful to keep the noise to a minimum.

The desperate cries intensified as he got closer. A little further, he could make out movement through the woods. A woman with her face against the tree, her hands tied around it, bawled. He couldn't make out what she said. Behind her was a man. His pants were down to his ankles, and he approached the woman. She screamed again.

The man slapped her on the back of the head and mumbled in Belarusian. "Shut up, woman. No one can hear you out here."

He crept closer. *The son-of-a-bitch is raping her.* His hand reached for his Glock. The thickness of a hefty branch on the ground snapped his thoughts away from shooting the man. He knelt down, picked it up, and sneaked into the clearing.

The fear this woman was experiencing angered him more as the man lifted her skirt as she pleaded with him to stop. *Okay, enough.* Stepping into the opening behind them, he was only a few meters away.

He drew back and sprinted toward them. The bough smashed on the back of the guy's head with full force. A loud crack and splinters flew as it broke in half. The man's body met the forest floor with a resounding whump.

The man rolled over and faced his assailant. Blake kicked him in the face. His jaw was now crooked and disfigured. There was satisfaction in causing the damage, and he smiled. The man lay on the ground; still conscious, but bleeding profusely from his mouth.

He drew his knife and stepped toward the woman. The whites of her eyes were prominent, locked on the gleaming blade.

He spoke to her in Russian. "Are you okay? Can you understand me?" Her dialect might be too different. Stepping to the tree's rear, he cut the rope. Before he could say anything else, the woman darted off and ran through the trees, yelling something he couldn't distinguish.

He turned back to the coward now lying on the ground. Anger filled the void from where the adrenaline had departed. Behind him was a dirt bike leaning against a tree. The man said something in Belarussian.

Blake drooped into a crouch. "Come on, asshole!" He drew his pistol and waved it at the man.

"Vstavat!"

The jerk understood and stood as ordered. He motioned the man to the tree. With some parachute cord, he fastened the man to the trunk. He left his pants down and walked around to the man's back.

"You don't mind if I borrow your motorbike, do you?" He reared back and kicked the man in the crotch as hard as he could. The man screamed and slid down to his knees.

"No? Didn't think so."

He hopped on, noted his location on his GPS and abandoned the man, still bound and moaning.

Blake spent the rest of the morning getting to know the lay of the land. He enjoyed the rolling hills and broad pastures as he traveled to the place where the meeting was scheduled. A ditch and some castle ruins will make for a fine place to stash his transportation once he returns to hide until whomever Al-Hamwi was supposed to meet shows up.

In the early afternoon, he was back in town, got something to eat, and filled the fuel tank on the motorbike. He purchased some apples, bottled water, and other snacks to take back with him. He wanted to make sure he was there plenty of time before anyone else showed up. If it were him meeting Al-Hamwi, he would be there at least four hours ahead of the time.

At sixteen hundred, Blake headed back out to the location and camouflaged the motorcycle with branches and leaves.

The castle ruin was what it was—a ruin. Only remnants remained, with mere fragments of crumbling walls scattered throughout the wooded area. He found a corner wall, sat on the inside, and waited. He had six and a half hours until the appointed time.

37

Hieraniony, Belarus
    June 30th
    22:49 local (19:49 GMT)

Blake remained hidden in the confines of the castle ruins. There came the distinguishing sound of gravel popping out from beneath the weight of tires. A vehicle approached. The driver gunned the diesel engine and pushed the truck through the woods.

He reared and peeked over the old wall. Beams of light bounced as the slow-moving transport trundled over the bumps and through the potholes in the road, about a hundred meters distant.

A set of headlights flashed to his left, sixty meters along the gravel forest road. As it closed in on the parked vehicles. The air brakes hissed as it came to a stop three lengths from the waiting car. Voices of several men reached his ears as they exited the back of the truck, and two more cars halted to their rear.

He crept through the woodland. Cutting the distance in half, a tall pine provided him cover, and he retrieved his night-vision goggles. The forest turned into a greenish hue and revealed much more than the thick brush. Opposite him, an elbow jutted out from behind a tree.

He scanned the woods on both sides of his position. There were no less than eight more men concealing themselves; all with automatic weapons. He reached into his backpack for a pair of night-vision binoculars with an integrated digital camera. Next, he took out a parabolic microphone with a set of earbuds.

Once nestled in his ears and the microphone strategically positioned toward the rumbling truck, he raised the binoculars to his eyes, homing in on his target. A car door slammed, and he panned to his left. Two individuals in dark suits had exited the vehicle facing him and walked toward the Mercedes.

Well, hello there. Who the hell are you two?

Zooming in, he snapped several close-ups of each person. It transferred the images to his phone automatically via Bluetooth, and then uploaded to the CIA's facial recognition database.

As voices echoed from his right, his gaze intensified through the binoculars. And there, standing resolutely, was none other than Al-Hamwi.

There you are, you sneaky bastard.

He adjusted the microphone until their conversation was clear.

The terrorist marched to the pair. "I am your contact."

One of the two men gazed at him for a moment. "I know who you are. Let's get on with it."

His eyes shifted to his phone. It identified the person speaking.

Oleg Shorets, Prime Minister of Belarus. What the hell?

He searched for the other man while he listened to them speak.

Al-Hamwi glared at him. "Your packages are in the back. Transfer the remaining balance and the truck is yours."

The other man stepped forward. "No. You need to show them to us first and how they work."

Blake snapped several pictures of all three men together. His quick look at the phone confirmed that it was still analyzing the image of the second man.

Al-Hamwi turned to the man behind him and spoke under his breath. He ran to the back of the vehicle and, with the aid of another, removed one of the smaller units. They brought the box to them and sat it on the ground. Another two individuals carried a wooden crate and opened the top with a pry bar.

"This is one of the compact weapons. It fires five point five six by forty-five-millimeter ammunition."

Blake zoomed in on it and captured more pictures. He checked his phone again. *Aleksandr Roshenko, Deputy Prime Minister of Belarus.*

What in the hell are these guys doing with a man like Al-Hamwi? And what are they buying the armaments for?

Zahmir bent over and flipped open the back of the box, then retrieved a tube from the crate. He held it up. "Here are the preloaded barrels. This unit holds thirty-six of them." He slid the barrel in until clicking into position.

"After you've loaded it with all the full barrels, close the back and press this button on top. Then your computer does the rest." He snapped his fingers and someone approached him with a stack of binders. He handed them to Aleksandr. "Those are the programming instructions. Everything else is there. You're free to inspect them if you wish."

Oleg turned to face two guys dressed in assault gear. He waved his hand, and they jogged to the back of the truck.

"While your people finish their inspection, we can complete the transfer of payment."

Oleg smirked. "What is preventing me from killing you and everyone here and just taking it?"

An arrogant smile creased Zahmir's face. "I've built in a safeguard."

Aleksandr studied his face. "What kind? What are you talking about?"

"These weapons require a thirty-six-digit password to access the firing program. I will give it to you after we receive the money and we are at a safe distance."

Blake looked on through the binoculars. The two men's eyes locked for several moments in a kind of silent struggle where each sized the other up. Oleg smiled and put his finger to his chin and shifted his feet. "No. I think you have the password on you."

Defiant, Zahmir crossed his arms, drew himself up to his full height, and glared at him. "I do not! Do not take me for a fool, prime minister! I will email it to the address of your choice. I have nothing to gain by telling untruths.”

Oleg stepped toward him and pointed at him. “Do not speak to me with such insolence again. You are lying to me.”

“What is it you think I am being dishonest to you about? Don’t you believe it needs an encrypted password or the fact I will send it to you after we are at a safe distance?”

“Neither. I think you have the codes on you now.” Oleg snapped his fingers.

The rustle of fabric and the click of safeties switching off came from both sides and in front of Blake. Over a dozen commandos emerged from the woods and opened fire on Zahmir and his men. They killed them all before any could return a single shot.

Wide-eyed and jaw agape, Blake continued to survey the scene and listen.

Aleksandr stepped back and threw his arms in the air. “What the fuck did you do? Why did you murder him? Now we don’t possess the codes!”

Oleg waved his hand down. “Calm down. He was bluffing.”

“How can you be so sure he was telling lies? Does the weapon not need an access code?”

“Of course, it needs one. He was truthful about it. He was lying about not having it on him.”

“How do you know?”

“Have you forgotten your interrogation techniques from the old days in the KGB?”

“What?”

“His tell. Everyone has a tell when they lie. Some can master deception and learn to cover them up. Our friend here hadn’t. His eyes went downwards and to the left when I asked him if he had them on him. It’s quite simple—he lied.”

Oleg kicked Zahmir’s dead body. “Contumacious little prick! I’ll locate it. Besides, he wouldn’t risk forgetting a code that long and complicated. It’s written down somewhere.”

A commando approached and passed something to him. “Sir, I found this tablet in the front seat of his car.”

The prime minister smiled and handed it back to him. “Excellent. I’m certain what we want is in this. Find it and get this weapon working as soon as possible. I want to have a demonstration no later than tomorrow afternoon. Search the other bodies for anything useful as well."

"Yes, sir." The soldier jogged off toward their motorcade.

Aleksandr scowled. "I hope, for your sake, you are correct."

"Trust me. They are there. Besides, I saved us over twenty million dollars by not having to pay him the balance."

As Oleg strolled away, he swung around and called out. "Take pictures of the corpses. We'll use them as evidence of our revenge on the terrorists daring to attack Belarus."

Another commando stepped forward and saluted. "What do you want us to do with the bodies, sir?"

"Dump them in the woods along the road and let the wolves have them. Minister Litwin has provided a place for us to store the truck for the next couple of days, so take it there."

He turned back to his partner. "Come, we have much to plan before Independence Day. Operation Spear Garden is in full swing now."

The two strolled back to their car and departed while their entourage of vehicles stayed behind to finish their work. Blake remained in the shadows and continued to snap photos of the men loading bodies into the back.

#

All the cars had gone ahead, leaving just the military vehicle.

I need to find a way onto that thing.

Kneeling on the forest floor, he kept a watchful eye on the two soldiers as they tossed the last two dead terrorists into the back. The soldier closest to him went to the front and stepped into the cab while the second one stood and faced the woods.

What the hell is he doing?

Urine splashing on the ground answered his question. He hoped the crackle of the fluid hitting the leaves would help to mask any noise he made. Slipping in behind the rear axle, he unfastened his belt, wrapped it around the undercarriage, and buckled it.

The last man got into the driver's seat, and the diesel roared to life. He withdrew the remaining parachute cord, pulled it around his back to support his shoulders and tied it to the frame. The heavy transport lurched forward as he finished tying the knot.

#

After an hour, they had traveled over seventy kilometers. The muscles in his legs burned from keeping his feet up. He would only get a rest when they stopped at a light or stop sign. As soon as the engine revved, he lifted them back and stuck them into a part of the truck's undercarriage.

Thirty minutes later, his muscles were on fire. Struggling to hold, a feeling of relief came over him when they slowed and turned off the highway. Blake held on with one hand and retrieved his phone. He thumbed the GPS application and waited for it to load. It showed he was two klicks from a nuclear power plant.

He unstrapped himself and fell. Wincing from the pain, he hit the ground; the vehicle passed over and he rolled off the side of the road onto his belly. Braving a glance, he sat up. The taillights gradually vanished into the distance, carrying with them the fading rumble of the diesel engine.

It left behind only the serene symphony of chirping crickets and the occasional hoot of an owl. With his night-vision goggles, he peered into the woods to a thick growth of young sycamore trees. Eyeing a sufficient place for cover, he stepped into the woodland. From his pack, he retrieved his satellite phone and called his boss.

"Mike Brennan."

"It's me."

"About fucking time I heard from you. Where the hell are you?"

"Belarus."

"Belarus? What in God's name are you doing there? The last time I talked to you; you were on your way to Slovenia. What made you go there?"

"It's a complicated story, but listen. Lots of things have changed."

"Such as?"

"Al-Hamwi is dead and the Belarussian Prime Minister killed him." There was a pause on the other end of the phone. Blake checked to make sure he hadn't lost the connection. "Did you hear me?"

"Yes, I'm here. I'm trying to figure out what he and Al-Hamwi have in common. Why would they be doing business?"

"From what I gathered, he hired Al-Hamwi to get the weapons and bring them to him. The question I have now is what is he going to use them for?"

They threw ideas back and forth at each other for a couple of minutes.

"Okay, well, this is going nowhere. It's still early evening here, so I'll make some calls and see what I can uncover. You're *sure* it was the prime minister?"

"Affirmative. I took pictures and used the facial recognition database. The PM was there and so was his first deputy."

"Okay, is there anything else?"

Blake pondered for a moment. "Yeah. He mentioned Operation Spear Garden."

"OK. We'll keep an ear out for any chatter mentioning it. I think you need to find transportation and get to Minsk. I'll call you as soon as I have something."

He studied his GPS and scanned the area for the nearest village. Astravyets was a town of about ten thousand people, twenty-six kilometers away. He made it his destination for the night. He would worry about Minsk in the morning.

38

Astravyets, Belarus
   July 1st
   07:50 local (04:40 GMT)

Blake awoke with a crick in his neck. The dirt floor in the shed he'd found provided little comfort. He cracked the door and a dusty beam of light shone through the thin opening. A spotted crake called and echoed over the lake nearby. A flannel shirt hung from a rusty nail on the far wall.

His all black attire wouldn't be the best thing to stroll around in. He whacked the shirt a few times and more dust dissipated into the air. A dead spider dropped to the ground. Flinging his pack over his shoulder, he left the shed.

After a short walk into town, he found a men's clothier in the middle of the block. A bell above the door rang as he stepped inside, and an older woman came out behind a row of almost bare wooden shelves. The old wood floors creaked as she approached. She welcomed him. *"Dobry dzień."*

He smiled at her. "Do you speak English?"

"Little."

"I need some new clothes. Can you help me?"

She nodded. A kind smile creased her face. "American?"

"Canadian."

"You are in Belarus, because?"

"It's for a documentary on the plight of the Belarussian people and how it's the last dictatorship in Europe."

She wagged a finger at him. "Careful. KGB is all places." She opened her arms. "You see, I have little."

She said something else but stopped. He suspected it could be out of fear. Instead, she waved him back to the little inventory she had. "Come, let us see if we can find you something."

Thirty minutes later, he changed into his clothes and purchased them with euros because she didn't take credit cards. At first, she refused the euros, but when he handed her more than twice the value of his garments, she accepted.

"Thank you for your help. Can you tell me if there is a place where I can hire a car?"

She gestured to his left. "Three blocks. But they are old. Junk."

He grinned. "It's okay. What about breakfast?"

Her brow furrowed.

"Uh—*Zaftrak?*"

"So, you speak Russian?"

"Yes, Ma'am."

A shaky hand pointed. "Around the corner that way. There is a café."

"Spasibo."

She smiled as he walked to the door. "It is *Sniadanak* in Belarus,"

After he finished his meal, he found the auto rental business. It was as the old woman said. They had four cars and one bus to choose from. Two of them were Volga's from the mid-eighties, which were known for their horrific reliability.

Third was a late nineties Fiat Panda and the last one was early eighties, a light blue Mercedes 300D. It had dented doors and mismatched wheels and its diesel engine belched black smoke, but it appeared to be strong enough for the short ride into Minsk.

Blake drove the one hundred and forty kilometers to his destination and checked himself into one of the best hotels the city offered. The Hotel Belarus was in the center and on the banks of the Svislach River.

The Executive Suite was vast, with Persian rugs covering the marble floors and a huge leather couch spread out almost as broad as the room in between the two fireplaces. A massive bookshelf was like a library, with books ranging from Russian poetry by Tolstoy to American classics, like *Gone with the Wind* and *Moby Dick.*

Double French doors led out to a balcony stretching the length of the two-room suite. He stepped out and took in the city's view. A glance at his watch revealed it would be a while before he heard from Mike. He considered that exploring the city to familiarize himself would be a productive use of his time. Perhaps he could also gather some information about the Belarusian interest in the weapons.

Families crowded the streets with cars and people on sidewalks as he made his way to the presidential palace on Pobedetelei Avenue, then to the president's office at The Palace of the Republic on Oktabratska Square. Touring the Partizansky, Central districts and other government buildings.

Hoping as he toured, it would clear his mind and give him some kind of idea of what the prime minister was planning. After a few hours, he relaxed at a café, admiring the enthusiasm of the people as they decorated the streets for Independence Day. On his way back to the hotel, he passed through Victory Square. They had erected an enormous stage in the center.

Upon entering, he stepped to the concierge's desk. A young woman with black straight hair and bangs sat behind the desk. Her hair accentuated her high cheekbones and her bright red lipstick highlighted her white teeth as she smiled. He leaned against the tall counter. "Hi, there."

"Yes, sir? How can I help you?"

He motioned with his arm. "Are all the decorations outside for Independence Day?"

"Yes, sir. It is in two days."

"Right. What's the stage in Victory Square for?"

"President Solonovich speaks there every year."

Ah ha!

He could almost feel it when the epiphany hit. "Right. Thanks."

He picked up his pace on the way to the elevator. Once on his floor, he ran along the empty hallway to his room; his phone was already out, and he pressed *call* as soon as he stepped into his room.

It was only 06:30 back home, but Mike answered immediately.

"Hey, glad you called. We're having a meeting with POTUS. The Joint Chiefs, Directors Slocum, and Thomas are all here as well. I'm putting you on speaker. Hold on."

After the brief pause, he continued. "Go ahead, Blake."

"Good morning, Madam President—everyone."

Her voice came over the line. "Mr. MacKay, Mike has filled us in on what you have told him so far. Do you have any further information else?"

"Yes, I do. This is only a hypothesis, but I think Prime Minister Shorets is planning to assassinate President Solonovich and then blame it on Al-Hamwi. I don't know his plan or have anything definitive yet."

There was a moment's silence. "Can you get proof to support this assumption?"

"It's something I'm working on. There's a definite connection with the stolen metal storm weapons and Al-Hamwi, but I want to get closer to the PM."

Director Thomas broke in. "I have an idea, but I need to make a quick call first. If it is all right with the president, I'd like to step out. It shouldn't take more than a few moments."

She nodded and waved him away. "Go ahead." The sound of the chair shuffling and the click of the door heralded him leaving the room.

Pennington returned her attention to him. "Can you describe to us what you saw and heard when you eavesdropped on the PM and Al-Hamwi?"

"Yes, Ma'am."

He described the meeting Shorets had with the terrorist leader. He explained the men hiding in the woods and the description Al-Hamwi gave about the weapon.

He told them how Shorets' people killed them all and took the weapons to the nuclear power plant and how he overheard the mention of Operation Spear Garden. As he finished, the sound of the door indicated someone had entered the room.

"Blake, this is Julian. We can find a solution for you. The prime minister hosts an invitation only party at his home on the eve of each Independence Day. There are all kinds of dignitaries from around the world coming."

"The call I made was to Canadian Intelligence. They've got much better diplomatic relations with the Belarusians than we do, and I've planned to get you an invite. You'll be going as the new minister for International Cooperation."

Blake chuckled. "Is it a proper position?"

"Yes, you would be responsible for overseeing the Canadian international development strategy. This is perfect because it is a brand-new post; so new, in fact, the Canadians haven't filled it yet. It will make building your background cover simple. But there's one more thing. You'll need to complete one tiny mission prior to going."

Blake's forehead creased. "Ok, what is it?"

"You're going to have to find a date."

There was brief laughter coming from everyone in the room. After it died down, a smile tugged at his lips. "Seriously, is it required or something?"

"Yes. The prime minister insists it is for dignitaries and one other. It's unavoidable. We suspect it is so he can do full background checks on both people attending. If you have to build a believable dossier on one person, it's relatively simple."

Julien cleared his throat. "Two people is more difficult. They have to appear to have been together and in a relationship for years. We don't have any female field agents anywhere near you that we could get there in time, so I'm afraid you're on your own. I know you have connections all over the world. Don't you have a relationship with someone in Mossad?"

Blake pondered the question for a second. "Yes, but I may have a better idea."

#

Pennington frowned. "This is most unconventional. I don't like this. Are you telling me we don't have any women assets within a day's travel?"

Veronica caught the Pennington's eye. "Madam President, we do have operatives in the area, but based on their current mission status, there is no way to get them away. It would compromise them and their current objective. I know this is out of the ordinary, but I can assure you this won't be a problem. We've used connections from foreign intelligence agencies many times in the past. Our people work well with others for these types of situations."

#

There was a brief moment of silence, and he hoped POTUS wouldn't shoot down the idea. He knew who he was going to get and was looking forward to it.

"Blake, this is Mike. Let us know who you get to be your escort. We can build a full background on both of you. Julian, are there specific details necessary for him?"

"None I can think of. Again, since this is a new position, we have a blank slate to work with."

He received the particulars of his contact; where and when to meet him to get his invitation. As the call was winding down, POTUS chimed in.

"Mr. MacKay, I know this is unconventional, but I feel it is necessary, given the circumstances. If a situation arises where you need immediate action, don't hesitate to contact me or my head of staff at the Secret Service. Understood?"

"Yes, thank you."

"The best of luck, Mr. MacKay."

The line went dead.

Blake dialed his pilot, Randy.

"Hey. What's up?"

"A lot. Bring the girl to Minsk."

39

Minsk, Belarus
  July 1st
  13:30 local (12:30 GMT)

The plane landed next to the old Mercedes. Blake's stomach turned with butterflies, giddy like a schoolboy. It had been a while since he experienced this emotion. It made him wonder if he loved her, or if it was because he couldn't remember being in a relationship for so long.

Stop thinking about this and focus on what needs to be done.

The engine shut off, and he waited for the door to open and her to descend the stairs. As soon as she did, he stepped out of the car to greet her.

"Well, hope you're happy." Her brows lifted.

"What? I promised I'd contact you and did. What's the matter?"

A wry smile accompanied her narrowed eyes. "Is it not obvious?"

Blake shrugged, puzzled by her response.

"After telling me you're coming, you jump out of the plane and tell me you'll call. For a day, nothing." She sighed and folded her arms.

He stared at her, chewing his lip, then opened his mouth to speak, but the words stuck.

"I didn't know if you were OK, or if you were lying dead in a ditch somewhere. Next, one of your pilot friends suggests I pack—I'm taking you to Minsk. How dare you ask what's the matter!"

She clamped her teeth in frustration and anger; her face turning red as she glared at him.

"Won't you say something?"

His lips curled as he struggled to suppress a smile. "You worried about me? You missed me." His eyebrows arched.

Adriana scoffed. "Ah, you're incorrigible." She brushed past him, opened the car door, and plopped into the passenger side.

He slid into the driver's seat and closed the door. Imagining her in different clothes, he stared at her for a moment. "Do you like shopping?"

Her gaze fixed straight ahead. Ignoring him.

"You like neat things, don't you? Stylish shoes, elegant dress—jewelry?"

She turned to him and smiled. "If you're trying to buy my acceptance of your apology, you should understand, I'm not materialistic."

He sighed and started the vehicle.

Shit.

"Come on, we've got some errands to do. I'll explain on the drive."

Traffic was heavy, and cars were bumper to bumper on the busy road. He weaved in and out of lanes, attempting to get to the square faster. He rolled his eyes and groaned as he tapped his fingers on the steering wheel. For a country in such dire economic straits, it still had its fair share of money. At street level, it's an attractive urban setting, but underground, the Stolica outlet mall shone with a vibrant light display.

Blake liked Versace, Gucci, Coach, Cartier, and Van Cleef & Arpels and he suspected she would too.

"We have a date with the prime minister."

As she turned to him, she raised her eyebrows. "How did you

arrange that?"

"I've been working on it for a while. Don't worry, we won't let the opportunity pass by. He purchased the weapon from Al-Hamwi."

"What does he want from it?"

"I'm not sure yet, but I think he's going to use it to stage a terrorist attack."

"An attack? On his own people? What for?"

"Well, that's what it'll look like."

Adriana swallowed and fidgeted in her seat.

He could tell she was upset. "The terrorist *thing* is a smokescreen for his plan to assassinate President Solonovich. And then he'll blame it all on Al-Hamwi."

"What happened to him?"

"Dead. They shot and killed him and his men when they delivered the weapon."

"Are you sure?"

He faced her. "Oh yeah. I saw it."

She shook her head. "So, what do we do next?"

"He throws a grand party on Independence Day every year. Several dignitaries are present, including you and me."

"But we're not dignitaries."

"Yes, we are. Well, at least I am. As Minister of International Cooperation, I represent the Canadian government."

"And who am I?"

Blake turned into the underground garage. "You, my dear— you are my smoking hot wife." He spotted her cheeks flush, and her smile.

She placed her palm on his thigh. "Sorry to break it to you, but I don't fit the profile. My Canadian accent isn't perfect."

He pulled into a parking spot.

"We've already taken care of that and built a dossier on you and your past."

"You have?"

"Yes. Your family escaped Cuba when you were sixteen. Your father wanted to relocate as far north as possible. He and the rest of your family settled in Vancouver, where we met, fell in love and got married.”

Adriana uncrossed her legs.

“They’ll send detailed files later for reading. I have a full history too, which I’m sure they’ll focus on, but we *both* need to read it and memorize it perfectly.”

“Oh, so what are we doing here at the mall?”

“Your job is to be stunning and keep the security team’s eyes on you. I will slip away and try to prove my suspicions.” He opened the car door. “Ready to shop?”

She sparkled in an off-shoulder, bright red Versace dress that hugged her curvaceous body like a glove.

With donned Ferragamo heels, a Gucci clutch and a sable shawl, she would wow the guests.

As she walked out of the dressing room, Blake’s eyes lit up.

He reached over with a trembling hand and gifted her with a single strand of pearls, ruby earrings, and a tennis bracelet.

To finish the outfit, he slid on her tiny wrist a Cartier watch and smiled. “Now, we’re ready.”

While the sales associates pawed all over her, thinking about their commissions, he witnessed her light up as she admired her stylish wardrobe for the first time.

Blake didn’t spend as much and purchased an Armani tuxedo and shoes. The bill was just under seventy thousand dollars. *The company* paid, of course.

After their shopping spree, they had a late lunch and strolled leisurely back to the hotel. A quick call to the concierge and he organized for a car to pick them up later that night for dinner.

Adriana placed her bags on the bed, turned around, and stepped toward him. She slid her arms around his waist and kissed him on the cheek.

She smiled. “What can we do for the rest of the day?”

He glanced at his watch. I’m heading out to get our invitations. “Stay here and relax. I’ve arranged for a limo to take us to a restaurant this evening. There’s a lovely quiet place right on the river.”

“It sounds perfect. I’ll take a bath while you’re gone.” She kissed him again, turned away, and disappeared into the bathroom.

He admired her curves as she closed the door and imagined her undressing before slipping into the bathtub.

Wow!

He shook the thought from his mind and left the room.

Blake located the meeting spot, a typical Belarusian sidewalk café with seating inside and out. He arrived early and sat at a corner table, watching the patrons. He didn't want his back to the door while waiting for his contact.

The crowd was a diverse group; from old to young, families to singles. The beautiful language and vibrant atmosphere, which he had not expected, struck him. His stomach growled as the steaming cooked food aroma wafted through the air.

After ten minutes, a man wearing a colorful shirt and matching hat appeared. He had a long, dark beard, and he carried a small bag under one arm. "Hey fella, do you know where to get a Bud Light?"

"Why would you drink such swill?"

"Perhaps you can recommend something?"

"The Alexandria is not bad. It's what I'm drinking."

Satisfied with the verbal confirmation, the man handed Blake an envelope and left. Inside was an invitation to *Mr. & Mrs. Dan Peart.* He slid it back into the cover and sipped his beer. For the first time, bringing Adriana into a secret world weighed on him.

She would have to play her part to perfection. One slip, one mistake could mean disaster for not only her, but for the entire mission. Were his affections for her getting in the way? Would he have the same ideas if another woman took her place? A trained asset or agent? One last gulp and his beer was empty.

The walk back to the hotel took longer than he expected. His thoughts drifted to this woman who had come back into his life. He'd felt the odd tingles and numbness months ago, but now she's with him. It's even more touching after admitting to killing her father.

Adriana's mind and heart were unlike any he had ever encountered before. The fact she forgave him spoke volumes about her character. And, to top it off, she was gorgeous.

Upon Blake's arrival, he found her wearing clothes he had purchased for dinner. The off-cut white blouse she wore accentuated her breasts, leaving just enough cleavage to spark his imagination. A loose-fitting, short black skirt cascaded over her well- shaped rear.

Her tan, shapely legs completed his image of the quintessential woman. She was the prettiest woman he'd ever seen. He felt the strange emotion again and realized with a start that he was in love.

"Wow!"

She spun around. "Like it?"

His jaw dropped, and he gasped. "You... Wow! Fantastic."

"Thank you."

"I recommend a sweater, though. It might get cooler this evening. Give me ten minutes to change and we'll go."

The enchanting restaurant was filled with classical music sounds. The walls were painted red, and the furniture was dark wood. They sat surrounded by a vibrant atmosphere, and the river view was breathtaking.

As they were still satisfied from their late lunch and the bottle of wine, they shared a meal. After dinner, they strolled along the bank and found a bench to sit on.

His fears swelled inside him, but he needed to ask. "So, what are you thinking now that you've discovered all these things about your father and your mother?"

Her chin dipped toward the bench. She brushed her hair back over her ear to reveal an earring Blake had purchased for her earlier in the day.

"I appreciate you asking." A smile creased her lips. "The way my mother raised me, before—before my father did what he did — was to forgive those who did terrible things."

Tears welled up in her eyes. "I forgave you. There are people in this world who would hate you for what you did, but... You had to do it. One day I'll absolve my father, but it's going to take some more time."

He put his hand on hers. "I'm sorry."

"Thanks." She cleared her throat and straightened up. Her eyes met his. "What about you? Are your parents still alive?

Do you have any brothers or sisters?”

“I’m an only child. My father was born in a village east of Loch Ness, in Scotland. He migrated to the United States when he was three.

“And your mother?”

“She’s a full-blooded Lakota Sioux.”

“Oh,   so it explains   where you got your dark,   exotic appearance.”

His face warmed. *Am I blushing?*

“I suppose. She grew up poor on a reservation in North Dakota. My grandmother passed away giving birth and my grandfather was a drunk. He abused her until he died of liver and kidney problems.”

Adriana placed a gentle hand on his cheek. “I’m so sorry.”

“Thanks. Her grandmother raised her, then she enrolled in college, where she met my father.”

As they continued to converse, they learned more about each other. Blake shifted between his smile, lines deepening, and he hung on to her words while she talked. Stories from his past flowed out of him without restraint. He’d never been so at peace with a woman.

When they returned to the hotel, he ordered a bottle of champagne and Beluga caviar with crackers. They sat on the floor next to the fire, drank the bubbly, and ate caviar. He leaned in and kissed her on the neck and lips.

Making love to her was an entirely unique experience for him. Every touch and kiss were more intimate and emotional than anything he had ever encountered before. His emotions were overwhelming, and it felt as if he were in a dream.

40

Prime Minister Shoret's Residence
Minsk, Belarus
July 1st
21:12 local (18:12 GMT)

The bottle made a thud on the bar after Oleg helped himself to a shot of vodka. He gulped the spirit back and poured another. "It angers me when I can no longer purchase my favorite spirit."

The raunchy liquid burned a trail down his throat as he strolled over to his partner, who sat on the couch next to the fireplace. He stopped and placed his glass on the mantle. "There is a complication."

Aleksandr took a drag on his cigarette. "What's the problem? Were you unable to find the codes for the weapon?"

"Those were in his tablet, as I predicted. We brought the weapons online and ran the targeting sequence. This is a fresh issue."

"So, tell me, what is it?"

"It appears there is a spy in our midst."

Aleksandr's eyes widened. "From Solonovich? Has he found out?"

"No. It's an American. His name is Blake MacKay."

His colleague stubbed out his smoke and sprung to his feet. "How do you know this?"

He smiled and shook his head. "I have my sources. Trust me when I say they are credible. He observed everything last night when we met Al-Hamwi. But do not worry, I will put my plan into operation."

Aleksandr couldn't help but voice his concern. "He was there? How much information has he got? What is your strategy? You must be straight with me. Do not keep me in the dark!"

He sensed fear and anxiety in his comrade's tone. "Fair enough."

Aleksandr banged his palm on the table. "Who is it? What are you going to do?"

He waved him off. "It is better you remain unaware. Besides, I have initiated an approach. I've allowed for this American spy to attend our party here tomorrow night."

"What? Are you mad? You can't—"

He raised his hand. "Wrong! It's *exactly* what I am going to do. We are the spider, and he is the proverbial fly."

"You're setting a trap?"

"Indeed."

"What is it?"

"He'll arrive as Dan Peart from Canada. At some point, I expect him to slip away and sneak in here. There will be a laptop with bogus data on it sitting on my desktop. I'll leave it turned on and make it easy for him to locate my password and discover some duplicitous information. And when he does—we come in and get him. Problem solved." Oleg drank the last of his vodka, peered at the empty glass, and returned to the bar.

Aleksandr fished out a cigarette and lit it. "How did he find out? Suppose there are more of them?"

"There aren't. This agent was tracking Al-Hamwi and stumbled on to our plot. My contact in America has been trying to dispose of him for weeks, but this operative keeps surviving his traps."

Aleksandr frowned. "What gives you the idea we can handle him?"

A broad grin spread across Oleg's face. "Because the others were stupid fools. They underestimated him. We will not. Once we get him, we'll press him for any knowledge, then shoot him in the head. Done and finished. Questions?"

Aleksandr shook his head and took another drag off his cigarette.

"Excellent. Now go home. We have a hectic day tomorrow."

After Aleksandr left, he turned on his laptop and created a folder several layers deep and put in a few files for the American spy to see; not giving him any detailed information, but enough to make him think he'd hit the jackpot and throw him off the trail.

Finishing his trap, he went and poured another vodka. Oleg sipped his drink and closed his eyes. He smiled and returned to his computer. Leaning over the keyboard, he renamed the file.

Spear Garden

#

Hotel Belarus
   Minsk, Belarus
   July 2nd
   20:00 (17:00 GMT)

Blake and Adriana spent the day making love and reviewing all the aspects of his plan. For once, he had a renewed spirit in his life. The last two days with her had been some of the best he could remember.

Mike had sent over a dossier he had compiled for both of them. In the records were bogus magazine and newspaper articles they had placed on the web. The majority of them were about Blake's alias, Dan Peart, but she had to know her part as Havana equally well. They sat on the bed and quizzed each other on the specific details of their aliases.

"When the party is in full swing, and most of the guests have had several trips to the bar, I'll slip away to find the prime minister's office. The guest to guard ratio will be at its best then."

"What if they have guards right outside of it?"

"I'm expecting it, and that's probably when you'll come to play. It will be necessary to improvise once I discover what I have to work against. I've been in situations like this before. It's part of the job. We'll have to deal with the hand we're dealt."

Her nervousness showed as she wrung her hands. "What do you want me to do?"

A hand on her shoulder revealed how tense she was. He grasped her clammy hand.

"Hey, it's okay. Treat this like any other party you've been to. Strike up a conversation with Shorets to keep him occupied. If I need you for anything else, you'll know it. Now take three deep breaths and calm down."

He glanced at his watch. "Time to go. The car should be here any minute."

The black Mercedes Maybach stopped under the hotel's portico, and the doorman opened the door for Adriana. She wore the red Versace gown and all the accoutrements *The Company* purchased for her. He stepped in the other side, sat and turned to her, his eyes inspecting every inch of her curves. Her tan thigh teased through the split in the dress. Her cleavage invited the eyes, daring for a peek.

She touched her hair and the corner of her mouth curled up. "What?"

He shook his head. "One thing's for sure. There won't be any problem for you to get the guard's attention."

She blushed and kissed him on the cheek.

He opened the wine chiller sitting between the seats, pulled out the bottle, inspected it and whistled. "Well, the prime minister has excellent taste in champagne."

"What is it?"

"It's a ninety-five Clos du Mesnil; about twenty-four hundred bucks a bottle—and extremely rare."

As he skillfully uncorked it, a delightful pop resonated through the air. As he transferred the golden liquid into her glass, it effervesced with a joyful fizz. Wanting to savor the moment, he poured himself a small amount and took a few sips, making sure to keep his wits about him.

While she finished her drink, Blake reached into his jacket pocket and retrieved a micro ear communicator. Holding one between his thumb and index finger, he handed it to her. "Here. Put this in before we get there. At some point, I'll need to use you as a distraction so I can gain access to restricted areas. We can communicate using these."

"So, where is yours? I don't see it?"

He shook his head and tapped the head of the pin securing his boutonniere.

"You will hear me, but I won't hear you. So unless you want to look suspicious, don't try to talk to me. I didn't want to take any chances and have someone spot it in my ear. Your hair will conceal easily conceal yours."

After a fifteen-minute ride, they halted in front of the prime minister's residence. KGB guards were everywhere; obvious ones and those not so apparent to the untrained eye. A modicum of worry crept in. He had to be successful, but in the meantime, he, more than anything, wanted nothing untoward to happen to Adriana, should things go wrong.

Men opened the doors on both sides of the car for them. A queue had formed outside the entrance, as they had set a makeshift security screening up, causing a slight delay in entering the home.

KGB agents searched women's purses. They frisked the males, and guards scanned everyone with a metal detector before they were allowed inside. He expected this, and despite hating it, left his Glock back in the hotel room safe.

The only thing he carried was a tactical pen. However, with the cap off, it exposed a needle with a dose of propofol large enough to knock out a 350-pound human being.

Upon entering the house, they encountered a line of guests eagerly waiting to be greeted by the Prime Minister and his wife. He took the time to peer around and scan for cameras and where the guards might be located.

The foyer was a grand entrance with black and beige marble tiles laid out in a checker pattern. The floor's center contained the country's symbol comprising ribbons in their flag's colors, ears of wheat, a red star, along with a map of the country inlaid with different colored marble pieces.

To the Prime Minister's back, a twin curved staircase led upstairs to the residence. Multi-colored velvet ropes blocked access. A lone KGB guard stood in the middle.

He spotted the doorway to the Prime Minister's personal home office. He nudged her.

"Don't turn, but to your right, behind the double doors. That's his office."

"How do you know?"

"Instinct."

And Mike sent me the blueprints.

Their hosts greeted them. Blake extended his hand. "Hello, I'm Dan Peart, the Minister for International Cooperation. And this—"

Oleg stopped him and said, "Yes, Minister Peart. You were a last-minute addition to my guest list. I am pleased you could come."

A tiny alarm went off in Blake's head. What Oleg said was true, but he couldn't read the man's intent behind his statement. Was it only matter-of-fact? Or could it be a warning?

"We will speak in-depth later; I have some ideas to throw at you. "And…" His eyes danced up and down Adriana. Blake could only imagine what secret desires ran through the man's head. He could feel his ire rising. "…I am looking forward to speaking to your lovely wife and learning more about you both." He reached for her hand and brought it to his lips. After a gentle peck, his eyes met hers. "And your name is?"

She blushed. "Havana. It is an honor to meet you both."

"Ah, of course. How could I forget? The name means heaven, I believe."

She tilted her head as her lips curled into a gentle, reassuring smile. "Yes. It does."

"I thought so. In the meantime, please—go in, have some champagne, vodka, wine, whatever you like. We'll be serving dinner in about ninety minutes."

The pair walked toward the massive room. He sighed. "Glad

we got through that," he said under his breath.

She leaned into him, grasping his arm and put her lips as near to his as possible. "I think you should have completed my wardrobe with a ring."

He said nothing in return as they stepped into the party hall, but his mind wandered for a brief space of time. Was she someone he could marry? Images of her caring for their children entered his thoughts. Past meaningful conversations raced across his memory as if playing in fast motion. Memories of her kindness lapped against the front of his thoughts, like waves on the shore. He glanced down at her beautiful feet and moved up her body to her angelic eyes and a smile which would light up the room.

Absolutely.

There were well stocked bars on three sides of the room. Life-sized oil paintings of previous Prime Ministers and other historical political figures adorned the walls. Despite being marble, they covered the floors with ornate oriental rugs. They decorated the antique Victorian furniture with gilded accents and had a color scheme of reds and blues. Sky blue velvet curtains draped the windows with gold braided ropes holding them back. In the center of the room was an enormous table with hors d'oeuvres comprising seared tuna, caviar, fresh cheeses, and crackers.

"Well, you can stand around, but I'm hungry." She walked over and grabbed a plate. He followed, got some food and then sauntered aimlessly and mingled with the crowd.

After twenty minutes, he glanced at his watch. He'd seen countless empty wine and vodka bottles thrown into the trash behind the various bars in a room packed full of people. The Ambassador from Sweden had taken too much of an interest in Adriana. She peered over her shoulder to him and indicated she needed rescued.

He dismissed himself from his conversation, meandered over to her, placed his hand on her back, and leaned into her ear. "It's time."

He extended his hand to the man. "Hey, sorry Ambassador, but I need to steal her away for a moment."

They shook hands, and she offered her hand, which the

inebriated man grasped, bowed and kissed.

A nervous smile creased her lips. "Ambassador. Pleasure getting to know you."

"Not nearly as much as it was meeting you. We'll speak again."

The smile vanished as she turned with Blake to walk away. "Thanks."

"Yeah, you looked like you needed rescuing. How many times has your hand been kissed tonight?"

Adrianna giggled. "You're not jealous, are you?"

He scoffed and glanced back, only to catch the man's eyes locked on to her rear. "Of what, such a scrawny little shit? No. He looks like he spent too many hours in a sauna."

After weaving their way through the crowd, he leaned toward her. "I think I have an idea. There is a restroom back this way. It is in the main foyer, underneath the staircase. I'll walk you there and during the time you're in the ladies' room, I'm going to check out the guard and see how he acts when I engage him."

They reached the bathroom, and she stepped in as another guest came out. The guard at the front of the stairs turned around and watched him while she was in the water closet. He attempted to chat with him, but the guard remained silent and stoic. When she exited, they both walked toward him. He noticed the hardware under the man's jacket and took note.

Thirty minutes later, he leaned in close to her and told her what his plan was.

He tapped the tiny transmitter on the end of the pin attached to his boutonniere. "Radio check."

A simple nod is all she gave in return.

She positioned herself in front of the restroom door and fidgeted with her earring. Blake was around the corner, out of sight. Adjacent to him was a closet. Withdrawing his tactical pen, he removed the cap and stood ready for her to call the thug over.

Adriana grunted in frustration. Her eyes shifted in the direction of the KGB agent she hoped to lure into her trap. His back was still away from her.

He suppressed a laugh as he shook his head. "A little louder.

You're going to have to sell it."

She sneered a response he couldn't make out. Stomping her heel, she let out a deep growl. "Arrr! Dammit!" The huge oaf turned to her. "Hey you." She waved him over. "Can you help me find my earring?"

As he walked toward her, she pointed to her ear. "The back." She directed his attention to the floor near where Blake waited. "I think it rolled over there."

As the guard leaned over to assist her, Blake slid in and injected the drug directly into his target's jugular. He dropped to the ground with a thud.

"Come on. Grab his ankles. We'll put him in here."

She grabbed his legs and strained to lift him. "He's heavy."

He chuckled as he latched under the man's armpits. "You wanna swap sides?"

"Uh, no. Do we have to tie him up or anything?"

They carried him into the closet, stepped out, and closed the door.

He wiped his forehead. "No. He'll be out for hours."

Looking around to make sure nobody saw them; he placed his hand on the small of her back. "Okay, I need you to go back to the party and be seen. If anyone asks, I'm in the restroom."

She leaned in, pecked him on the cheek, and went back to make conversation.

He reached what he presumed was the prime minister's office door. As he expected, it was locked. He pulled out an electronic lock pick and jammed it into the keyhole.

It clicked, so he cracked the door, slipped inside, closed and relocked it.

He went to the computer on the desk. It was on, but it had a screen lock. The username was filled in, but the password was blank. He attempted various spellings of the Prime Minister's wife's name, substituting characters for letters that were close. Unsuccessful, he peered around the office and at Oleg's bar. He tried multiple variations of the spelling for vodka, replacing common symbols for Alpha characters. This was also without success. He rested his elbows on a calendar blotter. Scrawled in pen in the square for July 3rd was *Spear Garden.*

He typed it in. It didn't work.

Fuck!

As he stared into the words and thought of the different possibilities, he had an epiphany.

Oh, surely not.

As he lifted the blotter, a piece of paper was stuck to the bottom. He peeled it away and laughed to himself as the word Password0306 was written in Cyrillic.

After examining the computer for various spellings of the weapon, in English and in Cyrillic. He looked for the name of the ship Al-Hamwi brought the weapon over in. He hunted for Hieraniony.

Goddamnit! I know it's here.

Leaning back in the chair, he sighed and leaned into the pin head. "Go ahead and find Shorets and mingle with him."

Like the first flash of lightning from an approaching storm, it hit him. He typed *Spear Garden* into the search box. It returned one folder, buried three layers deep in the *Faxes Sent* directory.

He double-clicked it and inside were schematics and information on the weapon. There was a map of Minsk with buildings circled, plus a number of other folders. Pressed for time, instead of cloning the entire drive, he only wanted the one folder. From his pen, he removed the cap holding the USB drive and started to copy the files.

#

Oleg stood in the corner of the ballroom with several attendees when one of the KGB henchmen strolled over and whispered in his ear.

"He's gone into your office and has accessed the file."

His lips curled up in a broad smile. "Thank you."

He turned back to his guests. "My apologies. Something has arisen I must attend to. Please, help yourself to more food and refreshments. I'll be back soon."

He and the agent marched across the room. "Call the other

men. It's time to take care of our problem."

#

When the red light on the USB drive stopped flashing, Blake removed it and rose to his feet. The French doors burst open.

Oh shit!

"Minister Peart, tell me; what could you be doing in my office? Looking for the restroom? Maybe something else to drink? Or a fine cigar? None of those?"

He stood and thought about what he could say or do to get himself out of this situation.

I have no clue what to say.

He squinted and cocked his head. "Printing up my boarding pass?"

Oleg laughed. "At least you have a sense of humor, Mr. Peart." The Prime Minister's smile faded.

"Or should I say—Mr. MacKay?"

What the fuck?

"How do you know who I am?"

"I'll ask the questions, Mr. MacKay, and to be honest, right now I don't have any. Take him."

He flinched and readied for a fight as two men approached him.

"I wouldn't try it. I have men outside all the windows, and I've ordered them to shoot, on site, anyone coming through them. Surrender to my guards and it will be less painful for you."

Oleg spun around and started to leave when he stopped and turned back to Blake. "Oh, and I have to thank you. Miss Vasquez will fit perfectly into my plans."

"You so much as touch her and I'll kill you." Blake's anger grew as his threat fell on deaf ears. He despised the arrogant smirk rolling across Oleg's face as he left the room. "Do you hear me? You're a dead man!"

He struggled against the grasp of the two men holding him and doubled over when a hairy fist slammed into his gut.

Outside the office, he overheard Oleg tell his head guard, "Tie him up in the basement. Beat some sense into him tonight.

Tomorrow morning, shoot him in the head and dispose of the body. I'm taking the girl with me. I'll be leaving when the party is over. Drug her, so she'll be quiet until then."

The sense of urgency and the seriousness of his situation shot through him. Slowing his breathing to keep from panicking, he had until morning to figure out how to get away. Realizing he had a beating coming, he hoped he wouldn't be too injured to hinder his escape.

He kept an eye on the man who walked in. With a shaved head and dressed in all black. The brute approached him and got in his face.

"We will have fun with you tonight. Enjoy."

"Yeah? How about this!"

He head butted the man in the nose.

The man stumbled back, put his finger under his nostrils, and wiped the blood off his upper lip. His brow furrowed and he grit his teeth. He lunged in and punched Blake square in the nose, followed by three more to the gut.

He coughed twice and laughed.

"Is it all you've got?"

The guy delivered two hard blows to Blake's jaw. He stepped back again and kicked him in the center of his chest. The two guards let go as the bald one connected. He flew back and smashed the coffee table as he landed on it.

Blake rolled over and propped himself on his hands and knees. The swelling in his face had started already. The pain in his chest was overwhelming.

I made a mistake. I need my wits. This guy is going to kill me if—

A knee to the forehead and everything went dark.

41

Belarusian Nuclear Power Plant
  Astravets, Hrodna Voblast, Belarus
  July 3rd Independence Day
  02:15 local (July 2nd 23:15 GMT)

Oleg's car and entourage stopped at the rear entrance to the power plant. When they neared the gatehouse, a head rose from behind the glass, followed by fumbling to grab a rifle. The guard emerged, scrubbing his face before squaring his shoulders.

He approached the man. "We're here to retrieve the truck. Open the gate."

"Mr. Prime Minister, you're here late."

"Don't worry about it. Get the damn thing opened so we can get what we came for."

"I'm sorry, sir, I do not know which truck you are speaking of."

He fought the urge to slap the incompetent idiot. He took a deep breath to calm his nerves. "Do as you're told, and it's possible I won't tell your supervisor about your sleeping on the job!"

He lowered his head as he nodded. "Yes, of course."

The guard fumbled with the electronic controls and opened the gate. When he reappeared out of the gatehouse, Oleg confronted him. "Where is Doctor Sakevich?"

"I am not certain, but it is my understanding he and his team are busy going through all the pre-tests to bring the reactors online."

Oleg pointed toward the plant. "Is the garage door unlocked?"

"No, I'll have to use my key card."

"Do it, and afterwards I want you to find Dr. Sakevich and fetch him for me. Do you understand?"

"Certainly, sir."

He motioned to his entourage to follow them. The guard swiped his keycard, keyed in a six-digit pin, and the chunky steel door creaked upward. Once open, the vehicles drove in. "Now, go get the Doctor. Have him meet me here."

The man made to depart.

"Wait!"

"Yes?"

"Downstairs. There are some empty rooms. Are they locked?"

The guard's eyes drifted in thought.

"Never mind."

Imbecile!

He snapped his fingers. "Give me your keys."

The man fumbled through the keyring. His eyes widened when he found the one he was looking for. "Here. This one will work on all the doors."

The guard handed him the key before turning to leave. As the man turned out of sight, Oleg motioned for the first two men exiting the vehicle. They hustled to the rear. It had been a long time since he had drugged someone. He hoped he got the dose right.

They removed Adriana's limp body, checked her pulse and nodded to Oleg, confirming she was still alive.

"What do you want us to do with her?"

"Follow me."

The red *Not Operational* sign across the front of the elevator added to Oleg's frustration. *Dammit!* He opened a steel door leading to a staircase. They climbed down eight flights of stairs to a level still under construction. They scooted along a long hallway with doors on each side, every fifteen feet. At the third door, he opened the unlocked door to find an empty room.

"Put her in here."

They constructed the rooms from poured concrete, lined with lead and were more than half a meter thick. The henchmen placed her on the ground.

He tossed a nylon rope on the floor. "Bind her and gag her."

They bound Adriana's hands behind her back. The taller of the two straightened up. "What do you want me to gag her with?"

He stepped out of the room and strode to some scaffolding. He grabbed a roll of duct tape, strolled back, and threw it to the guard.

"Here."

The sound of tape being ripped echoed within the confined space as he wound it around her head. After ensuring that the restraints were secure to his satisfaction, they closed the door, also lined with impenetrable lead, effectively sealing her within a tomb. The audible click of the lock reverberated down the hallway, permeating the surrounding silence.

As they exited the stairwell, Dr. Sakevich was waiting by the limousine. Thoughts raced through his mind of what to say. Having the sentry retrieve him was the only way it could assure him no one would witness them unloading their prisoner from the trunk.

"Ah, Doctor Sakevich, how are you?"

"I am fine, sir, but with all due respect. We are extremely busy and are working hard to make sure we can bring the reactors online in time for tomorrow's ceremony. What can I do for you?"

I know that, you idiot.

"Of course you are. I'm sorry to have bothered you. You're doing a fine job here. I wanted to get a quick status update and you've given it to me. I apologize. Please."

He extended his arm, indicating he could leave. Dr. Sakevich thanked him, turned and jogged off.

Discreetly concealed at the rear of the garage, the men whom he had entrusted with the task had retrieved the truck and positioned it at the forefront of the line, ready for departure.

He waved over to the driver.

"Are you sure you know what to do with the cargo?"

"Yes, sir. We have the list of buildings and the placement locations within them."

"Excellent. We don't have much time, so we need to leave now."

He gave the man an envelope.

"The cards in there will grant you access to the different premises."

He pulled out the keys and removed one. He handed it to the tall guard, who had put Adriana in her cell.

"Here. You stay here and make sure she stays quiet. Give her water once she comes to, but nothing else. Understand?"

The man took the key and nodded.

Oleg glanced at his watch. "Hurry. We have less than eleven hours before Solonovich gives his—final speech."

#

Minsk, Belarus
Home of Prime Minister Shorets
08:30 (05:30 GMT)
July 3rd

Aleksandr dashed up the stairs, into the mansion, and descended to the basement where he found the American spy held captive. A lone sentry sat on a stool smoking a cigarette.

"You."

The man snapped to attention.

"Have you killed him yet?"

"No. We're waiting for him to regain consciousness to extract information from him."

"Did you get anything off of him prior to him passing out?"

"No. He didn't say a word. Took quite a beating too."

Alexandr rubbed the back of his neck. "The prime minister asked me to squeeze a little more out of him. Give me five minutes alone. We'll do the good guy, bad guy thing like they do on

American TV.”

The former Spetsnaz grinned. “I take it you’re the good one?”

Aleksandr grabbed the guard’s hand and inspected his bloodied and bruised knuckles. The guard smirked, took a final toke off his cigarette, and tossed it to the floor.

“I think you’ve already established that. Now open the damn door.”

He complied and slid off the stool to unlock the door.

“Stay here. I’ll call for you when I need you.”

When he saw the captured spy, he was hunched over in a chair. He didn’t know if he was asleep, passed out, or dead. He raised the man’s head. His eyes were swollen, and blood trailed from his nostrils. His nerves started to get to him, and he wondered how this American agent would react with what he was about to tell him.

“Mr. Mackay.”

Aleksandr patted Blake’s bruised cheeks.

“Mr. MacKay!”

He reached into his pocket and pulled out some smelling salts. He broke them and waved them under the prisoner’s nose.

#

The scent of ammonia jerked Blake back to consciousness. His head pounded and his jaw ached. He couldn’t ignore the metallic taste in his mouth as he spat out the blood from his swollen cheek. He wriggled in his chair, but the cuffs kept him seated. The room was one he didn’t recognize.

“Where am I?”

“You’re in the basement of the Prime Minister’s house.”

Through narrowed eyes and a clenched jaw, he lifted his head. “Just to warn you, when I get out of this, I plan to kill you.”

“Please! I’m trying to help you. Listen to me. I’m your only hope.”

Blake squinted. He tried to focus his vision. “I know you. You’re the first deputy prime minister. What are you doing here?”

“If you want any chance of escaping here and rescuing the girl, you'll hear me out."

His thoughts rushed to Adriana. Was she okay? Did they torture her? "What did you do to her?"

"Shorets isn't only planning on assassinating the president; he is going to kill thousands of our citizens to make it appear to be a terrorist attack."

"Exactly as I thought. He going to blame it on Al-Hamwi, right?"

"Yes. Correct! As much as I despise our dictator, I couldn't live with myself if all of those other people died. There will be families there, women and children. It would be terrible. You have to stop them!"

He studied the expression on the man's face before him, the worry in his eyes, the desperation in his voice.

He's telling the truth.

Blake nodded. "I'm a little tied up at present."

"Oh. Of course." Aleksandr withdrew a handcuff key out of his pocket. He unlocked one cuff on Blake's feet and hands.

"Hey how about the other one?"

"One moment." He pulled out a silenced Beretta 9mm.

"I'll put this in the small of your back. It's loaded and one is in the chamber. I told the guard I had to get some information and I would be the good cop, and when I needed him, he could come and be the bad guy."

Blake chuckled. "You watch too much American television. How many are there?"

"Three, perhaps five at the most. When you get out of here, you can take my car. Please don't kill my driver. He's a family man and doesn't know anything about this. You could throw him out of the vehicle. Are you ready?"

"What is he doing with the weapons?"

"All I know is the prime minister has placed them in a circular pattern, all facing the center of Victory Square."

I knew it! "It's where Solonovich gives his speech, right?"

"Yes."

"How can I disarm them? Do you have the codes?"

Aleksandr shook his head. "I do not. They are being controlled by some men Oleg recruited. I do not know who, though. They will be a long way from Victory Square and far from the power plant. I am sorry I cannot tell you more. He was somewhat limited in what he told me."

"What time does he give his speech?"

"Fourteen hundred."

"What time is it now?"

"Eight forty-five."

"Well, we're running out of time. Let's do this."

As he watched Aleksandr leave to retrieve the man outside, a smile creased his face. He was looking forward to returning the favor to the man who beat him earlier.

The *dumb Russian*, as he thought of him, came in and rolled his sleeves to his elbows as he stepped toward him, his lips curled, as he anticipated his enjoyment.

"You want more, huh? Stupid American."

As he drew back his fist, Blake yanked out the Beretta and placed a bullet in the middle of his assailant's forehead. Brains splattered on the wall. The man fell backward onto the marble floor with a thump.

He stretched out his hands. "Take these cuffs the rest of the way off."

After Blake's restraints were removed, he knelt and searched the guard. He pulled his pistol from his holster and handed it to Aleksandr.

"Do you know how to use this?"

Aleksandr cocked the gun. "Of course."

He grabbed his wallet and cell phone off a table and paused. He turned to Aleksandr.

"I've got a question for you, and I'm giving you one chance to tell me the truth. I'll know if you're lying to me, and I have no problem beating it out of you. Understand?"

The man nodded. "Yes, what is it?"

"How did the prime minister know who I was?"

"He said he had an American contact; someone deep in your intelligence. Shorets made a deal with him for licensing rights for western businesses once we took over the government."

"You said *him*. Are you sure it was a *he* and not a *she*?"

"I'm sorry, no. I suppose it could be a woman, but I do not know."

He studied Aleksandr and searched for a bead of sweat, a small twitch under his eye, the direction of his stare, any sudden movement. There were none.

Well, shit! That doesn't help me out too much.

"I believe you." he started toward the basement door.

Aleksandr stopped him. "Wait, there is more."

"Okay, let me have it."

"I understand it is this contact who also arranged for the sale of the weapon we now possess. I don't know anything else beyond that."

"Well, this keeps getting better. All right, are you ready to do this?"

"Yes."

The two men silently approached the staircase door and ascended the steps, their backs pressed against the wall. Slowly, they made their way to the top, reaching the main level and arriving in the foyer positioned behind the imposing curved staircases. Peeking around the corner, he observed two sentries stationed in the middle of the lobby. He raised two fingers, receiving a nod of understanding from Aleksandr. Taking a deep breath, he swiftly emerged, hiding.

In an instant, both guards collapsed lifelessly to the ground, caught off guard. Aleksandr followed closely behind him.

Outside the front of the house, a sentry peered through the window, quickly reaching for his weapon and cautiously advancing toward the door. Darting from the foyer toward the door, he dropped to his knees. As the door swung open, he discharged three rounds, sliding across the smooth marble surface. Two bullets found their mark in the guard's chest, while the third tore through his neck.

Suppressed gunfire echoed from behind him, causing him to spin around and aim his weapon. On the floor lay the lifeless body of the guard who had emerged from the ballroom. He turned back to face Aleksandr.

Aleksandr nodded. "I got him. He should be the last."

"Thanks." *Now you've earned my trust.*

They hurried to the Mercedes. Aleksandr told his driver to get out and surrender the car.

Blake stepped in, started it, and opened the window. "Where did they take the girl?"

"To the power plant. You know where it is?"

"Yes. Do you know if she's okay?"

"She's alive, but they have drugged her. Oleg knows she is the daughter of General Vasquez. Information he'll use as part of his cover up. He and I will be there giving a speech when they are activating the reactors. It will be the same time as the presidents."

"Fuck!" he rubbed his hands through his hair. "And you are *sure* you don't know any way to disarm the weapons?"

"I do not. Prime Minister Shorets is your best bet."

"Okay. We'll, maybe I'll think of something else on my way there. Thank you for your help."

He put the car in drive and tore off toward the plant.

42

Minsk, Belarus
  July 3rd
  08:50 local (05:50 GMT)

The combination of rubber burning and brakes pushed to their limit, filled the cabin and Blake's nostrils. Tires squealed unforgivingly as he fishtailed around another corner and gunned the engine. The power plant was one hundred kilometers away. His mind bounced back and forth to different ideas on how to stop Shorets and save Adriana, never settling on any one particular plan. He reached for his phone and dialed an old friend at the Secret Service. A tired voice answered.

"Tim, this is Blake. I need your help."

"Blake MacKay? Dude, it's like—one in the morning. What the fu—"

"Shut up and listen to me. I have to talk to POTUS—now! It's about an assassination attempt on the President of Belarus. I don't have her direct number on me. Can you assist me?"

He heard rustling on the other end, as Tim must have straightened himself in his bed. "Yeah. Hang on. Let me get in touch with someone at the White House. Hold on, I'll try to do a three-way call."

There was silence. A long twenty seconds later, his friend came back. "I've got Jeff Lyons on the line. Go ahead Jeff."

"Hello Mr. MacKay, how can I help?"

"I need to talk to POTUS now. She will know what this is about. It's urgent."

"I'm headed upstairs now."

From experience, He knew outside the president's residence doors, there was a call panel. Inside was a phone connected to a telephone next to her bed. Blake could hear Jeff talking to her as his anxiety rose. A few seconds later, the door opened, and Pennington answered.

"Yes, Mr. MacKay, I assume this is about your theory in Belarus."

"Correct, Madam President. There is going to be an assassination attempt on the Belarusian president and Prime Minister Shorets is behind it. He's placed the Metal Storm weapons in multiple buildings around the city and is planning on firing them when he gives his speech in Victory Square today at fourteen hundred, Belarus time."

"What time is it over there now?"

"It's almost nine o'clock."

"Okay. What do you want from us? Let me know, and I'll do my best to make it happen."

"I have to have an expert on this weapon, either someone from the DOD or the manufacturer. We must discover a way to deactivate them. There's got to be an override code or something,"

"Ok, I'll get on the phone to them and locate their specialist. We'll get him or her on the line and ring back as soon as we have something."

"Thanks."

"What's your current status?"

"I'm headed to the nuclear power plant, where the prime minister is."

"Okay. Stand down once you get there. Don't do anything until you hear back from me in person. Do you understand? The last thing I want to do is start an international crisis."

"Yes, Ma'am."

#

POTUS disconnected and turned to Jeff. "Assemble the Joint Chiefs, get the Secretary of defense, get my intelligence directors here and have them meet me in the war room. And for Christ's sake, find someone who knows something about the damn weapon!"

#

Blake opened the directions to the power plant on his cell phone's GPS. He drove through the Belarusian countryside and thought about kicking anyone's ass who harmed Adriana. His phone rang and pulled him from his thoughts. The clock on the dash indicated it had been twenty minutes since he spoke to POTUS.

"MacKay."

"Pennington. I have the Joint Chiefs, Secretary of Defense Price, Director Slocum and Colonel Sherwin Cloonan. He is the resident expert on the Metal Storm system."

"Thank you, Madam President, everyone. Colonel, how can we disable these weapons?"

The Colonel's voice was filled with frustration. "I hate to tell you this, but there are only two ways you can deactivate them. First is to send a revocation command to the computer controlling the firing. Or, the other is to find them and shut them down one at a time."

"Well, the second option is out of the question. We don't know where they're located. Is there a universal method to power them all off simultaneously?"

"No, every unit or network of them will have their own code, which is set by the individual who initially programmed them. There is no factory override."

As Blake's anger surged, he slammed his fist against the dashboard, convinced that the resounding thud reverberated through the phone. For a moment, he could hear them mulling around with other ideas. Veronica was the first person to speak.

"These things work on electricity, don't they? Why not kill the power in that section of the city?"

Cloonan expressed his reservations. "No director, Slocum, they are made to operate independent from anything else, out in the field. They all run on batteries."

Blake's voice was quizzical. "Colonel, what about an EMP burst?"

Veronica's interjection rose to almost a scream. "What?"

"An E. M. P. an electromagnetic pulse."

"I know what an EMP is, and it's crazy. It would put the country back into the Stone Age. Besides, where are we going to get an EMP generator in enough time? Think of something different."

Secretary Price chimed in, "In my opinion, director, that's an excellent idea."

A smile creased Blake's face.

The president sounded puzzled. "Explain."

"We have a miniature EMP generator we can attach to the bottom of a helicopter. It's directional, and we can adjust the strength of the pulse. We can zero in to as small as a thirty-five-meter radius or expand it out to as broad as three kilometers."

Veronica coughed. "But where do we have one of those we can get to Belarus in time?"

Secretary Price responded. "Germany. We have one at Ramstein."

Blake concentrated on the road as he spoke. "That's fantastic, Mr. Secretary, but we've still got to find an aircraft to put it on. As far as I know, the fastest helo you've got there is an Apache. They can only go about two hundred and thirty klicks an hour. If you stripped it, you could perhaps get two hundred and eighty from it. It's over fourteen hundred kilometers to Minsk. There isn't enough time."

Admiral Thomas Andrews, of the Joint Chiefs, cleared his throat. "I believe we have an answer to your problem."

The president sounded inquisitive. "We're listening, Admiral?"

"We've been cooperating with DARPA and four

manufacturers to develop a better veetol aircraft."

"Veetol, Admiral?"

"Sorry, Madam President, V. T. O. L., or vertical take off and landing. We're working with Sikorsky, Boeing, Aurora—"

"Get to your point."

"Apologies, Ma'am. To be concise, we have one of these planes currently stationed on the Ronald Reagan in the North Sea. It's the Boeing Phantom Swift, capable of exceeding speeds of seven hundred kilometers per hour. I can ensure its arrival at Ramstein in a timely manner. Allocate the necessary time for fitting the EMP generator, and it could reach Minsk within two hours."

"I thought those were scaled down, unmanned prototypes."

"The original ones were, Mr. MacKay, but the one on the carrier can take a pilot."

Pennington's tone conveyed a mix of skepticism and hope. "That sounds cutting it close. Admiral, make the call immediately. I want that aircraft in the air within fifteen minutes. Secretary Price, contact Germany and instruct them to prepare the device. As soon as the experimental aircraft arrives, it should be fitted with the generator without delay. Colonel, collaborate with Secretary Price to determine the appropriate burst size needed to disable the Metal Storm weapons and mitigate any other damage to the area. We must ensure the safety of innocent lives, even as we strive to remove Solonovich from office."

Blake heard the mumblings of agreement in the room.

Pennington voiced her uncertainty. "Mr. MacKay, does this sound like we've taken care of everything?"

"As far as the weapon goes, yes. However, I'm almost at the power plant. I can still try to find out who's in charge of detonating it, and if things don't go as planned on your end, we'll still have a backup."

"Keep us informed."

"Madam President, there will be a lot of KGB. I could use some help from our side."

"Understood. I'll put together something and get back to you. For now, stay where you are."

43

Blake made it to the power plant in record time. The diplomatic plates on the Mercedes afforded him the luxury of driving fast without the worry of being pulled over by the corrupt police. They wouldn't dare stop or detain someone this high in the government for fear of losing their job or their life. Besides, attempting to extort money from the driver in lieu of a ticket would be pointless.

He sped past the turnoff. About a kilometer later, he veered the vehicle off the road into a patch of trees. The distinctive ring of his phone filled the interior as he placed it into park.

"MacKay."

"This is President Pennington. I've got some help coming your way. It's a group of marines. They were out on maneuvers in the North Sea."

"From the Ronald Reagan?"

"Yes."

"ETA?"

"Which information do you prefer—the good, the bad, or the worse?"

Blake shook his head, exhaling a deep sigh. Stepping out of the car, he heard the sound of crunching tall grass beneath his feet. He leaned with his elbows on the roof. "Let's begin with the bad news first."

"Well, as you guessed, they're on the Reagan, so they're a considerable distance away. It's going to take some time to get there."

"What's the best info?"

"They're on a much faster plane. They're scheduled to jump in under three hours and land in the field across from where you're parked."

He glanced to the sky and snickered. "You've got a satellite on me, haven't you?"

"Indeed we do, so don't pick your nose."

There was laughter over the phone.

"Yeah, I'll bear it in mind if I have to take a piss."

Pennington chuckled. "Excellent. Oh—Do not approach the power plant until your backup arrives. I know you would probably like to do some reconnaissance, but stay back. We can give you intel later from the sat feed as you're going in with your team. Do we understand one another?"

"Yes, Ma'am."

"We'll keep a watch on you. Check in if there are any changes."

"Madam President, wait. You said you had bad news twice. Was there something else you needed to tell me?"

"Right. Thanks for reminding me. In all our efforts to figure out how to diffuse this predicament, we forgot about the obvious. Calling the president's office and letting them know what the situation is."

"So, what's the problem?"

"Their Independence Day is like Christmas over here. Everything is closed down. No one is answering any damn phones. Even our back-channel coms are quiet. I guess what I'm saying is they may meet you with some resistance. With the Belarusian

Government not knowing what's going on and the current state of affairs with our relations with them, it will appear to be an American invasion. You'll need to be diplomatic."

"Understood."

He had to wait until the president disconnected the call. It took some time to camouflage the car with branches. Once satisfied, he opened the back door and laid down to rest while he waited. It was pointless, though. His mind split its time between trying to diffuse an impending attack and wondering about Adriana. The next few hours were going to be difficult.

#

Adriana came to and found herself surrounded in pitch black. She was groggy and her brain was lethargic from the drug's lingering effect.

She didn't realize her feet and hands were bound until she tried to move them. Her heart raced and her chest tightened. Fear enveloped her like a thick fog descending upon a tranquil lake.

Desperation welled within her, compelling her to unleash a piercing scream, only to have it stifled by the merciless grip of duct tape wound tight around her head.

#

Oleg was speaking to Minister Litwin about the ceremony taking place in under two hours when he noticed the guard he'd assigned to watch the girl approaching. He gave him a brief nod and continued his conversation.

"Everything appears to be in position. You've done well. Now, please excuse me for a moment. I have some other business I need to attend to."

Litwin turned and walked away. Oleg motioned for the guard to come closer.

"What is it? Has she awakened?"

"Yes, sir. I could hear her stirring."

"Alright. Let's go have a chat with our guest."

The line of light pouring into the room illuminated the woman on the floor. She squinted as her eyes adjusted to the brightness. Oleg stepped over to her.

"I know you are frightened, but listen to me and you may leave here unharmed. In two hours and fifteen minutes, I have to deliver a speech to the people of Belarus. It will not be about this power plant, but of the horrific and unfortunate terrorist attack in Minsk. I will be delivering the speech as the new President of Belarus."

Adriana struggled to say something. Oleg motioned for the guard to remove her gag. As soon as he did, she spat out.

"You bastard! You don't think for a minute you're going to get away with this, do you? I know someone and he will bring a team here to come and get me, and when he does, he's going to kick your ass and your stupid plan will fall to pieces. Everyone will know about your scheme."

Oleg scrunched his lips with a smug smile and chuckled.

Her eyes narrowed. "What's so funny, asshole?"

"Oh, my dear, if you could hear yourself. Your mumblings are so cliché of a bad American action movie, but this time, there will be no hero to the rescue." He paused for a moment to allow her to process what he said.

"Who are the people going to believe? Huh? Their new president—or the daughter of the man who sold Al-Qaeda the weapon unleashed on the people of Belarus?"

Adriana's gaze bore into Oleg's soul, her eyes devoid of any flicker of life or emotion.

That's right. Let it sink in for a moment.

Oleg enjoyed seeing the panic and confusion in her eyes. He let it fester for a few seconds more.

"Yes, my dear. I know who you are. And it was your father, General Hector Vasquez, who sold the weapons to Al-Hamwi. It was kind of him to send his daughter along to make sure they were delivered. Too bad you got caught. All of Al-Hamwi's men will have died in their gallant fight after the attack, but you, my dear— you will be tried for your part in the assassination of President Solonovich and for terroristic acts against the people of Belarus. Each offense is punishable by death. And, unlike America, we carry out our sentences with immediate effect.”

“It doesn’t matter what you say. As soon as my friend gets here, he’ll stop your plans. The truth will come out.”

Oleg scoffed again. “Oh, yes—your friend. Mr. MacKay, I presume?”

He leaned into her and asked, “Did you not understand me earlier?”

She turned her head.

He glanced at his watch. “Oh well, no matter. My dear, I’m afraid your little situation is not going to play out. You see, by now, Mr. MacKay is rotting in a field somewhere.”

He witnessed the color drain from her face as he delivered the news.

“What?”

“Yes. Do you think I would keep someone as dangerous as him alive? He would be a detriment to my plan and try to stop it. I gave the order to have him shot this morning. He’s been dead for hours.”

Her eyes burned into him before dimming. When she must’ve realized he wasn’t lying, she blinked several times. Each time, her eyes were wetter until a lone tear trickled across her cheek.

Oleg exited the room and motioned for his guard to come close. “You can keep the gag off her for now, but if she starts to make noise, put it back on. After I give my speech, kill her. Take pictures as evidence and afterwards dispose of the body in a forest somewhere on the way back to Minsk.”

The huge guy nodded. “Yes, sir.”

As Oleg walked off, the guard closed the door and locked it. Oleg went back to go over the final preparations for the simulcast and to find out where his partner, Aleksandr was.

44

Minsk, Belarus
July 3rd
13:50 local (10:50 GMT)

Captain Sutton eased the stick back to clear a tower. After it flashed under his stubby wing, he descended back to a low fifty feet above the Earth's surface. At four hundred knots, the countryside went by in a blur. Still, he was visible from the ground, and to those he flew over. The strange noise and odd shape caused those below to stop and gaze upward.

He'd entered Belarusian airspace thirty minutes ago and was only a short distance away from his destination when he saw the tail of a MIG-29UB blow past him at his ten o'clock. Checking his six, he spotted the first MIG's partner shadowing him.

"Blackout to base."

"Go ahead, Blackout."

"I've got two enemy jets on my tail and I assume they aren't friendly. Please advise."

"Acknowledged, Blackout. Switch to the emergency frequency and determine if they're attempting to raise you."

Jamie switched frequencies.

"To the pilots flying around me, this is Captain Jamie Sutton of the United States Air Force. Acknowledge."

"Unidentified aircraft. You are in Belarusian airspace. Follow us or risk being shot down. Over."

"Negative. There is a critical situation. I'm have no weapons. I repeat. I am unarmed. There is a potential terrorist attack about to happen against your country. We're trying to reach someone from your government."

"Captain., what is black object on bottom of craft?"

"Listen, I don't have time to explain. We have credible information a surprise attack and an assassination attempt is going to be made on your president in less than five minutes. I can get my CO on the line with yours if you think it's necessary, but I need to get to Victory Square."

"Yes, we will speak to your commander once you have landed. I ask again, what is attached to your belly?"

He clenched a fist with his left hand and hit the side of his canopy. "Fuck!" He pressed his mic button and responded. "It will disable the weapons that are about to be used against your people. Your president speaks in only four minutes and as of now, we're three mikes out. We have to act now!"

"Land immediately or we will engage."

That ain't happening. "Roger."

He started the landing sequence. The blades tilted to start hovering. One of the jets flew overhead. As soon as it passed, Jamie pushed the throttle forward.

"Spynits'tsa! We will open fire. Stop now!"

Sorry guys, I know you're just doing your job, but I've got to do mine. He powered on the EMP generator. The Phantom Swifts maneuverability was his only advantage over the faster and heavier armed MIGs. The ducted fans on the ends of the wings rotated back to airplane mode. He stayed low. The skyline on the outskirts of Minsk came into view.

Using the buildings on either side as cover, he navigated the craft around different structures, trusting the MIG pilots wouldn't fire in the fear of large-scale collateral damage.

I've got to get them away from this populated area. Their demands for him to land fell on deaf ears as he changed the channel.

He turned to head back in the direction of the countryside. Both jets flew toward him. Tracers exited their gun barrels and sped at him. He banked hard right and imagined bullets ripping the pavement and across a stone building, hoping no one was hurt or killed.

Off to his three o-clock, the Belarusian pilots were turning towards him. He executed a sharp left turn with a steep bank angle. Alarms bells rang. They had him locked on. Any moment, they were going to fire. The green light for the weapon illuminated and caught his eye. Taking a deep breath, he prepared himself.

Selecting vertical flight, the Phantom Swift stopped. With precision, the craft turned one hundred and eighty degrees and tilted its nose skyward. Jamie fired the EMP.

The older MIG's didn't have electronic fuel controllers and would still function without electrical power. However, everything else on the planes would be disabled. Both jets ceased their aggressive maneuvers and a wry grin appeared on Jamie's face as he watched them disappear over the horizon.

#

Solonovich stood at attention on the podium as he stared stoically at the Belarusian flag. The Central Military Band played the national anthem while thousands sang along and waved banners and flags. As the music continued, he peered out over the record crowd of over forty-five thousand people. A strange aircraft shifted his eye. He leaned in to one of his generals and pointed into the air.

"What is that flying over there?"

"I do not know Mr. President. It isn't one of ours."

He gazed on in silent wonderment as the odd craft climbed to a higher elevation.

#

Captain Sutton navigated to the altitude required to make the pulse spread wide enough to take out all the weapons. The affected area would be three kilometers in diameter. Everything electronic within that zone would be useless and would devastate Minsk, but at least thousands of lives would be saved, including Solonovich.

Discharging the weapon earlier drained its power. It was now a matter of waiting until it was ready. Jamie shifted his eyes to the clock on the instrument panel and then back to the charging gauge. He was at sixty percent and had only one minute. His chest thumped and his breathing intensified as he watched the EMP's capacity indicator crawl to its maximum setting. "Come on, dammit!"

#

Near the Belarusian Nuclear Reactor
    13:35 (10:35 GMT)
    July 3rd

The Marines landed in the field, across the road from Blake, as the president had said. He double-timed through the tall grass to greet them and found the man in charge. The man approached him and extended his hand.

"Mr. Mackay, Greg Olsky. It's a pleasure to meet you. I've been told by POTUS herself to do whatever you say."

He shook the proffered hand. "Thank you, captain." He pointed. "The facility is about one klick down this road. You can see the tops of the cooling towers beyond those trees."

"Right, we all got an excellent bird's-eye view as we descended. We've been briefed, but if you have something to add, I'm all ears."

"Our mission is to apprehend the prime minister. He is the one behind the planned attack. We need to assume the Belarusian Government doesn't know anything about this yet. So, to the KGB and other soldiers guarding him, it's going to appear we're attacking them. We're going to be met with resistance."

"The rules of engagement?"

"Don't fire unless I give the order."

"Affirmative." He turned around toward one of his men. "Yo, Taco! Bring me that forty Mike-Mike."

A short, but stout young man sprinted forward and offered the captain an M16 with an M203 grenade launcher attached to the bottom.

"I didn't know what kind of firepower you had with you, so we brought you this. I trust it will be—" A wry grin creased his face. "Sufficient."

He accepted the weapon, loaded a round into the chamber, and returned the smile. "Yep. Do you have any spare mags?"

He gave him three additional magazines and half a dozen grenades.

"Thanks. Oh—and one final thing."

"Yes, sir?"

"If this goes sideways and they fire on us, try not to mortally wound them."

"Understood. I know POTUS is still trying to reach someone within the government to let them know about the situation."

He nodded and then waved them on to move as fast as they could.

After double-timing it, they came around the corner to reveal the massive facility. Cars littered every spot; busses and news vans also congregated outside the plant's main gate. He took out his binoculars and KGB and other military personnel stood near the front entrance. A band played the national anthem and the sound of people cheering filled the air. The captain approached him.

"Sir? What would be wrong with just walking casually up there and telling those men what's going on?"

He glanced at his watch. "It's almost fourteen hundred. Let me get POTUS on the line first and ask if she's made any progress."

As he reached into his pocket, his phone rang.

"MacKay."

"Blake, Pennington. I've been in touch with the Belarusian Government. They're allowing us to use the EMP, and they're working on getting Solonovich out of there asap."

"Who did you speak with?"

"Aleksandr Roshenko."

He paused a moment. *Could he be trusted?* He remembered how Aleksandr rescued him and then saved his life by taking out the guard back at the Prime Minister's house. Had he been a willing player in this plot in the beginning, or had he been drawn in unwillingly? Regardless, Blake needed to tell POTUS.

"Madam President." There was silence. "Madam President, are you there?"

He turned to his wrist and saw it was fourteen hundred.

"Mr. MacKay. Is everything all right?"

"The line went dead. I don't have a signal."

The captain reached into his upper pocket and pulled out his phone. "Yeah, I don't have one either. Do you think it's the plant blocking it?"

"No. We were going to stop the weapon by sending out a small EMP burst into the city. The spread was wide enough to take out a few cell relay towers. I've got a sat phone back in the car, but it's too late to go and get it. Do you have one?"

"Negative."

"Fuck. Alright captain, down the line. Shoulder weapons. Follow my move."

Blake and the Marines marched straight for the front gates. They all hoped the guards would listen to reason and Aleksandr Roshenko truly was on their side.

They got less than one hundred meters from the gate when the KGB and other men opened fire.

#

Minsk, Belarus
13:59:23 (10:59:23 GMT)
July 3rd

The clock on his instrument panel counted down the time. The EMP was at ninety-four percent. At this rate, he would have just seven seconds until the time when the Metal Storm weapons would unleash their rain of flying lead and grenades. Tick by tick, he stared at the screen. "Come on!" He put his thumb on the trigger. The light turned green.

He mashed the button and moved the front of the aircraft in a sweeping motion for maximum spread.

#

KGB agents rushed the staged. People in the crowd started to panic. Solonovich glanced up again at the strange airship.

"Come, Mr. President. We need to get you to safety."

"What's going—"

A single shot flew silently through the air; fired from a building over one kilometer away, on the opposite side of Gorky Park. It ripped through the president's chest and the body of the agent behind him. Both collapsed on the stage.

45

Outside Belarusian Nuclear Power Plant
    July 3rd
    14:04 local (11:04 GMT)

Blake and the marines scattered on the road for cover, keeping their weapons in a non-threatening position.

"Hold your fire!"

"Captain, do you have a white piece of cloth or something? I don't want there to be any misunderstanding about our intentions."

"I think we're past that, Mr. MacKay. He rolled onto his back and patted his vest pockets. "I ain't got shit." he turned to one of his men. "Lieutenant, tear off part of your t-shirt."

"It's green, sir." He reached into his hip pocket. "I do have a handkerchief, though." He pulled it out and handed it to the captain. "Don't worry, it's clean."

He took the white cloth and tied it to the barrel of his weapon. Bullets plinked on the ground in front of them.

As the makeshift flag waved in the air, the firing stopped. With a deep sigh, relief washed over him. He waved to the men. "Okay, let's move."

Everyone rose to their feet and started a calm walk toward the gate. As they got closer, one of the perimeter guards shouted.

"Stop!" came the order in English.

Blake raised his hands, his rifle in one of them, with the handkerchief fluttering from the barrel. He motioned for the rest of the team to do the same. "Please, we're here to help. We have important information. It's about an assassination attempt on your president. First Deputy Prime Minister Roshenko can verify it."

The guard dipped his chin to his mic on his shoulder and spoke into it.

A minute had passed and a half dozen more men came to the fence. The gate opened and the Belarusian soldiers, plus a handful of KGB, approached them.

He turned to the captain, while keeping his attention on the approaching force. He whispered. "Tell your guys to keep quiet. Sling their rifles, otherwise, this could get ugly."

As they approached them with their weapons drawn, Blake and the troops to his back remained calm and still. The man in charge put a finger to his nose and scratched. "Who are you? What are you doing here?"

"My name is Blake MacKay and I work for the U.S. Government. There is going to be an attempt on the president's life, and we have evidence your prime minister is behind it."

The soldier scoffed at him. "Shorets? Bah, ridiculous. He's been here all morning. What is your proof?"

"Call Roshenko. He'll verify it. We need to get your PM in custody. He is holding someone here prisoner, and I want to make sure he doesn't harm her."

Pulling on his goatee for a moment, he used his radio to contact someone. When he finished his conversation, he studied Blake with a discerning eye and gazed past at the men behind him.

"My commanding officer is calling Mr. Roshenko to confirm your story."

"Okay. In the meantime, can we proceed toward your prime minister?"

He started to move, but the agent pushed him back.

"No."

The Belarusian soldiers emphasized their control with a quick shake of their weapons. Some chambered rounds. A young soldier stepped within a few inches from him.

He stopped. "All right. We'll do it your way." He swiped the rifle away from the inexperienced warrior and slammed him in the head with the butt of the weapon. Blake then pulled the KGB man in close and turned him to face his comrades.

He pointed the gun at the other troops. Some were youngsters. By the whites of their eyes, he suspected they'd never been in a situation like this before and had no idea what to do. Being careful not to set one off who may have an itchy trigger finger, he leaned into the agent. "I'm sorry. I didn't catch your name."

"Ivan."

"Well. We don't have time to sit around. We'll have to go ahead and move inside."

The agent's radio chimed.

"Can I answer? It is my commanding officer."

He held onto the guy while he spoke with the caller. He ended the call and told his men to stand down. Once he saw the weapons lowered and the soldiers more at ease, he released him.

"So, my story checks out. Your CO talked to Roshenko?"

"Not exactly. There has been an attack in downtown Minsk. It was an EMP. Not all, but most cell towers are dead, and they can't reach Roshenko. My superior did confirm there was a strange aircraft in Minsk. He believed it to be the source of the pulse."

A hint of a smile tweaked the corner of his lips. "Prior to that, we were in communication with your President Pennington, and they did back up your claim." With an obvious frown, the man appeared saddened. "It is a sad day for Belarus. Follow me."

Blake and the marines followed the KGB agent and other soldiers in double-time to the front of the plant where Oleg Shorets was going to be giving his speech.

#

Oleg was uncomfortable. "Why aren't those monitors operating? Why can't we hear what's going on in Minsk?"

The technicians scrambled to find out why they lost their feed to Minsk. "Mr. Prime Minister, everything here is working as it should. Something must have happened there. We can't get hold of anyone there to tell us if something has gone wrong. No one is answering their phones."

Oleg thought the weapons had gone off and now the city was a war zone. Any moment, he would be getting the call notifying him Solonovich had been killed and a terrible terrorist attack had fallen upon the people of Belarus.

As president, he would take charge and work tirelessly to restore the country's former glory. His first act would be to show the images of the dead terrorists and let his people know there was swift justice, with no mercy for their atrocities.

He was about to yell at the technicians again when he saw over a dozen soldiers heading in his direction, followed by U.S. Marines and a man he didn't expect to see alive.

He jumped off the podium and raced toward the nearest KGB agent. He ripped his AN-94 assault rifle from his hands, pointed it at Blake, and began shooting. Bullets pelted the ground. A ricochet went through the head of a spectator. People screamed and overturned chairs as they ran. The Belarusian troops were the first to return fire. Two of the technicians dropped dead off the stage.

#

Blake kept his eye on Oleg as he disappeared into the plant.

He grasped Ivan's shoulder. "You get in touch with your people and let them know what the situation is. I'll handle Shorets. I think I know where he is going."

Ivan nodded. "I'll need one of my guys to go with you." He waved to one of his other men and ordered him to follow Blake. They ran into the facility.

When they entered, they heard the clank of feet upon the metal staircase.

"He's descending the stairs."

After only three steps, bullets plinked off the railing. The other agent returned fire with two short bursts.

"Hold on. He's got a prisoner, and we don't know where she's at." The man acknowledged as the sound of footsteps continued to echo from the stairwell.

They descended, skipping every other step. Once at the bottom, they turned to their left. "Dead end." Then, turning in the opposite direction, they followed a long hallway lined with doors on both sides.

"Careful."

They moved along the corridor, scanning for any sign of movement.

In front of them was a corner. He focused his attention on it. If anyplace was fine for an ambush, this was it. They were completely exposed.

Something moved ahead and to their right.

"Gun! Get down!"

He hit the ground as the Oleg began shooting. He returned fire and placed three rounds in the wall next to where the shots came from. As the weapon vanished around the corner, the sound of hurried footsteps echoed in his ears, fading into the distance.

He sprang to his feet and ran. "Come on." When he reached the corner, he heard nothing from the guard who followed him. He turned back and saw the man lying on his back. Blood pooled on the cold concrete by his head. He closed his eyes and let out a sigh.

With exaggerated care, he placed one foot before the other, progressing at an excruciatingly slow rate. A faint scream brought him to a halt. He listened. Another followed it. He increased his pace until he came to a metal door on his left. Reinforced, it had a steel frame with a second panel welded to the front. It appeared to be more like the door to a safe than a room.

He knelt on the right side of the door and tried the handle. It was unlocked. Another shriek came from inside. He opened the door a crack. A bullet ricocheted off the inside.

"Adriana?"

"Blake? Thank God, I'm in here!"

"Shut up!" Oleg backhanded her. "Open the door and I'll kill her."

"You don't want to do that." He paused. "Your first shot ricocheted. You're lucky it didn't come back and hit either of you."

"I'll shoot her in the head."

"Wait! Hang on a second."

He stood as he took a deep breath and pictured what side she could be on. Was Shorets left or right-handed?

"Don't come in! I'll kill her."

He could sense the desperation in his voice. "You won't have a hostage, then. There will be nothing to prevent me from killing you. Hold on one—"

With his rifle raised, he kicked the door open. He pointed it at his target. Oleg was standing at the far end of the room with Adriana in front of him. His weapon pressed to her temple."

"It's over, Shorets."

Oleg smirked, "You mean president, don't you, Mr. MacKay?"

He tilted his head. "I wouldn't be so sure about it."

"What are you talking about?"

"Remember when all of your screens went dark outside and you couldn't reach anyone in Minsk? It wasn't because your weapons made the devastation you intended, it's because we used an EMP to disable them. Everything electronic got fried too, I'm afraid; unfortunate collateral damage."

"You are lying!"

"I'm happy to say I'm not."

He didn't know if their plan had been a success or not. He hadn't received word from Pennington, or anyone else, and it would be a while since the EMP disrupted communications for miles around.

He raised his chin. "You must lower your weapon, let the girl go and take your punishment."

"I don't have to take anything; MacKay and I'm not letting her go. As of this moment, I am the President of Belarus. I'm going to walk out of this plant, and when I do, you will be arrested."

He glimpsed at Oleg's right leg. It was the only thing not protected by Adriana's body. "I have a proposition for you, Mr. Shorets."

The man's eyes narrowed as he smirked. "You are in no position to—"

Blake lowered the barrel of his rifle and pulled the trigger. A single shot blew through smashed Oleg's knee.

Backing into the wall, he emitted a piercing scream of terror. Adrianna slipped out of his grasp, veering to her left. Oleg, straining against the unyielding concrete supports, fought to remain upright, stifling the urge to collapse onto the ground.

Blake's jaw clenched. He hoisted his weapon, and without hesitation, discharged three rapid rounds, finding their mark in the center of the man's chest. The impact propelled him backward, slamming him back again. His gaze wandered, fading with each passing second, until life itself abandoned his eyes. Traces of blood marred the frigid floor, marking his descent as he slumped down, defeated.

Rushing to Blake, she found solace in his presence. Unsheathing his knife, he severed her bindings. Faint sounds of approaching footsteps echoed from the hallway. Though his every instinct urged him to embrace and console her, he pushed her away and stepped toward the dead man.

"What are you doing?"

"Looking for intel."

Searching Oleg's pockets, he retrieved a small notebook. He slipped it into his pocket as the KGB agents rushed into the room. He stood and raised his hands in the air until he saw Master Sergeant Olsky walk into the room, who was the first to speak.

"Everything is under control outside. First Deputy Roshenko is taking charge. We still haven't heard any word from Minsk."

He nodded. "And we aren't going to if the EMP went off. We'll have to drive to Lithuania to make sure we can get cell service. Nothing there should have been affected by the pulse. How far are we from the border?"

One of the KGB agents knew the answer. "You're fifty kilometers from Vilnius and less than thirty from the border."

"Okay. Thanks. I need a vehicle."

Aleksandr Roshenko walked into the room. "You can take the Prime Minister's car. He won't be needing it."

Blake stepped over to Roshenko and held out his hand. "I'm grateful for your help."

"My pleasure, Mr. MacKay. We were able to escape what would have been a tragic event for Belarus."

He nodded and turned to Adriana. He held out his hand, which she took. His gaze returned to the captain. "I'll be back soon to let you know what I've found out. It shouldn't be any more than ninety minutes."

The marine nodded. "We'll be waiting."

46

Near the Lithuanian Border
    July 3rd
    15:32 local (12:32 GMT)

Adriana drove while Blake thumbed through Oleg's notebook. Scribbled on the pages were jottings about the president's speech and where his podium was located.

Notes describing the presentation and the fanfare he and Aleksandr were to give at the power plant. There were different scribblings about when other parties were to start, contact names and numbers.

They all had to do with the Independence Day celebration. There was nothing incriminating about the supposed terrorist attack or his address as president after the assassination.

She kept her eyes on the road. "Have you found anything that can help you with your investigation?"

"Not yet. I'm still looking."

"We passed through the border ten minutes ago. Did you want me to stop?"

When the last Soviet soldier left Lithuania in August 1993, the State Border Guard Service was already well established. It took five years to establish treaties on delimitation with all of their neighboring countries.

In February 1996, after a considerable diplomatic effort, they signed a treaty between Lithuania and Belarus. Crossing the line on major highways was as simple as showing an ID. On country roads, a wave would usually be enough to cross, but there wasn't always someone on duty.

He had been studying the notebook with such focus he hadn't realized how the time had flown by. He pulled out his cell and called the number for POTUS. The reply took seconds. "This is Kendall Price speaking on behalf of President Pennington."

"This is Blake MacKay. I need to—"

"I'm putting you on speaker."

He heard the phone clunk as she placed it on the table.

The next voice was the president's. "I'm here with the Joint Chiefs and Directors Slocum, Thomas, and Brennan. Where are you and what's your status?"

"I'm in Lithuania, across the border from the power plant. I assume the EMP was a success since no one can communicate via cell in Belarus. All the relay towers in Minsk are down and have disrupted most of the communications."

"Yes, it was successful in stopping the attack. Were you able to apprehend Prime Minister Shorets?"

"No, Ma'am, he decided he wouldn't give up without a fight. It didn't end well for him."

"I understand. I'm afraid we have some more bad news."

"Go ahead."

"We are unsure if it was Shorets' backup plan or someone else, but the president was assassinated at fourteen hundred hours."

Blake's eyes widened. "What? How?"

"A sniper from the opposite side of Gorki Park shot him."

His thoughts turned to Roshenko. *Could this have been his idea all along? Could he have arranged for the sniper and to turn-in Prime Minister Shorets? He's third in line and now he will become president.*

His attention went back to searching through Oleg's notes. He searched for any clues when his boss, Mike Brennan, came on. "You did a fantastic job. We want you to come home now for a full debriefing. We need you here tomorrow."

He came to a page in the notebook, stopping him in his tracks. He felt the blood drain from his head. Veronica Slocum spoke. "When can we expect you?"

He glanced at the numbers and tried to remember where he'd seen them before. Veronica asked again, but firmer. "I repeat. When will you be back here?"

Stunned by the implications of what he suspected; he was oblivious to everything until a gentle hand caressed his leg. Adriana stared at him with a frown. Was he as pale as he felt? "Sorry, I can't make it. I have something to take care of first."

Veronica's voice came through like nails on a chalkboard. "I'm not asking. I'm ordering you to be back here tomorrow!"

#

The line went dead and Veronica stood from her chair and lost it. "Goddamnit! That did it! His ass is getting arrested when he gets home if he's not here on time." She pointed a red nailed finger at Mike's face. "Do you understand me, Director Brennan? No more protecting your boy. He has to learn to obey orders! He needs to follow protocol!"

President Pennington chastised her. "Director Slocum, I suggest you get control of yourself. Let's see where this leads us. He must think there is something warranting this, and I will wait to pass judgment until he returns. If he had obeyed your instructions to come to D.C. instead of going to Cuba, this entire scheme never would have been uncovered. If you can't handle this, I can, and *will*, find someone who can. Do I make myself clear?"

Veronica stared at her like a schoolgirl who had been scolded and turned to the others around the room. All eyes were on her. Her cheeks throbbed as the blood rushed to them from embarrassment. "Yes, Madam President. I apologize. Excuse me, please. I have some tasks I need to attend to."

The president nodded.

\#

While Veronica retrieved her things, the Chairman of the Joint Chiefs, General Andrew Thomas, excused himself from the room. He closed the double doors behind him and thought about the news he heard regarding the assassination of President Solonovich. A satisfied smile crossed his face as he entered an empty room and pulled out his encrypted cell. When the voice on the other end answered, only two words were needed. "It's done."

\#

Lithuanian Countryside
   15:50 (12:50 GMT)
   July 3rd

The effects of his anger seeped in. His temples throbbed and darkness crept around the edges of the notebook. "Stop the car! I need to drive."

"Why? What's the problem?"

She pulled to the side of the road, and they switched places. Before he made the tires kick up gravel in a wild turn back to the border of Belarus, he removed the battery from his phone.

"The other day you were asking me about some bank accounts in your father's journal, right?"

She nodded. "Yes."

"And I told you they were for a numbered account in Zurich. Well, I found similar Zurich accounts in Shoret's book."

"Okay. So what does it mean? I am sure there are thousands of people with Swiss accounts; especially people like the prime minister. What are you getting at?"

He drove hyper focused, like a rally driver looking ahead and anticipating his next move well before he got there. "Two of them were the same as those I found in your father's journal back in Cuba."

Adriana's brow remained furrowed.

"There were three letters at the side of each account. I think they are initials to someone's name, and they weren't those of Zahmir Al-Hamwi or of your father. When I was speaking POTUS, she informed me a lone sniper had assassinated Solonovich after they stopped the attack. There is more going on here than what we are aware of."

"Ok, so what are we going to do?"

"We're going to Zurich."

Blake abandoned the plan to go back to the power plant. He figured the marines and others would get the information about what happened in Minsk.

They were still wearing the clothes and scars from their long night in captivity, so they drove back to the hotel to take showers and get back on the road. As he pulled out on to the highway, he turned to her. "We're going to have to drive the whole way."

She clasped her hands together and leaned forward, awaiting a continuation, but one never came. "To Zurich? Why? How far is it?"

"Close to two thousand kilometers. I think I'm going to be in some deep shit for disobeying a direct order, and if we get on an aircraft or train, there is a fair chance they will force me to go back to Washington. I can't risk it."

"Why not take a commercial flight?"

"Because you, my dear, don't have a genuine or a false passport with you. However, if you did have one, they know you're here with me, and as soon as it's entered into the system, it would be flagged and our trip would be over. All of my fake ID's were concocted by them so…" He remembered an old friend who owed him a favor. It was time to redeem it.

"I have an idea."

On their way back to Minsk, he stopped for fuel. He bought a half dozen pre-paid cell phones. With one of them, he made a call.

"Who are you calling?"

He raised his index finger. "One minute."

Matt Sharp was an ex-Navy SEAL he had been on several missions with in Afghanistan, Nigeria, The Congo and a few other places they couldn't identify. It was the kind of relationship that just clicked whenever they first met. Although they would only see each other once or twice every other year, they remained close friends.

After Matt retired from the military, he started a private sector business doing dirty jobs for the DOD and the CIA when the government had to be hands off.

All their funding came from hidden slush funds, disguised pet projects, and seized assets from the terrorists they took out. In his dealings, Matt had made contacts all over the world. Any of them could provide services for about anything imaginable. Creating perfect fake identifications was one such service.

"Blake MacKay. How's my brother from another mother?"

"Not at my best right now, I'm afraid. I'm in a bit of a jam and require some assistance."

"Where the hell you calling from? Did I see a Belarus country-code on the caller ID?"

"Yeah. Can you help me? I'm in a hurry."

"What can I do for you, buddy?"

"Is this line still secure?"

"You know it, Bro."

"I have to get to Zurich ASAP. Do you have anyone nearby who can get me four fake passports? I need two for me and two for a woman."

Matt snickered. "Up to your tricks again, huh? Is she hot?"

"Dude! Not now."

"Did you give her a little tickle pickle?"

Blake extended his arm and looked at the phone. "Goddammit!" He took a deep breath and brought the phone back to his ear. "Matt! Can you fucking help me or not?"

Matt laughed out loud. "Of course you did." After he stopped laughing, he got serious. "Yeah, I can help. Can you get to Kiev?"

"Yes, we've got a car. We're driving now."

"Excellent! Get yourself there. I've got a guy there who produces the best fakes I've ever seen. Better than what we can do. I mean, they are flawless."

"Can I trust him?"

"Dude. Seriously?"

"Sorry I asked. Let me have the address? Don't text it."

He scribbled it in the notebook.

"Can you give your contact prior notice we're coming?"

"Will do."

He ended the conversation, then removed the battery and SIM card from the phone. As he did, he quoted a slogan he heard from an accident attorney's television commercial he saw when he was in Atlanta.

"One call, that's all."

He lowered the window and tossed the phone out. At the first opportunity, he turned for Kiev. At their present location, it was four hundred and fifty-three kilometers away. They made it in less than four hours.

By the time they arrived, the clock was nearing 23:00. He passed the address Matt had provided, only to find it shrouded in darkness, with its doors firmly shut. Ironically, the establishment turned out to be a printing shop reminiscent of popular chains like Kinko's or Office Max in the States. They found a bed & breakfast still lit up and got a room for the night.

#

Kiev, Ukraine
08:00 (05:00 GMT)
July 4th

The pair sat in the car sipping coffee, parked across the street from the printers. It was on a central thoroughfare in between a florist and store and an electronics retailer. A flicker of lights inside got Blake's attention. "Someone is there. Let's see if this guy is as clever as Matt says he is."

They stepped out of the vehicle and closed the doors. While they walked, he checked the surroundings to make sure they weren't being watched. Relieved, he breathed a muted sigh as they crossed the street. The door was still locked when they reached it, but a clerk ambled over and twisted a lock. He spoke Ukrainian. "Good morning. What can I help you with?"

Blake answered in Russian. "Hi, we're looking for Vadim. Is

he here? Do you speak English?"

"I have a little English. He is busy. Perhaps I—"

"Could you please tell him, friends of Casper's evil brother are here? He'll understand and will want to come right out."

He smiled at the guy while the young man stared back with a furrowed brow before walking to the back of the store.

Adriana scrunched her nose. "Casper?"

"Yeah, Matt got the nickname for his ability to sneak in and out of places unnoticed. He hated nicknames. Someone suggested it. *Casper, the friendly ghost,* is a cartoon character back in the States. Another buddy of mine said 'friendly' wasn't in Matt's DNA, so he came up with Casper's evil brother as an alternative and it kind of stuck."

She smiled and placed a gentle palm on his chest. "You know some strange people."

He shrugged. *You don't know the half of it.*

A man of about average height and boney features came from the rear of the store. He had dark hair cropped short, narrow eyes and high cheekbones, typical of someone from this part of the world. He walked with caution. No doubt he was sizing Blake up. "Can I be of assistance to you?"

"I'm a pal of Casper's evil brother and he said you could assist us with some passports."

It was obvious from Vadim's mannerisms and the expression of "fake confusion" this man was unsure of their intentions.

With weighted trepidation in his voice, he tilted his head to the left. "And who is Casper's evil brother?"

He understood his apprehension and got right to the point. "Matt Sharp. He said—"

Vadim raised his hand.

"It isn't necessary. He called me last night. Follow me."

He and Adriana followed him to the back of the store. He had them both sit for individual photos and afterwards, went to work.

"Mr. and Mrs. John Morgan, from Indianapolis, Indiana." Vadim handed them their first set of fakes. He inspected the passports. Blake had seen plenty of false ones in his years, and these were exceptional. As he thumbed through the book, Vadim leaned forward, placed his hands on the table, and took a moment to collect his thoughts before continuing.

"I've put stamps in there from the past and for this week. You entered Ukraine eight days ago. Perhaps you are on your honeymoon or an anniversary trip. I will finish with the others in a moment. Mr. MacKay, what other languages do you speak?"

Blake rattled them off. "German, Russian, Spanish, Pashtu and Farsi."

Ten minutes later, the forger returned with the other two passports. He passed the first to Blake. "Detlev Vogt from Düsseldorf, Germany." He handed the other to Adriana. "Maria Sanchez from Bogota, Columbia."

He was amazed at their quality and accuracy. "What will happen now when they are scanned?"

"Give me an hour and all four will be in the system. Those will be as real as any other passport. Now hold on for one minute. I have something else for you."

Vadim returned and gave him a set of credit cards, all with matching names to the IDs he created for them. It was a combination of Visa's, MasterCard's and American Express'. "These all work, but go easy on them. They're all backed by an account Matt has. Whatever you spend, you'll have to repay him."

He raised his hand and gestured with an open palm. "How much do we owe you?"

Vadim shook his head. "Nothing. I still owe Matt for some things he's done for me."

They thanked him again and Blake put the details of Vadim and his store in the back of his mind in case he needed his services anytime in the future.

They left the print shop and drove to Boryspil International Airport, the largest in Ukraine and twenty-nine kilometers east of Kiev.

After finding a spot in long-term parking, he took an exceptional amount of time to wipe down the car and eliminate any fingerprints. As of now, there was no reason to do this, but he had a habit of erasing his tracks.

Inside, they approached the ticket counter, and he leaned in close to her. "Well, now we'll see how well these passports work".

He told Adriana to use the passport for Mrs. Morgan and they rehearsed the answers to the typical questions security asks. They'd been here for pleasure on their five-year anniversary, they hadn't been on any farms and they weren't transporting any produce. He used the American Express to purchase two first-class tickets to Zurich.

A few stomach twisting minutes later, they were issued boarding passes and passed through security. Before getting on board, he purchased an Android tablet from an electronics vending machine in the terminal. After seated on the plane, he removed his tablet and started researching the Bank of Zurich.

He found out the bank was not the average Swiss bank. All banks in Switzerland were renowned for their strict policies for keeping their customers' information private, however he discovered with this one, the typical person couldn't walk in and open an account. They operated by "Invitation only", and it extended invitations to its entire clientele. It was also known as "The B."

Blake sighed and massaged his face with his eyes closed until a gentle hand rested on his knee. The woman he'd fallen in love with smiled at him.

"Are you okay? What's bothering you?

"Oh, it's everything. Someone who I am close to might not be the individual I thought he was. I have to discover the name of this person in Shoret's notebook and tie them to your father. That's why we're going to Zurich. I have to find a way to hack into one of the most secure banks in the world."

47

Blake used one of his burner phones and called a trusted friend who worked in the CIA's Swiss field office in Zurich.

Stuart Tuttle handled the financials for operations which needed to stay invisible. He would move money from different slush funds or pseudo projects to be utilized to buy weapons, equipment, distinct assets or pay off informants. Whatever the need, he could supply the cash. All the things he purchased for Adriana in Minsk came from this fund.

"Stuart, Blake MacKay. I'm asking for a favor."

"What now? Are you buying a Lamborghini or something?"

"Not quite. This is a tall order—and keep this between us."

"Right. Aren't they all?"

"I mean, this one is private—you and me only. Can you get me access to an account in the Bank of Zurich?"

"Whoa, Dude. That place is locked up tighter than a snake's asshole in ten feet of water. I can't get in there."

Blake sighed. "Shit. I knew it."

He rubbed his temples with his other hand. "Listen, I've got someone who is going to go in there to inquire about moving her cash over to them. Once my asset is inside, I will find a way to breach their system. But I must have a convincing amount parked somewhere to spark their interest. I want you to create an account, or rather, an illusion, of one in another bank we can move money from."

"You know their requirements, don't you?"

"I do. I think four hundred and fifty million will capture their attention."

"No way—I don't have access to funds that large."

"I said the *appearance* of. Can't you make some kind of ghost account, or something? I only need them to see it exists. We won't transfer it. I want something for them to verify so my asset can gain entry."

There was a brief pause on the line.

"Did you die on me? Hello?"

"No. I'm thinking."

"Well, think faster."

"Okay. I'll set up what you're calling a ghost account. I can reroute any inquiry from them with your asset's alias to a VM showing the data. What bank do you want it in?"

"Any notable one in Columbia."

"Alright. It's doable. But it will be for an odd amount. Four hundred and fifty-six million, followed by a bunch of random numbers after that. An even number is too convenient, and also not too realistic. This will make it more believable."

"Well, since you *can* set up a phony account, add a two in front."

"Two *billion*?" Stuart asked, as he drew out the word.

"Yeah! Why not? It needs to be enticing for them."

"No. I wouldn't do that. Ever heard of Forbes' Billionaires List or the Bloomberg Billionaires Index?"

"No."

"Well, mark my words, they have, and they probably have memorized every name on there. Someone coming in with a name they don't know isn't realistic and that alone will be suspicious."

Blake scrunched his nose and thought for a moment. "Yeah,

you've got a good point. Let's just keep it at four hundred mil."

"Okay. Actually, I'll make it for nine hundred. That will get their attention. This should be interesting. Now, how do you plan on getting access to their system?"

"I was hoping you'd have a suggestion."

A long sigh came through the earpiece. "I do. I've got a device—it can get into their network. It's wireless. However, you have to have it sitting on, or next to one of their machines hard-wired to their system. If you don't have it directly on the computer, it's got to be right beside it. I'm talking millimeters away."

"Okay. Do you have a drop point?"

"The train terminal in Zurich. There are restrooms adjacent to the lockers on the main level. In the last stall, the cover over the flush button comes out of the wall. I'll put it in there."

"I need a piece, too. Glock 23 if possible."

"Geez. Ok."

"Perfect. Now, the next thing."

"Fuck, there's more?"

"Yeah. It's gotta be done asap. As in, now."

Another deep sigh. "Fine. Give me an hour. Is that all right?"

"Excellent. I owe you. Oh, and Stuart?"

"What?"

"We never had this conversation."

"Got it."

Blake disconnected the call, took the phone apart, and threw it in the trash.

Two hours later, the two sat outside the bank in their rental car. It was located on Talstrasse, in the banking district of Zurich. It was a less than impressive building, as were many of the buildings in this part of the city. Standing five stories tall, it curved around the block adjacent to the road. Constructed in off-white with plain looking windows, all with blinds in a varying state of opened or closed.

He handed her the box he retrieved at the train station. It was about the size of a laptop hard drive.

"Here is the device I told you about. Once you get in, you're going to need to get this right beside, or on one of their wired computers."

She took the gadget and put it in her purse.

His thoughts drifted to their intimate time together as she smiled back.

"I know. You've explained all of this already."

"Listen, we can't make any mistakes. Now, you have to get this next to the computer *before* he or she logs in. This has a keyboard logger as well, and it's the only way I can get a password. You'll need to meet with someone with executive status."

"Okay. Anything else?"

"We've made a dummy account at the Banco de la República. It's got more than nine hundred million dollars in it. It's in the name of your alias, Maria Sanchez."

She cupped his cheek in her hand, gazing into his eyes with a reassuring smile. "Don't worry, baby. I've got this." She pressed her lips to his in a tender kiss. Then she swung her legs out of the car, her heels hitting the pavement.

He leaned over the center console before she closed the door. "Hey. I'll be listening in. When the time is right, I'll have Stuart fax the account information to the main fax number listed on their website. Got it?"

Returning a thumbs up for confirmation, she turned toward the main entrance.

She wore a white, form fitting dress, similar to the one she had worn to the party in Minsk. Blake watched her butt as she strode away and thought to himself how amazing she was. Once she disappeared into the building, he opened his laptop and waited to get a connection.

#

Adriana entered the bank after they buzzed her in and stepped into a small waiting room. A security guard, protected by a thick, bulletproof window, greeted her.

"Guten Morgen gnädige Frau. Ihre Mitgliedskarte?"

She blinked, and her face creased into a smile. "I'm so sorry. Do you speak English?"

"Of course. Your membership card, *bitte.*"

She brushed her long black hair over her right shoulder. "I don't currently have one."

"This is a member only, madam. If you don't have one, you can't enter. Have a pleasant day."

The door behind her buzzed, initially a reminder she had failed at her task, but it also prodded her onwards, refusing to let her give up.

She quirked an eyebrow. "I have a sizable amount I wanted to deposit. If the Bank of Zurich is not interested, I'm sure another one will be."

The buzzing stopped.

"I am sorry, but you can come back if you get an invitation."

Blake had attached a tiny microphone into a broach she pinned to her dress, and she wore a miniature receiver in her ear to take instructions if needed. His whisper came through.

"Tell them how much money you've got for them."

Sliding her sunglasses down to the end of her nose, she fixed the guard with a defiant sneer.

"Maria Sanchez doesn't need invitations." As she slid the glasses back up, she spun sharply on her heel. "You can kiss almost a billion dollars goodbye."

Tugging on the door, it remained locked.

"Kindly buzz me out—now!"

The man behind the partition sighed. She turned to him and suspected, by his wandering gaze, he was digesting the number she told him.

"One moment." He picked up the receiver and dialed; his muffled conversation barely audible through the glass partition. After half a minute, he returned the handset, tone noticeably warmer as it filtered through the speaker.

"Please take a seat. Someone will assist you shortly."

Two minutes later, a gentleman entered and greeted her. Clad in a tailored navy suit, pink shirt with white collar and cuffs, the ensemble was accentuated by a beautiful blue silk tie. Diamond cufflinks glittered under the light, as did his rose gold wristwatch when he extended his hand.

"Hello, I'm Herr Schmidt, branch manager. You're interested in an account?"

Her lips curled into a bright, welcoming smile. She had to be as charming as possible. "Yes, I'd like to transfer my accounts. My business has grown over the years, and I want to maximize my savings. I'm sure you understand."

Releasing his firm grip, he continued smiling. "Of course, Miss...?"

"Sanchez, Maria Sanchez."

"Miss Sanchez, we only take on select clients, just a few each year. What amount did you say you wanted to deposit?"

Letting the number roll off her tongue, "Over nine hundred million dollars."

Schmidt's expression remained neutral. "Well, this is quite unusual. Let's discuss inside. We may find an arrangement." Motioning for the guard to buzz them in, he opened the door for her, and he followed. She could feel his eyes focused on her rear, which was what she hoped for. He came abreast with her. "This way, please."

"Herr Schmidt, I'd like to deposit the entire sum."

The branch manager sat at his computer. "Excellent. Can you give me your account information?"

Reaching in her purse, she retrieved one of the burn phones and pretended to be looking at something. "I have a message here stating all of my account information has been faxed to the bank here."

He cocked his head. "Really?"

Enjoying the expression of surprise on the banker's face, she allowed a meager smile to grace her lips and decided to stroke the man's ego.

"As I told your guard at the entrance, I don't need an invitation. I was confident, being the successful banker you are, you'd accept my deposit."

Schmidt straightened himself in his chair and played with his cuff links. "Miss Sanchez, can you tell me the number where it was faxed?"

She gave out the details as Blake whispered it into her

earpiece.

"Very well. It's on the second floor. I will call them and have someone bring it to us."

She needed to get him out of the room, and before a wave of panic washed over her, an idea popped into her head. "Herr Schmidt. As you can imagine, I like to keep my matters as private as possible. I don't want too many prying eyes looking at my business. As a professional banker of your caliber, I am sure you understand. I would feel better if you would collect the fax yourself."

"Yes, Miss Sanchez, of course. I would like you to know, however, we are extremely discreet here. Everything is confidential and—"

"Excuse me, sir, but I insist."

He smiled, placed both palms on his desk, and stood. "But of course, I will go and retrieve it personally."

"Thank you. And Herr—"

"Please, call me Ekkehard."

With a coy smile, she fluttered her eyelashes at him. "I'd love some water, Ekkehard. My throat is so dry."

After a moment of hesitation, he returned her smile. "Certainly, Miss Sanchez. I will be right back."

As soon as he left, she went around his desk. Removing the small box from her purse, she searched for the base of his computer. It sat under his desk on the floor. It was toward the back, and she couldn't reach it by kneeling. Getting to her knees, she reached back and placed the device at the rear of the box, out of sight.

Unbeknownst to her, Herr Schmidt had already returned to his office.

"What are you doing, Miss Sanchez?"

Startled, she backed out and raised her hands to the back of her left ear.

"I am so sorry. I bet it appeared absurd. My earring fell off and bounced under your desk. It was dark and a little hard to find, but I managed to locate it."

She held out one of the ruby and diamond earrings Blake

bought for her in Minsk. "Someone special gave these to me to me. I would have hated to of lost it."

The banker said nothing. Only a slight, tight grin.

She slid by him, purposefully allowing her breasts to brush against the man's chest.

He pulled out his chair and sat. "I've retrieved your account information, and here is your water. Now let's get started."

48

Blake focused on his laptop and started typing. He changed proxies frequently to avoid being tracked by the CIA. He connected to the B's network and waited on Herr Schmidt to enter a password. Once the key logger successfully captured it, he swiftly gained access to the highly secure bank system. With utmost precision, he began his infiltration by inputting one of the two account numbers he had obtained from General Vasquez's confidential journal.

The first one belonged to Al-Hamwi, no surprise. It was no wonder why the young jihadi was selling arms, as his balance was below the required minimum of 100 million. The bank flagged the account for closure for over thirty days. The balance showed twenty-two million, of which twenty million was the initial deposit Shorets paid for the weapons.

Entering the second number, the name Hedrick von Schumacher appeared.

Damn. Why does it sound familiar? It's rigging a bell.

He continued to mentally flip through the files in the back of his brain, trying to remember. Scanning through the PM's notebook, he identified a record where the initials "HVS" were printed. He couldn't shake the feeling he knew the name, but he couldn't pull from his memory.

It was one of those things if you dwelled on, it would never come to you., but eventually, it would flash into your mind in an instant. He dug deeper into von Schumacher's numbers and discovered multiple transactions involving the movement of money to and from the account. He noticed a deposit from Butterfield bank, in the Cayman Islands.

It was located on Fort Street, Grand Cayman, and was an institution he had hacked into when researching Adriana's father. Opening another window, he typed in the username and password he'd created, hoping they hadn't detected his earlier intrusion and changed their firewall settings.

After a few minutes of passing through safeguards and various secure systems, he was in. Searching the transaction date and time, it was also marked as being recorded in person.

In person, huh? Well, let's see if your camera system is any good.

The video surveillance archives were easy to get into. The logs were organized chronologically, so he chose the ones he needed and the recordings from several cameras came into view. He concentrated on the main door and fast forwarded to about twenty minutes before the timestamp on the deposit.

He witnessed people coming and going, and there was nobody looking suspicious or he recognized. A car went by and honked its horn. Blake turned away from his screen for a moment to investigate if anything interesting was happening. When he glanced back at the laptop, something caught his eye.

"Whoa. Hold on there. Who are you?"

He reversed the video and played it again. His heart leaped to his throat.

It can't be.

He opened different screens and searched for the person he thought was familiar. The suspect was wearing glasses and a hat, so he chose a camera with a better angle. One of the frames displayed the subject, greeting someone and afterwards removing his hat.

Blake froze the frame and zoomed in. He confirmed his suspicions and felt as if a freight train had hit him. The memory of hearing the name slammed into his brain and came to a screeching halt.

"You son-of-a-bitch!"

#

Adriana listened to his mumbling through her earpiece and desperately wanted to find out what was happening. She glanced at her phone.

"Herr Schmidt. I apologize, but I received an important text. I'm stepping out to make a call."

"Take your time. Miss. Sanchez. I still have some forms to fill out."

As she stood and left the room, she emulated calling someone while speaking into her mic.

"Hey, what is it?"

"I found out what I needed to know. Get out of there as soon as you can. We have to leave immediately."

She stepped back into the manager's office. "I am so sorry. This is an emergency. Can we schedule an appointment for another day?"

He raised his head from his computer. "It isn't a problem, but Miss Sanchez. Is something the matter? Can I help in any way?"

She shook her head. "No, thank you. I'm afraid it is something I must deal with back home."

He flipped through his calendar. "Ten in the morning. Is it convenient for you?"

Adriana didn't care what the time was. "Yes, it's fine. I will see you then."

"I will need to escort you out." He stood from his desk and gestured for her to step out of his office first. He escorted her to the main door and presented his card to her. "Until tomorrow."

Once outside, she started for the car, pulling the annoying piece from her ear.

#

Relief swept through him when she exited the bank. The first thing on his mind now *was* going home to handle the situation he'd been dealt. The amount of trouble he was in for disobeying orders would be overshadowed by the information he ascertained. In a world where reality often surpassed the wildest imaginations, the age-old adage that truth was stranger than fiction had never rung truer than in this extraordinary moment.

The roar of a motorcycle rumbling to a stop pulled his gaze to the side mirror. The broad shouldered Ducati's driver was clad in black leathers and helmet. He unzipped the jacket and put his hand inside.

Blake glanced at her as she moved ever closer. Back in the reflection, he saw a weapon.

Oh, shit. He spoke directly into the mic. "Adriana, get down."

She continued along the sidewalk, unaware of what was developing. The man on the bike gunned the throttle and closed the distance.

I don't think so.

He readied his hand on the door handle.

"Listen to me! You have to get down!"

He focused on the rider in the mirror. "The biker at your two o'clock!"

He shot his eyes back at her. His plea fell on deaf ears.

"Can you hear me?"

The engine wailed a high pitch as it approached. He cracked the door and laid back across the center console, placing his feet against the door. The helmet of the suspect came into view. A swift kick flung it open, and the assailant slammed into the door, nearly ripping it from its hinges. He flew through the window and onto the pavement. Blake righted himself and saw the biker's weapon skitter along the street.

He leaped from the car and ran toward the man lying on the road. He turned his head and witnessed Adriana slide out between two parked cars with wide eyes.

"What happened?"

The strong exhaust note of a diesel engine pulled his attention from searching the biker. A white van came from the opposite direction.

It screeched to a halt next to her as its rear doors flew open. Two men in ski masks rushed in, grabbed her, and threw her in the back. It sped past Blake and accelerated as it skidded on to the crossroad and out of view. Its tires barking in anger against the pavement.

Snatching the weapon from the road, he sprinted back to his vehicle. He leaped inside, hit the ignition, slammed it into gear, and stomped on the accelerator, rubber wailing, as he peeled out. He ran over part of the bike as he did a one-eighty and took off in pursuit of her kidnappers.

Rounding the corner, he spotted it ahead, leaning as it screeched onto a side street. His engine whined in protest as he set his sights on the upcoming turn. Pedestrians jumped out of the way as he blazed through a red light and drifted around the bend. Drawing his Glock, he rested it in his lap, closing the gap as the captors loomed a few hundred feet in front of him. This was it— he was within reach.

The van weaved its way through traffic before making an abrupt left at the next intersection. It sideswiped a taxi and nearly flipped over. Blake negotiated the corner with better skill and slid past the cab. He fired two shots at the van's tires from the window but missed.

Stuffing his pistol under his leg, he grabbed the steering with both hands. Accelerating, he tried to ram the back of the van, but it sped up as he closed in. He maneuvered the car to pass on the right. A parked truck blocked him, and he jerked the wheel back, missing it by a paper's width.

As he veered to the left, he accelerated. A sudden jerk in the opposite direction caused his front right bumper to collide with the rear left quarter of the van. The impact forced his target to lurch right and smash into a street vendor's cart. Pretzels and drinks flew through the air.

The captor's vehicle strayed in his direction.

Oh shit! He dodged. He pressed the accelerator and attempted to get level with the window. A man of middle eastern descent glared at him. Blake fired two shots. The glass shattered.

The barrel of a machine gun protruded out of the open space and opened fire. He braked hard. A line of bullet holes stitched the hood before dancing up the windshield. The van swerved to the right and made a skidding turn at the next corner. Slamming on his brake pedal, he turned the wheel and pursued.

He mashed the accelerator, gaining on the men who took his love. He rammed into the back bumper, pushing the larger vehicle into the small compact ahead. The van's driver pounded on the brakes. Blake's car smashed into it once more, the force triggering his airbag. Undeterred, the kidnappers accelerated again, trying to shake their pursuer.

Stunned by the airbag's concussion, he watched as they pulled away, plowing the tiny auto out of the way.

"Son-of-a-bitch!"

He stabbed his knife into the deflating bag and pressed on in pursuit. A block later, he had them back in his sights as it neared a large junction. Barreling through a red light, it plowed into a sedan crossing. The four-door spun out, careening to the roadside as horns blared all around. Weaving seamlessly through the intersection chaos, Blake kept hot on the van's trail.

His mind was racing. Who were these people? Why did they want Adriana? What were they going to do to her? His fear and anger flowed through him and renewed his intensity to catch them and find out.

Dodging left as a Volvo came from the opposite direction. The rear of his vehicle clipped the other, and he spun out and the engine died, as his vehicle sat crosswise in the street. Tires screeched as oncoming cars attempted to avoid a collision. Horns honked. Drivers gestured and yelled.

When he managed to get the motor restarted, he sped around the pile-up on the sidewalk. A small coupe blocked his way.

"Get the fuck outta the way!"

He waved his arms in a motion for the driver to reverse out of the way.

His jaw tightened, a muscle working furiously in his cheek. "To hell with it!" He floored the accelerator. His battered sedan plowed into the smaller one, shunting it out of the way as the van finally cleared the far end of the intersection.

As they got closer to the next junction, once again the signal changed to yellow. This time, her captors slowed to a crawl.

What the fuck are they doing?

As the light turned red, they accelerated and went through the crossing. Halfway through, the side doors opened and Adriana flew out and rolled across the pavement.

"Oh, God! No!" Blake's heart was in his throat.

He stared helplessly as she tried to stand.

Rubber screamed as an oncoming car approached, but its inertia was too great. It hit her as it slid through the intersection.

"No!"

He stopped as fast as he could and ran to her. When he reached her, she was coughing blood. It oozed from her ears and mouth. Both legs were in unnatural positions.

"Adriana! I'm here. Somebody call an ambulance! Help! Please get an ambulance now!" Blake carefully grasped her and held her in his arms. Crimson stained her lips as it oozed out of the corners of her mouth.

Oh, dear God!

"Sit tight baby, help is on the way!"

A crowd gathered as voices in multiple languages surrounded them. He pleaded, "Stay with me!"

He shot a glance at the countless pairs of eyes surrounding them and yelled for medical assistance again. Someone in the sea of faces told him EMTs had been called and were on their way. He put them out of his mind and concentrated on her. She was trying to say something, but he dismissed it. "Don't talk, sweetheart, sit tight." *Oh my God, please don't die. I couldn't bear it.*

A gentleman handed him a rolled blanket and assisted in putting it under her head. She still tried to speak. He leaned over to hear her say, "I'm sorry."

He stared into her eyes while he stroked her hair.

"No, don't *you* say that. You have nothing to be sorry for. You were perfect. It's entirely my fault. Hold on, baby. Help is coming. It will be here any moment. Stay with me. You're going to be okay."

Despite her weakened state, she persevered, attempting to communicate once more. Leaning in closer, he strained to catch the mumbled sounds. As understanding dawned, his brows furrowed in confusion. "Brother? Who's brother?"

The distant wail of sirens intensified, creating a backdrop of urgency. With her fleeting gaze fixed upon him, she fought to convey something of utmost importance, her determination refusing to waver.

He lowered himself, pressing his ear against her quivering lips, straining to decipher the faint words that escaped her breath.

"Al-Hamwi."

As he stood tall once more, his eyes fixated on her fragile form, a realization struck him like a bolt of lightning.

"It was Al-Hamwi's brother?"

Their eyes locked, conveying an affirmative response through a subtle nod. But before he could react, her body convulsed, consumed by an uncontrollable tremor.

"No, no, no! Stay with me, sweetheart! Help is coming! Stay with me!"

The sounds of the sirens grew closer, and he assured her she would be fine, and to hang on a little longer. Her convulsions stopped. As her eyes met his, a glimmer of affection danced within her eyes. With a tender smile gracing her lips, she gently reached out, her hand stained with blood, and caressed his cheek. As he locked onto her gaze, he carefully deciphered the words forming on her lips.

"I... love... you."

Her voice was filled with a heartfelt sentiment.

"Move!"

Three EMTs rushed through the throng with a gurney. With a supportive hand beneath him, one of them assisted Blake in rising to his feet.

One of the Emergency Medical Technicians raised his voice, projecting over the growing crowd.

"We've got her now. Everyone, please give us some space."

Working in tandem, the remaining two secured her onto a

spine board, ensuring her head remained stabilized. With precision, the taller one of the three auscultated her heart with his stethoscope, while the other inserted an intravenous line.

One of the three called on his radio. "We've got severe head trauma with lacerations on her left arm, torso, hip, and both legs. I'm worried about the head. We need to get her to—" At that moment a car alarm went off and he didn't catch the next words of the conversation. The last sentence was. "We need to transport her immediately."

He stepped forward, his concern evident. "Where are you taking her?"

"Are you a relative?"

As they gingerly placed her onto the gurney, the shorter one focused on securing her with buckled straps.

He turned to Blake. "You know her? What's her name?"

"UH—no. I—I came upon the accident and tried to help her."

They wheeled her into the waiting ambulance.

He tried again. "Where are you taking her?"

As the medic replied, the driver switched on the siren and the reply was drowned by the sound. The door slammed closed.

The blaring sirens once again pierced through the air and the ambulance sped away.

He stood, feeling nothing. All sounds faded into the distance. Blood covered his shirt and pants. His body was numb. He thought he might vomit. These feelings for someone were something he'd never experienced.

He shuffled back to his car. Police were now converging on the scene, as were more and more bystanders. There were people pointing in different directions, all speaking of their accounts of the events unfolding in front of them.

He leaned against the door and put his hands over his face. For the first time in years, he felt absolute pain and heartbreak. Sure, he'd lost friends and other people he'd cared about, but nothing like this. This was a woman Blake was falling in love with and he was actually allowing it to happen. He welcomed it, and now she might be taken away and the only person to blame was himself. He started going through the typical "What if's" and "I should have done...".

Of course, it all sounded great in class when he went through this part of his training, but until now, he hadn't understood the power grief had over the human soul.

He turned his head over toward the accident. Officials were interrogating the driver of the sedan that hit her. They would approach him at any moment to take a statement. Something he couldn't allow. He needed to get away now. He'd check in with the hospital later. There will be hours and multiple surgeries to repair her broken body *if* she survived.

Blake grabbed his bag from out of the trunk and slipped away when no one was looking. He went around a corner, removed his shirt and threw it in a trash bin. His undershirt was covered in blood as well, but not as much. Strolling by a men's clothier with racks of clothing outside, he snatched the first one his size.

Stumbling from the pain and shock, he went into an alley and pulled out one of the burner phones. He called Randy, his pilot, and told him where he was and asked they come and get him as fast as possible. Once he ended the call, he knew he needed to get to the airport, but his feet wouldn't move. The power of his emotions took over. He leaned his back against a wall, slid to a sitting position, put his face in his hands and started to weep.

49

Zurich, Switzerland
July 5th
13:21 local (10:31 GMT)

Blake ended the call. He had lost track of all the hospitals he had called, asking about any unknown or recently admitted Jane Doe. None of them had any record of a woman being brought in or treated with Adriana's injuries. It's as if she disappeared into thin air.

The plane pulled into the hangar, and the stairs lowered. Shoulders drooped, he trudged up; every step, a painful reminder he would be getting further away from his missing love.

Chuck opened the cockpit door. "Hi, Blake. Where's the girl?"

Emotionless, he kept his head down. "I don't know. Missing. I'd rather not talk about it. Take me home." Both pilots gave each other a concerning stare. He shuffled to the rear of the cabin.

A second passed. "I'm sorry." Chuck's words followed him to the back.

"Me too," Randy added.

After the plane departed and leveled out, he came forward, thanked them and poured himself a double I. W. Harper bourbon on the rocks, prior to returning to his seat.

Only Adriana was in his thoughts. The loss was overwhelming. The emotional pain was greater than his bumps and bruises. His body was sore, but his heart was destroyed.

Countless questions surged through his mind, akin to a relentless tidal wave crashing against the shores of his consciousness. What happened to her?

Where did they take her? Was she still alive? Sleep beckoned him, and he needed it to clear his mind and plan his next move.

On the ride back home, he did nothing but rest and reminisce about the time he'd spent with her. He replayed his memories of their walk in Belarus. Her smile as she tried on the clothes, the night they made love in front of the fire.

From his pack, he pulled out her passport they had printed in Ukraine. He opened it to reveal Mrs. Morgan. It was the only picture he had of her. All the "What if's" started playing back in his mind. What should he have done differently was the dominating question cutting and slicing at his guilt.

To rid his pain, he forced himself to think about the betrayal he had endured by one of his own, but the thought only got his adrenaline pumping.

He knew when he returned, there would be an excellent chance he would be arrested, so he made a call to his buddy, Tim, in the Secret Service.

He told him of the information he'd found, and his pal also confirmed he was, in fact, to be taken into custody, all due in part to Veronica Slocum.

She'd passed word to the president, and the orders filtered through to him. His friend would arrange to have a team there, ready to take care of the traitor.

"Do me a favor and keep this confidential. I want to make sure the son-of-a-bitch doesn't get wind of this."

"Not a problem. I'll be there when the plane lands. I'll see you a little later."

"Thanks."

#

He managed to get a few more hours of sleep and was

awakened when Randy came over the com system and said they were approaching Andrew's AFB. Blake readied the information he gathered as proof of who was behind everything; so he thought. As he studied the intelligence, a lone transaction in the history of the bank account caught his attention.

He booted his laptop and started to trace the money. The transfer went to a corporation registered in the Netherlands. After combing through records, he discovered a name. He grabbed the last burn phone he had and made a desperate call.

After the aircraft turned off the runway, he noticed the five black SUVs with dark tinted windows.

Look who all came to welcome me home. Well, I've got a surprise of my own.

As they got closer, he could see "the Bitch" Director Slocum, Director Thomas and his boss, Mike Brennan, plus about fifteen Secret Service.

Randy's voice chimed through the cabin speaker. "You've got quite the welcoming party."

He allowed himself a brief chuckle.

The plane taxied to the hangar and stopped. While the engines were winding down,

Randy stepped out of the cockpit with a friendly smile. "I want you to know whatever happens out there, it's been an honor to serve with you. And I don't hold any grudge to what you did when you forced us to go to Cuba. You did a brave thing, and because of it, a disaster was averted. I know Chuck feels the same way."

He put his hand on Randy's shoulder and shifted his eyes between the two of them. "Thanks guys. But I suspect you'll be seeing me again real soon."

Randy nodded, opened the door and deployed the staircase.

With a measured stride, he descended the stairs, his heart brimming with eager anticipation for the impending encounter. As he reached the final step, a figure emerged from the shadows, none other than Veronica Slocum. Her gaze, icy and piercing, locked onto him.

"Mr. MacKay, I am placing you under arrest for disobeying orders three times in the course of this mission. Your days of trotting around the globe; doing whatever you feel and ignoring the commands of your superiors are over." She nodded to the Secret Service, and they stepped in behind him and grabbed his arms.

"That's ok Director. At least I can sleep at night knowing I did the right thing. How about you?"

She scoffed as she stared into his eyes. "I sleep fine."

"Would you sleep as well if you arrested the wrong person for the wrong reasons?"

Asserting herself, she closed the distance between them; her face, mere inches from his, exuding an air of arrogance. With a hint of disdain in her voice, she posed a challenging question, "If I am indeed mistaken, pray enlighten me. Who, in your esteemed opinion, should be the target of my apprehension?"

You stupid bitch. I'm about to rock your world. Blake pointed his eyes over her shoulders. "Him."

She turned and was facing Mike Brennan. Two Secret Service men, one of whom was his friend Tim, approached Mike and reached out to seize him.

A quick elbow to the face of the nearest agent gave Mike the separation he needed. He lunged and wrapped an arm around Veronica's neck and used her as a shield. The black steel of his weapon pressed firm against her temple.

"Fuck you, all!"

Her eyes widened, darting from one onlooker to another, her mouth agape in a mixture of shock and desperation. "Somebody *do* something!"

Agents drew their weapons. Blake twisted out of his hold, slammed an open palm into the chest of the man behind him. With swift and ruthless force, he tore the pistol from the agent's grasp, his movements fueled by a surge of adrenaline.

Without hesitation, he pivoted on his heel, aiming with deadly precision. The deafening sound of the gunshot echoed through the air as the bullet found its mark, piercing Mike's skull just above his left eye.

His lifeless body collapsed onto the pavement, the impact resonating with a sickening thud. As the life drained from him, a crimson tide spilled forth, cascading from the back of his head and seeping into the cracks of the concrete.

Veronica stood frozen in a state of profound disbelief. Her gaze lingered on the corpse before shifting toward Blake. In an attempt to steady herself, she inhaled twice, her eyes closing as her hand found its way to her chest. With a resolute determination, her eyes flickered open once more, ready to face the grim reality in front of her.

He turned and gave the pistol back to the agent and locked eyes with her. "You're welcome."

"What? What in the *fuck*—happened?"

He shifted on his feet and pointed to the body on the ground. "It was him."

Director Thomas stepped forward. "Do you have evidence?"

"Other than how he reacted? Oh, hell yeah, I've got proof. How about a Swiss account with the Bank of Zurich with one hundred and twenty-five million dollars in it? How about a book I pried from the dead Prime Minister's cadaver with Mike's account information in it? I have pictures of him making a massive deposit into a bank in the Cayman Islands and transferring it to the account in Switzerland."

Veronica chimed in. "What led you to all of this?"

Blake stole a glance at the man he used to call a friend and let out a sigh. "Scouring the notes in the notebook, I came across the name Hedrick von Schumacher. It was familiar to me, but I couldn't place a finger on where I'd heard it before."

He paused, raised his hand, and rubbed his chin. "When I saw him on the bank's video, it came to me. It was an alias he'd made use of in East Berlin, back in the days of the Cold War. It came out in a conversation we were having one night when we were doing some heavy drinking. I remembered."

He paused and took a deep breath. "Mike didn't. It was during his time in Germany, he met a young Oleg Shorets who was working for the KGB. It would appear they developed a friendship that would last throughout the years."

He glared at the body on the ground. "When Oleg presented the idea if he were to become the President of Belarus, he would be in charge of granting licensing rights to western businesses. If you had the right connections, you could open shop and reap the rewards of a monopoly."

Director Thomas stood, shaking his head in disbelief. "That's incredible."

Blake chuckled. "I'm not done yet. In exchange for getting them the metal storm weapon, Mike would be the sole owner of all those rights for a wide variety of companies operating in the West. He could lease the permits to companies like McDonalds, KFC, Starbucks; the list goes on. Hold the rights to enough businesses and it had the potential to be worth hundreds of millions of dollars."

She leaned in closer, her eyes widening and eyebrows arching in surprise. "Are you one hundred percent sure?"

He furrowed his brow, his eyes narrowing in frustration. "Seriously? The man tried to kill you and you're still questioning me?"

She turned away and expelled a frustrated breath. He watched and waited for some kind of pathetic response. She spun around. "I'm sorry. I want—"

"Shut up, Director. Since you still have doubts, you have to shut the fuck up and allow me to finish."

She stood wide-eyed again.

Director Thomas interjected. "I think what we must do now is—"

"You shut up too." He glanced over at Tim and nodded in the direction of the Thomas. Two men grabbed his arms.

He rotated his head from side to side, his eyebrows furrowing in a mix of confusion and surprise. "What the hell is this all about? I didn't have anything to do with this."

"Oh, is that so? Well, let me ask you this." He took two steps toward him. "Does the company Three L Consulting ring any bells?"

He hesitated. "No!"

"Are you certain? It should. You're the proprietor and that's the business Mike made a substantial transfer to."

"I am not the owner of any company. You don't know what

the fuck you're talking about and you're making a *huge* mistake!"

He smiled, stepped to him, and gave him two gentle pats on his cheek. "Well, perhaps Julian Thomas isn't the boss, but Oscar Van Wey is."

He enjoyed the fear rising in the Thomas's eyes after he heard the name. "You need to understand, Director; I know you contract out a lot of work; including document forgery."

A bead of sweat carved a path across the man's face.

"I had the pleasant opportunity to meet Vadim, in Kiev. You know him. He's the one who provided Adriana and me with our documents. I knew you wouldn't utilize an internal team to create your alias. It would be an insult to your intelligence to think that. No… You'd use an outside source, and only the best. I made a quick call to Vadim before I landed, and he confirmed my suspicions."

He shot a glance at a shock faced Veronica prior to turning back and continuing.

"You and Oscar Van Wey are one and the same." He leaned into the director's ear and whispered. "Who's fucked now?" A sly, knowing smile curved his lips as he locked eyes with the man, who swiftly came to the disconcerting realization his fate was sealed.

He turned and walked back to Veronica. "There's more. Brennan gave the order to terminate General Vasquez, tying up any loose ends on his side. Shorets would kill Al-Hamwi to eliminate any problems possibly occurring on his side, while blaming Al-Hamwi for the assassination and terrorist attack in Belarus."

He glanced around at the others. "All would be happy, fat and rich until Mike and Julian realized I was requested personally by the president and assigned the job of eliminating Vasquez. They couldn't overrule the request and assign a less capable agent."

He stepped over to Mike's body and focused on his well-placed shot. "That's when Brennan started using his connections to give anyone in my path information about my mission. Every step of the way, I was compromised."

He cleared his throat. "From the night I tried to take out General Vasquez to the night I met my asset in Afghanistan; the raid on Al-Hamwi's house, the police firing on me on the way to the airport, Prime Minister Shorets capturing me at his house."

He paused and raised his index finger to make a point. "In each phase, someone was trying to stop me from completing this assignment, and Mike was the one giving info to the enemy. Hell, he even knew I was in Zurich. How, I don't know. But he tipped off Al-Hamwi's older brother, Osama."

He returned his attention to Julian and gave him a scornful glance. "To be honest, I can't believe I made it back here alive."

Veronica cleared her throat. "How long has this been going on?"

"I'm sure after a full investigation, you'll find out this isn't their first time to the dance. Do you remember when the North Koreans invaded Attu Island and stole the warhead last year?"

"Yes."

"Mike was the one who tipped them off about it and sold them the information. The money trail doesn't lie."

She motioned to the Secret Service to place Director Thomas in the car and take him away.

He raised his hand. "Wait." He stepped to the disgraced man and gazed into his eyes. The amount of contempt and hate he held for this man was immeasurable.

Veronica's fingers tightened into fists as she watched him approach the disgraced man. "Careful."

Dismissing her with a wave, he sighed.

"You prick! I trusted you! Go to Hell!"

Julian lowered his chin, stared at his feet, and kept quiet. Blake stood over him and glared through him. *That's right. Squirm. You're going to pay for what you've done.* After a moment, she had Director Thomas removed.

She took a decisive step closer to him, her touch wrapping around his arm with a tenderness he hadn't witnessed before.

Blake was shaken, suspicious of her intent. He couldn't help but wonder if this newfound display of vulnerability signaled a deeper level of respect and gratitude toward him for saving her life.

However, he dismissed such thoughts, feeling a jaded

indifference creeping in. What did it matter anymore?

At last, she broke the silence with her words, her voice filled with remorse. "I apologize. I understand the significance he held in your life." She gestured at Mike's body, her expression reflecting the weight of the devastating loss impacting them all.

He stood and listened. He didn't care about what she was saying, and he didn't need to be patronized. After she said a few more things, he didn't pay attention; he turned to her. "May I be excused?"

"After your debriefing, excuse yourself for a couple of weeks. I hope that's an order you'll follow. Come back here after some time off and we'll figure out what to do. Okay?"

He nodded, reached for his bag and got into one of the SUVs for the ride back to Langley.

50

July 24th

In the aftermath of Julian Thomas' apprehension, a series of revelations unfolded, sending shockwaves through the tight-knit community of Langley.

The realization that two of their most esteemed and trusted colleagues had been compromised resulted in the service reeling. How could individuals who had forged deep bonds of trust betray their comrades in such a profound manner?

The audacity of their actions left everyone questioning how they could have ever believed they would escape unscathed.

Because of these disclosures, Veronica Slocum found herself thrust into a new role, assuming the position of head of the CIA, albeit under the guise of a temporary arrangement. In this capacity, she became Blake's interim handler, navigating the uncertain terrain of clandestine operations while decisions were being made about his future.

With Julian's trial looming on the horizon, the realization of the U.S. justice system no longer imposed the ultimate penalty for treason settled in. Instead, the traitors were destined to spend the remainder of their lives behind bars, forever locked away from society.

With each count weighing against him, Julian faced the prospect of serving multiple life sentences consecutively, resulting in a staggering total of almost nine lifetimes of captivity.

As a final measure to ensure his permanent confinement, an additional three hundred years were to be tacked on, leaving no room for doubt he would never taste freedom again.

#

Julian found himself confined within the walls of his own home, a fortress of security enveloping him like a silent sentinel. House arrest, a begrudging gesture of professional courtesy, held him captive, amplifying the weight of his impending trial, set to commence the following day. The echoes of his wife's departure weeks prior reverberated through his thoughts, a painful reminder of the fractures irreparably breaking his once-whole life.

In a moment of contemplation, Julian's trembling hand reached for the crystal vessel, housing the amber elixir, offering a temporary escape from the harsh realities encircling him. His gaze drifted to a photograph resting at the corner of his desk, a snapshot frozen in time, depicting the happiness and unity of his family. Gingerly, he lifted the frame, his fingertips tracing the edge with a bittersweet tenderness, before returning it to its rightful place.

With a heavy heart and a final sip of scotch, Julian relinquished the empty glass to the surface again, a silent symbol of the emptiness permeating his existence.

#

Positioned a mere half mile distant, the sniper found solace in the sturdy embrace of his harness, suspended halfway up a towering cell structure, nestled beneath a cloak of camouflaged netting. Attuned to the atmospheric conditions, he gauged the wind's subtle nuances, accounting for the humidity lingering in the air. With unerring precision, he calibrated his scope, ensuring every variable aligned with total accuracy.

With laser-like focus, his gaze homed in on the intended target, his eyes scrutinizing the vivid imagery laying before him while relishing in a momentary respite, indulging in a sip of a well-deserved libation.

As the world around him faded into insignificance, his heartbeat gradually descended, settling into a steady cadence, a testament to the resolve coursing through his veins. Taking a deep breath, he embraced the rhythmic pulsations resonating within his chest and timed the beats.

In the fleeting space between heartbeats, a precise and deliberate pressure caressed his finger, culminating in an effortless squeeze of the trigger.

#

One month later
Greece

Perched upon his stony balcony, the assassin's gaze was captivated by the ethereal spectacle unfolding as the sun emerged from its slumber, casting its golden glow on the tranquil expanse of the Aegean Sea. In this moment of serene beauty, a sudden interruption shattered the tranquility—the piercing ring of his phone jolted him from his reverie.

He reached for the device, his fingers pressing the answer button, yet he chose to remain cloaked in silence, allowing the voice on the other end to unfold its tale.

"Two kills accomplished. The operation in D.C. was a success, but Minsk was most impressive."

He remained silent.

The speaker continued with an air of finality. "The money has been transferred to your account. Our paths will cross again."

The call concluded, the assassin sliding the phone into the concealed pocket of his robe, preserving the secrecy shrouding his existence.

Turning away from the breathtaking vista, his eyes fell upon the slumbering figure of a woman, her vulnerability contrasting against the backdrop of his dangerous world.

With a mixture of detachment and admiration, he observed her for a moment, the allure of her naked form a stark juxtaposition to the darkness consuming his reality. Resolute, he stepped into the shadows of his abode, leaving behind the remnants of his clandestine encounter.

END